SISTERHOOD

CATHY KELLY worked as a journalist before becoming a novelist. Her debut novel, *Woman to Woman*, became an instant No.1 bestseller and since then she has published twenty-two novels, which are loved by readers all around the world and have sold millions of copies globally.

In addition to her writing, she is a UNICEF Ambassador and lives in County Wicklow with her family and dogs.

Join the #Sisterhood
Sign up for Cathy Kelly's newsletter here:
smarturl.it/CathyKellySignUp

Cathy KELLY

SISTER HOOD

HarperCollins*Publishers*

HarperCollins*Publishers* Ltd
1 London Bridge Street,
London SE1 9GF
www.harpercollins.co.uk

HarperCollins*Publishers*
Macken House, 39/40 Mayor Street Upper,
Dublin 1, D01 C9W8, Ireland

First published by HarperCollins*Publishers* 2024
1

A catalogue record for this book is available from the British Library

ISBN: 978-0-00-854495-9 (HB)
ISBN: 978-0-00-854496-6 (TPB)
ISBN: 978-0-00-867261-4 (TPB, AU, NZ, CA-only)

Set in 12.5/16.8 Sabon by HarperCollins*Publishers* India

Printed and bound in the UK using 100% Renewable Electricity by
CPI Group (UK) Ltd

To PJ, Dylan and Murray, plus the four babas.
I could not have got through the past few years
without your love.

Prologue

Everyone loved Whitehaven Beach.

The sea, the rocks, the creamy curve of white sand . . . No matter how the wind raged in from the Atlantic along the rest of the Cork coast, there was a calmness about Whitehaven Beach and the overlooking Mermaid Peak.

Lou Fielding adored them both. For her entire existence – fifty years now – the beach had been part of her daily life. Dad used to take her there when she was a toddler, taking off her socks so her plump little girl toes could dig into the sand with glee. She'd gone there with her younger sister, holding Toni's hand as they searched for shells and constructed sand citadels.

As an adult, she'd walked the beach in all weathers, sometimes finding pieces of driftwood she used to decorate the cottage, sometimes trying to make up her steps. There were always friends on the beach: Lou knew everyone in Whitehaven. Despite being allegedly a town, it really was a village. Lou had walked there with her husband, Ned, with their daughter, Emily, and had even jogged along it with her best friend, Mim. They'd decided eventually that jogging was hard, possibly bad for the knees, and no sports bra had ever stopped Lou's breasts behaving like wayward basketballs. Walking was the answer, they'd decided; only mad people actually swam in the Atlantic.

Since Mim had died, Lou walked alone. Her capacious crossbody bag always contained a hat, a rolled-up rain jacket and a handy bag for rubbish so that seals and sea birds wouldn't swallow a sliver of plastic bag or get tangled in a piece of junk on her watch. Nobody would ever say that Lou was unprepared or unready to help. But being prepared and being ready to help meant *nothing*, she thought now, standing on the beach in the wrong shoes, staring at the sea as if she could stop the waves with the intensity of her gaze.

It was Saturday morning, the night after her fiftieth birthday party. Lou hadn't slept. She'd lain open-eyed on her bed for the whole night. Hadn't removed her make-up, hung up her dress or worried about flossing her teeth. Why floss? Why do *any* of it? Where had being a good girl ever got her? Absolutely nowhere.

'What did I do wrong?' she said out loud.

The wind was howling now and her words were quiet.

She tried it louder: shouted.

'What did I do wrong? Tell me!'

The wind from the Atlantic whipped across Lou's face and she wondered if the rain was going to come in. Rain would be good now. It would match her mood. Or perhaps hailstones would be better. The sharp pain of a thousand tiny stones hitting her skin . . . That was exactly how last night had felt as, one by one, the people in Lou's life showed precisely how much they truly valued her. Her mother, Lillian, her husband, Ned, even her employers - the people she'd worked with for twelve hard years. They'd all shown her that she wasn't special or a huge part of their life. She was the wife, daughter and employee who'd do anything for anybody and never asked for anything herself. 'Good old Lou', the family fixer so desperate to be liked that she'd never noticed that they didn't respect her.

Lou felt the shame of her stupidity flatten her, just as a cloud burst overhead and the rain finally arrived. Lou let it pummel her, uncaring that she was getting wet and that her dark hair was plastered to her forehead.

The sea was unusually rough and waves threw themselves wildly against the beach, green and brown tangles of seaweed washing in and out.

Her mother had made an art installation out of seaweed once. Her mother . . . Out of the pain of last night, her mother's revelation was the worst. She'd taken Lou's childhood and in one sharp move, smashed the perfect memories.

'What did I do wrong?!' Lou screamed at the ocean.

The ocean ignored her and continued its giant swooping of water onto the beach; one sad woman standing in the rain was not on its agenda. Lou kicked at the sand, scattering dark lumps like demerara sugar all around.

'I. Hate. Everyone.'

She stared at the sea and the dark and frightening thought snaked back into her head. It had been there last night, rippling around in her aching heart, flitting in and out of her brain like a slow-acting poison as she lay in her bed, dry-eyed.

She could gently go, she had decided. She wouldn't walk under a bus, no. That was not her. But if a bus flattened her when it veered out of control, that would be OK, right? She'd cease to exist and all this pain would go away . . . Was that a terrible thing to think?

Emily, Toni and Gloria would miss her.

But Emily was grown up, happy in college and living away from home.

A mother had to be there for her child.

Except Emily was a wonderful grown-up now, gentle, kind, loving, funny. Lou could leave her peacefully, knowing she'd done her best. Toni and Gloria would be there for her, and Ned. He was a good father, for all that he thought Lou was a piece of the furniture. Would Lillian be there for her granddaughter? Who knew.

Lillian used people, it seemed.

Like so many of the people in her life had used Lou.

In all her years of fighting depression and anxiety, Lou had never felt the way she did now: as if she was suddenly, frighteningly, teetering on a precipice.

How many times had she been on this beach and felt alone? Yet she'd never in her life felt this alone.

'Wish you were here, Mim,' Lou said into the wind.

She'd never have felt alone with Mim around. Mim had been that rare creature: a soul friend who understood everything about Lou. Lou hadn't had to try to explain anxiety and depression to her. In general, explaining it was hopeless. People who'd never felt that way rarely understood the fear of the dark hole a person could fall into. They never grasped that anxiety or depression were not things she could 'get over', that they were constantly throbbing inside her body, waiting for the right moment to emerge.

Mim had understood. But Mim wasn't here.

Lou began to cry at the enormity of her thoughts. She couldn't do it, not to any of them. Lou loved them all too much, but she hurt so much too . . .

'I knew you'd come here.'

The shock of the interruption made Lou whisk around at lightning speed, and she rapidly wiped away her tears as she faced her sister. Toni stood behind her, a waterproof fisherman's hat jammed on her head keeping the blade-like blonde hair dry. Her tall, slender figure was enveloped in a bulky padded coat that also appeared to be rainproof because drops of rain were sheeting off it. Even in crisis, Toni looked perfect.

Toni would never recover if Lou walked into the sea. Or Emily . . . her darling Emily.

What had she been *thinking?*

She could never do that, not to her family.

'I came here to be alone,' said Lou and, almost immediately, her instinct was to add, *Sorry – that sounded rude.*

Even now, in this dark place, she was ready to apologise. But Lou held her tongue. It took enormous effort, but she did not say 'sorry'.

'Course you want to be alone,' Toni said. 'But I can't let you. In case—'

'In case what?' demanded Lou, and again she had to shut down the instinct to apologise.

'In case you needed me.' Toni's tone was easy. 'Don't want you walking out on us all. I might, if I'd had a night like the one you had last night. It was quite a party.'

Lou stifled a noise and she wasn't sure if it was a sob or a wail.

Whatever she had been expecting from her sister, it wasn't that.

Toni was more of a 'cheer up' and 'we'll cope with whatever happens,' sort of woman. Not that Toni was like their mother in most ways but in this, she was: neither she nor Lillian did comforting.

'Where would I go?' Lou asked.

There was no reply. The ocean in front of them roared. The sisters stared at its welcoming depths.

'I wouldn't do that,' said Lou quickly, but even as she said it, she knew this wasn't true.

She'd felt the pull of the sea, the nothingness of it all, how easy it could be to end the pain . . . Or was it the hardest thing ever? She'd never felt that before. Never even understood the lure, but her heart just ached so *much* . . .

'I know you wouldn't do anything silly, Lou,' said Toni gently, but she put her arm around Lou's shoulders as if to hold her to the shore. 'What do you say to a cup of coffee? It's chilly and we need something warm.'

'Don't want to go home,' said Lou, aware that she was speaking the way a child might. 'I don't want to see anyone after last night. The whole town will know by now. I might as well be on the front of the local paper.'

'I know.' Toni squeezed her sister's arm. 'I know, but—'

'I'm not going,' Lou interrupted. 'I can't.'

'Then . . . how about we take off, just the two of us?' Toni said, surprising her utterly.

'And go where?'

'Anywhere we want,' said Toni. 'Nobody but us. We just *escape*.'

Lou felt some of the weight on her heart lift. As if a little light still glowed within her. A spark of life still burning.

'Just leave . . . ?' she asked.

She thought of all the things she had to do and how many tasks she normally needed to complete before taking even the smallest of holidays. She organised cover for work, made nutritious meals for her mother, left endless instructions because, without her, who would run things?

'Let's just go,' said Toni eagerly. 'Everyone will be fine without us.'

Astonished at this notion of simply leaving, Lou scanned her mental list: her mother, Ned, her work. They had all let her down horribly.

'You're right,' she said, holding her head up to face the wind. Her new life would start now: nobody would take advantage of her again, she decided with unaccustomed ferocity.

She thought of what Mim used to say: *If you can't have a good day, just have a day. Get by.*

Today, Lou could get by. Today, she would be as strong as Mim had been.

She smiled tentatively at her sister and nodded.

'Let's go.'

Part One

Chapter One

Three days earlier

Today was not a good day for the Barking Dog, Lou decided as she walked up Academy Street in the morning sunshine. She had an interview with Oszkar, her boss, for the newly created company strategy manager job, and it should be nothing at all – she'd worked for Blossom Flowers for twelve years and Oszkar and Bettina called her 'the backbone' of the company – but anxiety ran to the beat of its own drum.

Breathe, you nincompoop.

But as she turned in the direction of the flower shop, she heard the noise of a morning delivery truck rumbling on an adjacent street, and without waiting for her conscious mind to figure it out, the Barking Dog had flicked the danger switch inside Lou's head. It was the heavy, menacing thrum that did it: hurricane? Plane crashing into Cork? Lou's dog didn't differentiate between

11

the grumbling of a heavy truck and a plummeting flight. It went for the worst possible case in all instances.

Lou gave herself a mental shake and started her thoughtful breathing. Today was not a day for catastrophic thinking. *Breathe in for six, hold for three, out for nine.* She had to stop walking to do it because the 'out for nine' bit was hard unless you were very fit. *Breathe in for six, hold for three, out for nine.* It was working, slowly. It seemed to be the only thing that did.

Toni had once suggested that Lou give her anxiety a name: 'so you can shout at it. Tell it to leave you alone . . . no?' Toni simply didn't get it. Toni thought anxiety hit like menstruation pains – once a month possibly, and then it was gone – mostly because she'd never had a moment's anxiety in her life, a fact which astonished Lou. How could two sisters be so different? Same parents, seven years between them and nobody would have even guessed they were sisters. Toni was utterly self-contained and confident, while Lou could fit her self-confidence in one of the tiny, enamelled pill boxes their aunt Gloria collected.

Toni never said sorry. *Women live in a world of muttering 'sorry'*, Toni had said so often that it was one of her most quoted statements; that and *What I look like is the least interesting thing about me.* Which might be easy to say when you were forty-three with dewy skin, perfect bone structure, and a body that seemed to burn calories effortlessly – but it also happened to be true, since Toni not only had a wildly popular TV show, she also mentored as part of the Women in Business charity. She had everything – of course she couldn't understand Lou's anxiety!

It was Mim who had taught Lou her breathing exercises. Mim explained that you had to inhale deeply, fill your belly and exhale slowly, all of which put the frighteners on the amygdala, AKA the Barking Dog, which was the bit of the brain that entirely hijacked a person's sense of peace.

'How are you so good at this,' Lou had said to Mim, who never suffered from anxiety, who was always so serene, calm, strong.

Lou desperately wanted to be all these things and had fooled most people in her life that she *was* all these things. Except for Mim. While most members of Lou's family appeared to think that Lou was a rock of sense with an occasional foray into nervousness, Mim – who she'd only met for the first time when their daughters were five – had instantly intuited that Lou was a walking timebomb of fear and anxiety.

'Talk radio,' Mim had explained lightly. 'I listen a lot and you hear lots of useful things. That's why I know about the amygdala and all that stuff.'

It was a little longer into their friendship before Mim explained that her father had suffered from anxiety and depression.

'Thank you for telling me,' Lou had said gratefully. 'It's really helpful to hear about other people who feel the same. I don't talk about it much because . . .'

'Because people don't understand or they ask you how you can be depressed when you have so much, like a husband and daughter and are clearly only experiencing first world problems.'

Lou nodded fervently. 'Exactly.'

She'd wondered at the time why she could say all of this to Mim and not to her husband, mother or sister, but then she reasoned that Mim understood because of family experience and nobody in Lou's family had ever apparently felt the way she did. Plus, Lou didn't like worrying the people she loved – she was a problem-solver, she liked to think and that meant not bothering other people with her worries.

Now, Lou raced past the Pandora store, which had pretty troll beads in a grape hyacinth colour that might be a nice present. Ned was bad with birthday gifts and she knew he hadn't got her one yet and he'd be embarrassed at the party when he realised. She should have reminded him and—

Damn. She'd stopped the breathing.

By half eleven, when she was due to meet Oszkar for her interview, Lou had put out several metaphorical fires, had gulped half a cup of cappuccino and had managed five minutes to talk to Sarah, the company's accountant, who was dealing with a wildly out-of-control situation involving her extended family and a great-uncle's will.

Money, reflected Lou sadly, was more easily weaponised than uranium.

'Thank you,' sobbed Sarah at the end of the call, after Lou had advised stepping back from the situation entirely.

'You're not a lawyer and everyone will just get mad at you,' she'd said. 'Your poor uncle! He must have been sad at the end to have made such a muddle.'

Lou liked to give people the benefit of the doubt – he can't have meant to cause such trauma.

Nobody would do that on purpose, surely?

'You're so forgiving,' Sarah said guiltily.

As she hung up, Lou fought back a yawn. She'd always taken care of people – friends, family, colleagues – but it was exhausting. Being everyone's go-to person took it out of her. She took a reviving sip of coffee and sat back in her chair, but the phone rang again.

She dealt patiently with the new caller and then raced up to Oszkar's office, which was on the second floor. Lou had dressed up today in a chic A-line navy cotton dress which skimmed her figure in a forgiving way. A-line was her friend, along with her signature watermelon pink lipstick and a dash of sheeny blusher on each rounded cheekbone. Even when her uncurated collarbone-length dark hair was sticking out at all angles, the lipstick, blush and severe dress made her look put together. With tortoiseshell glasses over her chestnut brown eyes, she had the look of an academic, her daughter, Emily, liked to say.

'Your dad's the academic,' Lou reminded her daughter ruefully, because Ned was an engineering professor and was academia through and through.

'But you look it in those glasses,' Emily would say.

Lou didn't have a college education, unless her secretarial course counted. She'd planned to go to college but her mum had been involved in a painful car accident just before, so Lou had put off the term start for a year and somehow, she'd never made it to college.

Upstairs, Oszkar's office was empty, so she went to the window to look out at the busy street below and waited. Oszkar was always late.

'Lou, sorry. I was getting coffee,' he said, five minutes later, rushing into his office, his startling height dwarfing even Lou, who was five ten.

He sat down with a sigh, and Lou did the same, making sure her posture was upright and her smile friendly but professional – this was still a job interview and she wanted to do it properly. She'd written a proper new résumé for the application, even though she'd been with Blossom since they'd started up and they all knew each other inside out. She smiled to herself, thinking of Oszkar back then: he'd been so young, tall and skinny and finally making his dream come true by opening a flower shop.

The company had until then been based out in the sticks in an industrial estate, which was a million miles away from their current swanky town centre premises. Oszkar's wife, Bettina, had just given birth to their first daughter and Lou had taken care of baby Bianka many times, babysitting so her young employers could go out. She'd even stood in for godmother when Bettina's mother got stuck in the airport in Budapest because she'd left her passport back home in the family home in Dabas.

Lou had saved the day for the company often, including when Blossom had teetered on the verge of collapse because of a misorder for a hugely important wedding, the one that had put them on the map because it was a grand movie star one with paparazzi in attendance. Lou knew she'd rescued it all that day: an entire night spent on her feet making up the emergency bouquets and table settings because the delivery of precious white Vendela roses had not come so Lou had begged for hundreds of white O'Haras from all her florist friends.

Not that she minded: it was what she did. Fixing things brought her joy.

She smiled at Oszkar now.

It would be a whole new chapter for them all. The previous office manager had taken a better-paid job and Lou had plans for enlarging their current business and—

'The thing is,' Oszkar rubbed his pale blue eyes. He suffered dreadfully with dry eyes, which was not an advantage in a florist.

'Will I get you some drops?' she asked solicitously. She always kept some in her drawer.

Oszkar sighed.

'No,' he said. 'Lou, I am sorry, we cannot hire you for this new job.'

Lou stilled.

'You are an excellent worker, but . . . we need someone with a business degree and you do not have such a thing. A strategy manager needs degrees.'

Oszkar was still speaking in his very formal English. He and Bettina spoke Hungarian when they were working together, a fluid rush of language that had always sounded like mysterious music to Lou.

'It is not that we are not grateful for all you do, but we need more experience if we are to expand.'

'I understand,' said Lou, flattening back all the emotions. She would not cry. Not now.

He was probably right, after all. Of course he was right. Blossom needed someone else. Why had she been so foolish as to imagine she was it?

Oszkar spread his long fingers. He had huge hands, perfect for hand-tying bouquets.

'I wish it was not this way, Lou, but I must think of the shop. You understand?'

'I understand,' said Lou, holding the tears in.

Oszkar would be upset if he thought he had upset her. He and Bettina must have worried themselves sick over this decision. It could not have been easy. She would not make it worse.

'I understand,' she repeated, more in control of herself. She could handle disappointment, couldn't she?

'I knew you would,' said Oszkar, relieved.

In the open-plan office where staff took orders for ordinary bouquets and finalised details for big events, Lou stared blankly at her computer for a while. She could hear the bustle of the shop floor beneath her and hum of voices from the back room where the cooling room kept valuable flowers at their peak. Emails pinged in rapidly but she couldn't make herself look at them. Not crying was taking up all her energy. She tried her deep breathing, but it felt suddenly impossible. She felt . . . she searched around for the right word. Hurt, that was it. Hurt.

She did so much for Blossom, for Oszkar and Bettina. In the early days, she'd run the company single-handedly when her employers went on holiday. Twelve years she'd worked for them, did that mean anything? Her sister's voice came into her head: *But you never asked for anything, never asked for any position or share in the company, did you?*

I shouldn't have had to, Lou answered silently.

But still Toni's voice was in her consciousness: *Not everyone is as kind as you are, Lou. People let you down. You have to fight for things.*

Toni had said this to her before. It was another of her sister's mantras. Toni identified what she wanted and then went for it, like a heat-seeking missile.

Lou's approach was more organic – what was for you, wouldn't pass you by. There was a reason Oszkar hadn't given her the job. Something better was coming along. She wasn't ready to be an office manager. If it's for you, it won't pass you by, she told herself over and over. The universe would provide. Wouldn't it?

Chapter Two

Fresh from her twice weekly early morning blow-dry, Toni Cooper led the way up the stairs past the indifferent watercolours on the walls and into the smaller of the upstairs offices of Women in Business. As a high-profile mentor for the charity, she could have asked for the bigger office but Toni, who'd worked for years in radio broadcasting and then TV – interviewing celebrities, business magnates, sports stars and politicians – knew that the size of a person's office meant absolutely nothing in the grand scheme of things. Big offices often just meant big egos.

It was a snug room, but the view made up for it: from the desk, Toni could see the whole of Dublin's rooftops in what she called the art-and-market part of the city. WIB was a charitable organisation and had no money to spend on fancy offices, so their base was on the third floor and attic of an old warehouse, with a set designer and two sculpture studios beneath them and a herb importer across the road. Today, the scent of rosemary was palpable in the air, and Toni took in a deep breath as she placed two mugs of instant coffee on the low table and grabbed her notebook from the desk. Folding her long limbs elegantly, Toni settled herself into an armchair and looked at the woman opposite her.

Fragrant, fluttery and lipsticked, she decided.

Toni was good at coming up with three-word descriptors for people. Oliver, her husband, had thought it was like a party trick when they were first married and used to make her do it for all guests in their home. But nobody liked being reduced to three words, Toni had found. People liked to think they were mysterious and rounded, worthy of scores of adjectives, and so most of the time Toni kept the skill to herself.

The woman in the office smiled tentatively at Toni, who swapped 'fluttery' for 'tentative' and took a grim sip of coffee. It was not easy to be a success in business if you were tentative. Business success generally required ovaries of steel, a phrase which quite often shocked people when Toni said it aloud.

'Nobody ever complains about "balls of steel",' Toni would regularly point out to her board. From the beginning, she had felt the board would all benefit if she didn't mince her words, and in the past year and a half since she'd taken up her new role, they had been shocked non-stop.

Men thought that testicles were the strong bits and ovaries were delicate, while the actual possessors of ovaries knew that ovaries pumped out eggs that could grow into actual humans – it was incredible what the female body could do, Toni often thought, even though she had never grown a human herself and was glad of the fact because she still had a pelvic floor and could sneeze without wetting herself. But still. Balls and men were not made of steel. Women were.

Oliver loved it when she held forth at parties about how women were the stronger sex.

'Did I rattle on too much about men not appreciating women?' she'd asked in the taxi home after a particularly raucous dinner party some months ago. 'It's the mentoring. I get so annoyed at how women are treated. You wouldn't believe the stories I hear.'

Oliver wrapped one long arm around his wife in response and leaned in, his patrician face looking effortlessly handsome, even after he'd let his greying hair grow long for the part of a detective on television.

'You're magnificent when you're arguing, Toni,' he murmured, nibbling her earlobe.

Toni felt the flutterings of desire in her belly. Nothing was more erotic than a man who loved you for who you were.

In the small Women in Business office, Toni's mentee began to speak.

'You see,' began Ms Tentative, who was there for an hour-long mentoring session and had waited six months to get seen by Toni Cooper herself. 'I want to be taken seriously in my company or else I have to move. I'll have no option.'

Toni nodded. The woman, whose real name was Susanna, was fully stocked with intellect and degrees.

On paper, she was perfect. In real life, she had long chestnut hair that gleamed silkily, was petite and had an undeniable beauty which she was trying to hide with heavy-framed glasses and a long skirt suit with a jacket a size too big – covering herself up like an antelope hiding from big cats at the watering hole, and Toni understood the impulse.

The twin attributes of being beautiful and petite could definitely be a problem. Tall people, like Toni herself, were taken more seriously. Unfair but true. Nobody would ever dream of sitting on the edge of Toni Cooper's desk and smiling benignly down at her the way they did to so many other Women in Business. Any that tried were instantly sorry, and in consequence, some men called her a ball-breaker.

They weren't real men like her husband, she thought. Oliver had never been emasculated by her success.

'Tell me,' she said now, looking at Susanna, who was watching her eagerly, a notebook on her lap, ready to write down the pearls of wisdom because, damnit, Toni Cooper was fabulous, and if she couldn't help Susanna, nobody could. 'What is the word you use most? In general conversation?'

'Sorry?' Susanna blinked.

Toni held up a hand.

'You don't have to say another word,' she said. '*Sorry* – it's the Woman's Mantra—'

'No, that's not the word—' began Susanna.

'It's the first thing you said when I asked you a question, so yes, it *is* the word.'

She angled her head, turning catlike sea green eyes onto Susanna, who folded.

'OK. It's the word but I – you know . . .' she finished pleadingly.

Toni knew. Unbidden, her sister Lou came to mind. Lou was the most golden person Toni had ever met and 'sorry' was her default word, too. Goodness shone out of Lou, she spent her life helping other people – and what did that get her? Nothing. Absolutely nothing. She ran around after their mother as if Lillian was a feeble little old lady instead of a fearsome woman who had never seen a door or a rival she couldn't flatten.

It was Lou's fiftieth birthday party on Friday and Toni had arranged to have her TV show recorded instead of running live so she could be there. She still hadn't bought Lou a present yet. It wasn't so much a case of what you got the person who had everything but instead, what did you get for the person who never asked for anything?

'Is my hair too long?' asked Susanna suddenly.

Toni's razor-like brain returned to the issue at hand and she felt the familiar weariness at the issue itself.

Hair, nails, the wrong shoes – why couldn't women be judged on the right things instead of on the surface ones? She saw nothing wrong with having her hair professionally dried twice a week. But one profile had nastily worked out how much this luxury had cost her.

'Can you explain why this worries you?' she asked.

'It's very pretty and my friend says it's—' Susanna paused. 'Cute. I don't want to be cute,' she added hotly. 'I do everything I can to dispel any notion that I'm—'

'Female?' asked Toni.

'Yeah,' said Susanna with a sigh. 'I like my hair and I've always had it long.'

Toni paused.

'How you look or what way you do your hair shouldn't matter,' she began, 'but it does. Some of us – women, people of colour, people who dress certain ways because of their religious beliefs – get judged on what we wear, how we look, what lipstick we like, what gender we're attracted to . . . The list is endless. It's wrong. None of it affects how we work, but some people judge us on that and find us wanting. So we need to be strategic. Tell me about your work life.'

Susanna sat poised with pen and notebook.

Toni wished she could say that society needed to change but this would not be a helpful statement. Once she'd helped Susanna, then Susanna could be a Women in Business recruit and help other people. Person by person they'd change the world.

And nobody would have to explain their hair choices, why they wore flat shoes or high ones or a headscarf or not.

One day.

The church bell was ringing to announce ten o'clock morning Mass as Gloria Cooper stood outside Whitehaven Helps charity shop and polished the glass in the front door. Holding onto her walking stick with one hand as she cleaned, the town's news drifted past her as people hurried along Main Street. News travelled fast in Whitehaven. Always had.

Gloria, who was gently freewheeling towards eighty-five, could remember when the news came via Old Mac with the milk in the morning as well as from Mr Johnson, the postman, who brought Dr Cooper's letters as if each was a medical emergency in itself.

Both men knew that Gloria's father, Dr Cooper, never gossiped, no matter how they waited for a titbit.

Still, news moved just as quickly then as nowadays when everyone had a phone surgically attached to their hand.

Whitehaven's Main Street was busy and as people walked by, snippets of conversation came to Gloria as she wiped slowly. There was to be a party, people were saying.

'Marco from the Gin Palace is outraged about it . . .' muttered one woman into her phone as she walked past.

A couple were discussing how Jess from the bakery was wondering if she could get an invite. Three forty-something women in leggings and trainers walked past the charity shop with their yoga mats, exhausted after their morning Iyengar class which had stretched their muscles to pure fluidity.

'It's Toni Cooper and her husband,' one of the women was saying in between sips of water. 'He was in that Netflix programme about Armageddon. Awful muck but he was good in it, wasn't he? You wouldn't kick him out of bed for eating crisps, even though he's no spring chicken . . . !'

'Toni's mother, Lillian, is getting an award. I bet that's it. She must be seventy if she's a day. Looks amazing,' a second yoga lady said. 'I think she's had Botox and some stuff in her lips. Not a line on her forehead but no face lifts. Definitely has sex appeal. The men are still mad for her, my mother says. You know my mother: loves a gossip. Says there's a trail of men in and out of that house, although Lillian apparently insists she hasn't looked at a man since poor Bob died. I mean, Too Much Information. Imagine sex at her age . . . Blast! That's his sister over there . . . shush!'

Gloria kept on serenely cleaning the door, adopting the manner of a woman who hadn't heard a word. When Lillian was your sister-in-law, the ability to appear deaf had always been an asset. It had from the very first moment. Even at Lillian and Bob's wedding, Gloria could recall the bridesmaids venting in the ladies' room about how they looked like green armchairs in their high-necked pouffy, damask frocks while Lillian was a vision in slender white chiffon and a deep 1970s V-neck that revealed her untethered full breasts.

'Channelling a Van Eyck painting my foot! She made us wear these hideous dresses on purpose so we'd look like pregnant overblown Madonnas and she'd look fabulous by comparison!' one bridesmaid had hissed, unaware that Gloria was in the bathroom, too, and when Gloria had sailed out of the cubicle later, it had been with a sedate smile nailed to her face.

Assumed deafness had been a boon when it came to Lillian and, true to form, fifty years later, nothing had changed.

Gloria looked at the shop's window, assessing it for any dirt that could mar the excellent window display, which was all flowers and pink prettiness in readiness for Mother's Day in a couple of weeks. Gloria's niece, Louise, had decorated the window on Saturday, bringing early roses from her own garden and tying cunning little paper flowers to each corner of the window with ribbons fluttering down. Like everything Lou did, it was completed quickly, without fuss – and afterwards, Lou had determinedly waved away thanks.

'It's nothing,' she said, standing back as Gloria and Aoife, who was the shop's manager, admired the window.

'It's not nothing,' Gloria replied, patting her niece gently on the shoulder with a thin hand. 'It's beautiful.'

'Gloria, stop,' said Lou, blushing. 'Anyone could do it.'

'But anyone didn't. You did it.'

Even though Lou had a full-time job, a daughter, and countless else to do besides, she had come to help – while Lillian had declared herself far too busy sculpting. And why should Lillian exert herself for others when she had Lou to do her charity work for her?

Gloria closed her eyes and said a quick prayer for forgiveness. It was a prayer she said a lot, and almost always about Lillian. When Bob and Lillian had become engaged, Gloria had made a promise to her dear mother, always to be kind to her.

'She's not like our family, but Bob loves her,' her mother had said, and Gloria had agreed.

She was as kind to Lillian as she could be. It wasn't always easy. After what Lillian had done, all those years ago, Gloria hadn't thought she would ever speak to her again. But there hadn't been an angry word between them for years now. They had buried the past with great success and now there were only three people alive who knew the whole story – or perhaps only two – and that was for the best. Her nieces could never know.

Gloria sighed. It was better that way. Far better for all concerned.

'Miss Cooper! You shouldn't be cleaning the door and windows,' said Aoife, the shop's perky manager, arriving now with her rucksack and the inevitable black sack of donations – when a person worked in a charity shop, everyone and their lawyer had a black sack of old clothes for them.

'It was a five-minute job,' said Gloria easily. 'I wouldn't have done it if I hadn't felt able.'

'But you're—'

Gloria smiled. 'Old? Yes, Aoife, I know. Rubbing a cloth over the glass in the shop door isn't going to make me older. I love the town in the morning. When you're quietly outside, everyone passes by, nobody notices you and you hear all the news.'

'What news?' asked Aoife, following the slightly stooped figure into the shop.

Gloria adored Aoife, who she knew considered Gloria a beloved relic of the past – a being who might drop dead at the drop of a hat. Young people were very scared about the elderly, Gloria found.

Aoife often worried when Gloria had one of her chests and fretted about her tripping over Sugar, Gloria's tiny dog. At her age, Gloria found there was no point in worrying anymore.

'There's great chat about the party on Friday,' said Gloria now. 'Half the town thinks it's Lillian's party and she's being presented with some award. The other half think it's Toni and Oliver's bash and that most of the glitterati will be there.'

'But it's Lou's fiftieth,' said Aoife. 'Don't people know that?'

'Apparently not. There are people in life who get overlooked,' said Gloria.

'How could anyone overlook Lou? She's an angel.'

Gloria bent very slowly to attach Sugar's pink tartan lead to her pink tartan harness. Sugar was a rescue dog: part chihuahua, part mystery. She was small, white, soft as an eider duck, quivered a lot and had great big eyes that spoke of early cruelty. Gloria idolised her and Sugar idolised her mistress in return.

Sugar was a wise little dog and adored Lou. She sensed the gentleness and fragility that other people usually missed when it came to Gloria's niece.

'That's the crux, isn't it,' said Gloria to Aoife, picking up Sugar. 'Nobody ever sees angels or notices what they do.'

Aoife nodded.

'And sometimes,' Gloria went on thoughtfully, 'even angels get fed up.'

Chapter Three

Lou repeated her mantra as she drove to her mother's house on Wednesday evening: 'The universe will provide, the universe will provide.'

She hadn't told anyone about not getting the strategy job. Not her family. Not Ned, who was planning a trip to Munich for an engineering conference the following week and was so busy that he hadn't mentioned her birthday party or what present he was getting her. Not Emily, who had a college assignment due and who was coming home on Thursday night to be with her mother for the big celebration. And Lou had definitely not told Toni, who would undoubtedly explain where Lou had gone wrong in her approach to the entire thing. If Toni had worked for Blossom, it would be multi-national by now and Toni would be managing it from a yacht somewhere as well as running for president of Ireland in between writing her memoirs. No, Toni definitely didn't need to know that

Lou hadn't been hired for a job she was basically already doing. It was too humiliating.

The worst moment had been when Bettina had hugged Lou sympathetically, reassuring her that she would like the new employee, the one with the degree who apparently knew way more than Lou.

'She is a woman, and young! You will get on with her and help her!' I know how wonderful you are at helping people, and she will need help because the job will have such long hours. I think it would be too much for you or me! Bettina had beamed as she spoke, her youthful face full of pleasure at how things in her world were working out, and how she obviously felt that Lou was too old for such a strenuous new position. Lou had been momentarily lost for words. They'd already hired someone, it seemed, before telling her she hadn't got the job, and thought that Lou would assist the new – young – company strategist who would move Blossom into a whole new dimension. Lou would even help her understand how the company worked. Fantastic!

Lou buried this mortifying information safely inside her and did her best to ignore it. But she couldn't.

'Universe, I do hope you know what you're doing,' Lou said out loud as she drove, negotiating the winding Pine Hill in the evening light. 'Mim, could you keep an eye on Universe in case She's busy and has forgotten about me?'

Lou never told anyone that she still talked to Mim, but the one-sided conversations gave her comfort. Mim had been such a unique person that Lou knew she'd never be able to think up what Mim would say in any given situation, but she could intuit it. Mim was still with her, she knew that.

Lou pulled in at the peeling white gates to her mother's house and parked behind Lillian's car, an elderly SUV that was perfect for transporting oddly shaped wire and iron sculptures, but not so perfect for parking. The car, once blue, was now dotted with silver and white from the myriad dents and scrapes where the paint had been bashed away. Lillian was blasé about her parking accidents.

What was the point of leaving notes on people's cars telling them she bumped into them.

'People don't care,' she'd say cheerfully. 'What's a little scratch when the world is falling around us. We need perspective. Look at . . .' and she'd draw everyone's attention to whatever the important world events were and make everyone see that a car – a mere car – hardly mattered.

Emily, child of two careful drivers, had always been fascinated by her grandmother's blithe disinterest in the state of her own car or anyone else's.

'Lillian's funny,' the little Emily had said.

Unlike Ned's mother, Ruth, who was Nana, Lillian was never called *Granny*.

'I'm a feminist! I can't be defined by my relationship to other people!' Lillian would say. 'Perish the thought of a child calling me Granny. I'd rather die!'

Lillian had made her daughters call her by her given name once they'd been teenagers.

Mummy had sounded so *old*, she'd said once.

'Women are defined by words. Grandmother would define me as old in a way grandfather does not. No, I choose to define myself,' she'd said regally, and had later repeated it in an interview with a local newspaper when she opened an art exhibition for one of her friends.

Lillian Cooper made excellent newspaper copy because she always had an opinion on everything.

'When I'm a grown-up, I won't have a car,' Emily said when she was little, 'but if I did, I'd have one you can bump into things with, like Lillian's.'

Lou got out of her own never-dented old Nissan and carefully avoided the nettles that grew happily beside the dog roses to one side of the driveway.

Valclusa was on a corner, a two-storey farmhouse that had expanded over the fifty years that Lillian had lived in it. Early photos had shown a neat house with sparkling windows and a tamed garden. In one of her favourite pictures, Dad was holding the toddling Lou's hands as she made her way around the garden. He'd been a tall man with a kind face, fair wavy hair and the sparkling sea green eyes that Toni but not Lou had inherited. He was always smiling in the photos with his first-born, pride and sheer happiness all over his narrow, thoughtful face.

Then came photos with little Toni: being carried around, then toddling, while Lou looked on proudly. She'd adored being an older sister.

Initially, she'd wanted a rabbit instead of a baby but Toni, a fair-haired little sprite with those curious cat eyes and tiny little fingers that clamped onto Lou's hands trustingly, had been the best gift ever.

Lou still loved those photos and had an entire family wall on her upstairs landing covering her and Toni's childhood and long after, right up to Emily's twentieth birthday party last year, with Christmases, holidays and school plays amid it all.

Family was where the heart was.

People who said differently just didn't understand.

That thought often held Lou together. She was so lucky. She had a wonderful family, people who needed her. The job was just a job, after all.

Thanks, Mim, she said mentally. *That's just what I needed to think. It was just a job. I have so much more in my life than a mere job.*

Being at her old home solidified this notion in her head.

Of course, Valclusa looked different these days than it had in her childhood.

For a start, since Dad had died, the tidying regime had gone out the window. Lou's mother was excellent at making a mess but had no interest in cleaning up. That was her artistic side, Lou thought fondly.

The garden was no longer tamed unless Lou had a go at it. Lillian had built a slightly ramshackle studio onto the side of the house. A wooden structure with two huge windows, it had been bitterly cold the previous winter and talking to a builder about insulation was on Lou's never-ending to-do list. Her mother would never get round to it and Lou felt it was her duty to do so. Lillian also had a plan to build a giant rockery, though Lou wasn't sure at what stage of planning this was. It was amazing having this wonderfully creative person as a mother, but creative people had marvellously inventive ideas about their surroundings and naturally expected other people to bring them to fruition.

'Lillian!' she called as she reached the black kitchen door, where several dying plants, still in their garden centre pots, were sitting haphazardly beside an old Belfast sink that Lillian had rescued from a skip.

There was no reply. Unfazed, because not getting a reply was quite normal, Lou took the spare keys to her mother's house from her handbag and unlocked the door.

The kitchen was ablaze with lights and the scent of cigarettes mixed with wet dog hit her as soon as she entered. Something was in the oven and, peering over to look, Lou saw that a pile of frozen chips had been shoved in recently. The cooker top was a mess and, instinctively, Lou moved towards the sink and the cleaning stuff before remembering that she had to say hello first. She could tidy up afterwards. Lillian forgot stuff like cleaning.

Her mother and three guests were in the living room, ranged on the two big couches, all holding wine glasses and cigarettes. A small dog, something in the Dachshund department and clearly the source of the wet canine scent, lay on the floor holding a stick in its mouth as if daring anyone to take it away.

'Hello! We're celebrating,' said Lillian.

Tall and statuesque, Lillian Cooper had held onto her 1950s bombshell figure with the help of cigarettes and clever underwiring. Her hair had once been jet black and swept back from a high forehead, but now it was dyed black except for a shocking white streak that the hairdresser said was impervious to dye. Her lips had the unnaturally full curve of injected hyaluronic acid, which made Lou nervous on Lillian's behalf, and were now outlined only faintly in Moscow Red liner which she made Lou order for her on the internet. Today, she was dressed in one of her trademark long white shirts with an armful of silver bangles, and black ankle-length trousers. The heavy clogs on her narrow feet were the only hint that she worked with metals.

It was, Lou thought with a sigh, easy to see why her mother attracted people so easily and also to see where Toni had got her looks. They had the same catlike eyes, the same way of making people look at them.

'This is my daughter, Lou. No,' Lillian said to the man with the damp dog at his feet, 'not the one with the career and the famous husband. Lou works in flowers and is the milk of human kindness, aren't you, darling?'

Lou smiled around. Her mother always said that Lou was *the milk of human kindness*.

Lillian had been saying it since Lou was eight and Lillian came down with pneumonia one summer after a Bacchanalian art festival which had included midnight sea swims, much smoking and no sleep. All hell for the immune system.

Dad had been away, Lillian had been confined to bed and three-year-old Toni's nursery school had been closed for the holidays. Only Lou could step in. Lou adored being in charge, being needed. Adored being the milk of human kindness. How many people got to be called that? It meant you were appreciated, loved. She'd basked in the words, and still did.

'Pull up a chair,' said one of the men.

'Meet Timothy, Charles and Peadar,' announced Lillian. 'I totally forgot they were travelling round this way. I mean, who can cope with putting things in a diary? I certainly can't. They're staying in The Ashling B&B on the Dublin Road, but nasty old Mrs Butler won't let the dog in.'

'Your mother offered me a bed here,' said one of the men cheerfully.

'Lovely,' said Lou, wondering if the men were staying for dinner. She didn't want to ask in case it sounded rude, yet she had to ask, for her mother's sake. Lillian hated cooking these days and the chips in the oven would hardly feed everyone, would they?

'You couldn't make up the bed in the red bedroom, could you, sweetie?' cajoled her mother. 'And bang some sausages or something in a pan? I've found oven chips, but they look dreadfully old and we're all ravenous. Peadar's got an exhibition coming up. We're celebrating it and planning the guest list.'

'Yes, of course,' said Lou. The flutterings of anxiety abated. She knew what to do: all was fine. If there were no sausages, she'd go out. Lou to the rescue.

Upstairs, she looked in at the airing cupboard and poked around. It had been months since she'd tidied it. Months. At the time, she'd replaced some of the more ripped sheets with perfectly serviceable ones she'd ordered from IKEA. Not that she'd said this, although she'd agonised over the decision. Lillian was very attached to her old and expensive high-thread-count ones. But it hadn't mattered. Lillian hadn't actually noticed, which meant Lou had made the right choice.

One large grey sheet, a very seventies flowery duvet cover and two matching pillowcases later, the red bedroom's slightly sagging double bed was made up. Lou eventually found the vacuum cleaner in the studio, where it was plugged in with little evidence of it having been used, and ran it over the red bedroom floor. She dusted quickly, then looked around to see where the little dog would sleep.

Her mother was not an animal person. Dogs had never lived in Valclusa. Nor cats, for all that Lillian admired their elegance and had once had a cat-sculpting phase. The Bast phase, she'd called it, after the Egyptian half-cat goddess. Lou had wanted a dog from when she was very small, but she knew it wasn't allowed. Her mother was scared of dogs and she thought they were messy things too.

'Dogs are dirty,' Lillian said. 'I am not cleaning up after it.'

So, no dog unless you were a guest, obviously. Lillian was a wonderful hostess.

Lou made a nest of old towels on the floor near the radiator, which was the warmest spot in the room if the wind howled, which it could do in March. If the dog needed water, she assumed the owner would sort that out. Was that the right thing to do, she wondered.

'I'll run to the corner shop,' she yelled when she was finished, had checked the fridge and found it empty. Nobody replied.

Sausages, eggs, milk, some raspberries and yogurt for breakfast, along with brown bread and a tin of dog food later, she was back at Valclusa.

'Very kind of you,' said one of the men, coming into the kitchen to replenish the bottle, and seeing the tin of dog food on the table. The dog followed him.

'I had forgotten about Monty's dinner.'

Lou, who was quite immune to shock, stopped cutting the cellulose casing connecting the sausages. The words came out of her mouth almost before she could stop herself: 'You hadn't got anything for him to eat?'

If she'd had a dog, it would certainly eat before she did. Lou believed that true love meant others came first and if she'd been a pet owner, said pet would be cosseted the same way she cosseted the people she loved.

'Monty and me can survive!' the man said cheerfully.

'Oh, dogs will eat anything,' agreed Lillian dismissively, following him in. 'Well done, sweetie. Perfectly decent dinner. If you could cook it and then off you trot. I'm sure Ned's waiting for his dinner. Her husband's an engineer,' she added to her guests, in a vaguely *sotto voce* manner. 'Very boring. There's no art in numbers, no matter what they say.'

Lillian and her guests all laughed.

Lou smiled too because it was stupid to take offence, her mother often said.

'Sweetie,' Lillian went on to Lou, 'I might run up to Dublin with the boys tomorrow for the weekend. I want to go shopping. There's a lovely rumour' – she beamed at her guests – 'that yours truly might be the first female recipient of the Kennedy Art Prize! I know . . . Utterly thrilling. So I'll need an outfit. But I think I have boulders for my rockery coming sometime next week. I can't recall the details. You can ring and ask, can't you, because somebody needs to be here for the delivery —'

'Lillian,' said Lou, and she found that her voice was ridiculously quivery. 'It's my party on Friday night.'

Lillian's mouth fell downwards.

'This Friday?' she asked.

'Yes,' breathed Lou.

Lillian paused, calculating. She did not look pleased.

'Boys, you'll have to go without me,' she said finally, but her face was taut with displeasure. 'Now, more wine?'

As Lou drove off twenty minutes later, the meal cooked and ready to go, she wished she'd eaten a few of the sausages herself. She was ravenous, and Ned wasn't waiting at home for his dinner. He was out at a work event tonight but, even if he hadn't been, Ned's habit was to eat whenever he got hungry and he never expected Lou to cook for him. The corollary was that he never cooked for her either. When it came to food, he was entirely self-sufficient and grazed endlessly.

Still, her mother hadn't known Ned was out and Lou hadn't wanted to press herself upon her mother and her guests. She was 'the milk of human kindness', too. She hoped that not leaving water for the dog was the right decision.

Near home, the phone rang and Lou, who feared being stopped by the police, rapidly pulled into the side of the road.

'Lou. Glad I got you,' said Ned's cheery voice. 'I tried the house, but you were out.'

'I was over at Lillian's,' she reminded him, although she'd mentioned it that morning. Ned would forget his head if it wasn't attached.

'Of course,' he said quickly. 'Anyway, are you home now?'

'No,' she said, and hopefully added, 'are you on your way?'

'Hell's bells, no,' he said. 'I'll be hours. Listen, I can't believe I've forgotten this but—'

Lou began to smile. Dear Ned. He'd finally thought of her birthday present. He was hopeless at gifts and he'd need a bit of a steer. She'd mention the gold bangle or tell him about the hand-dyed silk scarves in the Things of Beauty shop in town . . .

'I'm lending the big computer power bank to Barry because he's off on that cycling trip at the weekend and if you don't put it out in the hall, I'll forget it again. Could you grab it from the study and put it out where I'll trip over it?'

'Sure,' said Lou, feeling utterly forgotten for the second time in half an hour. 'Will do.'

'You're a treasure, Lou,' said her husband. 'Bye. Don't wait up!'

Not everyone was a treasure, Lou reminded herself as she set off again.

She'd have a me-time night, she decided. Maybe a bath. If she was braver, she'd think about what to wear to the party, but she didn't feel all that brave. She and Mim had talked about reaching the grand old age of fifty and being fit and toned. Now she was there on the cusp of fifty and she wasn't even vaguely toned. Her A-line dresses were a necessity now, elegant cover-ups to hide the results of every bar of chocolate and poor food choice. While poor Mim was gone.

I'm sorry, Lou said to her friend. *I am so sorry, my darling. You'd have done anything to reach fifty. I'm just a complaining old cow and ignore me. Promise?*

How could Lou worry about a silly job, her mother momentarily forgetting her birthday or about Ned being incapable of remembering her birthday gift? They were silly problems. Not real ones.

Lou turned into her own drive, brightening up as she always did at the sight of the cottage with its painted veranda. The clematis cirrhosa was already coming to the end of its winter flowering, the glossy evergreen leaves making the pretty cream bell-shaped flowers stand out.

Lou knew she was so lucky in so many ways. Her beloved Emily would be there the next night to help her pick the outfit, and Lou breathed in the relief at that thought. She missed Emily in a way she could never explain to anyone. Her darling daughter had flown the nest and while it was wonderful that Lou had taught her how to fly, it was incredibly hard to watch her do it. Still, they'd have precious time together from tomorrow evening. And Friday *would* be a fabulous night because it would have all her favourite people there – apart from her father and darling Mim.

Lou would just have to keep Oszkar and Bettina away from Toni, in case they spilled the beans about hiring someone else. Toni would not take that well. Neither would Ned. But these were minor concerns, Lou knew. If she could smile at her employers, and she was the one who hadn't got the job, then her family would have to cope with it too.

People missed out on jobs all the time, after all. There was no point getting upset about it.

After all, she was going to be fifty and that was the important part. Not everyone was lucky enough to reach fifty: it must be celebrated. The universe was watching over her and how could she have doubted it.

Chapter Four

Three hundred and fifty miles away, Toni rushed up the steps of the Dublin theatre foyer to catch up with Flossie Ryan, her oldest friend from the world of acting.

'I'm late because the traffic was a nightmare,' said Toni, embracing Flossie, who was wearing her lucky preview coat, an indigo velvet piece.

'I whizzed in because I got a taxi,' said Flossie, beaming at her and wriggling out of the coat, which was too hot in the warmth of the foyer. 'Drinkies afterwards!'

Flossie draped her coat around her shoulders and Toni helped her adjust it.

'It's getting so worn,' said Flossie, adjusting a threadbare sleeve where the nap of the velvet had worn away to reveal just bare blue fabric.

'But you have to wear it,' finished Toni, grinning. Flossie had worn the coat many years ago for the preview of the wildly successful Oscar Wilde season both their husbands had been in and now, in the superstitious world of actors, the coat was a necessity. Flossie had to wear it, her husband, Bernard, insisted or the play would be a disaster.

Toni was just glad that she hadn't been around all those years ago and thus confined to wearing something she'd long outgrown fashion wise. She was wearing an elegant camel coat over a sleek cream woollen dress which showed off her slender legs in knee-high tan leather boots. Simple and chic: that was Toni's style. Once she put clothes on, she forgot about them.

Tonight was the first preview of *King Lear* and the show proper wasn't starting its run until the following Thursday. Therefore, tonight, dinner and many bottles of wine were inevitable and the cast would post-mortem the whole production.

Flossie, like Toni, was married to an actor, although in the hierarchy, Flossie's husband Bernard was several fathoms below Oliver Elliott. Bernard was a character actor, with a face described as 'interesting' and not a hint of the leading man about him. Whereas Toni's husband Oliver, with his flowing dark hair with the hint of grey at the temples, clever grey eyes and Roman orator's profile, was very much leading man material. He was, naturally, playing Lear.

'Haven't they done a completely gorgeous job of the repainting,' said Flossie, leading the way into the theatre, a delicious cachepot of a theatre that resembled a French cake: pastel curlicues and baby blue pillars all lovingly recently redecorated with painted-on ivy and improbably large flowers.

'Yes,' agreed Toni, not appreciating it all.

She always felt a huge wave of trepidation at play previews. Actors were such sensitive souls and a preview was a time when their hard work was laid bare for everyone to see. They were laying themselves wide open for everyone else to skewer them. Having been married to one for years and having spent many hours among actors, Toni would not be one for any amount of money. Oliver was such a strong character: determined, brilliant and wise. Yet even he could be felled by a harsh review, though it had been years since he'd had one. The worst he received nowadays were the critics saying he was wasted in the role.

'Oliver Elliot shone in an otherwise lacklustre production,' was a common theme.

'Bernard says it's a fabulous production. Majestic, he said,' Flossie went on, holding onto Toni's arm. Flossie was one of life's affectionate people. She liked to pet her friends and acquaintances, stroking their hair and their arms.

'He says Oliver's magnificent,' Flossie continued.

Toni smiled with quiet pride. Oliver was always magnificent. He had been ever since Toni had met him when she was twenty-six. He'd been forty-four. She'd seen him at a Yeats' poetry recital and at the after-event party he'd made his way over to her with laser-like intensity.

She was fresh from work but had changed briefly into a draped shift, swimming-toned arms and long hair, making her look like an Amazon just back from a bit of archery.

'When I spotted you, I felt that I had to meet you. I deserved a treat,' Oliver had said, looking her up and down with hunger in his gaze.

Toni was tall but he was taller. Six foot four with charisma oozing out of every pore.

'I'm positively ancient compared to you,' he added in that famous gravelly voice, his eyes implying that he thought no such thing.

'I like older men,' Toni said boldly. 'In fact, I don't know if you're old enough for me.'

Wrong-footing people was something she was working on at the time – her mother was an expert at it – but Oliver had simply raised one eyebrow, smouldering. He'd recently starred in a French film with a César-winning actress and they'd scorched the screen. Despite an abundance of self-confidence and a determination to have a successful career before she even thought about any man in a serious way, Toni had fallen for him.

Seventeen years later, she still adored her husband, but she wasn't blind to his faults. When he was rehearsing, Oliver became the character he was playing and, in preparation for this Lear, he'd been rampaging around the house declaiming. It was easier when he was playing the television detective for the BBC Northern Ireland show because the detective was a thoughtful man who did not feel the need to rampage at dinner. In his detective persona, Oliver wore his hair long and bought her flowers and perfume, but as Lear, he shaved in such a way as to leave manly stubble as per the artistic director's instructions and scowled at dinner. He'd been less scowly lately, though and more . . . distant, yes, that was the word, Toni thought. He spent a lot of time in their shared work office, staring at his old laptop.

'Research,' he'd mutter whenever Toni asked what he was up to.

She'd left him to it, but she'd felt she was being excluded in some way, which was irrational, she thought, given the way they'd always lived their lives. Their marriage worked because they had different professional lives and each respected the other's work ethic. They were separate beings but had a shared life. Toni had no time for couples who did everything together.

'Oliver and I complement each other but we're not tied together,' she liked to say.

Yet recently she'd felt that perhaps the healthy distance between them was stretching.

She'd only felt that once before when Oliver had been on a two-month film shoot in Brazil. She'd worried – irrationally, it turned out – about the hours spent with his younger co-star, Alba, a Spanish actress with the broodingly sensual dark eyes of a Goya model.

'I would never look at another woman, you should know that,' Oliver had said when he was home again, when too much wine made Toni admit what she had barely admitted to herself. 'Why would you worry about Alba?'

'We're here,' announced Flossie now as they reached their row near the stage and sat down to discover that right behind them was an excited gaggle of beautifully made-up women in their twenties. Their clothes sparkled as if they were en route to a nightclub, and every one of them had eyelashes that fluttered like butterfly wings.

Toni briefly wondered if she was getting old because she didn't want false lashes and then decided that no, she wasn't old. Just not twenty.

'I bet they're some of Marissa's party,' whispered Flossie, who always knew everything about everyone in a play.

'Marissa?' said Toni, wrong-footed. She had a fabulous memory, was known for it. There was no actor named Marissa in the production.

'Sheila's understudy,' said Flossie. 'Sheila's Achilles tendon snapped at yoga. Very painful, apparently. Marissa's just had two weeks to take over. It's a huge break for her, playing Cordelia, the most important female character, when she'd only had small parts up to now. Bernard says she's luminous. Oliver didn't tell you?'

'He probably did,' lied Toni.

Why the hell hadn't he told her?

'I've been so busy,' she added.

Someone had once said that Toni's most fabulous skill was being able to handle tricky people. In fact, her most fabulous skill was the secret one of being able to lie on demand, which was almost but not quite the same thing.

'You never stop working, do you?' Flossie said, patting Toni's hand in the over-familiar way that Toni would not have permitted from anyone else.

'As usual,' agreed Toni, her game face on.

Something was pinging in her brain, trying to come to the surface, but she ignored it, joining Flossie in speaking to the cast's friends and families until, finally, the lights were dimmed.

Relieved that all the talking was over, Toni sat quietly and waited for the curtain to lift. What was in her brain? She tried but couldn't reach it. No matter. She'd let it process quietly. The magic of the world of a play swept around the theatre, and the darkness enveloped everyone except the people onstage.

Toni caught her breath as she watched, but it wasn't because Oliver was playing the best Lear of his life or because she was admiring the work of the cast, all of whom she'd seen before.

Her breath had stilled at the sight of Marissa playing Cordelia, King Lear's only loving daughter. It was not for Marissa's acting but for her ethereal beauty. The pinging in Toni's brain became more insistent.

Far younger than the actress she was replacing, Marissa was also shorter. When she stood close to Oliver onstage, her slender blonde head bowed, she looked young and vulnerable. The set design was 1920s and the exquisite dresses that Lear's three daughters wore flowed beautifully in bias-cut symmetry over flanks and breasts. Marissa, in pale lilac satin, was a poem.

Not that Oliver appeared to notice. His Lear was commanding and brooding, the ageing king still trying to control. And yet, was he noticing Marissa but pretending not to? Theatre was all pretence, after all.

'Fabulous,' whispered Flossie to her.

'Yes, they all are,' Toni whispered back.

It was the automatic pilot response. Everyone was fabulous, nobody was ever a dud. Loyal to a fault, the cast's family and friends never said a bad word about any performance.

The language, taken from the ancient by the skill of the actors and made understandable, flowed over her but she barely heard the words. Instead, she watched as the vulnerable Cordelia stood beside her father, the king.

All directors interpreted things differently. This production involved much physicality. At that moment, Cordelia reached up to touch her father's face. Toni felt rather than saw that this touch was not one actor in character touching another. Marissa's young face burned with hero worship. Was that it? Was she overawed by her big break and her role opposite this titan of stage and cinema?

There was something magical about theatre, Toni had always thought. Magic that was so difficult to describe. There were no three words for it. It was always different. The suspension of disbelief and the sense that alchemy from one small stage could transport the audience into a whole other world. And yet, tonight, Toni was not transported. She felt a tingle of fear, as if every goosebump in her body suddenly raised in anticipation of a threat. She thought of Alba, the Spanish actress, and how she'd worried over Oliver's closeness to her. She'd been wrong then, so she was probably wrong now, too – wasn't she?

At the interval, shaken but pretending not to be, Toni led the way to the bar.

'Can you make vodka martinis?' Toni asked the barman when she and Flossie had made it past the throng.

'Can I make vodka martinis?' he asked back, obviously wildly outraged at such a suggestion. 'I can make a martini that would make an angel sing or take the sight out of your eyes.'

'We'll have two of the angel versions,' Toni said grimly. 'I need my eyes in my line of work.' She leaned closer to the barman. 'Could you make mine very strong?'

The pretty young women beside them were discussing manicures when Flossie and Toni went back to their seats, Toni heavily fortified with vodka from two industrial-strength martinis.

One of the women was displaying a hand with each fingernail decorated with a flash of silver and then a swirl of neon pink.

'Aren't the young so funny with their twinkly manicures,' said Flossie, and Toni realised, in a rush of horror, that Flossie had linked the two of them together. Together in their aged-ness, even though Flossie was well over fifty and Toni was ten years younger.

Alba. Alba and Marissa. The two younger women danced in her imagination.

The curtain was being drawn back and, before the lights went down totally, Toni looked unsteadily down at her own hands. Enormous work went into keeping herself slim and young, but the hands never lied when it came to age. The veins on the back of her slender hands were raised up, blue and knotted.

Her nails had no youthful flash of neon pink. She hadn't done much to her nails. She kept them simply manicured in a nude shade because she'd never wanted any commentary about her fingernails either. If she'd been all about her hair or her shoes or her manicures, then people would have boxed her into that compartment where women were ridiculed for certain things. Men with bad haircuts or ludicrous beer bellies never had these commented upon. But a woman in the public eye could not be so lucky. A woman in the public eye could not imagine the pain of her husband choosing a younger version, either.

Toni looked up at the stage and waited for her husband and Marissa. She would not rush to conclusions. Seventeen years of history could not be erased because of hero worship. But still, she felt unsettled. What if Oliver had finally succumbed to a younger woman? What then?

Toni felt the vodka settle into her body, calming her down in a way she knew was nothing but temporary. She'd settle for temporary at the moment; it would have to do until she could compute her way out of this.

As the alcohol did its thing, fake bravado flooded her: she was Toni Cooper. She had everything. What was she doing imagining crazy scenarios?

Oliver adored her. She was absolutely sure of that.

She would find out why he'd been distant. Face it head-on.

Not for Toni the head-in-the-sand approach to life.

She'd worked so hard to get to where she was now: a powerful, strong woman with a career, a loving husband, security and respect. She would not throw it all away because of Oliver flirting with another woman. Toni Cooper was stronger than that. She would fight for what was hers.

Chapter Five

Dawn was breaking, sending slow shoots of colour into the sky as if the Early Morning Goddess was racing around the east with a Zippo frantically lighting candles to spread light into the waking world. Lou sat curled up in the cushions on the wooden seat on the veranda that faced her small back garden, a fleece blanket wrapped around her, and a mug of lemon tea cradled in her hands. It would be warm later, the gentle warmth of late March, but now the morning was cool and, wrapped up and clutching her hot mug, Lou was able to enjoy her precious early moments of calm before she had to shower and race out the door.

She and Mim had begun the morning reset over ten years ago. They'd discussed a way to start their hectic days peacefully.

'I read something about sitting outside, if possible, and spending five or six minutes just being still and setting your intention for the day,' said Mim. 'Not that I can repeat that phrase to anyone but you.'

They both laughed loudly at how some of their more prosaic friends would scoff at such a notion.

'Martin would roar his head off at the notion of *setting your intention.*'

Mim's husband worked in sports management and viewed the world through the prism of the sports calendar and complex travel arrangements for various events.

'Ned would think I'd lost my marbles and he'd mention it to his mother, Ruth, by mistake and she'd be round like a flash with new rosary beads,' said Lou, grinning. Ruth was an old-school religious lady who liked Mass on Sundays and was wildly disapproving of anything she hadn't read in the *Whitehaven News*.

'Like praying? Is that what the five minutes is about? Prayer is what you need,' Ruth would declare. She was devoted to the church and was frustrated that none of her family were in the slightest bit devout.

'How 'bout we keep this just for us?' said Mim. 'Five Minutes of Peace.'

For ten years, nearly every weekday morning, both naturally early risers had sat outside their homes for the requisite five minutes and let themselves be calm. Mim was instinctively good at it. Her ability to sit and let peace flow through her was breathtaking. It had been harder for Lou, who felt the rising frisson of anxiety if she was sitting without a to-do list at her side. Thoughts kept breaking into her calm . . .

She had things to do.

Or 'Things To Do: IMPORTANT', as it said on her list.

Get the boiler serviced. Shop for food – buy stuff for the green soup diet. It worked, everyone said. Tasted disgusting, but it worked. Pounds dropped off when you lived on green soup. Call her friend Jackie, who was going through a tricky marriage break-up. Organise her mother's taxes because Lillian 'didn't do government things'. The government was 'an embezzling crowd of bastards!' when they wanted tax and miraculously transformed into 'those sweet politician boys' when the local county councillors had given her freedom of Whitehaven.

'Lou, it's only five minutes,' Mim had said. 'Five minutes of not thinking about anyone but yourself. No worrying about Emily or work or Ned or money or what complex mission your mother is planning for you.'

Mim didn't approve of Lillian.

'Ah, you just don't understand her,' Lou would say. 'She's had a tricky life. Dad looked after her and she's a bit lost since he's gone.'

Somehow, Lou had learned how to sit. Five minutes had become ten.

The summer that their daughters – school friends since the age of four – had unaccountably fallen out over a boy, they'd sometimes finished the morning reset with a quick phone call to discuss the intricacies of the teenage brain.

'Emily wants to dye her hair pink,' sighed Lou one morning. 'Kev likes pink . . .'

'What Kev likes most is setting girls against other girls,' groaned Mim. 'That boy is a menace to young women. I am waiting for the moment when Simone tells me she's fed up with him and she must have been mad to let him come between her and Emily.'

'Should we interfere—' began Lou.

'No.' Mim was firm. 'They have to sort it out themselves. They're nearly seventeen, Lou. It's a hard lesson. We can't learn it for them.'

The girls had figured it out. Kev was history.

And sadly, so too was Mim.

It would soon be two years since she'd died. Two years of no beloved Mim to talk to, to run things by, to relate how her day had been. It had been like having another sister: except that Mim wasn't high-powered in the way Toni was or constantly on the phone to some important person discussing a movie star's preferred questions about their new movie/husband/clothing range. It wasn't that Toni was an absent sister, but she had a big life and, by contrast, Lou felt her own life was small. Mim had been present in Lou's life on a daily basis in a way that Toni couldn't be.

Now Mim was gone.

Lou would be facing into her fiftieth birthday alone.

She didn't mind the age bit. Getting older was an honour Mim had been denied. But sometimes – feeling selfish at even thinking it because Mim's family had lost her too – Lou wanted her beloved friend with her just for another hour. Just to say . . . *I feel a bit lost, Mim. Now that Emily's gone to university, I'm not sure what I am anymore. Who are you when you're a mother and the person you mother has moved on? I wish you were here and we could be empty-nesters together, worrying about Simone and Emily.*

She'd woken early and a litany of sad things had sprung into her brain: her not getting the job; her mother forgetting about her party; the fact that Ned still hadn't got her a present. If he had, he'd have said something, tapped his pocket endearingly and said, 'Guess what I've got in here!'

But joy superseded the sadness – Emily was coming home that night, which was wonderful. Having Emily at home made Lou feel that her life was almost back to the way it had been.

Emily was seeing a new boy – well, a man, Lou corrected herself. Evan was twenty, the same age as her daughter, and he was someone she knew from Whitehaven. Lou knew Evan and his family and the Barking Dog in her head could come up with no dangerous scenarios with regards to him.

'Funny to go to Limerick to fall for a guy from round the corner,' Emily had said happily on the phone the previous night. 'I'll introduce you to him tomorrow night, Mum. It's not that serious,' Emily had added.

Lou finished her tea, put it down on the veranda rail and picked up the Tibetan worry dolls that hung from the wall. Mim had given two sets to her. One for the veranda and one for beside the bed.

'You need something to tell your worries to when I'm gone,' Mim had said.

She and Lou had loved things like worry dolls and little amulets. Between them, they had a store of bracelets and necklaces with Greek evil eye talismans, angel wings, Hands of Fatima, tiny ankhs, triple goddess moons – you name it.

'All tat,' Mim would say fondly, when they were shopping and found something else, a spindly bracelet or necklace of metal painted gold, dangling with charms and all set to tarnish in five minutes.

'But such lovely tat,' Lou would add, equally happily.

When Mim had died, Martin had found the ones she'd loved best and laid them on her hands in the coffin.

She hadn't seen him for ages, Lou thought guiltily.

Phone Martin needed to be on a list, so she grabbed her phone for her list section. The lists were colour coded – house ones for groceries, another house one for things like 'phone alarm company for inspection', work ones, personal ones and the over-arching 'MUST DO!' one which ravaged her brain at night.

She added Martin's name to MUST DO! and closed her eyes to say hello to Mim. She was definitely listening. Lou could feel her friend's presence. There were signs too: a white feather or a butterfly. She rarely said this to anyone because people would think she was bonkers. Sensible Lou believing in all this woo-woo? Fairies, angels, goddess moons? Really? Nobody would believe that she believed in 'signs', but then nobody would believe that she suffered from anxiety or took antidepressants, either.

When Mim was diagnosed with pancreatic cancer, Lou found that she couldn't sit still in the morning. The Fear hit her whenever she sat down. The diagnosis and subsequent investigations and treatment happened with speed. Mim was in and out of hospital. Her morning five minutes of peace became a phone call.

'Not as picturesque here as at home,' Mim said one day, her voice weak but her spirit still sounding strong. The window in her ward's little TV room, which was quiet in the morning, faced another wing of the hospital. The view, which Lou knew, was concrete accessorised with more concrete and squares of windows.

'Nature is represented by pigeons shuffling around and the odd seagull dive bombing past my window. The night staff keep dropping in, though, which is lovely. They've had a dreadful night with an older gentleman who is going fast. Poor pet. He's terrified.'

'You're so brave,' said Lou quietly.

The *unfairness* of it all. She was snug in her seat outside her home, her family were safe inside and the chattering birdsong from the two Japanese maples in her garden sounded as if the birds were planning a rave. Her reality was so different from her best friend's, and that difference seemed vast this morning.

Mim said nothing for a while.

'I'm not brave, not particularly,' she said finally. 'I have no option. This is it, Lou. I'm going to die. I can sob or I can keep going until my body decides it's over. For Simone, for Martin, for you—'

Lou caught her breath.

'I should be there for you, not the other way round,' she finally said, feeling something in her chest that made her think that hearts did, indeed, break.

'You're there for so many people, including me. Your presence in my life is enough. You don't have to *do* anything.'

'But you're fighting—'

'Do you know, I've come to really dislike the *cancer-fighting* motif,' said Mim suddenly. 'That, if and when you die, you haven't fought enough, the implication being that you *lost* the battle. People aren't expected to fight tsunamis or volcanic eruptions or famines. They just kill everyone in their path. So why do we have to "fight cancer". We have no control. When cancer has broken your body, you die.'

Mim had died two years before. It felt like years and moments simultaneously.

Lou still fretted and worried about the same things.

Now Lou sipped her tea and let the sights of the garden fill her senses.

Mim had sent her a card, delivered when she was dead, and it had been full of Mim's straightforward advice.

Take care of yourself. If you can keep resetting the day the way we used to, it would be wonderful. Could you do that?

Lou did her best to live up to her friend's request.

'I'm going to make fifty fabulous in honour of you, Mim,' she said into the sky.

Toni and Morag, her second-in-command in Women in Business, had arrived at Epsilon Radio at nine and had been drinking indifferent coffee in reception for the past thirty-five minutes.

'Is this normal?' said Morag, looking at her watch again.

Toni shrugged. Toni's day job was broadcasting in the prestigious AJH Television and Radio studios. Their guests often had to wait to go on-air but were offered decent coffee and an explanation of why they were waiting – but nobody had come to explain why their allotted slot was delayed. Toni was at Epsilon to appear on a panel discussion about a new report on the startlingly low figures of women in managerial positions in businesses. And she had a message to get across. She'd brought Morag because she needed to work on her media skills, but her deputy had to be in the WIB office for a mentoring session at half ten. And Toni had to be in her own studio for work by eleven.

Another nine minutes had passed, and Toni was about to stand up to leave when a harassed producer came out to bring Toni into the studio.

'What was the delay about?' she asked as she followed the producer into the studio, but before she got any further, a loud male voice was heard proclaiming: 'The traffic was dreadful. I hope you didn't mind waiting.'

There was a split-second while Toni tried to decide whether to be honest. Her fellow guest would have the interview to himself if she bailed.

There was nothing to be gained by appearing irate. Nothing at all. She was in the studio to discuss the report on women's lack of representation in senior roles in companies. Professionalism was the order of the day and there was no point in making an issue about the other guest, a businessman who ran a big company, making her late with his timekeeping. Sitting down, she fought hard not to shiver. The air conditioning in Epsilon's studio was on full blast but no one else seemed to notice. The latecomer was heavily insulated with the muscular bulk that came from schoolboy sports and probably plenty of hours in the gym where men were men and anybody who ran from the communal showers was considered a wuss. Now was not the time to explain that women felt the cold more than men because men's core body temperature was higher.

'So you're saying that despite everything, reports still show women in industry – in all jobs, you'd argue, Toni – aren't in the top jobs?'

'That's exactly what I'm saying,' Toni said.

They'd got precisely one minute into the ten-minute segment before Gerry Lanigan, her fellow guest with the poor timekeeping skills, got fully into his stride.

Ignoring the report on women in management entirely, he happily interrupted Toni.

'Ah now, you see,' he said cosily to the show host, 'I know it's an uncomfortable truth, but I have to say it: Toni and her ladies show that the world has gone crazy about being "woke". There are women in business in every company in the world, but feminists keep pretending it's not the case. They want all the management people to be women, which makes no sense. We need equality on both sides, not just for women's rights. It's all women's rights in my home.' He smiled as if at some great joke. 'My wife tells me what to do and my home is very female-oriented. Herself makes sure of it.'

There was laughter from the host.

'Gerry, I bet it's a full-time job keeping you in line.'

Toni, freezing cold and late for her next meeting because of this idiot, did not smile. She knew more about Gerry Lanigan than he thought. At Women in Business, they were quite well aware of companies where the corporate policy and public relations spouted one thing and the real-world experience was something else. In her role in WIB, part of Toni's job had been to rattle the cages of people like him. She was very good at it.

'Gerry, tell us about your team, your top team,' she said silkily. 'I presume because you're here this morning that there are many wonderful women on it?'

She watched with interest as Gerry's chest puffed up and his chin edged forward as if he was planning on banging it on the desk to show how hard he was.

'My team are wonderful,' he declared proudly. 'They'd follow me anywhere. On our recent team building weekend in Donegal, we were out all night on an exercise where we were all frozen but in high spirits. Orienteering is tough but, I have to say, it's a very bonding experience. We modelled the exercise on an army Ranger programme—'

Not male-oriented at all, Toni thought sarcastically, looking at Gerry's face. He honestly thought he was winning this one. Poor lamb.

'That Donegal trip sounds excellent,' the host said, 'and I'm sure your team would follow you anywhere,' he added.

It was time to interrupt.

'To return to my original point,' Toni said, reining in the host like she was lassoing a wayward cowboy, 'I know the army-style exercise sounds like good boyish fun, but the listeners want to hear about what Gerry's female management employees add to the team. That's the crucial thing in such a female-friendly company and, as Lanigan's have a lot of women executives, you can explain the benefits to listeners who run businesses that aren't so women-friendly.'

She waited a beat. There was the sound of silence.

'Obviously, you have women on your management team?' said Toni politely. 'Don't you?'

She waited again. It was like shooting fish in a barrel.

'How did the female members of staff fare on the bonding exercise?'

'Uh, the thing is . . . uh women work for me, of course,' Gerry stuttered.

If she'd been on television, Toni would have directed her clear gaze at the person she was about to eviscerate but this was radio and gazing was no use. She needed to paint the picture.

'I'm a little confused, so I'll rephrase.' Toni had many years of experience as an interviewer and she knew that one should be calm when one went in for the kill. 'I'm not getting the sense that you have female executives after all, Gerry. I must have misunderstood. Can you clear it up – do you have employees at managerial level who happen to be female?'

She waited another beat.

'Right,' she said in meaningful tones. 'If there are no women in management positions in Lanigan's, perhaps you could tell us precisely what is the turnover of women employees in your business? I can understand that you might not want to give out such statistics, but in companies without women in management roles, the turnover of female staff generally reflects whether what a company says publicly matches the actual facts.'

She smiled then at Gerry, who, too late, recognised an apex predator in the jungle.

'We can't let out important business information like that,' he muttered.

'We're here to discuss Women in Business and how you feel the world has become too "woke" as you put it. You implied that the world of business, especially in your own company, is an equal opportunities paradise. Information on how many women hold key positions in your company is surely vital to that.'

'True,' agreed the radio host. 'How many women are in key positions in the company?' he asked.

'Now . . .' Gerry looked harassed. 'I mean, we did . . . but she didn't work out—'

'*No* women in managerial positions, then?' said Toni. 'Apart from one person who may feel libelled at it being announced on the radio that her employment – what was it you said? *Didn't work out.*'

'I didn't come on the radio to be ambushed—' began Gerry, rage spreading like the red of sunrise on his face.

'You came on to tell us that there was no need for organisations like Women in Business to further the rights of women in business and that pro-female organisations are pandering to the concept of "wokeness",' Toni said, mask off now. 'You told us your lady wife runs you –

and my congratulations to her – but in fact, by your own admission, you have no women in key positions in your business, despite your previous assertions to the contrary. Your company's male bias certainly appears to be proof that the report we've seen today is an accurate one.'

She rearranged her papers significantly, taking one up as if she was about to read from it.

Gerry took the bait, assuming that she was about to launch a broadside with actual details of precisely who worked for him and what gender they were.

'Of course we need organisations like yours,' he said, in an attempt to sound humble. 'It's not always easy to know what various voluntary bodies do—'

'Women in Business is a network of women,' Toni explained, 'and we talk as openly as we are legally allowed to about our jobs and our industries. We mentor women, we share information on what we get paid and correlate that to real-world analyses of what men in the same positions get paid. I hope a time will come when society won't need us, but right now, clearly, it does.'

'Well put, Toni,' said the host, spotting a moment to close and move on. 'Thanks to Toni Cooper, inimitable mentor lead of Women in Business and one of Ireland's most successful broadcasters. And thanks to Gerry Lanigan . . .'

Gerry Lanigan gave a terse nod. He was glaring at Toni with absolute venom.

She had made an enemy there, Toni thought. She gathered her belongings and was out the studio door in a flash. She had no desire to hear the inevitable tirade when

Gerry got to his feet knowing he'd been made to look foolish on national radio. That was on his head, not hers.

'Why do they come on the radio to bluster like that?' asked Morag, as she and Toni left the building at speed.

'He came on the radio because the fact of being invited makes him feel important,' Toni said, thinking that she was somehow going to pay for showing up Gerry Lanigan on live radio.

Her phone rang and she answered quickly.

'Toni—' It was Oliver.

The strange pinging in her brain happened again. Oliver rarely phoned during the day unless he was working abroad or wanted to tell her of a change in plan.

'Yes?'

There was a pause, a scary pause.

'Darling,' said Oliver, 'we need to talk tonight.'

Neither the company boss she'd just eviscerated on-air or the radio host would have recognised Toni at that moment. Her face went white and masklike.

'What's wrong?' she said quickly, then remembered she wasn't alone. 'Actually, no – let's talk tonight. I'm in the city with Morag.'

'Fine,' said her husband tersely and hung up.

Fine? Toni felt her jaw clench. Something was wrong. Very wrong.

Chapter Six

Lou moved in the warm cocoon of the bed and felt Ned beside her reach for his phone to switch off the alarm. It was early morning and the dawn chorus soaring from outside made it feel as if the birds were singing inside the bedroom.

'Shit.'

She heard Ned's muffled swear as he saw the date and realised, as Lou knew he would, that it was her birthday. And that he hadn't got her a present.

She wouldn't get upset. *Don't sweat the small stuff,* she reminded herself.

'Lou, you awake?' he whispered.

Lou moved in the bed and reached a hand out over the covers. Her husband caught it, his hand closing over her slightly smaller one.

'Happy Birthday, Lou,' he said fervently and kissed her hand. 'I'm really sorry but I haven't—'

'I know,' she interrupted, not wanting him to have to go through the whole apology. 'I know.'

'I meant to,' he began again, 'but I didn't want Emily to have to get it because that's just outsourcing it, and you know how useless I am at things like that.'

'I know, it's fine,' she said and sat up in the bed.

Ned turned and pulled her into his embrace.

'I'm a useless husband,' he murmured into the cloud of her hair which always looked as if she'd had a spiral perm first thing.

Lou breathed in the scent of Ned, partly the musky scent of his skin and partly the smell of sweat because he'd gone into the garden the evening before and spent an energetic hour in the dusk sweeping the path and the driveway. He knew Lou loved everything to be tidy and he loved her enough to do boring things like sweeping up leaves and random garden detritus in order to make her happy. Those were the marks of love, she felt: the genuine thinking of another person. Not buying gifts.

'You're not a useless husband,' she said, which was what she always said.

Ned was anything but useless in so many ways. However, he was incapable of purchasing so much as a paperclip without express instructions. Plus, she had already known he'd got her nothing: had overheard the conversation between him and Emily in the kitchen the night before.

'Dad,' said Emily, exasperated, 'you can't have forgotten.'

'I didn't, it just slipped my mind because it was a busy day. You know how hopeless I am at buying gifts—'

Lou paused outside the kitchen and listened to her husband and daughter. Emily was a lot like her aunt Toni: one of life's doers. Emily's room had always been immaculate, her homework was always done and her clothes organised. Emily had birthdays, dates of assignments and reading weeks carefully logged in on the calendar on her phone diary. Ned, by contrast, had endless Google Keep lists on his phone and never collated any of them. He overbooked himself socially and was known for having to leave one college event early in order to get to another.

On one momentous occasion, he'd almost missed his parents' golden wedding anniversary lunch because he'd booked himself into the Glasgow engineering education symposium without connecting the dots. Lou had caught him leaving the house on the morning in question, high-tech rucksack in hand, absent-mindedly checking that his passport was in his inside pocket.

'Where are you going?' she'd asked.

'Glasgow. I told you, didn't I? I'm on the eleven fifteen.'

'You'll be on a platter, dead, with an apple in your mouth if your mother realises you've forgotten what day it is,' Lou had said, having to smother a laugh.

Ned's mother adored him.

'Her genius,' she called him and told everyone he was a professor, 'the first in the family!'

'What day is it?' asked the professor, bewildered. He scanned his phone calendar. 'It's Tuesday . . .'

'Fifty years ago today, your parents got married,' Lou reminded him.

Ned has slumped against the wall.

'Today. I forgot. She'll kill me.'

Even Ned knew that no professorial conference would make up for Number One Son not being at the special Mass for the married couple, followed by a big family lunch in Whitehaven's prestigious Old Court Hotel. He'd cancelled the conference, naturally, and his mother had loved the big lead crystal vase that Lou had bought for the golden wedding anniversary couple, fulsomely thanking Number One Son for his thoughtfulness.

Lou had said nothing. The background suited her.

'I'll make it up to you, birthday girl,' Ned whispered now. 'What time is the party?'

Lou snuggled into her husband's shoulder.

'Eight,' she said. 'You're driving your mother and her friends from the church, so don't forget.'

'I value my life too much,' said Ned, kissing her neck. 'I hate to get up now, but I have to. Early tutorial. Till tonight, my fifty-year-old flower.'

He moved out of the bed and Lou would have thrown a pillow at him, but he'd vanished into the bathroom.

He might have the memory of a goldfish for certain things. But he loved her.

And she accepted him fully and understood that he wasn't one of life's great gift-buyers. Acceptance was the key to a happy marriage.

Yet . . . the feelings she so rarely allowed to reach the surface popped up. She would have liked a gift from her husband on this special birthday. Even a card to say he loved her. How hard could that be?

It was 3.15 p.m. on Friday when Toni swiped her pass at the outer door to the studio and walked in with a smile bolted to her face. Normally, she loved filming her show: loved the buzz, the energy of knowing they'd a great line-up of guests, the meetings beforehand to nail everything down, the calm in the make-up chair when she allowed herself to settle perfectly into being Toni Cooper, interviewer. This afternoon, she was faking it all. Every smile, every upbeat conversation, was a lie.

Toni had no other choice. She could not tell anybody what had happened the night before. Nobody could know. She barely understood it herself. Her life was crumbling around her and Toni didn't know how to fix it. But she had to. Lou wasn't the only fixer in the family. Toni would figure out how to get everything back on track. She had no other choice.

'Hi Toni, tonight's your sister's big night?' said one of the production team as Toni stalked down the corridor.

'Yes,' said Toni brightly. 'I won't be around for the post-show drinks. Have to drive to Cork.'

She put her stuff in her dressing room, grabbed a speedy coffee and was ready for the pre-record meeting with the team with her game face on. When they taped *Tonight with Toni Cooper*, they taped 'as live'. Which meant that if someone screwed up – even Toni herself – it still went out that night: unedited.

'Keeps people on their toes,' said Cormac Wolfe, the show's executive producer, a tall, sinewy man whom Toni had long ago decided was 'ethical, driven, steely'.

'Steely?' he'd asked when she'd told him – breaking her rule of keeping everyone's three words to herself.

Cormac could handle the truth. 'You said I was driven and focused years ago.'

'Once even . . .' he'd shot her a look, 'I was hot.'

'I was young and foolish when I called you hot,' said Toni.

They'd been on the verge of a fling at the time – pre-Oliver, of course – but it had never happened. They'd both been ambitious and yet junior in their jobs, she in radio and him in TV. Toni knew that work affairs were so easy in their careers and that untangling professional relationships after said fling was a nightmare. Who knew if they'd work together in the future, she'd thought.

At least she'd got that right. They'd worked together for years now and a tricky relationship in the past would have made life difficult even for such professionals as she and Cormac Wolfe. His being steely worked in her current show's favour, though. No matter how much of a car crash an interview was, Cormac never allowed anyone to retape.

Today, they were taping at five to allow Toni to leave the studio at six fifteen in order to drive to Whitehaven for her sister's party. Toni was unusually quiet all afternoon, so much so that make-up's newest member had asked if she had a headache.

'No,' said Toni, trying to smile. 'I'm just a bit preoccupied, that's all.'

'What are you going to wear to your sister's party?' asked Liz from wardrobe, who was a genius at both ironing and working out where a particular shirt needed a hidden nude popper because it had been made for a woman with AA-cups.

'I have a grey sheath dress,' said Toni, who normally looked at her hair from all angles but this afternoon, couldn't summon up the interest in such a thing. 'It's simple.'

'That one from Zara?' Liz had a microscopic knowledge of what was in the shops at any one time. 'It's a bit day-timey, isn't it?'

'It's my sister's night,' Toni pointed out. She had planned her plain outfit because she knew how easy it was to outshine other people at their events if you were in any way famous. If anyone was going to suck the oxygen out of the room, it was her mother. It would not be Toni. Worrying about that family drama seemed insanely banal now. Who was the woman who had put so much thought into a dress?

Toni closed her eyes, and prayed, something she rarely did. *Please let me get through this, whoever you are up there. Just keep me going until I'm in the car and can relax again.*

Toni wasn't sure who she was praying to. Unlike her sister, she didn't believe in any divine beings or have any faith in mystical symbols, ankhs, or dangly things made of tin in the name of random goddesses. But if there was anything up there, Toni fervently wanted it to help her. *Please let me get through this.*

By 6.20 p.m., making her way across the studio's car park, Toni felt about a hundred years old.

Her mind was racing, so much so that she barely noticed the heavy-set man nearby.

'You made me look like a moron yesterday!'

The man loomed in front of her. A tall muscular man who looked angrier than he had been the previous morning on the radio station: Gerry Lanigan, possessor of a company with no women in managerial positions.

He'd picked the wrong day to hijack her, Toni thought grimly.

'Don't creep up on people, especially not women,' she snapped. 'And what are you doing here?'

He loomed closer. Toni's sense of unease rose.

'I'm here for you, bitch,' he hissed.

'Don't talk to me like that,' Toni fired back.

He was calling her a bitch? Really?

'I didn't make you look like a moron: you did,' she said, failing to keep the contempt from her voice. 'You know you have no women executives. Why go on a radio show to argue that you do?'

Even as she said it, she knew she'd made a mistake. This big angry man shouldn't be here. He'd clearly been waiting for her. He looked enraged, his face red with anger and she was suddenly aware of how physically strong he was. For all that she was a tall woman, her stature had nothing on his musculature. He was angry and frightening.

Determined not to let him cow her, Toni nevertheless moved back a step. She'd been in the public eye long enough to know that people didn't always behave coherently. She didn't think Gerry would go so far as to hit her but then, you never knew. Her fingers found the side button on her watch. She had an SOS number programmed in – it rang the local police. Her fingers touched it, but she didn't press the button.

'You have no business trying to make me a laughing stock,' he said furiously. 'I run a bloody successful company and I don't want do-gooders like you whining that there aren't enough bloody women in it. You've damaged me and my company with your whining, you bitch. Women don't understand business. You're nothing but a jumped-up bitch who thinks she has power. You have no power. Real power is money. I can destroy you, and I will.'

The threats did it. That and the mention of money. Rage flooded Toni's body. After last night, she felt as if she had nothing to lose. Everything was being taken from her and this bastard was trying to threaten her? How dare he?

Years of training fled Toni's brain. All the lessons she'd taught herself about thinking before she spoke just vanished. Along with the lessons about how men were physically stronger than women and the danger that this implied.

'I called you out because you're like so many fucking men,' she hissed furiously. 'You think you can pretend to be one thing and really be another. I'm fed up with all of you, all the smarmy businessmen pretending to employ and care about women. When I know it's all bullshit.'

Her eyes were glittering with rage now.

'I know exactly how many women people like you actually employ. You pretend you like women but really, you hate us, *you fear* us. I have news for you, Gerry

Lanigan. I will bloody well destroy you and your fellow misogynists. I'll enjoy it, I'll be laughing as I do it. I'll be doing it for all the women you've discarded in your bloody company because they made the fatal mistake of not being bloody men! You have no idea who I know and how easily I can let everyone see what a self-satisfied pig you are. All I need to do is a bit of research and you and your precious company are finished. Finished,' she repeated in case he hadn't got the point.

'Ha!' Gerry looked triumphant. Toni stared at him – she didn't understand. Until he held up his phone.

'Gotcha, Ms Cooper, you fucking bitch. Got what you really think of men in that last bit!'

Toni felt the rage haze leave her and she looked at his phone. She recognised the recording app.

'That last little bit will play very well, bitch. I wonder who I can sell it to or whether it's worth going to Epsilon or your own TV company with it?'

He leaned over her, frighteningly close so that she felt the fear again, and breathed, 'Fuck you.'

One hard finger stabbed into her chest, shoving her off balance and then he stalked off. Toni put a hand on the bonnet of her car and the other onto the sore place on her breastbone where he'd jabbed his finger. It was painful. Lanigan was strong. He could have done anything to her, and she'd provoked him. She hadn't used her damn brain when faced with an enraged man.

Anything could have happened. She willed herself to breathe deeply, her entire body numb. All it had taken was two minutes to completely destroy her career. He had a recording of her words and, no matter what he'd said or done, there was no evidence of that. It would be his words against hers.

She'd just committed career suicide and a man who hated her had it on tape.

The car tyres scattered gravel as Toni drove in the gates of Mermaid Cottage two hours later. Usually, the sense of peace of coming close to Whitehaven began to sink into Toni's bones as soon as she crossed the border into County Cork. Tonight, she felt no welcoming joy. Just a sick feeling in the pit of her stomach.

She had bought the cottage as a bolthole years before: a run-down hovel with a lean-to for a toilet, bushes growing on the inside and most of the blue roof slates scattered on the ground where wild goats grazed.

'You'll need a magic wand or lots of money,' Lillian had commented when she'd seen it.

'It has such a lovely spirit about it,' had been Lou's verdict. 'An oak tree and a monkey puzzle in the garden. A huge rosemary bush and look . . .' Lou had stood outside what was the existing kitchen window – if only its pane of glass was not smashed – and pointed at the view in front of them. 'You can see why it's called Mermaid Cottage. You can see the headland from here.'

'Pots of money,' Lillian had said again, waving a negligent hand. 'It should be called Derelict Cottage. Why not buy something nicer in town? I'm sure you can afford it. My friends could stay when they come and they won't need cars if they're in town itself.'

She'd glanced sideways at her daughter, which Toni noticed but did not acknowledge.

'This is on the outskirts of the town, and I like that,' Toni had said with studied calm. When people wanted things from you, things you were disinclined to give them, it was easier to pretend you hadn't noticed them asking. Then they had to repeat the request and you could look at them quizzically and say, 'I must have misheard . . .'

Worked a treat every time.

Lou, lovely human being that she was, had never learned how to do it with anyone. Lou gave everything she had to everyone, especially their mother.

That day, Lou had grabbed her companionably as they'd stood in the damp kitchen. 'I'll help.'

Now, with its whitewashed walls, front door and windowsills painted Farrow & Ball's Setting Plaster pink, all set off with two olive trees in cream wooden tubs outside the door, Mermaid Cottage was, much money later, the stuff of idyllic rural fantasy. Although so much of Toni's professional life was up for grabs, she'd never allowed anyone to photograph her Whitehaven refuge, insisting that all 'at home' photos of her and Oliver took place in their modern Dublin city house.

People seeing the ceiling-to-floor windows, poured concrete floors and vast canvases on the walls of their home overlooking Dublin Bay could not have imagined the coolly professional Toni Cooper being happy in a house with gingham curtains and a herb garden. But the separation of both lives was part of the firmly controlling hand Toni kept on her life. There was work

Toni and there was Whitehaven Toni and ne'er the twain should meet.

Toni dumped her bags on the cream couch beside the curved window in the small living room. There was a low ceiling, a stone fireplace with logs stacked underneath the stove, and walls covered with seascapes of the area. Unlike the Dublin house with its specially made couches, the cottage was a haven of comfort with tapestry cushions, an old ottoman on which books and candles sat in pride of place in the centre of the room, and a small round table stacked with novels. The lamps were all old with warm-hued silk shades and Lou had found a big kilim rug online as a present for Toni and Oliver.

Toni longed to light the stove, sit down and stare into its depths for the evening but she couldn't. She'd grab a quick cup of tea before going out, she thought, and went into the kitchen, where a vase of wild flowers sat on the scrubbed wooden kitchen table. There was milk in the fridge, too. Lou must have been in during the week, Toni thought, near tears for the first time that whole day.

Staying in control mattered to her. She'd lost it earlier today and she felt herself shaking at the stress of the incident in the TV car park. Her life was spiralling out of control and it was terrifying.

Toni put the cheery yellow kettle on to boil, found her favourite pottery cup and made tea. Then she took a deep, calming breath: it was Lou's party and she wasn't going to desert her sister. Her own disastrous life could wait. She would sort it out. That's what she did. Toni Cooper never waited for anyone to save her. She saved herself.

Chapter Seven

Whitehaven was out in force on Friday night, and as the sun set over Mermaid Peak, a steady stream of cars and taxis were making their way to the Haven Barn. Once a simple haybarn, now a rustic setting for big parties, the Haven Barn looked particularly beautiful that night, covered inside and out with twinkling fairy lights, floral bunting made from old saris and silk and paper flowers in giant colourful garlands. Inside, the sanded-down wooden tables and benches were accessorised with bright tablecloths and old-fashioned oil lamps, and the waiters and waitresses were all dressed in jeans and plaid shirts as if about to run out and bring in the hay in between taking your order for sweet potato fries.

It had been Emily who had suggested the barn.

'It's fun and casual, Mum,' she'd said. 'Not stuffy. Everyone likes this place.'

Lou agreed. There was a lovely informality to a barn, and it had been so cleverly transformed so that it was warm even in March and if people wanted to sit outside and smoke, IKEA fleece blankets were there for the most ardent puffers.

On the dot of nine, a buffet would be whisked out and the partygoers would have their choice of the Barn specialities like pulled pork buns, chipotle sausages, sweet potato fries and their famous butternut squash, pomegranate seed and feta salad. There were slices of roast beef served with carrots, mash and Yorkshire puddings for those who liked plainer food, and roasted edamame beans, mushroom stroganoff and a whole menu of vegan delights for the vegans and the vegetarians.

Even though the barn had been booked out for Lou's party, its smaller sister, the Mini Barn was still open and it was as thronged with locals as Whitehaven itself on a Paddy's Day weekend. The Cooper party was providing satisfying food for conversation as they watched the guests arrive.

Jess the baker, a Whitehaven stalwart, and the nosier members of her bridge club had decided to have a quiet drink in the annexe to admire the party guests. They weren't invited but they weren't going to miss Lillian's big party . . . Of course, the Grey-Haired Women Against the Patriarchy could be there.

Tired after a busy morning cleaning out the Gin Palace, Alice and Vera, who ran Whitehaven's busiest cleaning business, poked their noses into the barn.

'It's very full,' said Vera nervously, looking at all the dressed-up people, particularly the women with leather handbags worth twice what the pair of them earned in a month. 'I think we should go, Alice.'

She and Alice had been brought up to know their place and to believe that only certain types of people fitted naturally into the world of big parties. Alice and Vera would clean any party premises, no problem. But walking into a party as a guest was another matter.

Knowing their place was a lesson that had been drummed into Alice and Vera so harshly that no stain remover would ever eradicate it.

'Vera and Alice, hello! How lovely to see you,' said a gentle voice.

It was Gloria Cooper, Lillian Cooper's sister-in-law, walking slowly in through the main barn door on her cane, a peony pink silk wrap around her narrow shoulders and stooped figure.

'Gloria,' they both said guiltily.

'We were only—' began Alice.

'We didn't mean—' began Vera simultaneously.

'Are you coming into the party?' said Gloria, leaning in to give them each a gentle kiss on the cheek.

'No, merciful hour, we're not invited,' said Alice, shocked.

'It's only that Alice's little granddaughter, Solange, would love an autograph if there's anyone famous, that we're here at all.'

'Well come in, then,' said Gloria gently. 'It's Lou's party. Her fiftieth, and she'd be delighted to see you both there.'

'Lou? I thought it was something for Toni and Oliver. That's what everyone says . . . No, we couldn't come in,' squeaked Alice.

'Nonsense, you must,' said Gloria firmly. 'Who helped out at the water station during the charity half-marathon for cancer that was in honour of Lou's best friend, Mim Kerrigan? You both did. Lou said she knew she'd mistakenly leave out some of the people she meant to invite to this party and that I was to keep an eye out for anyone she had forgotten. She'll be devastated if you don't come in.'

'But—' protested Vera.

Gloria was strong for such a frail-looking old lady. She swept the two of them along with her, past Jess the baker and the bridge ladies who had decided that they might as well be hung for a sheep as for a lamb and were ordering cocktails in jam jars and plates of nibbles. Gloria smiled sweetly at the bridge ladies but did not invite Jess in. Having been the subject of much gossip many years ago, Gloria didn't like it. Back in the old days when Bob, Gloria and Lillian were young, there had been plenty of gossip and Jess's mother had been keen to spread it.

Gloria had been raised to forgive her enemies, but she remembered their names.

Lou waited nervously for the first guests, touching her hair self-consciously. She and Emily had been to the hairdresser earlier. Her hair was blow-dried so that it looked elegant and had no fly-away hairs fluttering in front of her eyes. Emily, whose own long dark hair had been curled into glossy waves and who wore a fitted dress with a skater skirt, had insisted that her mother wear mascara. Emily was determined to make her darling mum make the absolute best of those beautiful big dark eyes and had even taken out her eyelash curler to start the process off properly.

'It's like an instrument of torture,' protested Lou.

'But it curls them up beautifully,' said Emily, concentrating hard as she curled her mother's lashes. 'You have such long lashes but they're straight. Now, mascara and look: aren't you gorgeous.'

Lou blinked at herself in the mirror and smiled. What was gorgeous was that she had a daughter who loved her enough to help her tonight. That was her gift. It even surpassed the little magnolia tree Emily had given her.

'I thought we could plant it in the garden close to where you sit for your morning reset time,' Emily had said proudly. 'Mim had a magnolia tree, and you can think of her and me when you sit in the morning.'

Emily had also got a huge card on which she'd written a beautiful note telling how much she adored her mother.

'I don't know who I'd be without you, Mum,' it finished. 'Have a wonderful day: you deserve all the love in the world, love Emily.'

There was also a keyring with an obsidian stone: 'To protect against mean people,' Emily had said happily, and a rock salt lamp for the top of her mother's bookcase where she kept her self-help books.

'Thank you, darling,' Lou had said tearfully.

Emily's gifts were the epitome of thoughtfulness and thinking of them made Lou smile now as she saw the first few people start to come in, her aunt Gloria looking elegant and talking to two other women. She took a deep breath and prepared to mingle.

When it was your party, you were supposed to sparkle, mingle happily and have in-depth conversations with all the people you hadn't seen for ages. In reality, Lou felt, when it was your party, you worried that the group of friends from your book club would be horrified by the lack of bookiness of your friends from school. The school friends would be talking about that holiday to the Canaries where strange men were snogged senseless on the dance floor and the only book talk would be about how someone had once memorably tried to recreate the goldfish scene from Shirley Conran's fabulous book, *Lace*. And then there was the issue of whether people would think she and Ned were mean as hell for not paying for a free bar for the whole night. Toni had offered to foot the bar bill, but Lou simply couldn't accept such generosity, it was far too much – but maybe she should have? Lillian had warned her it would look cheap, hadn't approved of the barn as a venue at all actually and maybe she was right . . .

Breathe in for six, hold for three, out for nine.

Lou took a moment to check her spiralling thoughts. She reminded herself that Ned had said that light beer and jugs of the barn's classic fruity wine punch was perfect, and the barn's head barman had agreed.

'Free bars are a mistake,' he advised with the air of one who had had to haul out far too many horizontal guests who'd over-availed of free bars. 'Light beer and the punch, which is quite weak, are the perfect choice.'

Her mother was already installed in a corner of the barn with a few of her cronies and even if Lillian would have preferred a more salubrious setting where expensive wine was available she seemed fine, now. They had plenty of jam jars of cocktails on the table, as well as boards with the barn's special sourdough and baba ganoush, and she had waved regally at Lou in a way that suggested she was happy. Lillian had a special code for when she wanted rescuing from what she called 'art groupies'. The signal was a little wave and then she'd blow a kiss at Lou. So far, her mother had not blown any kisses her way, but Lou knew it would happen. Lillian found people overwhelming sometimes.

Lou looked around now for Ned, but he appeared to be missing. Ned was a natural at parties: he was so easy-going that he could chat to anyone, and she missed his presence beside her. She spotted Emily with Simone, the tall and rather shy Evan, and a few other young people, and headed over there to see if Emily had noticed where her father was.

Ned was wedged into a corner of the bar with his brother, Tommy, who'd ordered a couple of Heart Starters for the pair of them 'to get the night going'.

'It's a party, we might as well enjoy ourselves,' said Tommy, a man who was only let out by his wife on very rare occasions. Given this fact, Tommy felt it was important to get maximum enjoyment in early before Siobhan, who ran a tight ship and had no truck with wasting the family's money, caught sight of him and dragged him home for a lecture on being a bad influence on their children. With this in mind, he had found a corner of the bar where he and Ned were almost hidden from view by a decorative barrel with a silk flower arrangement on top of it.

'Sheesh, this is strong,' said Ned, taking a sip.

Tommy had reliably informed him that the Heart Starter was a combination of brandy and port and was guaranteed to reanimate the dead. The young barman had needed the explanation too, as he'd never made such a drink.

'It's an old classic,' Tommy advised them both.

Old people were mad, the barman decided. Imagine mixing strong drinks like that so early in the evening.

'Get it down you before Siobhan sees me,' hissed Tommy to his brother.

'Ah Tommy, this is lethal stuff. If we drink these, we won't know which day of the week it is—' began Ned.

'Drink!' said Tommy with urgency.

Ned gave up and drank, catching sight of Lou on the other side of the barn, which was now filling up fast. She looked beautiful: he was a lucky man. If Tommy had forgotten a gift for Siobhan's significant birthday, he'd be recuperating in hospital with some vital organs missing. But Lou . . . she was a treasure.

The Heart Starter wasn't that bad, either, he decided, feeling a nice glow after he finished it. Normally he liked just a beer or two but still, it was a party after all. Tommy said port and brandy was almost medicinal, and ordered them another pair.

Through the happy haze of a second round of Heart Starters, the brothers admired the party. Their mother, Ruth, was at a table with her cronies, mineral water in their hands and eyes narrowed as they surveyed the guests, some of whom were swaying gently and tapping their feet as Hot Chocolate crooned 'You Sexy Thing'. Ned knew from the looks on their faces that they didn't approve of the liberality of the drinks, or the Barn as opposed to Whitehaven's elegant Old Court Hotel. He could see that they were talking out of the side of their mouths, undoubtedly making horrified remarks about the scanty outfits and general behaviour of the rest of the guests.

Ned loved his mother, but he'd hate to have married a version of her, which was what poor Tommy had done. Siobhan and his mother were both devoted churchgoers, always doing novenas and worrying about what the neighbours would think. Which was more important: what God thought or what the neighbours thought? He knew they'd never work it out to their satisfaction.

He could see Lou and Emily near the door, Lou looking lovely in some sort of loose purple dress with her dark hair all neatly pretty because Emily had insisted she go to the hairdresser. Ned felt a twinge of guilt again.

What did you get for your wife when she was fifty? Nobody in the university was any help. His closest work friend wasn't even married or dating anyone, so he was no help in the advice department. Earrings? Special gold ones with diamonds? Ned was at a loss as to what to buy, plus he'd left it too late because the whole party thing had slipped his mind in the first place and then today, well, it had been mad at work.

Lou hadn't minded at all, anyway, as it turned out. She knew what he was like. Lou was both the social secretary and the purchaser in the family. She bought gifts for everyone, including his mother – Ned wouldn't have known where to start – and never seemed to hold that against him. Gifts just weren't his strength.

Two friends who'd come from Cork city arrived at the bar with himself and Tommy, who happily began ordering more Heart Starters all round. Siobhan would kill Tommy when she got hold of him, Ned decided, but he didn't care. It wasn't his problem. It was a party. They were allowed to enjoy themselves.

Gloria spotted her niece and grandniece welcoming guests, and there was that nice young man that Emily had just started dating. Evan. Tall, a bit shy, but a total gentleman. Gloria knew his grandparents. Decent people with a small farm, and his grandmother sang in the choir.

Gloria looked further into the fairy-light-spangled barn and spotted Lillian. Even across the room, it was clear to her that Lillian was not entirely on form. Gloria recognised the signs. Her sister-in-law's eyes were narrowed and in between drinking liberally from a jam jar of clear liquid which Gloria suspected was neat alcohol, she was staring around at the party crowd as if planning a murder that even Poirot wouldn't be able to solve.

'Look, it's Lillian,' said Vera happily and started off towards her. 'We should say thank you—'

'I wouldn't,' cautioned Gloria. 'Let me get you a drink instead.'

'No!' protested Alice.

'Yes,' Gloria insisted. 'You can tell me about your grandchildren. How old is Solange now? Eleven?'

A Lillian who was not enjoying herself should be avoided at all costs. Lillian liked to be the centre of attention at all events. If she wasn't, she might lash out at someone, and Alice and Vera were two gentle souls who could do without seeing Lillian buzzed up on booze and rage.

'Aunt Gloria,' said Emily, leaning in to whisper to her great-aunt. 'Is Lillian OK? She was fine earlier but one of her Crazy Grey-Haired Ladies just came in and now she looks a bit grim.'

'Really? Has she blown a kiss at you yet?' said Gloria, who knew all her sister-in-law's little foibles.

'Well, no—'

'I'm sure she's grand,' Gloria added.

Lillian did look a bit grim. She was wearing one of her cream silk shirts with a long tight skirt, and a necklace of red crystals that looked as if someone had just dug them up and not bothered polishing them. Lillian's face was pale but there were two red patches on her cheeks, as red and angry as the rough crystal stones on her necklace.

Chapter Eight

In her flat grey ballet pumps, Toni hurried towards the barn, past the smokers outside with their beers and lit cigarettes. Seeing someone running made people think twice about stopping you to chat. She waved at a few people and was in the barn before the owner, who was a big fan of her show, could get out to grab her.

Because she was tall, she could see over the heads of the smaller guests and instantly sighted Lou standing near the buffet tables urging people to partake.

Even now, late and still in a state of shock, Toni felt the slowing heartbeat she associated with her sister. Lou had been like a mother to her – she would want to help. Toni could tell her everything, now, and Lou would no doubt drop everything to help her. Which was exactly why she had to keep quiet for a while longer. She would tell Lou everything, but not tonight.

It did not occur to Toni to confide in Lillian, instead. Her mother did not like hearing about other people's problems. She would never say so, but she didn't have to – she pulled herself away, creating a barrier few dared to breach. Her mother was very successful at only worrying about what she cared to worry about, Toni reflected. A neat trick if you could do it.

'Hello birthday lady!' said Toni when she reached her sister.

Lou looked up and beamed at her.

'Hello you,' said Lou and hugged Toni. 'You look beautiful. How did the show go?'

'Toni,' interrupted Emily. 'I know you've just got here but Lillian's upset about something. Her face would stop a clock and if you go over and calm her down, it means Mum can mingle.'

'Emily, I can do it,' said Lou.

Toni put a hand on her sister's arm, knowing that Lou would race off to tend to their mother if she had the slightest feeling that Lillian was upset.

Not tonight: this was Lou's night.

'No,' said Toni. 'It's your special night, Lou. Leave Mother Courage to me.' And she headed over to their mother and her gang.

Toni grabbed a glass from a passing waitress. She thought that a drink might help her relax – plus it would help in dealing with Lillian.

She fixed her professional smile onto her face and greeted her mother and her cronies.

'This is the fun part of the party, then?' she said cheerily.

'Is it?' snarled her mother.

It was going to be that sort of evening, Toni realised, with a sinking heart.

'You look lovely Lillian. Doesn't she?'

Toni had found that complimenting her mother could cheer her up, but it was not to be the case tonight.

'Fat lot of good it does me!' hissed Lillian, downing her drink in one.

Toni wondered what level of storm was about to ensue and determined to keep her mother well away from Lou.

Just one peaceful birthday party – was that too much to ask for?

'How gorgeous that you came!' said Lou, still stationed near the barn entrance as Magda and Indira, two of her workmates from Blossom appeared.

'We are late, sorry!' said Magda, who still had the faintest Polish accent.

'Bettina and Oszkar sent these,' said Indira, whose accent was pure Cork. She gingerly held out the tiniest bouquet, so small and limp that it made them all silent.

'This is from us,' said Magda hurriedly, handing over a big, beautifully wrapped box.

'The flowers are not from us,' emphasised Indira. 'The box contains something that might break.'

'I'll take it,' said Emily cheerfully.

Lou found herself holding the limp little bouquet and she stared at it in astonishment.

Bettina and Oszkar couldn't have sent just this, could they? Not that she was into presents but it was so small, and even . . . insulting?

'The food is gorgeous, Lou!' said a couple passing by. 'Delicious!'

'Have you seen Tommy?' Siobhan, Lou's sister-in-law, had her eyes narrowed as she scanned the room.

'No,' said Lou truthfully.

She told herself to stop worrying about Lillian or her bouquet and ate some food with Emily, Simone and the lovely Evan, who was keen to impress upon Lou that he respected her daughter fully.

'Evan, she knows that,' said Simone, laughing.

Emily found her father in the corner of the bar with her uncle and dragged the pair of them over to her mother.

'I'll get them to play music you like, Mum,' she said, 'and you can dance. Siobhan was looking for you, Tommy.'

Tommy looked alarmed and headed back to the bar.

'I'm not sure I can dance,' said Ned, a bit unsteadily.

'You can, Dad,' said Emily.

'No really. You know me, not much of a dancer.'

'It's Mum's party,' Emily said, and Lou watched as her daughter almost pushed Ned onto the dance floor.

'It's the Eurythmics,' said Lou hopefully to her husband.

'Ah, sorry! You know I'm not a dancer,' said Ned, apology in his voice, and he sloped off towards the bar.

Lou stared after him. Couldn't he have made a bit of an effort?

'Mum,' said Emily in cheering tones, 'we can dance even if Dad isn't in the mood.'

They danced for fifteen hot minutes until Lou was fanning herself with a cocktail menu and they tried to leave, hand in hand, in the middle of 'Dancing Queen'.

'Lou, no!' yelled Simone. 'You can't leave now!'

Someone pushed a glass of water into her hand, she downed it and, beaming, joined the gang to shake her thing to a medley of Abba.

Toni arrived, holding a cocktail made up of something pink and fizzy, drank it and then began dancing, too.

'I love you,' shouted Lou.

'Love you too,' shouted Toni over 'Money, Money, Money'. Lou stopped caring that Ned was being Mr No-Fun and stopped caring whether her mother was having fun or not. Tonight was about celebrating.

Over the next hour, the party moved up a gear as people abandoned seats to dance.

Lou sent love and smiles up to darling Mim in heaven on her sparkly unicorn, and said thanks to the universe that *she* was around to celebrate her fiftieth.

'Thank you,' she yelled at Emily at one point.

'For what?' said her daughter.

'For being you,' yelled Lou, hugging Emily, feeling the heat from both their bodies after such glorious dancing.

In the background, the buffet was being cleared away and the cake Emily had ordered was coming out. The Barn could supply simple cakes with sugar flowers, white icing and pretty sparkly things on top, and Emily had said a lilac cake with rich amethyst flowers, a colour which suited her mother, would be perfect. Everyone ooh-ed and aah-ed as it was carried to a small table beside the buffet.

The music was turned down several notches so that the chattering of delighted guests could be heard and people turned to watch.

'You don't have to do a speech,' Emily said. 'We can just cut the cake and let everybody sing.'

Lou nodded gratefully – the idea of having to say anything in front of so many people was terrifying – and reached for the knife.

Just then, Emily grabbed her arm. 'Mum,' she hissed. 'It's Lillian, she's coming this way. She's been doing her signal, waving at us, she's blown several annoyed-looking kisses and she definitely looks angry.'

The two sisters and Emily turned to see Lillian, holding onto a jam jar of liquid, storming over towards them.

Lillian glared at both her daughters.

'Have you heard?' she demanded fiercely.

In the quiet of the music having been turned down, everyone could hear her.

'Heard what?' said Lou anxiously.

She glanced at Toni and saw that her sister looked unusually tense. No matter what was going on with Lillian, Toni always appeared in control and calm. But not now. What was happening?

In her anxiety over the strange look on her sister's face, Lou did the wrong thing: she turned towards her mother in an attempt to make sense of it all and somehow called Lillian 'Mum'.

'Mum, what's wrong?'

The silence in the room seemed to be magnified.

'Mum?' said Lillian in a voice that wouldn't have been out of place during the Inquisition. 'I'm Lillian. Never bloody *Mum*. I meant have you heard about the prize. The Kennedy Art Prize. Worth forty thousand euros.'

Lillian was hissing now and Lou saw Toni take a step back. How strange, Lou thought absently. Toni never retreated from anything.

'That bitch Concepta O'Brien has won the Kennedy. The first woman painter to win it. The first woman!' Lillian had stopped hissing and was now shrieking.

Their mother didn't notice Toni's silent withdrawal any more than she noticed Lou reaching out to put a hand on her mother's arm.

'Lillian,' began Lou, but her mother interrupted her at full roar.

'I should have been the first woman to win it! ME! I set up Grey-Haired Women Against the Patriarchy! I made people sit up and notice older women artists! She just joined in, followed me. Concepta's a follower, that's all! I did it. Me! It should have been me!'

Lillian was blazingly angry now and the people nearest to them were engrossed in the scene.

'Lillian, of course you should have won—' began Lou, clicking instantly into protect-Mama mode.

'Oh for fuck's sake—' Lillian howled, and Toni could hear intakes of breath all round at the profanity. 'What do you know about it?'

Shocked, everyone took a step back except Lou, still holding onto her mother's arm.

'You know nothing! You know I gave up everything for you. I should never have had children. The enemy of good art is the pram in the hallway! Bloody Cyril Connolly was right!'

'Lillian, stop this immediately,' said a severe voice.

Aunt Gloria stood there, white-faced but stately.

Beside her was Emily, who'd clearly run to get the only person she felt could handle Lillian Cooper in a rage.

'This is Louise's party and you shall not ruin it. I do not care who has won which prize. Who knows how these things are judged!'

White-faced, teeth bared, Lillian turned on her sister-in-law.

'You're here to tell us about the art world and about where I went wrong, are you, Miss High and Mighty?' she said. 'What do you know about the pram in the hall, you with your barren womb?'

'I know it has nothing – nothing – to do with your daughters,' Gloria said, face stony.

'You sanctimonious bitch,' Lillian hissed.

'Mum!' Lou couldn't help it. Calling Lillian 'Mum' seemed like the only way to stop this torrent of rage. Her mother's temper was legendary. Anyone who stood in the way would get blasted tonight. 'Prizes aren't the only important thing. You're such an amazing sculptor,' she said, attempting damage control. But her mother appeared to hear nothing.

Lillian's gaze was focused laser-like on Gloria, and Lillian's now faded crimson lipstick was barely visible around bared, ferocious teeth.

'You didn't want me to have Angelo's baby in the first place, did you? You wanted everyone to be as dried up and empty as you!'

There was a general sharp intake of many people's breaths. The music was no longer playing even at a low

101

volume, Lou realised, so the shouting could be heard all over the barn. Every hideous word was audible to everyone.

'You were right, after all. Bob's baby was fine.' Lillian gestured in the hollow silence towards Toni. 'Everyone wanted Bob's baby by the time she came along, by the time we were married, but not so much Angelo's brat.'

Again, the gesture: this time towards the now-horrified Lou, who was still holding on to her mother with that tender grip. Toni, who'd never fainted in her life, swayed briefly, and held on to a wooden beam for support. Was she hearing this correctly?

'Lillian!' Gloria was saying. 'Stop this immediately!'

'Stop why?' snarled Lillian. 'About time everyone heard the truth. People have talked about it for long enough. Your sainted brother said people would forget, but they didn't, did you?'

She stared furiously round at the assembled guests, all of them staring at her, aghast.

'Nobody thought how it would affect me as an artist having a baby when I was just starting out. Nobody thought about that! "I'll bring her up as my own," Bob said, like it was a great sacrifice. What about *my* sacrifice? I had to teach, I needed an ordinary job.' Lillian's catlike eyes were flashing with rage. 'Me, being ordinary! I couldn't dedicate myself to my art. *That's* why I'm not winning prizes now! That's why I've never been recognised for what I am!'

In one quick, dramatic movement, Lillian threw her jam jar glass onto the ground where it smashed with maximum noise. Gazing around at everyone as if she was determined to make a grand exit, as if she wanted every eye on her and her horrible words, she turned on her heel, the long red stone necklace she wore swinging ominously.

'What are you all looking at?' she hissed at the first group of people in her way. They parted mutely and Lillian stormed off, leaving silence in her wake.

Lou didn't move. Her hand was still outstretched as if she was touching her mother. What had Lillian said? She'd heard everything her mother had said. Everyone had. Every single person in this room had heard – but it couldn't be true, could it?

Lillian had said a man called . . . Angelo was her father. Surely not. Surely that was wrong.

None of this made any sense. Dad had adored Lou. He was her *father!* A person couldn't imagine that closeness. She'd held his hand in the hospice, he'd smiled at her lovingly and when he'd gone, the loss had been unimaginable. She and Toni had clung to each other, sobbing, hardly able to believe their beloved and kind father was not on the planet with them anymore, caring and loving, while Lillian had been outside in the sunny garden, chain-smoking her way through the French cigarettes some other artist friends had brought, not able to bear the pain of watching him die.

Bob was Lou's father. Bob Cooper, beloved Bob.

Lillian could be irate when she'd been drinking and perhaps—

Lou felt a soft hand on her shoulder. She turned and saw Gloria's face, which was full of pity. Gloria's expression was the one people used when something dreadfully painful happened. Like death.

Gloria's face meant that Lillian wasn't lying and this was a death after all. Her mother had been speaking the truth. An unknown man was her father. Bob Cooper was not. And everyone at the party had heard it, which meant soon everyone in Whitehaven would know.

'I'm so sorry, darling Louise—' Gloria began.

'I'm fine,' Lou interrupted, shaking her head. 'I'm fine.'

The words were automatic. Lou was always fine. She was the carer, the fixer.

'Lou—' Toni reached for Lou's arm, but Lou backed away.

'I'm going to find Ned and go home,' she said.

'You'll want your flowers,' said one of the waiters eagerly, handing her the limp bouquet from Oszkar and Bettina.

Unable to think of any response, Lou took it and hurried towards the entrance and found her husband coming back from the loo, swaying slightly.

'Lou!' he said delightedly. 'I've been looking for you. I'm sorry about the dancing but you know me: two left feet!' He laughed the happy laugh of a man nicely marinading in alcohol.

He leaned towards her for a kiss, boozy fumes emanating from his breath.

'D'ya know, you're an amazing wife, Lou, not like Siobhan because she's going to carve out Tommy's heart with his blood donor pencil because he's drunk. She'll want diamond earrings when it's her fiftieth, but I told Tommy that you don't need that sort of thing. You're a trooper. You don't expect anything. You don't even mind me not dancing! Good old Lou, I told him. I could buy her a pot plant from the supermarket and she'd be happy because she just doesn't need—'

'I do!' shrieked Lou, turning on him. 'I do need things! I need proof that people care about me just like everyone else does! Why does everybody think I don't need proper flowers or earrings or people to say, "Thank you for helping me, Lou?" I deserve thanks! I deserve birthday presents!'

Her head was exploding with shock and grief. Why had everything gone so wrong?

Ned was too drunk to comprehend this long, complex complaint but he stared at the flowers Lou was holding in her hand.

'Oszkar and Bettina got you those?' he asked, pointing. 'Oszkar phoned, said they couldn't come – I forgot to tell you – I thought they'd send something, but not those.'

Ned, buoyed up on unaccustomed alcohol, laughed at the hopelessness of the bouquet.

Lou looked down at the flowers. 'Yes, they did send these,' she said. 'This appalling bouquet wouldn't make it to the website under any circumstances. It's so obviously an emergency, we-have-nothing-prepared-but-this-will-do bouquet. Not even the twenty-five-euro one. Oszkar and Bettina didn't think I deserved even the twenty-five-euro bouquet for my fiftieth – but it's still better than what you got me, isn't it.'

She glared at Ned, tears in her eyes.

The music system cranked up again and the people who'd watched the whole Lillian saga at the back of the barn and followed Lou's progress to the door did their best to look away. But it was hard. The entire night was like a live episode of *Outraged Housewives of Beverly Hills* combined with *Long Lost Family: The Intro.* Nobody could tear their eyes away.

The waiters hovered at the cake trolley, unsure what to do next: cut it up or wheel it back into the kitchen.

'I'll get you flowers,' said Ned, slurring a bit. 'Ouch!' He staggered back as his mild-mannered wife began to hit him with her bouquet.

'But you didn't get me flowers at the right time,' shrieked Lou. 'For future information, Ned, you buy the person flowers *before* the party. Not after. Before. *For* my birthday, you big moron. It was my birthday today. Although nobody, my mother included, seems to realise that.'

'Whasha matta?' asked Tommy, arriving in time to get a belt of the green stems for his trouble.

'Mum,' said Emily, appearing with Gloria and Toni by her side and Simone and Evan bringing up the rear. 'We're leaving. Will you come with us?'

'No,' said Lou. 'I need to be alone. I need to think.'

She set off quickly before anyone could follow her. She couldn't bear to be with anyone right now.

Outside the barn, she saw a taxi which had just disgorged its passengers and she threw herself into it.

Why has nobody ever told me this before, she asked Mim silently. *Why now? Why explode my world now? Why would Mum hurt me like that?*

Part Two

Chapter Nine

Lou felt the wind on Whitehaven Beach whip her face and heard her sister speaking to her.

'What do you say to a cup of coffee? It's chilly and we need something warm.'

'Don't want to go home,' said Lou, aware that she was speaking the way a child might. 'I don't want to see anyone after last night. The whole town will know by now. I might as well be on the front of the local paper.'

'I know.' Toni squeezed her sister's arm. 'I know, but—'

'I'm not going,' Lou interrupted. 'I can't.'

'Then . . . how about we take off, just the two of us?' Toni said, surprising her utterly.

'And go where?'

'Anywhere we want,' said Toni. 'Nobody but us. We just *escape*.'

Lou felt some of the weight on her heart lift. As if a little light still glowed within her.

'Just leave . . . ?' she asked.

'Let's just go,' said Toni eagerly. 'Everyone will be fine without us.'

Astonished at this notion of simply leaving, Lou scanned her mental list: her mother, Ned, her work. They had all let her down horribly.

'You're right,' she said, holding her head up to face the wind. Her new life would start now: nobody would take advantage of her again, she decided with unaccustomed ferocity.

She thought of what Mim used to say: *If you can't have a good day, just have a day. Get by.*

Today, Lou could get by. Today, she would be as strong as Mim had been.

She smiled tentatively at her sister and nodded.

'Let's go.'

As the two women walked back along the beach in silence, Lou could sense her sister glancing at her.

'Emily is amazing and will be fine,' offered Toni. 'And I bet Ned is still in bed with a hangover. What on earth was Tommy giving him to drink?'

'Something called a Heart Starter.'

Toni rolled her eyes. 'Heart Attacks, more like. He'll be OK, Lou. Let's get away from Whitehaven, just you and me. We need a bit of distance.'

'I can't simply walk out on people—' began Lou and then stopped, realising she was slipping back into her default position.

Why couldn't she walk out on people? After all, people had metaphorically walked out on her. Like Ned with his muttering about how she was such a superbly non-complaining type of person that she didn't need a fiftieth birthday present – as if that excused him from making an effort. Could he not have got her something, a little bracelet, something in the costume jewellery line, nothing expensive. How much effort would that have taken? Very little. Instead, it was 'Good old Lou: she won't mind.' Well, actually, she *did* mind. He hadn't even got her a card, not even flowers.

The thought of flowers brought her to the infamy of Oszkar and Bettina. Her pulse began to race as another blast of unfamiliar temper hit her. They hadn't come to her party, had sent an excuse and a paltry bunch of flowers. Yellow carnations. Lou's least-loved flowers. If she'd been making a bouquet for an important member of staff, she'd have created a sumptuous marriage of creamy calla lilies, Vendela roses and tender eucalyptus stems all held together with sprays of lisianthus and phlox. Not a few limp carnations fluffed up with a bit of gypsophila. Thoughtless.

Toni began to lead Lou up the path to where their cars were parked.

'I was going for the office manager's job and I didn't get it,' Lou blurted out. There was no point holding it back. Time for all the shameful secrets to tumble out. Time for everything to come out, actually.

Toni stopped walking briefly.

'Why not?'

'I don't have a business degree.'

Lou felt another blast of temper surge. How dare they?

'That didn't worry them when you were running the place single-handedly every time they're not there.'

'Exactly.' Lou allowed the anger to flood her instead of stopping it at the pass. It felt very strange. She was never angry or, if she was, she flattened the anger down. Nobody liked anger. Nobody liked anxiety, either, which was why she flattened that down for other people too, just experienced it herself without telling people how she felt.

'Lillian was the worst,' Lou said, and suddenly the anger gave way to pure rage, which surged through her body in a strange and unfamiliar way. 'I can't get my head around it, Toni. Can't believe it. How could she do that? And to tell me last night, like that . . . ?'

Toni sighed. 'Our mother is tricky,' she said.

They were at the cars now. Toni's all-electric luxury car sat alongside Lou's old Nissan.

'I know but—' began Lou, and then stopped. 'Actually, I didn't know. I had no idea. She was like a stranger last night. She's always been a bit temperamental, but she's artistic, that's what they're like, right? I took care of her, adored her, wanted to be like her. Do you realise that I have done everything Lillian ever asked of me, no matter how inconvenient? I didn't go to college because of her – and has she ever apologised for that? No. Last night it was like she didn't care if she hurt me or not. How could someone do that to a person they loved? How could she do that to me?'

Her mother's face the night before appeared in her mind: Lillian enraged and not caring who she hurt.

Beside her, Toni said nothing – what was there to say?

'I honestly can't believe what she said, in front of everyone, like that.' Lou was still unravelling it all. 'I mean, is it true? Was she joking? It was like she wanted to hurt me?'

Toni didn't answer; instead, she opened the passenger door of her car and settled Lou into it. She peered into Lou's car. It was locked, no handbag or anything else on the seat. Toni frowned. Lou never moved without a handbag of some sort, one with plasters, a spare protein bar, handkerchiefs, handwipes, plastic bags for the beach, paracetamol should someone else need them. Lou's handbag was full of things for other people. She must have been incredibly distressed to leave home without one.

'I'll drive,' Toni said. 'Where shall we go?'

'Will Oliver mind you going away?' Lou asked suddenly, as if the thought had only just occurred.

'No,' Toni said shortly.

'I don't want to disrupt your life,' Lou said. 'Just because mine has gone all . . .'

At this, Toni felt a bitter laugh rise in her throat – as if her life could be disrupted any more than it already was – but she squashed it. Lou would ask questions and she wasn't ready to talk, yet. Because if she did, she might cry, and Toni Cooper didn't do tears. Not now, not ever.

'Toni?'

'Don't worry about me, Lou,' Toni said firmly. She wanted to get away more than anything else in the world. This was her chance.

Toni turned the key in the ignition, and turned to look at her sister.

'Where to?'

'Can we talk to Aunt Gloria, first?' said Lou. 'If Dad wasn't my dad . . . I have to know the truth.'

'Sure,' Toni agreed – anything to avoid thinking about her own life – and pulled out onto the road.

'I don't know what I'll do, if it's true,' Lou said quietly. 'My whole life, a lie.'

Toni didn't answer. She didn't know either.

Whitehaven was quiet, with none of the coffee shops open yet, so Toni pulled into 24-Hour-Snacks and got two coffees, bog-standard, out-of-the-machine things with no fancy milk or fluffing up for cappuccinos.

'I wish I didn't like nice coffee,' said Toni, sipping a bit before putting the cup into the cupholder. 'It adds a whole new level of effort to life. Have your hair done properly, don't look too young but not too old either, find your favourite coffee and get it into the routine so it's part of "me time" . . .' She trailed off, realising that she was talking as if she was doing a chatty interview on TV. An intro to a piece on modern women, perhaps. She glanced across at her sister.

Lou, whose hair was back to its normal state of uncurated dark wildness, would not be interested in conversations about hair. Certainly not now. But then, Lou never seemed bothered with whether she looked too young or too old. She just was who she was, just Lou, something Toni secretly envied. Lou wore the same sort of clothes all the time, her A-line dresses in navies and aubergines with flat shoes, long cardigans in matching colours and the same tortoiseshell glasses she'd favoured for years. Her make-up was lipstick and whatever she used to bring a blush to those high cheekbones, a rosy colour which set off her dark cloud of hair.

The hair. Lou's hair had always been different to the rest of the family's.

Their mother's hair was still mainly jet black, though Toni knew it owed a lot to little bottles of colour in the salon, and Dad's had been a pale ashy colour, the same as Gloria's in old photos before they'd both gone white. Lou's hair was a rich tone that owed nothing to artifice. Toni had occasionally wondered where in the family Lou's hair colour and those warm dark eyes had come from – was this the answer?

Toni remembered listening to a podcast a few months ago about the percentage of children who were not related to their apparent fathers – and how the rise of genetic testing was opening up lots of cans of worms. Maybe there was truth in all of this.

Aunt Gloria still lived in the old house on Worcester Road, which sat perpendicular to Main Street. Her father, the girls' grandfather, had been the town's doctor for many years and had run his surgery in the basement of the old house. Gloria and Bob had grown up with the knowledge that their father's mission in life was good works. Their mother had been the same. A natural nurse, she'd been there to help whenever the doctor was out. Dorothy Cooper had been a practical, kind woman who loved people, remained serene no matter how much blood spurted out of a wound and understood that what was said in the surgery was sacrosanct.

She had delivered two babies herself when her husband had been out on emergencies.

Toni and Lou's father hadn't followed his father directly into the noble art of medicine but had helped in a different way as a pharmacist. For years, he'd worked in Cooper's, the small pharmacy he'd established, with its wooden shelves and quirky old bottles that stood high on the shelves with all the modern medicine underneath. When they'd been younger, Toni and Lou had sat behind the counter with their father on occasion and Toni's biggest thrill had been being allowed to arrange the flowery perfumes and the boxes of soap that some of the customers loved.

Toni was glad Bob Cooper was no longer around to witness this family scandal, she reflected as she parked a few doors down from their aunt's house. He'd been such a gentle and dignified man. He'd have hated Lillian's outburst and truly hated that his beloved Lou had been hurt. No matter what the truth of the matter was, Toni was in no doubt that Bob Cooper was her sister's father in all the ways that mattered. But, she acknowledged, knowing that he potentially wasn't her biological father was a huge deal to her sister.

'Are you sure you want to do this?' she asked carefully. Lou might have changed her mind.

Lou nodded. They got out of the car.

The door to Aunt Gloria's house was a rich, comforting russet colour: the colour of beech leaves in autumn. Bright plants had always sat in white pots outside the door, along with an elderly bay tree that appeared to have flourished in the Cork sunshine. Lou remembered her grandfather saying that patients liked a welcoming sense when they arrived at the doctor's home.

'One of a medic's most important tools is the ability to make people feel at ease,' Grandpa had apparently said often when he sat smoking the pipe that he knew, medically speaking, he should not have indulged in.

'In that respect, Henry James was right,' he liked to continue. 'The most important words in the English language are kindness, kindness and kindness. Medicine and a wise ear help. But if we can't put them at their ease, we won't hear the full story.'

Of course, if everything her mother had said was true . . . then Dr Cooper was not her actual grandfather. And Dad, who had dispensed cough bottles, antibiotics and kindly advice to the people of the town, was no longer her father. Lou raised her face to the sky, trying to hold back her tears. The anger she had felt on the beach was gone, and in its place waves of grief were flooring her. She felt as if she was losing her dad, her grandfather, her childhood, all at once.

Breathe in for six, hold for three, out for nine . . .

But no breathing exercise in the world could help her today. The Barking Dog was going off, and there was nothing Lou could do to stop it. She felt so terribly afraid that she was shaking.

The russet door opened slowly and Aunt Gloria looked every inch of her eight and a half decades as she appeared before them.

117

'Come in, my girls,' she said, her voice shaky and her face even more lined than usual with sleeplessness.

She held out her arms to Lou, who embraced her gently.

'Oh Louise,' Gloria soothed.

Lou was determined not to cry, even now with Gloria holding her, but she felt the comfort of her aunt's embrace. It helped with the fear. Gloria loved her. That was unchanged.

'Lou has some questions,' said Toni, shutting the door. 'Shall I put some coffee on?'

Her voice sounded over-bright against the wrought atmosphere in the hallway, and Gloria shot her a look over Lou's shoulder. Gloria missed nothing.

'Are you feeling all right, Antoinette?' she asked.

Lou turned to look at Toni, too, wondering what Gloria had noticed that she hadn't.

'Fine,' said Toni, smiling widely and leading the way through to the kitchen. 'Coffee?'

'I only have decaf, I'm afraid. I think real caffeine would kill me nowadays.'

When the decaffeinated coffee was made, the three of them sat in Gloria's front room and the radio in the kitchen could be heard gently in the background playing the classical station that Gloria preferred. Sugar, Gloria's little rescue dog, perched on a pink fluffy dog bed at her mistress's feet with her tiny nose delicately between her paws.

Lucky to be a dog, Lou thought. Dogs didn't have to worry about things, except for where their next meal was coming from. Dogs didn't feel the way she did: shaky and unreal.

'I feel . . .' Lou paused, as if trying to sum up how she felt. Broken, scared, hurt . . . 'I feel as if my world has fallen apart.'

'It hasn't,' said Gloria at once, 'not really, Louise. The essentials are the same: we all love you.'

'They're not the same, Gloria,' said Lou shakily. 'Nothing is the same. The essentials are totally different and I feel I'm on the edge of a cliff right now. With one step I could fall off it. Do you know how terrifying that is? I couldn't sleep last night.'

She turned her gaze on both of them.

'Not a wink. I kept going over it in my head – the way that everything in my childhood was a lie and nobody told me – not Lillian, not Dad, not even you, Gloria. And it's not just that: everything's falling apart.'

She stared into the distance bleakly. 'Ned didn't buy me anything and that shouldn't matter, and it doesn't. It's a first world problem for sure but it's what it says about him and me. It says I don't matter. That's what Lillian was saying last night at my party – I don't matter so she can ruin my party because she's in a bad mood. How could I have never seen that in her before? She was horrible.'

Nobody spoke.

'I didn't get the job in Blossom,' Lou blurted out. 'I'm basically the office manager but when I went for this new job they've come up with – strategy person working out where the company goes in future, well, Oszkar told me I couldn't have it because I don't have the right degree. I'm under qualified. I didn't even argue with him,' she added, and there was a hint of crazy in her voice. 'I didn't want to upset him. Imagine – he wasn't giving me the job I was already doing, and I'm so stupid, I was worried about *him* being upset. I thought being kind meant kind things happened in return. I thought the universe would provide. And look where that's got me.'

Finally, Lou's stream-of-consciousness was over and she sat back against the couch, empty and bleak.

Gloria and Toni exchanged a look.

Toni was not sure what to say. She'd never believed in the inherent goodness of the universe, like Lou. She loved the notion of this magical thinking, but it never seemed to work for, say, people trapped in endless poverty. If they, desperately wishing for something, couldn't manifest more money and a job, then desperate hoping was clearly not the simple key to getting things. Employment law – now that was a force she could believe in. Oszkar deserved being hit with a lawyer's letter to put manners on him.

'You could always sue . . .' Toni began, but Gloria shook her head.

'Not the time for that,' she murmured, and moved so that she was sitting beside Lou on the faded purple velvet couch. Gloria took Lou's hands in her own thin, aged ones.

'My dearest darling Louise,' she said. 'Not everyone recognises the talent of people under their noses. That Oszkar doesn't see how much you do for the company is an example of this. It's nothing to do with the universe, sadly. I do like to think that the universe provides some things, but we have to provide a lot of the rest. The trick is knowing which is which. I . . .' Gloria paused, considering her words.

'I want to share something with you both. It may help. I was deeply in love once and then . . .' She paused again. 'My heart got broken the way women's hearts do, and there was no other man for me because I'd loved this man so much. Neither was there any point in spending my whole life regretting him. I had to live, Lou. Not wait for another man, no. But have a happy, fulfilled life. I have done that,' she said, smiling at the idea of her very full life. 'My friends, my choir, my charity work in Whitehaven, you two, my dear nieces and darling Emily – *you* have become my life. Better that than waiting for the universe to provide another man.'

Toni listened silently. She'd never questioned why Gloria wasn't married. She'd simply assumed that her aunt was one of those older ladies who'd never bothered with the male of the species, happy with charity work and her garden, her rescue dogs and the choir where her delicate soprano was such a feature. What a foolish assumption that had been. Of course Gloria had once been young and vibrant. How insensitive of her not to think of that.

'I'm so sorry, Gloria,' Lou said, her instinctive kindness pulling her out of her fugue state. 'You didn't deserve to have your heart broken. I don't understand why people do hurtful things. I hope he knows what he lost. All these secrets—' She broke off miserably. 'Did you know, Gloria? Did you know about my father not being my father? Is it true?'

For a moment, Gloria didn't speak, looking down at her lap as if seeking wisdom there. Finally, she admitted: 'Yes.'

Lou let out a tiny sob. 'Why did nobody tell me?' she said hoarsely.

'It wasn't my place to do so,' said Gloria, still speaking slowly as if she was choosing her words very carefully. 'My brother was your father because he raised you and he loved you.'

'That's not what I meant,' Lou interrupted.

'He was not your biological parent, but he was your father, Louise,' Gloria's voice was stronger now. 'Trust me when I say that. Nobody loved you like Bob.'

'But this Angelo. Did you know him? Who is he?'

Gloria looked down before speaking.

'He was here for a while,' she said cautiously. 'He was a painter from Sligo. An artist rather than a house painter,' she added with a small laugh, as if Lillian would ever fall for someone with as normal a job as being a house painter. 'He went back home to Sligo and nobody has seen him here since.'

Lou realised she had been holding out hope that Gloria would deny the story, that Lillian's behaviour had been the result of anger and too much gin, but it seemed not.

Darling Bob Cooper was not Lou's father after all.

Toni was her half-sister.

Gloria was no relation to her at all.

Lou shuddered. It was all too horrible and shocking. The Barking Dog could not have come up with a catastrophe like this – this was the stuff of Lou's nightmares. That her precious family weren't hers at all. That almost everything she loved was a lie.

'What was his surname?' asked Toni.

'His name was Angelo Mulraney,' said Gloria quietly, reaching down to stroke her little dog, who was now bored with her bed and wanted to sit on someone's lap. 'And yes, he's your father.'

There was a long, long pause. Lou stared at Gloria, her eyes filling with tears.

'I want to meet him,' she said at last. 'I need to see him.'

She turned to Toni.

'Will you take me?' she asked.

'Yes,' Toni said at once. 'Yes, of course.'

If this was what Lou needed, then she would do it in a heartbeat. And it was what Toni needed, too.

'Are you sure you want to do this?' Gloria asked Lou. Her voice was tremulous, her face very pale. 'I'm not sure it will help . . .'

'I want to hear it from him,' said Lou in a high shaky voice. 'I want to hear him tell me he's my father because I don't believe my mother. In fact, I'll never believe anything she tells me again.'

She burst into tears. She felt broken inside. The smiling Lou Fielding was gone and in her place was the fragile version that very few people had ever seen.

Chapter Ten

Lou jerked upright in the passenger seat as the car stopped and looked out her window. She'd been asleep on and off for hours, ever since they'd left Cork city. Outside, the landscape was harder, colder than the gentle Whitehaven coast. The fields were small, dotted with stones and there were no rolling hills, only a stand of bent trees in front of them and dry-stone walls lining the road. Had they arrived in Sligo already?

Lou looked out the driver's side window and realised that they'd stopped on the forecourt of a pub, a long low building with a thatched roof.

'Here?' she asked, confused. 'Is this a pub? Is this where we were heading?'

The pub was set on the side of a high road. To one side was a vast car park and to the other was a sandwich board proclaiming *Food served all day!*

Was this it? Aunt Gloria had given them the name of a place in Sligo: Easkey. Nothing more.

'No, this is not it,' she said, undoing her seat belt. 'But Angelo's last place of residence was here in the town of Easkey and people who run pubs know everything about everyone. It's the first rule of journalism – apart from being able to ask the correct question at the correct time and know how to fill in your expenses forms. Come on,' she added. 'We're going in.'

Slowly, Lou undid her own seat belt. This had been her idea, and she still wanted to find Angelo – but it felt as if everything was moving so quickly. As soon as they had left Gloria's, they had been on their way – with only a brief stop home to pack a bag, hug Emily and explain where they were going – and now they were here, she did not feel at all ready. Lou liked preparing, liked having all her things with her on trips, felt anxious otherwise. This speedy departure from her normal life in Whitehaven, which felt right earlier, seemed foolishly unplanned now.

'Come on,' Toni said, rapping on her window. Slowly, Lou got out of the car.

The pub was named Margo's Bar and Lounge, an establishment with the painted wheels of an old-fashioned cart on the white walls as decoration. There was also a Kelly green water pump from ye olden days and wooden tables and benches surrounded by enough pink and white begonias in tubs to fill several gardens.

'It's adorable,' said Lou miserably, searching for why the sight of this pretty place made her feel sad.

Then she got it: normally, she'd be here with Ned and Emily on a little family weekend away. Now she was here with Toni to search out a man she hadn't known existed until the night before, with her whole life in disarray. No wonder she didn't feel very cheerful. But then, she hadn't had enough sleep, either, and she was hopeless without sleep. It made her feel nauseous, the way she felt now, in fact.

'We could have lunch,' Toni was saying as she locked the car.

'I don't feel hungry,' grumbled Lou.

'You can watch me eat, then,' said Toni sharply and marched in ahead of her sister. 'Come on. The country pub is a place where everyone knows what's going on. It's like Facebook with Interpol tendencies.'

The interior of Margo's Bar and Lounge had been hit many times with the same cute stick as the outside. Prettiness abounded. If Margo was a person, Lou guessed that she'd trawled the length and breadth of the country looking for adorable Irish bric-a-brac with which to adorn her premises. There were elderly china chamber pots hanging from hooks and old spinning wheels nailed precariously to the wall, with a cluster of cherub-adorned holy water fonts hammered into a wooden beam near the door in case anyone felt the need to bless themselves several times in one go. The stone walls teemed with hung *objets trouvés* and behind the bar were enamelled signs from days of old, promising fabulous pints, marvellous cigarettes and train journeys to places that were now bypassed. None of it matched precisely and the hanging decorations were all in danger of concussing the taller customer, but somehow, the kitschy chaos worked.

A dark-haired girl in her twenties was behind the bar supervising a couple of old lads holding tightly to pints as if some mysterious person might steal them if not held tightly.

'Good afternoon,' said Toni briskly to the girl. 'Can you help us? We'd like the lunch menu – and I wonder if anyone around here knows Angelo Mulraney?'

Standing behind her sister, Lou felt her body vibrate with a sudden rush of anxiety.

She didn't actually want to meet Angelo Mulraney, she decided abruptly. She wanted life to go back to the way it was before, when her father was her father. Bob Cooper was her father, not some randomer her mother had casually become impregnated by. The nausea was back and she closed her mouth in case she was sick. This was hellish, every nightmare she'd ever had. Lou liked things to remain the same. Change made her anxious and this was change with knobs on.

From behind the bar, the dark-haired girl handed over two menus and then yelled 'Ma! There's a woman here to talk to you,' in the general direction of the back of the premises.

Toni passed her a menu and Lou took it automatically. If they left, she could pretend last night hadn't happened.

'Can we go—' she began, but before Toni could turn and tell her no, which was what would inevitably happen because Toni was so bossy, an older woman appeared.

A glamorous vision with dark hair, lots of lip gloss and with a black apron covering skin-tight jeans and a clinging T-shirt, the woman was a version of the bar girl, but twenty years older and with suspicious eyes.

'What can I do for you, ladies?' she asked crisply.

'Are you the Margo who owns this gorgeous place?' asked Toni, using her television voice. 'I adore it. You've done fabulous work. Has anyone ever filmed anything here . . . ?'

Apparently, there was no trowel too thick with which to apply flattery when it came to pub decor. It was indeed Margo and she blossomed under the trowelling.

'Sadly no . . .' she began, and then looked closely at Toni.

Lou had seen the television metamorphosis before and it still amazed her. Ordinary Toni stood up taller, flicked her platinum blonde hair, deepened her voice and kowabunga – people recognised Toni Cooper, TV star extraordinaire.

'You're . . . Toni from the telly?' said Margo, shocked.

Toni waved a hand as if batting away the career she'd fought tooth and nail for.

'Oh, we're here privately,' she said, in a voice that hinted at great secrecy and men with walkie talkies outside handling her security. 'My sister and I. We're doing a little trip and we thought we'd look up an old friend of our aunt's, an Angelo Mulraney. Dear Auntie G mentioned him, and we thought since we were here, we'd say hello.'

Lou sat shakily down on a bar stool and, despite her anxiety, was able to admire both her sister's ability to fib and her expensive dentistry, which was getting a good showing.

'I love your programme,' said Margo, 'although we don't always get to see it, what with running the bar and all.'

'You must be so busy,' cooed Toni. 'Don't let us hold you up. We're going to have something delicious from your menu but if you do think of where we might find Angelo, that would be wonderful.'

Margo whisked around to the sisters, shook Toni's hand delightedly and showed them to a round table where there was a definite chance of them being knocked out by low-hanging chamber pots. Both sisters ducked cautiously.

'We've a lovely fish pie on today. Salmon from the Moy and as it's still fine to eat winkles at this time of the year, chef scattered a few in. They were picked early this morning. Hard work picking them off the rocks, though: they're tiny things and they sell them by the kilo. You want to see the women doing it. Out there in all weathers in their wellington boots, frozen with the cold.'

Lou could see interest flaring in her sister's eyes at the thought of someone filling a giant bag of tiny molluscs. Toni loved stories. She couldn't help herself. Even in this time of stress, Lou knew Toni would want to find out more about the winkle-picking ladies.

'Fish pie sounds wonderful,' Toni said finally. 'And,' she added casually, as if an afterthought, 'Angelo . . . ? Aunt G would love to know we'd tracked him down. She doesn't travel anymore herself. Elderly.'

Lou bit her lip. Despite her age, elderly was not the first word people would use to describe Gloria, although she'd certainly seemed old that morning. Lillian's screeching revelations had shattered her too.

'Angelo Mulraney?' Margo's eyes with their lacquer-like coating of bronze eyeshadow, narrowed a bit as if considering whether to divulge anything or not.

Some decision was clearly reached. 'My mother will know,' she said.

'Very exotic the Mulraneys were,' said Margo's mother, a neat little woman with her daughter's shrewd eyes and skin like ivory crepe paper. Once she was installed beside Toni and Lou with a pot of tea beside her, she was keen to help. 'There was talk that one of the Mulraney women fell for a soldier from General Humbert's French army.'

'French army?' said Lou, startled.

'They came to help the 1798 Rebellion,' went on Margo's mother, as if only a complete idiot would not know this.

'There's a monument down the town,' added Margo proudly.

Lou could feel Toni longing for her notebook and pen.

'Great. But back to the Mulraneys,' Lou said.

In spite of herself, she was interested. She still wasn't sure that she really wanted to find her putative father or not, but the story Margo's mother was telling was interesting. Yet these Mulraney people could hardly be related to *her* – Margo's mother was speaking of people who'd lived over two hundred years ago because of the General Humbert reference.

'And then there was Spanish blood in them as well from the Armada—' Margo's mother went on.

'In the sixteenth century?' posited Lou, searching her brain for Spanish Armada information. Perhaps the pub was a stop-off for people on genealogical tours. Name a family name and, even if they were all long dead, the history would come out.

'Yes, and they were all very good looking as a result,' said Margo's mother. 'All that foreign blood, very exotic. The Mulraney boys were always lookers.'

This sounded more recent, Lou thought.

'When I was young, they had their pick of the local women, I can tell you.' Margo's mother smiled mistily. 'Obviously not myself,' she added, with a hasty glance at her daughter. 'I knew better than to let one of the Mulraney lads near me. I was a good girl,' she added, as if her virtue was being questioned.

'So there was an Angelo?' asked Toni.

'Oh yes, there was,' said Margo's mother softly. 'Gorgeous lad. Eyes that would melt the clothes off you.'

'Mam!' exclaimed Margo.

'I'm only saying what's true. He was clever but was full of notions. Fancied himself as an artist. There's not a lot of money in that, I can tell you. His poor mother's head was worn with worry because he wouldn't settle down to some trade. Then he left the West, went off down south and there was talk he was getting married down there, to some lady in Cork.'

My mother, thought Lou, feeling herself come down to earth. The link was there. Cork. Her mother. It was beginning to connect.

'Then it was all off, he came back here and he wasn't the same. Couldn't settle. Couldn't paint, he said. Went off again and hasn't been back since his mother's funeral. They all left. Nobody in the homestead now except his niece by marriage, and she goes off to the heat for her arthritis. I can tell you where the family home is, but I doubt there's anyone there now. Last I heard, Angelo was in Sicily.'

'Sicily?' said Lou, surprised at this turn of events.

'I suppose you won't get to see him, then,' said Margo's mother, looking mistily into the distance as she remembered Angelo. 'Some island near Syracuse. Can't remember the name. Oh, what a fine man he was . . .'

Outside the pub an hour later, stuffed with both fish pie and local knowledge, Lou wandered off to look at the view. From the high road, she could see the sea in the far distance and the faintest scent upon the air of somebody burning turf. People still did, even though the ancient Irish turf fires were mostly gone. The boglands were protected, Lou knew. But that smell . . . it was evocative of another Ireland. She'd smelled it on a visit to Achill Island years ago with Ned and baby Emily. Achill was southwest of them now and Lou realised she'd been unwittingly close to her real father's home all those years ago.

Real father – did she believe that yet? No, not yet, she decided. She would believe it if and when she saw him. Then, she'd know.

With Lou a safe distance away, Toni took a deep breath and finally turned on her phone. It exploded into a litany of missed calls, unseen text messages, WhatsApps and twenty-seven emails all shrieking 'urgent'.

Toni, you were looking for me with regard to your finances. We need to talk, urgently, said a brusque email from her pension adviser.

132

What happened between you and Gerry Lanigan?
demanded an email from Cormac, her producer. *He rang
to tell one of the lads in the newsroom that he 'can shaft
you properly now' that he has you insulting him on tape.
What the hell, Coop? What does Gerry the Muppet have?
He implied that he can ruin your career. We can't help
unless you tell us what's going on. So – what's going on?*

Toni couldn't help it – the thought of the confrontation
made her shiver. Gerry Lanigan had been terrifying when
he'd appeared in the TV station car park, but she'd made
a cardinal mistake in answering him back with such rage.
If only she'd kept her mouth shut.

'What's wrong?' asked Lou, walking over to her,
impatient suddenly to leave.

She was shivering in the grey puffa coat Emily had
given her to wear over the jeans she'd pulled on that
morning. Her unflattering Mom jeans, which Emily liked
to tease her were the ones she'd been wearing since long
before Mom jeans became fashionable. At least she'd
ripped off her party dress in the morning. Nothing would
say 'complete nervous breakdown' like a woman wearing
a sheeny evening dress by the side of a Sligo pub in a cool
March breeze.

Toni had pulled a cashmere hat on over her platinum
hair and had wrapped a matching scarf round her neck,
but it was still cold: the wind seemed to be coming in
from the sea with a severe chill factor. Toni stared at the
screen of her phone as if it contained the secrets of the
universe. She turned the phone off again. What was the
point keeping it a secret from Lou?

'Someone taped me when I was ranting at them about being a sexist moron, more or less, and if they release the tape, my career is in shreds.'

Saying it out loud made it seem more real than ever and it had been pretty damn real in her head. She'd been scared too, scared of Gerry Lanigan, but there was no point saying that. Toni barely wanted to admit it to herself. For all that she knew men were stronger than women, she'd rarely been aware of it in her own life, which made her lucky, she knew. She'd heard stories of women who'd learned the hard way that a strong man could overpower them. But she'd thought her brain power could protect her.

Her brain power hadn't protected her from Lanigan – or from what Oliver had done, either.

'But Toni, can someone do that legally? You're powerful, you have a TV show, people behind you. Nobody can just end your career.'

Toni snorted. How little Lou knew of her world. People thought that fame and success made one inviolable. How wrong they were.

'Yes, they can end my career. Legally and realistically are two very different things. This person can do what they like because, while taping me without my knowledge is illegal, if the tape gets out and everyone hears it, then the law won't matter. He'll release the tiny bit of the tape he wants.'

And not the bits where he was threatening her.

'The court of public opinion will try me and find me guilty. My career will be over. Cancelled.'

Lou gasped. 'What can we do?'

The 'we' touched Toni.

'We could find him and kill him,' she deadpanned, 'but I'm not sure that would help. He'd probably get that taped or filmed too and carving my initials into his cold, dead forehead while some third party tapes it for the news at nine will not help my career. No, I have to figure out what to do next.'

She had no idea what that was, either. Normally, her quick-thinking mind loved problems. She would analyse at speed and would have a solution while most people were still making bullet points of what the issue was. But not now. Now, she felt weirdly frozen. She had two separate problems, both huge, and for the first time in her life, Toni had absolutely no idea what to do.

'But you need to be back in Dublin . . .' began Lou. 'This whole road trip is crazy, Toni. I don't want to find Angelo Whatever His Name Is. I was sleep-deprived this morning when I agreed to it. I need to get back to Emily, Ned, Lillian and work—'

'No,' said Toni firmly. 'You do not need to get home to fix everyone!'

Whatever happened, she would make her sister take at least the weekend to figure out that she did far too much for everyone. Otherwise nothing would change and Lou would be a doormat all her life.

'Get in.'

Lou got in and Toni began to fiddle with the satnav.

She was inputting the details Margo had given them. Directions to the Mulraney home.

Lou felt herself get irritated. She didn't know if she wanted to go there. She needed to think about it first.

And Toni needed to deal with the catastrophe in her life. That was important, not haring off around the country looking for some possible father.

'Toni, let's go home,' she said. 'I don't think I'm able for this.'

Ignoring her, Toni began to drive. Under usual circumstances, Lou would have kept silent because Toni was the 'doer' sister and she was the one who went along with the plan, but not now.

'I don't want to do this,' she said again, more loudly.

'Well we are,' said her sister flatly.

Lou experienced something she rarely felt: utter fury.

'You are not listening to me!' she shouted. 'I said I don't want to do this!'

'What is wrong with you?' asked Toni, sounding shocked.

'I am fed up with nobody listening to me!' said Lou. 'And if you're going to be cancelled, then you need to get home, too. So let's abandon this crazy road trip and go home.'

She sat back in shock. Where had this come from? She never shouted, not even that time Emily had emptied her entire bottle of rose bath oil down the sink when she was five and she and Simone were 'making perfume'. Not even last night when her mother had destroyed her memories of a happy childhood with this hideous revelation.

Although she was mildly impressed that her sister was finally finding her voice, Toni wanted to scream with frustration. Lou thought that all Toni needed to do was just snap her fingers and everything would be fine again. Except it wouldn't. Not now, not this time.

'I don't need to be back home because – because it won't help.'

'But why—'

Toni exploded. 'It just won't.'

'You don't have to shout,' shouted Lou.

'I do,' shouted Toni. 'And you've been shouting!'

'I don't shout!' shouted Lou.

The car began to go faster because Toni's foot was really pressing down on the accelerator, and the sisters sat in fury beside each other. They never fought. What was wrong with them?

Nothing, Lou decided. Shouting was not forbidden by the Nice Woman police. She could shout if she wanted to. She could stand up for herself, the way she should have stood up to Oszkar for a start, and the world wouldn't implode.

Toni was definitely in trouble, Lou sensed it. Her sister was a machine, for heaven's sake: she was afraid of nobody. There was something else going on, there had to be.

She was not going to go on a mad search for bloody Angelo. They had to sort out her sister's career.

'Why won't it help if you go home?' she demanded. 'And don't fob me off this time.'

And she was done with being polite.

Toni would have closed her eyes and laid her head back if she hadn't been driving the car and such a thing was not in the road safety manual. Lou watched her sister try to start a sentence and stop again. It was as if Toni, who had never been at a loss for words in her life, couldn't speak.

'The night before your party . . .' she began. 'Oliver said we needed to talk, and I went home and . . .'

She paused, as if unable to continue. Lou had never heard her sister sound like this before, so scared.

'Toni?' Lou asked.

'Oh, Lou,' Toni said. 'I've spent years trying to control everything and I missed what was under my nose. Everything is ruined.'

Chapter Eleven

Toni had been waiting for Oliver when he got home from rehearsals on Thursday night.

'We need to talk,' he'd said on the phone when she and Morag had left Epsilon Radio. She'd known it was serious. Oliver never rang like that.

It was Marissa, she knew it. It had to be. As she waited, she felt her worry levels creep higher and higher, and that made her even angrier. She was not a worrier. She was happy, successful, calm – how dare he put her off course like this! How dare he cheat on her!

Toni toyed with the idea of opening a bottle of wine, but knew that alcohol and what she had to say wouldn't mix. She wanted stone-cold sobriety when she kicked him out for sleeping with another woman. A younger woman. Marissa. A woman with no age lines on her face, no strange new aches in her body, one who hadn't had to clamber up the mountain of success with nothing but her own abilities to recommend her.

Toni was sitting at the dining room table when Oliver arrived. She'd made a pot of green tea, drunk half of it and watched it sitting on the table, cooling, as she waited. She never normally waited up if he was late. Toni Cooper did not believe in waiting for other people. She had her own agenda and her own things to do. She had her life and Oliver had his. It was how their marriage worked. She did early mornings and he did late nights. They came together for dinner, talked on the phone, left handwritten messages on the pad beside the fridge because Oliver had never liked texting.

She was still dressed in her elegant suit from earlier, though she'd taken off her heels and her lipstick had long since gone. She was tired and, from the look on his face, her husband was too. He looked rumpled, weary, the dark leonine hair was greasy and he had puffy bags under his eyes. His shirt was unbuttoned and she could see the white T-shirt he wore underneath, a glimpse which added vulnerability to the picture. The strong King Lear, the titan of the stage, was nowhere in sight.

Toni pushed her tea away.

'Tell me the truth, Oliver,' she said in the tones that had put the fear of God in many interviewees. 'What is going on? Is it Marissa? I need to know and there's no point in lying to me as *I will know.*'

She rasped out the last words. She would know from the look in his eyes. Oliver might be a great actor, but he could not lie to her. She knew his every tell, knew every plane of his face – the craggy and noble face with the wise Shakespearean eyes – and he could not lie to her. Toni fixed him in place with a stare, waiting. All at once, the noble face crumpled, and all the strength seemed to go out of his body. He sat weakly on the armchair nearest to her, close but still removed.

Nothing he ever did physically was uncalculated. He needed space from her. Toni felt her stomach tighten. It was the girl. She'd so hoped it wasn't. Hoped he hadn't done the clichéd thing of falling for a girl young enough to be his daughter. Because she would never be able to forgive him for this. Never be able to truly love him if he'd had an affair.

She was only forty-three but, in her world, perception was everything. At forty-three, a male TV anchor was young. A female was not. The rules were entirely different and henceforth, she would be Toni Cooper, famous for being the click-bait woman whose actor husband left her for a younger woman *who looked just like her*. Nice.

Much would be made of the fact that her replacement was a woman without subtle creping on her eyelids, a woman who did not need secret visits to the dermatologist for filler and botulism, a woman who didn't need to push her body through endless barre classes to keep it taut.

'I'm glad you know,' Oliver said, shoulders slumped as he sat in the armchair. 'If you knew how often I wanted to tell you because it's been killing me—'

'Killing *you?*' Toni said, her voice rising even though she'd spent years perfecting her modulated television tones. Nobody shrieked on TV and made a career out of it. 'I'm the one it's killing, you cheating bastard.'

'Toni, it has been killing me. I am so sorry. I had no idea how to tell you and I have let you down but,' he looked up finally.

'With that girl . . . ?' she asked.

To her complete astonishment and disbelief, he shook his head. 'Girl?'

'Marissa!' she yelled.

Her words appeared to penetrate his brain.

'Me cheating on you with Marissa? No, no,' he said urgently. 'There's no girl! It's nothing to do with Marissa. I mean, she wanted to, it's the hero worship thing, but I'd never do that. She's a kid. I mean, I was so broken that I didn't realise for ages that she was caught up in the whole play magic, but I couldn't do that to you as well. What sort of a man do you think I am? No, I wouldn't dream of that, not when what I was doing was—'

Toni was confused.

Broken? As well? What was he talking about?

'As well as what?'

'Gambling,' he said in almost a whisper.

Finally, he was looking at her. She was his confessor and he was ready to recite his sins.

'I am so sorry, Toni. It's been getting worse, and I kept losing. I was trying to put money back so I could win back but my luck had changed and the debts were racking up so quickly. You have no idea how quickly the money goes . . .'

The words didn't seem to sink in. Gambling? Oliver never looked at sports, unless he was with some of his more macho actor friends who wanted to watch something sporty. Then he could roar knowledgeably at the pitch because he could act anything.

'What are you on about?' demanded Toni.

'I'm a gambler. I can't help myself,' he said bleakly. 'I thought I could stop but I can't. It takes over. It's like it's not me making the decisions. I have to do it.'

'Have to do what?'

'Play the games.'

Toni was used to applying verbal shock treatment to other people. But now, she felt it herself.

'Games?' she repeated.

Oliver bent over on his armchair so that his torso was leaning forward onto his knees. 'Everything. I started on casino games, went on to the Premiership—'

'Football?' she asked, astonished.

'I was a VIP member online. Could have gone to games because I got sent tickets, but I never cared about the game – it was the buzz, it was about winning. Eventually, I got into online poker too.' He laughed a weak little laugh. 'It's called the crack cocaine of gambling.'

Toni stared at him. If he'd said he was taking crack cocaine, she wouldn't have been more surprised. Oliver – gambling?

'But you never go to the races—' she began.

'Racing is boring in real life,' said Oliver quickly, as if now he'd started he couldn't stop the words tumbling out. 'All that standing around, and you only get to bet a few times. I mean, how many races are there at your average meet, but online games – that's where it's at. It's so fast that there's speed, the rush that comes from that . . .' He stopped, sitting up, his face flushed and guilty. 'I've tried to give up, I really have. Eamonn plays this stupid bubble game on his phone – you have to burst bubbles.

He's always on his phone. Everyone is. Nobody notices . . . and you can lose so much. The money's hideous. You get sucked in . . .'

'Into popping bubbles?'

'No. In poker, in online gambling. If only I'd stuck to bloody bubbles, but no, I play the casino games and poker. Or poker played me. I think that's what happens.'

He wasn't talking to her anymore. He was talking to himself, on some mantra he'd practised many times before. 'You start playing and then you're hooked, and it's playing you. The sites have you hooked, the debts have you stuck. I mean, someone killed himself last week over his debts. He lost everything.'

Oliver got up and began to pace.

'People talk about drugs and booze, but you can lose everything with gambling, you can lose your whole livelihood, you can die . . .'

Toni let her oddly confused mind roam over these facts until she came to the important point.

He'd mentioned debt.

'Money,' she said finally. 'If you gamble compulsively, then you lose money, right?'

Toni knew very little about gambling. She'd seen a documentary about casinos once. There was one simple rule to gambling: the house always won. The people playing kept coming back for more, desperate to win again, then desperate to win back some of their lost money. But the casino or the bookies or the poker professional won the money.

Money.

They had joint bank accounts. They both had access to their investments. Toni was a wonderful businesswoman, but she let those things slide. She paid her taxes, got an accountant to do it, but the money was all carefully put away and she only looked at it once or twice a year. She liked knowing it was there. The bills pinged out on direct debits and she had enough, always, for her needs.

Financial security was vital. Women needed it. She needed it. Had worked for it.

Oliver's lower lip quivered in a way it had never quivered in his onstage or onscreen career.

'I'm so sorry, Toni,' he said. 'I'm so sorry—'

'What is the part you're sorry about?' she demanded, even though she knew. The question was, how much?

'I've lost money.'

'How much?' she rasped.

Then he began to cry. Not the tears that had won him a Golden Globe nomination in the affair with the French actress. No, these were broken real tears and Toni began to feel very afraid.

'I don't know. Hundreds of thousands, Toni. Investments all over the place. I didn't want to look but lately, things got very bad. I was in trouble and I borrowed from someone and then I lost that too. Not just my money but yours too . . .'

They'd been driving slowly for about fifteen minutes along busy roads. Toni turned left and stopped the car on a tiny road that led to a beach named Lacken, according to an old sign on the verge of the road. She got out of the car now and stood with the wind rippling around her, blowing her blade-like hair and whisking her coat against her slender legs in their black jeans. Her cashmere scarf blew in the wind. Close by, the beach was not precisely a beach but was more an inlet of sedimentary rock creating vast horizontal slabs of grey stone around which the sea crashed mercilessly.

Lou got out and stood beside her, put an arm around her sister.

'How much has he lost?' she asked.

Toni shrugged helplessly.

'I don't actually know. I went onto my online bank and that has been quite comprehensively cleaned out.'

Toni sounded matter-of-fact but she was horrified. There had been almost no money in the account. Just enough to cover the electricity bill, perhaps, and the dustbin removal. Not much else. It had been shocking to see her account so denuded.

'Most of the money's gone. I withdrew all the cash I could yesterday. A lot of my money goes into a long-term savings account. There's some in the current account we share, but I have investment accounts and a pension. I can't access those online. I made some phone calls on Friday morning to find out what's gone on in those accounts, but nobody phoned me back before the weekend.'

One of them was looking for her, though, via email and it felt ominous.

'I couldn't say "I think Oliver's lost all my money – so this is urgent and could you check?"' Toni went on. 'I know your banking details and investments are supposed to be secret but nothing's secret, not really. Someone might hear and then where would my career be? Either I'm a moron for having a husband who's gone through all our money, or else he's up to his armpits in money-lender debt. Either way, that's not a good look for a person who regularly grills politicians and business people on my TV show. I'll be cancelled times two – once for saying what I think on tape and another time for being so stupid as to have my husband gamble away our life savings.'

'He borrowed from money lenders?' interrupted Lou.

'Oliver admitted that he borrowed from some guy named Big Jimbo Connor. Yeah,' said Toni bitterly, 'sounds like a pillar of the banking establishment to me, too. This guy hangs around a private gambling club in town, so add possibly illegal gambling to the mix, as well as someone who is probably in organised crime.'

Lou held on more tightly to her sister.

'We might have nothing left and there will be no way of getting it back. The investments were shared. Illegal gambling, money lenders, organised crime . . . and then I finish it all off by getting taped telling some horrible businessman that he's an ass. Which he is, by the way, but nobody will be championing me for standing up to him. No, when all this comes out, Oliver and I will have the police round our house to find out what happened, and nobody will believe that I didn't know. *The wife must know*, I always think when scandals break. *I'd know*, I tell myself. And I didn't.'

Lou leaned against the bonnet of Toni's car.

'Did you have any idea how easy it is to gamble with a smartphone? No, me neither. But smartphones have been around for nearly twenty years and the legislation on gambling is much older. So anyone can put every penny they – or their wife – own onto a poker game or slots or bet on a football match, and there are no rules. How did I not see this?' she asked. 'I feel like a complete idiot.'

'You're not an idiot,' Lou said softly.

'I am,' said Toni. 'Let's go before I throw myself into the water.'

'You wouldn't,' said Lou. 'You're not the type.'

'I know,' agreed Toni.

'I'm more the type,' Lou said softly.

The very idea was so scary that Toni had to change the subject.

'Come on. Back in the car.'

'Where to?' asked Lou.

'To look at the house, of course,' said Toni.

'Why?' asked Lou. 'They're gone. You heard what Margo's mother said.'

'But it's . . .' Toni searched in her head for the right phrase. 'The house is a piece of family.'

Too late, she realised that this was not, in fact, the right thing to say.

Her sister stopped and looked at her in horror.

'I can't believe you said something so callous,' Lou said. 'You're calling this place a part of my family?'

Toni had long wanted her sister to be less passive but as she watched her become enraged, she wished Lou wasn't losing her temper right now.

'Family?' repeated Lou. 'How is some house in the middle of Sligo a sign of my family? Angelo Mul-blinking-raney was not my family. He was a sperm donor!'

'I'm glad there's no one around to hear us,' Toni said evenly, glancing towards the nearest cottage, about six hundred metres away.

'Why? Because I said sperm donor? I'll say it again: he was just a sperm donor. Bob was my father! You don't get to have him all to yourself now.'

'Don't be angry,' said Toni wearily and drove off the Lacken road and onto the main one again. She was worn out with talking about Oliver and how her life was in shreds.

Where was the Lou she knew and loved? This new version was very mercurial. A few moments before, she'd been soft and vulnerable. 'I simply meant that we could look at the place where—'

'Where *my* father came from, so that you could have Bob all to yourself?'

'You're being ridiculous – and stop shouting!' shouted Toni.

Honestly, it was like being four again, all this shouting.

There was silence in the car.

'Drive for one point five kilometres, then turn left,' intoned the satnav lady.

'You can shut up, too,' yelled Lou.

Obligingly, the satnav lady shut up.

Ignoring the fact that they were on a main road with no hard shoulder, Toni pulled in. The satnav lady objected to this behaviour and Toni, fearing another explosion from her previously calm sister, quickly turned Ms Satnav down.

Searching in her pocket, she found the piece of paper with the address of the Mulraney family home and Margo's directions to it.

Lou ignored her and stared out the window, her shoulders shaking.

At home, the sea on Whitehaven Beach could be wild but here, not too far in the distance, it looked as if a storm was raging. The same Atlantic plunged against both coasts but the Western seaboard did not have any of the sense of shelter of the southeast coast. Here, with the next stop being three thousand miles away and nothing but plunging waves between the two land masses, the small stone houses and cottages of Easkey seemed to lean away from the ferocity of both the sea and the wind.

Toni ignored her sister. She'd seen people behave like this before: suddenly realise they were allowed to get angry and then come down from the rage rush feeling shaky.

'We're going the right way,' said Toni, looking at satellite navigation details and her written ones. She flicked a switch to keep the directions silent. No point having another blowout.

'OK,' said Lou. 'Let's go, then. And sorry – I'm a bit fragile. I'm really sorry about Oliver and your job. It's awful. But I hate feeling that you're distracting yourself from that with looking for my supposed father.'

Ouch, thought Toni.

'I'm not distracting myself,' she said tautly, which wasn't entirely true.

'I can't believe a random guy can ruin your career. And you don't know all the financial details yet, do you? There's got to be a way out of it.'

'Of course,' said Toni automatically.

There was a way out of it – she just hadn't worked it out yet. But she would, she always did.

Lou stared out the car window as her sister drove. Something about the wildness of the landscape made her protests about not wanting to see the house seem oddly insignificant. Here, human beings had struggled to survive in spite of living off fields dotted with rocks where nothing but sheep could graze and where the harsh climate flattened all but the toughest of plants.

Margo had talked about people picking tiny shellfish like winkles for a living, trudging on the shore to fill huge bags for which they were paid a pittance. The very wildness of the west made Lou feel as if she had no right to stamp her feet like a pampered lady and refuse to look at the house where her father had been born.

Strong women had been raising children on this land for centuries, battling famine and social injustice, determined to rise above it all. Nobody had taught them how to breathe to get over anxiety. What must it have been like then? Lou couldn't imagine. Your children starving and you had to keep it together without any help, any medication. If this was the place where her birth father had come from, then Lou decided she owed it to her newly-fifty-year-old self to find where he'd come from.

You'd absolutely want to visit his home, she said silently to Mim, wherever Mim was in the sky. On a unicorn, probably, with pink sparkles in the long blonde hair she'd have to replace the tufty baldness at the end of her life. Mim had hated losing her hair. She'd definitely have long blonde rippling hair now. *You'd find the place – and you'd find him.*

Mim was indomitable. Had been indomitable. Rounds of chemotherapy and watching her hair fall out in clumps and feeling the pain rip through her body had not stopped Mim's determination to keep living as long as she could. Mim would not let the mere fact that this information about a new father was a shock stop her.

Lou imagined the conversation with her best friend: 'So what if it was a surprise? Go find where he was from. Find him. It'll be an adventure, Lou!'

I can't find him because he lives in another country, Lou told Mim, who was probably sitting happily on her unicorn, head tilted. *But I suppose that Toni and I can visit his house. Is that good enough for you? But what then, Mim? What do I do with this information? I want Bob to be my father because it's what I've known all my life and he was a safe harbour. But this new person, how can he replace Bob? What is my family now?*

Mim, busy with plaiting the unicorn's tail or her own sparkly hair, didn't answer.

She never answered when Lou talked to her, but it was comforting to have the one-sided conversation all the same. Mim had never let her down. Not once.

Mim had gone with her to the doctor when the world had felt too much for Lou.

'You're depressed, lovie. I think you need some professional help. Can I do something?' Mim had said, something nobody else had said.

Not Toni, who probably wouldn't have recognised depression if it had hit her with her straightening irons. Not Ned, who, for all his brilliance, had a slight fear of anything 'mental', induced no doubt by a mother who believed a reliance on God was all a human being needed and 'Hadn't He put us on earth to suffer?'

The antidepressants were in the small bag Emily had packed. Emily and Ned both knew about them, but if he'd been asked to pack a bag for her, he would never have remembered them.

Not Lillian, who only noticed her own ailments. Her mother had no idea that Lou was on any antidepressant medication. Why had she never told Lillian?

Why indeed.

And as for Toni, Lou had failed to tell her sister that far from just taking the tablets for a few months after Mim died, when she felt shattered with grief, she was still on them. Possibly always would be. She'd been scared that Toni would judge her. Toni would never need any pharmaceutical help to get up in the morning, Toni would not need to gently up the dose until it was working, or deal with the side effects. Toni might work on a TV show where she talked about mental health with somebody, but as to discussing it with her sister . . . that had never happened. Was it Toni's fault? Or Lou's for making her own needs so minuscule that nobody remembered them?

The sisters drove along a straight road, past tiny turn-offs with no signposts and past a little chapel with a tractor parked neatly outside. A girl on a bike flew along the road beside them, dark hair flying in the breeze made by her movement, and as Toni slowed on the narrow road, they both saw that a small dog wearing a blue ribbon on its topknot sat in the basket on the front.

'I always wanted a dog,' said Lou suddenly as they passed the girl on the bike. 'Lillian had one in the house during the week. Some artist friend of hers had a little dog and he couldn't stay in The Ashling B&B with it, so Lillian invited him to stay with her. I thought she hated dogs.'

'Lillian doesn't hate dogs.' Toni negotiated the first left turn, which took them down an even narrower road. 'She hates extra work. Anything that puts her out: that's what she hates.'

Lou stared out the window at the view. The road had carried them to a point where they were now facing the ocean. She thought of the change of perspective of her mother. She didn't merely have to negotiate the concept of a different birth father. Her vision of her mother had been turned quite upside down, and that was utterly bewildering.

'Lillian implied she was scared of dogs.'

No, not implied. Her mother had definitely once said she'd been bitten by a dog and that was why she didn't like canines in general. There had been a palaver about seeing where the dog had bitten her leg, Lou was sure of it. But her mother hadn't pulled up her cigarette-leg pants to show the mark. They were tight above her shapely ankles. Lillian loved her ankles. No matter what dirty work she was doing in the studio, or before, when she taught art at a girls' school, a job she loathed, Lillian was always beautifully dressed. Sexily dressed, now that she thought about it.

'Lillian was bitten. Wasn't she?' Lou hated that she was doubting her mother now.

A new father, dogs . . . what next?

'She wasn't bitten,' said Toni without thinking. 'My friend Jules used to bring Pogo, her lurcher, around when he was small before he became all leggy and huge. When he grew up, Julia couldn't walk him on her own then because he was too easily scared and hard for her to hold onto. But Lillian quite liked Pogo. He was that silky grey colour she painted the studio in. You know: the purpley grey colour? He was beautiful, she liked that. If Lillian was going to like any sort of dog it would be a very beautiful one, all gleaming musculature like a bronze.'

Lou stopped admiring the ocean and sat very upright.

'So – Lillian was never bitten by a dog?' she asked, just to be sure.

Toni's own emotions were too close to the surface for her to be able to protect her sister's.

'No,' she sighed. She felt a headache coming on. The stress of the day was making her jaw tight with tension. Talking about Oliver made it all very real: the betrayal and the fear that came with it. She would have to start again to make money to feel secure.

Weary anger made her blunt.

'Lillian wasn't bitten, Lou,' she said. 'I've seen her with dogs. She's not scared. I'm sorry. I've told you that not everyone is wonderful and honest. I really thought you'd figured our mother out. She's a dreadful fibber.'

'Why would she lie to me?' Lou asked, aware that she sounded like Emily, the small child version.

Why is the sky blue? When will I be a grown-up?

'Because she felt like it on the day in question,' replied her sister bleakly. 'You wanted a dog and she didn't. Lou, you can't have believed everything she ever told you? I didn't. Mind you, I should have learned that lesson better. I believed my own husband, I *trusted* him, and look how well that's worked out.'

Lou wished she could ignore the dreadful ache inside her.

Her mother had lied about many things. But then *she'd* lied too. Her mother knew vaguely about Lou's anxiety but not that she took medication for depression . . . Why had she kept that a secret? Why did she feel that she had no right to bother other people with her problems when they had no problem bothering her with theirs?

Toni was being no help: her mind was totally somewhere else.

The only sure bit of information Lou had to hold on to was that her mother lied about lots of things. Had lied about the dog and had lied about Lou's father, although she could still be lying about this Angelo man. A lie within a lie.

Who knew? Lou wasn't sure she knew anything anymore. Her mother was no longer the beloved woman who called her 'the milk of human kindness', the woman Lou did her very best to please. In her place was a temperamental mother who'd blithely destroyed Lou's peace of mind at what should have been a special occasion. This version of her mother was one Lou didn't recognise.

'Look, we're here,' said Toni.

Here was precisely as Margo had described it: an old-fashioned two-storey farmhouse painted a muted grey with a small walled garden to one side and some run-down sheds with galvanised roofs to the other side. White-painted rocks formed the edge of the driveway, which was filled with grey pebbles. One ragged rose clung to a bit of trellis to the left of the door and was trying to bloom.

'We can't simply drive in like this,' said Lou, feeling the familiar surge of anxiety. 'Somebody might be here.'

They might be shouted at or get into trouble for trespassing. Lou's fear of getting into trouble was strong. It was why she never walked across the road without waiting for the traffic light's green man; why she parked before answering her phone in the car. Someone might shout at her, and Lou spent a lot of her life trying to avoid that possibility.

'There's nobody here,' Toni said. 'Margo or her mother said they thought it was empty at the moment. I'd say a blade of grass doesn't grow around here without the pair of them knowing about it. Trust me: nobody's home.'

She parked on the pebbled driveway and got out of the car. After a moment, Lou got out too, following Toni toward the little walled garden. It was built with the cool grey pieces of rock used in all the dry-stone walls in the area, but in order to make a taller structure, these stones had been fused with thin layers of concrete. The gate was a warm green which was now flaking, and inside the garden were crab-apple trees, what might possibly be a cluster of fruit bushes and a long vegetable patch.

Someone had clearly been in and planted something recently in the vegetable patch, though Toni, who knew precisely zip about where food came from until it was on the shelf in a shop, had no idea what it could be at this time of the year. Those insanely big leaves on one side were from rhubarb, she thought, recalling a programme she'd done once on the Irish Countrywomen's Association. Rhubarb leaves were like something from a dinosaur movie: giant things.

'Should we be in here?' asked Lou tentatively, standing at the green gate as if waiting to be given a ticket for admittance.

'We're not here to steal anything,' replied her sister in exasperation. 'Margo said we could come up here—'

'But it's not her house,' protested Lou. 'Who knows if there's anyone here or not. There might be someone inside phoning the police as we speak!'

'There isn't,' said a voice from behind Lou.

It was the girl they'd seen on the bicycle. Slim from all the cycling, early twenties with the small brown fluffy dog at her heels. Delighted to see new people, he ran into the garden with his topknot bouncing, yapped a bit at Lou and then leaned against her legs to be petted.

'Hello little doggie,' she said, leaning down to stroke his fur, then stood up anxiously as she remembered that they were trespassers. 'We're just here to see the house. We were looking for Angelo Mulraney—'

'It's grand,' said the girl, waving a long, dismissive hand accessorised with a jewelled, hippie-ish bracelet. 'They're not due back for months. Mrs Mulraney likes the Canaries in the winter. She comes back the colour of mahogany from hours on a sun lounger and makes everyone jealous of her tan.'

'Sounds like a good plan,' said Toni, because even though they were in the shelter of the walled garden, there was quite a breeze blowing in from the ocean. This place would be Baltic in the real winter and the thought of the Canaries was beguiling.

'Mrs Mulraney . . . is she Angelo's wife?' asked Lou tentatively.

The girl considered this. 'No. I think Angelo's the uncle. I don't know him. He lives abroad.'

'Sicily,' supplied Toni.

'I'm going to Greece when I've done my finals,' said the girl, perking up at this new bit of information. 'I wonder is there a ferry linking them? My mother keeps an eye on the place for Mrs Mulraney and I could go and kip on Uncle Angelo's floor so we could have a look at Sicily. There's only going to be three of us. He wouldn't mind, would he?'

'How could he?' said Toni easily, as if she knew Angelo intimately instead of only having heard of his existence the night before. 'How many Irish people have travelled the world sleeping nowhere but on distant strangers' floors?'

The girl nodded enthusiastically. She liked this plan.

'Listen,' went on Toni, 'do you have Mrs Mulraney's phone number?'

Toni was on home ground here. Searching out phone numbers and contacts for people was one of the many things she was good at.

'I could ask my mother, but she's off with her walking group for a week. Never looks at the phone. We're having a party every night!' The girl laughed and Lou could see her sister beginning to look annoyed.

'We'll track him down another way,' Toni said grimly and began to scroll.

'Good luck with that,' said the girl cheerfully, and Lou, left to her own devices, looked around. Now that someone who knew the family had given the imprimatur for Lou and Toni to be at the house, Lou felt some of the tension leave her. Not that she or Toni could possibly resemble the sort of people who'd rampage through the house and steal things, but it was better to have someone know they were there. How was it that Toni didn't have a shred of anxiety about being in a stranger's garden when she was riddled with fear at being caught there? How could they be so different – was that Angelo's doing? His genes?

Lou gave the little dog one last pet and left the garden to walk around the house. It was clear why the walled garden was a necessity: at the back of the house, the wind from the ocean had nothing to stop its progress. There were no trees and only a few bushes in its path. The view must have looked the same, Lou thought, as it had a hundred years ago. Nothing could have changed, except that perhaps erosion had made the sea closer.

Lou realised there were ruins just metres away at the bottom of the land on which the house sat. The ruins were probably the remains of the original Mulraney homeplace. The same white-painted stones were placed around its front door but there was only a shadow of a cottage left. One gable wall was gone entirely, and ivy and moss clung ferociously to the remains of the house. Despite its destruction, there was peace surrounding the mossy ruins.

Without knowing why, Lou took out her phone and began to take photos. She and Mim had always believed that places could contain memories. It was why they'd loved all their tatty jewellery talismans and stories about ancient Celtic sites. They'd gone to the Hill of Tara and Newgrange, as well as many holy wells and the Druid's Altar, the stone circle in Drumbeg. They'd felt something in each place. The memory of the past, a distant echo of other lives lived.

Lou now felt something here, although she could not have put words upon it. If Angelo was her father, then his family had lived here, and they were her family too. Had her ancestors farmed this rock-strewn land? Had they looked out onto the sea every day, trying to make a living, wondering why they yearned for the heat and thinking they'd never reach the stunning Spanish land from where their relatives had come?

Lou ran a gentle finger over the ruins. *Am I from here?* she wondered.

'Lou, there's a dark cloud coming and my app here says it's going to rain for sure. Time to go. Come on.'

They made it just beyond Skreen before the rain truly came down and soon, the windscreen wipers couldn't keep pace with the furious torrent.

'We have to stop,' Toni said, but it was ages before they came upon a suitable place where the car would not be flattened. The stopping place was on the outskirts of Ballysadare, a gleaming mobile Winnebago of the type that had done huge business in the pandemic and boasted signs all over that said it sold coffee and stunning ice cream. A little further along was an actual café, with Wi-Fi, and as soon as they sat down Toni began googling for mentions of the Mulraney family and of Angelo. Then, when she could find nothing, she began looking up articles about people discovering they were not genetically related to some of their family members.

'This is amazing,' she said to Lou. 'Look, this woman thought it was a laugh to do his and hers DNA tests with her boyfriend and they hoped he had Viking blood because he was blue-eyed, tall and very blonde. In fact, he was 4 per cent Viking and she found that the person she'd thought was her sister was in fact her mother! Her nephew was her half-brother. I can't believe I haven't interviewed anyone about this before.'

Lou shot Toni a jaundiced look.

'This is not a research trip,' she said. 'This is my life, Toni.'

'But still,' went on Toni, oblivious to Lou's agitation, 'it's thrilling stuff! We don't have a number, we just have a name and a destination: it's a quest!'

She didn't notice her sister glaring at her.

'It's my life!' said Lou in icy tones. 'Not a stupid programme idea.'

'What is wrong with you?' demanded Toni. 'You're being a bitch.'

'Why is it that when I stop being a doormat, you think I'm a bitch?' Lou countered.

They stared at each other.

Toni reached out and grabbed her sister's hand.

'I'm sorry,' she apologised. 'Whatever happens, if Lillian is telling the truth, you'll always be my true sister. Lou. My soul sister in every respect. Even if you're being an awful cow.'

Lou couldn't help it: she smiled. So did Toni.

'This new spiky you is going to take some getting used to, Lou,' she said.

'Again, sorry,' said Lou, sighing. 'Nobody has ever called me a cow before. I've always been Ms Sensible, Ms Lovely, and I've spent years being terrified that people won't like me or will think I'm a cow.'

'Nothing wrong with a bit of a cow or even bitch,' said Toni. 'Too many women are scared out of their minds to say what they think in case people think they're demanding. If a woman stands up for herself, she's instantly labelled a "bitch", which . . . I guess I just did, too. Sorry. Of all people, I should know better. Look.' Toni held up her phone, which was showing a blast of scary rain-inducing weather on the satellite picture. 'There are going to be floods this evening, Lou. We should just find somewhere lovely to stay—'

She paused. Was it wise to be spending money on 'somewhere lovely' right now? When the money she'd earned over the years might all be gone – but Toni refused to think about that now. 'I need to charge the car too.'

Lou thought about it. She had everything she needed for one night. She had Toni, Emily loved her, and she had her medication. She'd manage.

Somewhere lovely seemed like a gorgeous plan. Was it running away? She didn't care. She was going to start playing by new rules. Now. If running away helped, then she'd run.

Chapter Twelve

Lillian parked the car at an angle on the corner of Whitehaven's Main and Miller streets. She got out and looked briefly at the rear, which stuck out into the bike lane perilously.

Tough shit to all the people on bikes, she thought grimly. Only people who couldn't afford cars used bloody bikes. Without locking the car, because who would be nuts enough to steal it, she stomped off in her metalwork clogs towards the small expensive supermarket. She couldn't face the big one: all those families doing weekly shops – hideous.

On sunny Sundays in Whitehaven, the town was full of people meandering from brunch in the direction of the small food and craft market in the park at Mermaid Peak. Lillian normally avoided the Sunday market like the plague, but today, lack of food in the house and the lack of Lou to get food for her had forced Lillian out.

For as long as Lillian could remember, her elder daughter had been on the other end of the phone, ready to drop whatever she was doing to get food, drink, a canister of gas for the heater in the studio – whatever Lillian wanted. But not today. Lou wasn't answering her mobile phone. Lillian had rung four times – four! – in ever-increasing outrage.

'Where's your mother?' Lillian had demanded of Emily when she'd given in and phoned Lou's home number and had been irritated to find her granddaughter answering. Emily was a great kid, feisty and sharp, but she wasn't biddable like her mother.

'Mum's not here,' said Emily. 'Can I leave her a message, Granny?'

Granny! Cheeky girl, thought Lillian. Calling her Granny.

It was a very definite snub. Something to do with Friday night, no doubt.

'Tell her to call me when she gets back,' said Lillian loftily, not even responding to her granddaughter's rudeness. Then she hung up. She liked hanging up on people: made them worry if they'd been cut off or confused about whether they'd upset her. Lillian liked a bit of confusion. Except when the confusion ball was in her own court.

Lillian had to admit to herself that she was still slightly hazy about Friday night. Something had happened for sure, and she had a niggling feeling that she'd unleashed a stream of truths in her rage at hearing about the Kennedy Art Prize, but nobody had phoned her to fill her in, so who knew what she'd blurted out.

Still, she'd long made it a habit never to ask how she'd behaved at any event or party.

Such things were very bourgeois, an old art teacher had told her decades before, and Lillian had loved the idea of never having to explain or apologise. Artistic people were always going to be a little outrageous and people needed to get with the programme.

Bob had found her tricky at first, but he'd learned to deal with it by smiling in that almost paternalistic way. She definitely drank more now that he was gone – Bob had toned down her wilder excesses, but he was dead and she was grieving, so tough bananas to the rest of the world.

Friday might have been a bit chaotic, on reflection. First, there had been the consumption of a new botanical gin with hints of borage and elderflower, she recalled.

'Light and airy,' said one of her old pals, Peadar, who did his best as a painter and sold ugly landscapes to tourists who knew nothing about art. It paid the bills, he liked to say.

He'd brought a litre of said botanical gin to the party because he said the Barn had very dull drinks, no decent wine and only old slop of punch. No way Lillian and their crew would manage a whole night drinking what the plebs were drinking. Typical Lou, to have her fiftieth in such a whimsically pretty location without a decent bar. Before she'd heard about the award – and Lillian's jaw ached from grinding her teeth at the very thought of Concepta winning it – Peadar had been pouring jam jars of the gin for the four of them. Then someone had come in and, this is where it got hazy, Lillian had heard the news. Who'd told her? Was it Ivanka who made those felted pictures? God, she hated felted pictures. They were so twee.

Lillian knew that news of the Kennedy going to Concepta – fifty grand to that derivative cow who'd never had an original thought in her life! – had made her angry, as it bloody would. Then Gloria, stupid do-gooder, had tried to calm her down. Grabbing a basket in the supermarket, Lillian's nostrils flared at the thought of Gloria telling her to shut up. When had she ever listened to her bloody sister-in-law?

As she sailed past the vegetable aisle on her way to the ready meals, Lillian thought she saw a couple of women staring at her. Jess, that busybody from the bakery, was one of them. She wasn't staring in the way Lillian liked to be stared at, either. Not an 'aren't you fabulous, feminist sister, standing up for older women!' sort of look. No. More of an 'are you daring to show your face in public?' sort of stare. Lillian didn't like that.

She glared back at the women, stuck her tongue out and then stomped off to get something to eat. Carbs and cheese, she decided. Some homemade Italian thing, perhaps, and damn the diet. It was hard keeping the old waist slim once one hit seventy, but to hell with diets.

She'd get wine too. She hadn't planned to because yesterday's hangover had been monumental. That type of newly distilled gin was always lethal, but until she had a vague feeling about what had really happened on Friday, a few glasses of vino would help. On her way back to the checkout, she might stick her tongue out at those two bitches again. That would show them. Nobody snubbed Lillian Cooper and got away with it.

For a brief moment, she thought of Lou. Where the hell was she? Lillian needed her. Whatever had gone on at the party. Lou would get over it, surely?

A fragment of memory infiltrated Lillian's consciousness.

Angelo. She had talked about him. She'd sworn to keep the secret to her grave. Bob had begged her. It was hard to remember Friday properly. There had been a lot of gin. After the party, they'd had wine in the Gin Palace, which she hated but which had a decent bar and that hot Italian boy running the place.

'You went a bit near the knuckle, Lillian, my darling,' Harry had said cheerfully when they were on their third bottle.

'Never explain, never apologise,' Lillian had said loudly.

Whatever she'd said or whatever she'd done, Lou would get over it. And hopefully soon, because the house was a bit of a mess. Dog hair everywhere from that damned Monty, and every glass in the house used. She'd be drinking wine out of teacups next.

Lou would sort it out. She always did.

They'd stayed the night in a big hotel on the outskirts of Boyle in County Roscommon and now Lou sat in the hammam in the swimsuit she'd bought in the hotel spa reception and wondered what she had been doing to miss out on this sort of feeling all her life.

'I adore this,' Lou said to her sister, allowing herself to luxuriate in the feeling of bonelessness that came from blissful wet heat after an invigorating swim.

Toni had insisted on them getting up early on Sunday morning and using the hotel's facilities.

'They've an adult's pool as well as a children's one, a hot tub, and – bliss! A hammam!'

'We've nothing to wear,' said Lou.

Toni had stared at her.

'We can't swim nude,' Lou added.

'We can buy swimsuits,' said Toni, as if she was talking to a child.

'Pardon me for not knowing how to behave in swanky hotels,' said Lou, slightly stung.

Somehow, they got down to the pool area without fighting and then, in their new suits, swam lengths. Instantly, all irritation fled.

Lou had not swum for a long time and she remembered that she loved it, slicing through the water in silence, feeling her body move like a seal was almost as good as meditation. Even better was the hammam.

'I have to get out,' gasped Toni. 'It's getting too hot for me. Coming?'

'No,' said Lou, stretching languorously. 'It's still perfect.'

When was the last time she'd done anything like this? Years. Years since she'd taken time out to do anything as physically relaxing. She and Mim had swum in the hotel pool on a weekend away in Florence some years ago. They'd taken Emily and Simone, who were both studying art history.

'Time in the Uffizi is what we need,' Mim had said. 'Think of how you can make sense of the Renaissance there by seeing the paintings in the flesh.'

'Is there an outlet mall nearby?' Simone had asked wickedly. 'We could spend time there too . . . I need some retail research in the flesh!'

It had been a glorious weekend.

'I didn't fulfil my promise to live life to the full,' Lou muttered to Mim, with her eyes closed. 'I can see that now. It's still a work in progress because I'm a bit mixed up but,' she got to her feet, having suddenly reached peak boiling point, 'I'm going to change. Promise.'

They were finishing up a relaxing brunch, having vacated their room, when Emily phoned her aunt. Seeing her niece's name come up, Toni got up from the table and walked over to the window to look out. To one side was a mini crazy golf course and it was jammed with exhausted adults and their energetic charges.

The hotel was very much a family one with an entire corner of the breakfast room given over to a soft play area complete with a ball pit. At the window, she could talk away from Lou.

'Granny rang the house,' said Emily.

Toni laughed. 'Granny? Since when do you call her Granny?'

'Since she upset Mum,' said Emily. 'I know I'm supposed to look up to her and respect her but . . .' Emily stopped. 'Respect has to be earned.'

Toni felt an unaccustomed pang at her childlessness at that moment. It happened rarely but sometimes, only sometimes, Emily behaved in such a way as to make Toni wish she had an Emily of her own.

But then, kids were never yours, were they? You reared them and they moved on. Toni had seen it happen time and time again in all areas of her life. Previously sensible women were made insane with grief at their empty nest when the children left.

'Have I ever told you how much I love you, Emily?' she asked, returning to the topic at hand before she could answer. 'Bet Granny didn't like being called Granny and not Lillian.'

'And I care why . . . ?' said Emily, unrepentant. 'How is Mum?'

'You can talk to her yourself—'

'Not yet,' interrupted Emily. 'Let me get this out of the way first. I don't want to wreck her time away with this stuff. You can choose to tell her or not. You judge. Dad is upset because he knows he hurt her—'

'Your father is an idiot,' remarked Toni.

'I know and I told him so,' Emily went on. '"How could you not buy Mum something for her fiftieth?" I said, but he's hopeless. He says he can't shop.'

'We both know that's a useless excuse. *Can't do something* applies to specific skills like brain surgery or nuclear physics,' said Toni caustically. 'All he had to do was walk into any perfume place or clothes shop, bleat that his wife was fifty, and an avalanche of lovely shop assistants would have helped him out.'

'This is not news to me, Toni,' said Emily impatiently. 'I know he's an idiot and I've told him so. Before I forget,

172

Oszkar from Mum's work has rung several times. There's some panic over a wedding planner who left a message for Mum on the office phone: they're all going mental because none of them have a clue what she's talking about and Oszkar's bleating that he knows it's the weekend but he must talk to Mum immediately.'

'Do him good to lose some business because he treated Lou badly,' said Toni. 'After all the hours your mother had put into that company, imagine not giving her the big job. I know she's been basically doing it anyway.'

'I agree. Oszkar is totally ick.'

'Ick?'

'Awful, in old people language,' Emily said. 'Mum is way too forgiving, so don't tell her about Oszkar. She'll want to help out.'

'She might surprise you,' Toni said, smiling as she looked over at her sister, blissfully relaxed.

A few hours later, the sisters collected their meagre luggage and went to check out.

Automatically, Toni handed in her credit card and tapped in the PIN, speaking to Lou over her shoulder.

'It's not going through, Ms Cooper.'

Toni looked down at the card reader and the words 'declined' on the little screen.

'I have another one,' she said lightly, her hand beginning to vibrate as she found her wallet and searched for another card. Then, worried in case the next card wouldn't go through either, she added shakily: 'but there was a problem with them all yesterday. I wonder if my account has been hacked?'

'You did mention that,' said Lou, realising what was happening and reaching for her own wallet.

'I'll pay so you can phone the bank and cancel the cards properly. Hackers,' Lou said to the receptionist, 'it's dreadful what can happen these days.'

'Dreadful,' agreed the receptionist, taking Lou's card.

'Do you want another coffee while you sit in the bar and get onto the bank's emergency number?' Lou instructed her sister. 'You don't want your accounts cleaned out!'

'Ha! Imagine that!' said Toni with an air of hysteria. Lou was turning out to be very good at making stuff up at short notice. That was a turn-up for the books. 'We might have to kill the hacker!'

'I have gardening shears that might do the job!' said Lou cheerfully.

Both sisters laughed so heartily at this that the receptionist briefly reconsidered his belief that reception was a promotion from being in charge of the small kiddies' pool. Customers were mad, no two ways about it.

They went back into the restaurant, where Lou took charge and ordered an espresso for her sister.

'Can you check your credit card balance online?' Lou whispered to her sister.

Toni nodded. There had been money in her normal accounts on Friday and she'd taken out as much as she could but, stupidly, she hadn't checked yesterday. She'd been too busy avoiding the phone and the texts and emails. She didn't want to speak to Oliver. She couldn't bear to talk to him yet. She logged onto her bank and inhaled swiftly.

'My credit card's on stop,' she breathed. 'The balance is—' She could hardly say the words: 'Nine thousand euros and change. I only just paid the bill on Tuesday. No way have I spent any of that in the past few days. I used the card for parking in town, and got lunch the other day. Thirty euros max. I've spent nothing else . . . Oliver has taken money out. Look – cash withdrawal. He must be mad! Taking cash out of this credit card means you're instantly paying interest. It's insane.'

Toni's breathing was becoming quicker and quicker.

'It's addiction,' said Lou quietly. 'What are we going to do?'

Toni squeezed her eyes shut. She had wanted to bury her head in the sand, had wanted to run away from the problem as long as she could. But it felt real now. And she couldn't run anymore.

'I need to go to Dublin,' she said. 'Talk to the pension and investment people – speak to Oliver.'

The task ahead felt overwhelming. She turned to her sister, her eyes wet with tears.

'Will you come with me?'

Lou nodded.

'Of course.'

She'd been thinking that she had to stop fixing people's lives for them. But this was different. This wasn't doing a small errand for Toni to save her time – this was being there when Toni seriously needed her.

'Of course, I'll come. You need me.'

She thought for a minute. 'I'll phone Emily and get her to pack a bag with more stuff – but how will we get it to Dublin?'

Toni took back control. 'I'll get it picked up,' she said. 'Leave that to me.'

Chapter Thirteen

Trinity Rose McNeil took all the cash from the fake can of cola on the shelf behind her boyfriend – ex-boyfriend's – desk and stuffed it into her zipped purse. It was mostly twenties, with a few fifties. Possibly six hundred, because Pete was saving for a car. Or at least he'd said he was saving for a car. She was currently of the opinion that he was actually saving for a new guitar. Because what else would a guy want all that money for? Not for a sensible future, no. But for worldwide fame and a career onstage – that was the future!

Trinity found she was pursing her lips the way her aunt Dara did and almost laughed. If Dara could see her now, she'd be angry. Trinity had screwed up. She'd believed everything Pete had said. So much for thinking she was a clever cookie. She was an idiot. Well, not anymore.

Trinity decided she'd count Pete's money later. She didn't have time now and time was money, she thought with a slightly crazed laugh.

'Girl, you're losing it,' she told herself, opening the drawers in Pete's desk to see if there was anything useful she could take.

His bone-handled penknife was there but she left that. She hated knives. There were pens, receipts and the old bottle opener he'd got from Orlando when his family had gone on that US trip when he was fourteen. That was coming. Bottle openers were useful. Plus, Pete would hate that it was gone and, even though Trinity was not a bad person – she'd been on the college entertainment committee for the past two terms and had been voted Friendliest Ents Officer Ever – she wanted to upset her erstwhile boyfriend. Ex-boyfriend. He needed to suffer.

Of course, she could always damage his guitars, but the noise of smashing a Gibson Les Paul, standard '61 in classic ebony might attract attention. The desk yielded a wallet with dollars and sterling in it, which she imagined was money from relatives abroad. Where had that been at Christmas when they'd been so broke? She removed the cash and put it in another part of her rucksack. Pete deserved to be cleaned out.

When she'd gone through the tiny flat and taken everything she thought she could possibly need, she packed up her big box of leftover possessions, taped the lid and dragged it outside the hall and up to Ferdie's apartment. Ferdie was out – she knew because she'd run to his door as soon as Pete had gone to work – but she left a note on the box: *Ferdie, please take care of this stuff for me? Do not give to Pete. Will explain and will call. Trinity xx. PS If on the weird off-chance that my aunt Dara phones, tell her nothing, promise? Love ya.*

Ferdie had been amazing to them when she and Pete moved into Boyle. Ferdie was a transplant too – a hair colourist from Belfast and running away from a chaotic love life and the bosom of his family.

'They all want to set me up with friends' sons and nephews,' Ferdie groaned. 'It's the gay wedding thing: straight weddings are dullsville and everyone wants to go to gay ones. I'm flat out saying I'm never getting married. I mean, really? Can you see me married?'

Trinity had laughed. She could totally see Ferdie married, possibly him and his bridegroom dazzling everyone with matching white dinner jackets.

'White?' said Ferdie when she told him. He shuddered dramatically. 'No, hon. The eighties called and it wants its look back.'

Ferdie was a breath of fresh air in Trinity's life.

'Never colour your hair, darling,' he told her that first day, his expert hairdresser's hands zhuzhing it so that it fluffed up around her face. 'It's almost impossible to get that natural shade.'

They'd been in his apartment and she'd looked at herself in his big mirror, trying to see the long auburn waves through his eyes. She was very pale, never tanned and freckled like her poor mother – Aunt Dara always said 'your poor mother' and somehow, Trinity had got into doing it too – but now, with her hair all wild and her green eyes outlined in Ferdie's gold eyeliner, she looked like a maenad from a fantasy book illustration. She liked it, liked the slightly unusual look because, for so many years, Trinity had been a straight-A student, the girl most likely to succeed. Now that she had come spectacularly off the rails, it made sense to change her look.

She was sorry she wasn't getting to say bye to Ferdie, but she knew she'd see him again. They were twin souls, she felt. Pete, on the other hand, was a different matter. Maybe she would do something to his precious guitar, after all. She skipped downstairs after dropping off her box, took the last of the chocolate – two full packs of Lindt white chocolate, her favourite – from the cupboard and found a felt-tip pen. Then, when she'd left the message, she headed off into the afternoon.

There were no buses to Dublin right now, but she'd hitch. Everyone said hitching was insanely dangerous. But then, moving hundreds of miles from home to be with your childhood sweetheart was not supposed to be insane and look at how well that had turned out. Therefore hitchhiking was possibly wildly sensible. If anyone tried to attack her, she'd stab them with the Orlando bottle opener. Correction: stab and twist. She practised the movement as she walked down the tiny path of the apartment block.

Yup, she could do it.

Hurt me at your peril, she thought, and pulled her woolly hat down on her head. It was cold but she was undaunted.

Hello, New Life. Goodbye, Old One.

They spotted the girl as she walked along the Dublin Road just outside Boyle, rucksack on her small frame, one hand stretched out with a thumb up.

'Is that girl—' began Lou.

'—hitching,' finished Toni. 'Yeah. She must be mad.'

'It's not safe to hitch anymore.'

'Don't think it ever was,' Toni agreed.

Without thinking about it, she began slowing the car down.

'We should pick her up,' Lou said. 'Imagine if it was Emily.'

'Emily would never be daft enough to hitch on a country road,' sighed Toni, and stopped the car.

The girl ran towards the car and arrived panting at the passenger window. Her rucksack was nearly as big as she was. She was in her twenties, a sprite of a thing in jeans and a puffa jacket, with freckles, red hair in two plaits and a grey woollen hat pulled down on her head. She beamed at them as if they were her very own personal angels sent to keep her safe.

'Where are you going?' asked Toni.

'Away from Boyle,' said the girl.

'More specifically?' Toni continued, her voice sharp. She had no time for this right now.

'Where are you?' the girl said, still beaming.

'Dublin.'

'Can I come?' said the girl.

In reply, Toni flicked the switch to unlock the back door.

'You're lucky we came along,' she said as the girl got in. 'You have no idea what sort of weirdos are out there.'

'Oh I do,' said the girl eagerly. 'I totally know but today has been unexpectedly strange, so I thought I'd risk it. The safe people have turned cray cray, so I thought it was probably fine to hitch. 'Cos like, opposites, you know.'

'No, I don't,' said Toni, still disapproving. 'Hitching is not safe.'

'But you found me!'

Lou smiled slightly. Toni was expecting this to be a teachable moment, but the girl was on a different wavelength.

'Are you from Dublin?' asked Toni.

'No,' said the girl. 'I'm from the Planet of Trinity!'

Lou laughed out loud this time.

'Where are you going to in Dublin?' she asked the girl.

'I don't know. A hostel?'

With her eyes still on the road, Toni said: 'You can stay with us.'

After all, she thought, she had a big house and who knew how much longer she'd have it. Might as well have guests in.

'Wow, I love this place. This is yours?' said Trinity, as Toni clicked the electric gate zapper and the big wooden gates slid seamlessly back to reveal Elliot Lodge, the house that one obsequiously flattering magazine profile had called 'a modern home designed with the essence of Art Deco'.

'Yeah,' muttered Toni, throwing the gate zapper into the front of the car. The closer they'd got to Dublin, the more her anxiety had increased.

Was she mad to bring Lou and Trinity here? The house was possibly the property of the bank now. Or maybe a loan shark? Or possibly the Criminal Assets Bureau, because if Oliver's borrowings had been from some organised crime guy and who knew what other stupid things Oliver had done in his gambling mania, then she and Oliver were unwittingly funding organised crime? Perhaps some hoodlum would emerge from the front door and warn them off? Art Deco cost a fortune and it now belonged to somebody called Big Jimbo who might appear with a baseball bat and tell them to 'eff off'.

'It's big,' Trinity went on as they drove in the gate and the house faced them, the beautiful and wildly expensive cloud tree still sitting in the flower bed to the left of the vast glass front window. At least nobody had dug the tree up and taken it, Toni thought, staring at it with narrowed eyes. That was something. The cloud tree had cost thousands.

The entire place had been a money pit that they'd managed to keep going because Oliver liked the good things in life.

'We need to be seen living in the right sort of place,' he'd said every time Toni winced when a new bill came in for the extensive renovations. 'People in our line of work have to have a home that reflects us.'

Toni had loved the house, but she hadn't needed it to reflect any part of her. She'd liked it because it was luxurious, proof to herself of how much she'd achieved. It was the same with clothes or handbags – they weren't there for anyone else, just for her. Oliver had wanted this house too, had loved it. But if he'd lost as much money as he'd said he'd lost, it would be gone. Oliver had ruined it all.

And if his removal of nine thousand from her credit card was anything to go by, her money was probably all gone. Her safety and security. It was only in the losing of it that Toni finally realised how important her financial security was. Money meant nothing until you didn't have it.

'How many of you live here?' asked Trinity carefully as she took in the size of the house.

'Just myself and my husband,' said Toni grimly.

She felt Lou's comforting hand on her leg, patting it.

'You don't know anything for sure, yet,' Lou said.

Toni sniffed. Since they'd picked up their passenger, Lou had reverted joyously back to being the lovely, kind sister Toni had always known. It was as if having a young person in the car had made her forget all her random irritation and grief and become cosily kind again.

Like a mother. Not *their* mother, obviously, but a good mother.

Toni turned the car before parking. Just in case they had to make a getaway. Lou didn't appear to notice this bit of forward planning and for that, Toni was grateful. She unlocked the hall door and went in, finding to her utter surprise that the alarm was on. No hoodlums then?

'Wow,' Trinity said yet again. 'This is an amazing house, Toni.'

Toni might have liked the admiration for her beautiful home had she not been about to lose it. She normally loved people cooing over the poured concrete floors, the giant Japanese walls where Oliver had indulged his love of Yamato-e art.

The pictures, three huge pieces painted in delicate golds and autumn colours, Oliver's favourites, had cost a fortune and what were they worth now . . . ? Probably damn all. Like expensive jewellery: nothing. She felt a sudden pang that she had never been interested in things like Chanel handbags. Now they were things worth collecting. Vintage Chanel flap handbags in old leather made money when you kept them and sold them years later. But not – she looked down – handmade carpets in the same colours as the Japanese art. They were probably now worth the same as nylon office carpet tiles in resale value.

'I can see you calculating every item,' whispered Lou.

Toni closed her eyes and wished she could stop doing it.

'I am,' she said. 'That couch . . .' She gestured into the open-plan lounge where a deep couch in the same bluey-green colour of Monet's lilies dominated the room.

Each room has a different shade, the obsequious article cooed.

'The couch cost fifteen thousand because it was handmade for the space . . .' said Toni, feeling numb now. Fifteen grand. They must have been out of their minds.

No, she must have been out of her mind. Or else drugged on the insanity of having enough money and success to buy such things. She should have put the bloody money under the bed. But then Oliver would have just found it and spent it. Or spent it and borrowed more from Big Jimbo.

In her head, Big Jimbo had arms like hams and a posse of enforcers who took back whatever he could when his debtors couldn't pay up.

'Stop,' said Lou again.

'I can't,' Toni murmured.

'Come on,' said Lou to Trinity, 'I'll show you to your room. Is Oliver not here?' she asked her sister.

'Apparently not,' said Toni, drifting into the kitchen as if in a dream. She'd half expected him to be there, and she hadn't known if she was going to throw him out if he was, but it appeared Oliver had left to lick his wounds in private. The nine thousand plus euros he'd removed from her credit card account was in her mind. Perhaps he was staying in a city centre hotel in a gorgeous suite, going to the casino in a last-ditch attempt to win their money back. If he'd done that, she'd really kill him.

'This house is really cool,' said Trinity, following. She put her battered old rucksack on a wire-framed cream leather kitchen chair, unwound the batik silk scarf from her slender neck and then looked around. In the modern, expensive space, she looked like a teenage model brought in to advertise a soft drink. All they needed were a few more young people, some soft drinks and an art director hustling Toni and Lou, far too old, out of shot.

'Is there a kettle?' said Trinity. 'I have some herbal tea bags.' She waved a small box. 'Ginger, if anyone wants some.'

'No kettle,' said Toni. 'There's a special hot tap.'

She went to the sink and demonstrated the thousands of pounds' worth of plumbing magic that dispensed boiling water.

'This is so amazing,' said Trinity. 'I've seen the adverts on TV but never saw one in real life.'

'Don't calculate it,' Lou warned her sister.

'One thou,' said Toni bitterly.

'I give up,' said Lou. 'Trinity, we can see your room, or do you want to help me make supper?'

'Food! I'm ravenous. If—' Trinity looked her age for a moment, 'if you're sure it's OK for me to be here? I don't want to impose. Getting the lift was fantastic but—'

'It's lovely to have you here,' said Lou firmly. 'Without you, myself and Toni might have gone mad.'

'Thank you.' Trinity beamed gratefully. 'Supper? I can cook.'

'Let's look in the freezer,' said Lou happily.

Toni left the two of them to it and went into the office.

Like everything in her life, the files were perfectly organised, and it didn't take long to find the financial documents relating to pensions and investments. Toni knew that having bits of paper relating to money and having the money were different things, but she found a certain pleasure in finding that she still had documents relating to various investments. Until she found Oliver's laptop still in its bag and papers stuffed in the side of it.

There were sheafs of paper with seals on them, filmy bits of paper and lovely banking quality card all stuffed in together. On many pieces of paper were places where her signature was scrawled. Not her signature but a forgery, the sort of thing a husband would be able to do when he'd lived with her for years and had seen her write her signature endlessly.

Antoinette Lucinda Cooper.

All hope of things being sorted out disintegrated. If Oliver had forged her signature, he was guilty of fraud.

Even if he threw himself at her mercy and the mercy of the courts, she would never see the money again.

She was ruined.

In the kitchen, Lou and Trinity were busy.

Trinity had been right: she certainly knew her way round a kitchen and was already expertly dicing shallots she'd found in Toni's utility room.

'We've got frozen fresh pasta and look, porcini mushrooms,' said Lou delightedly. 'Trinity's going to make garlic mushroom pasta.'

'It's really easy,' said Trinity, moving on to crush some garlic cloves with the flat blade of a knife.

Toni gazed blankly at them. She was holding two things: a bottle of 1961 Dom Pérignon that someone had given Oliver when he'd won his BAFTA and his rarely used American Express card. The world was falling around her ears.

'I had an idea,' she said, and even to herself, her voice sounded slightly crazed. 'Things are going to be a bit bonkers here for a while so I thought we could go to Sicily and find Angelo.'

'Sicily?' Lou looked up from where she was stirring the now-soaking dried porcini.

Toni nodded.

She had never run away in her life. Never. But no matter which way she tried to work the problems out, they were insurmountable. Sicily, with golden sun and beaches and the azure gleam of the Mediterranean, was calling to her.

'Italy,' said Trinity. 'I know this sounds a bit mental, but I'm sort of trying to get away at the moment too. Could I come? I mean, I've got money. I'll pay my way.'

'Nonsense,' said Toni, popping the Dom Pérignon expertly. 'I've got my husband's AmEx. It's a charge card and it comes out of a sterling account he keeps for work. I bet there's still money in there because he always forgets he has it. About time he paid, don't you think, Lou?'

Oszkar Gottschall looked at the email with some agitation. It was addressed to Lou from one of the country's top wedding planners, and it appeared Lou was on very friendly terms with this woman. The woman had phoned on Saturday looking for Lou, but the message she'd left had been vague.

Oszkar had tried to track Lou down to no avail.

Now this blasted woman had emailed and things were worse. Her email made no sense.

Thank you so much for the chocolates, Lou! Dark cherry centres – my favourite, but you knew that, you star. I'm back at work now and about the Kennedy/Schenkmann wedding: the couple love the sound of your idea. Plus, Cinnamon is the name of Fiona Kennedy's family dog! Who knew? But because Michael's grandmother really does only have a few months left, they have moved the date of the wedding to Saturday week. I know it's crazy but they so want Michael's granny there before she becomes too ill and is bedbound. He says the idea of being at the wedding is keeping her going. I phoned on Saturday but you weren't around, so maybe we can talk later? Izzy xxx

Oszkar read the email again.

'What is this about cinnamon?' he said, mystified. 'This email makes no sense. I do not understand.'

Mindy, the new office manager, with a degree in business studies and three years working for her uncle's building company behind her, stared at her new boss and thought of shrugging but quenched it.

It was her second day and things had been a bit hectic since she'd joined Blossom. She adored the shop floor, although, behind the scenes, the bouquet part of the business was very hectic, dirty, and seemed to involve lots of standing for hours on end. It wasn't what she'd thought the flower business would be about, but she was upstairs in the office most of the time so far.

Mindy loved flowers, which was why she adored the shop with its lovely bouquets waiting to go and ranks of flowers, cut and with excess greenery removed, in serried ranks of rainbow colours. Yellow flowers were her favourite. Her Instagram account was a hymn to sunflowers and lilies.

Her obvious love of flowers and the fact that she was twenty-five and a cheap hire had helped her get this job. She didn't have much experience in the world of floristry, but business was business, right? She was totally qualified to be a new business strategy manager.

'You can learn on the job,' Mr Gottschall had said in the interview. 'We have a good team. Lou Fielding will teach you the basics of what we do.'

But now it seemed this Lou lady had vanished, and they wanted her urgently. Lou was normally in on

Mondays but there had been no sign of her. They'd checked her emails but this one, which was important, was stressing the boss and Mindy had no idea how to sort this all out.

In McCondren Builders, Uncle Toby always knew what to do about things. Or if he didn't, he had a person working for him who did. Maybe this Lou woman was one of those people who knew how everything worked?

'Could we phone Lou?' said Mindy, meaning that *she* would not phone Lou, because she didn't know her, obvs, but that Mr Gottschall could do it. Or his wife, who said their little girl's birthday was coming up and Lou knew the name of a face painter who was amazing. '*You* could phone her,' Mindy added, to make sure he knew what she meant.

'I have tried to phone Lou!' shouted Mr Gottschall. 'But she does not answer her mobile and she is not at her home.'

Mindy couldn't help it: she shrugged. Her new boss glared at her, and jabbed at the computer screen. Mindy wondered if the flower world was for her. For all his flaws, Uncle Toby was not a shouter.

'You do it,' he said. 'Email this woman back and find out what she means. She is very important. I did not know that Lou knew her so well. You must say she is ill . . .'

When he was gone, Mindy forwarded the email to her own desktop. She read back over the email and then looked up the wedding planner lady, who turned out to be ultra-cool with a fabulous Insta page full of celeb weddings. The missing Lou Fielding went up in Mindy's estimation.

She began an email to the wedding lady. She was not going to lie. If Oszkar Gottschall wanted lying, he could do it himself. Lou had gone missing: that's what she would say.

Lillian Cooper heard her front doorbell ring and as she fumbled around for her glasses, she knocked something over on the bedside table and heard the crash of a cup. Shit.

She sat up in bed, winced at the pain this invoked in her skull, and looked around. The tang of red wine told her that she clearly hadn't finished the cup of wine she'd dragged up to bed the previous night. The glasses were still all dirty and she hated putting them in the dishwasher. They were precious, especially the ones from TechBite, who'd been so pleased with her MotherBoard sculpture that they'd presented her with leaded crystal white wine glasses.

Lou was excellent at washing glasses. Nobody got a sheen on glass like Lou. Lillian herself couldn't really be bothered with washing things by hand. It was such a waste of time. Where the hell was her daughter? This was no longer funny.

The doorbell rang again, more insistently.

'Yes?' shrieked Lillian, hauling herself out of bed.

She made it to the window, opened it and yelled down: 'Yes!'

'Delivery. Boulders,' roared a voice back at her. 'And sand.'

Lillian closed her eyes and let her hand rest against her forehead briefly. Boulders, of course. She was making a rock garden because it was an easy way of maintaining that stretch of grass to the right of the studio.

Lou was normally here every second Tuesday morning because it was her day off and she helped Lillian with the chores. That was why Lillian had organised the delivery for today. Bloody Lou. What was she playing at? She couldn't still be upset about Friday night?

Damn it. Lillian had moved on. She knew her know-it-all sister-in-law would fill her in chapter and verse if she asked, but Lillian hated asking Gloria anything. She would not ask.

'What do you want me to do with the delivery?' roared the delivery guy again.

Lillian felt her head ache some more. Ageing was not for sissies, as Bette Davies had said. Nor was drinking, for that matter.

'Wherever,' she yelled in bored tones and shut the window, on a mission to find some high-quality painkillers to dull the ache in her skull.

The room reeked of wine now, which was horrible. She thought she might throw up, which was worse.

The man at the door looked around Lillian Cooper's property. Wherever, she'd said. Easiest spot to dump the sand was just inside the rusty, once-white gate. The boulders were trickier. The grabber on the second truck could put them just to the right of the old dear's car. She probably didn't go out much in it. And she was rude.

The sand started off in a nice hill but by the time the truck with the boulders had manoeuvred in and placed them, the sand had shifted a bit so that it was spilling slowly and inexorably down behind the old dear's car. *Karma's a bitch*, he thought, and waved his mate off before getting into his own truck.

Part Three

Chapter Fourteen

Lou slept on the plane and woke as it banked gently over the Mediterranean like a giant hand was gently waking up a sleeping baby. They were coming down out of the sky, moving through the soft clouds so that Lou could see, past Trinity who had the window seat, clouds shaped like a giant duvet stretching in front of them so they could float deliciously down to earth.

'Are we here?' she said, stretching and dislodging Toni's winter white cashmere throw she'd wrapped around herself in the early coolness of the flight.

'Nearly. We've about fifteen minutes to go,' said Toni, who was folding up her own throw, a similarly expensive cashmere version in old gold which was always very useful on holiday in case the nights were cold.

'Thank you for this,' said Lou happily, pulling the throw around her and luxuriating in its expensive glory.

She closed her eyes again happily, not even wondering why she wasn't feeling her usual panicky self as the plane descended. This was generally the time when Lou's Barking Dog went into overdrive. She had never seen Plane Crash Investigation on TV but she didn't have to see it to imagine it: all crunching metal, screaming people and body bags. Take-off and landing were the most dangerous times of plane travel. Normally, she'd be sitting bolt upright and white-faced as they headed towards the airport. But not today.

Instead, she was snuggling into cashmere which was scented with some sexy perfume of Toni's, an exotic haze of oud, amber and tobacco mingling with something like attar of roses, perhaps? Lou liked her perfumes floral but in this new bizarrely laid-back incarnation – and she had no idea where this had come from, but she'd woken up feeling this way – she found herself wondering if this sexy perfume would suit her. It was probably called Femme Fatale. Erotica. Molten Honey. She grinned happily to herself and snuggled deeper.

At least half the clothes she'd brought were Toni's, far more expensive than her own wardrobe, and she'd borrowed things with stretch because Toni was a far leaner creature than Lou.

'Mum, I couldn't find most of your summer stuff,' Emily had written on a ripped piece of paper attached to the couriered bag. 'Did you put it all away? I found flip-flops, a sarong, two summer dresses – but I think you wore them in the garden . . . ? I added in your necklaces, though, and some stuff from your bedside drawer. Plus some books.'

Lou, who normally loathed packing because her anxiety came to a head when faced with the notion of all the catastrophes that might take place, and how unprepared she was for each, had astonished herself by laughing at the diverse bits and bobs her daughter had sent.

'Look at these!' she said, grinning and holding up two cotton sleeveless dresses with scoop necks, one navy and one silvery grey, which had been washed so often that they were fit only for gardening or being turned into dusters.

In the holdall was a pair of ancient off-white Converse with filthy laces, an actually decent pair of Havaianas, a white linen shirt, a multi-coloured sarong and khaki shorts that no longer buttoned at the waist. Emily had added her mother's jewellery pouch, which contained all her little hands of Fatima and ankh bracelets and necklaces, along with the rose gold pendant for self-love, and the silver necklace made with tiny aquamarine and amethyst beads for anxiety, one of the things Mim had given her.

Plus there was more of her antidepressant medication, her valerian drops, her Rescue Remedy, her Peruvian worry dolls, the books from beside her bed and her big notebook with its purple pen where Lou wrote her gratitude lists.

'I've got ribbons for those Converses,' said Trinity, picking the shoes out of the pile and carefully beginning to unlace them. 'They're an aquamarine colour. They're for my hair but they'll look totally adorable in these shoes.'

Lou had been about to say: 'I couldn't take your hair ribbons,' when she stopped herself.

Trinity was delighted to be able to offer something.

Having the younger woman around was proving to be a joy. She had no idea what Trinity was running from, or indeed, if she was running from anything, but she was young and even though she was quirkily independent, Lou felt she needed someone to, well, mother her a bit.

Not like an actual mother, Lou thought, being firm with herself. She could not fill the gap of Emily's absence with Trinity. That would be wrong. But she could be . . . an auntie. Yes, that was it. A surrogate auntie helping Trinity navigate whatever was going on in her life. Lou was going to get to the bottom of it, but for the moment she was asking no questions.

'What's going on with her?' Toni wanted to know.

Toni, for all that she knew everything, simply had no idea how to handle the young, Lou thought. It was very confidence-boosting to think that there was something she was better at than her younger, sharper sister.

'She'll tell us when she's ready,' Lou had said.

'But what if she's on the run?' Toni had asked as they sat at the airport gate and waited for Trinity to return from the loo. She went to the loo all the time, even more than Lou with her menopausal bladder.

'On the run from what? Europol? The Gardai? The paparazzi? You used her passport to check her in online. If she was wanted for a crime, someone would have picked her up by now,' said Lou, as if to imply that Toni was behaving in a very paranoid way.

At Catania airport, they hired an ice-cream pink Fiat 500 and Trinity sat in the small back seat with the luggage.

'It's cosy,' said Toni, who was in the driver's seat.

Lou peered into the back where Trinity was perched with all the bags settled on the other seat as if they were considering flinging themselves onto her.

'Very cosy,' she grinned. 'You OK, darling?' she asked.

Trinity beamed and gave her a thumbs up.

Toni liked to quickly adopt the driving style of her holiday country so was revving the little Fiat and waving in irritation at anyone who gestured or honked their horn at her as she negotiated the roads around the airport.

With Lou being the Google Map reader, they left Catania and were soon out in the countryside with Mount Etna's snowy peaks in the distance.

'It's very fertile land,' Lou said, admiring the landscape with its vineyards, olive tree groves and exotic plants she'd love to grow in her own garden. 'They've got tamarisk trees,' she added, looking up the flora and fauna on her phone. 'I love them – they're pink flowering trees. Impossible to grow at home.'

Toni ignored this – she had no interest in floral things – and after a while, Lou stopped looking things up. Winding down her window, she sat back in silence, basking in the heat and the difference of this unfamiliar island with the scent of lavender, lemon and wild rosemary drifting in the open windows.

By the time they'd reached Syracuse, close to where the island of Ortigia lay and which Toni assumed was the island Margo's mother had told them about, she'd acclimatised herself totally. The city was beautiful with its honeyed Greek and Roman-style buildings, pretty balconies overflowing with flowers and plants, and tiny streetside cafes where people were sitting, letting the balmy Mediterranean sun heat them.

'*Turistica!*' Toni shrieked, ignoring the relaxed atmosphere to gesticulate at the other drivers, who all continued to drive as if either in the Monaco Grand Prix or a slow bicycle race.

Finally they made it across the city towards Ortigia, which could be accessed by three bridges. When roadworks obscured the route they'd planned to take, Toni swerved into the side of the road and slammed on the brakes. Lou, sleepy in the heat, appeared to be just staring out the window now.

'Let's ask someone,' she said and yelled, '*Ciao, parla inglese?*' to a passing young man.

This golden-haired young man turned, revealing the face of an Adonis and a tan like toffee. He leaned against the Fiat and gazed at the three occupants in turn. It was a leisurely gaze, as if he was assessing them on some Sicilian scale of beauty and giving marks out of ten.

'The bridge to the island closes soon. You must drive to park quickly,' he said to Toni, who was clearly scoring quite high on the scale, given the purr in his voice as he looked her over.

Toni had travelled in white jeans, a white silk T that did not quite disguise the expensive lace bra underneath, and her platinum hair hung elegantly over her shoulders. She looked expensive, as if someone was travelling behind with her Louis Vuitton steamer trunks instead of having piled a couple of very battered chain-store suitcases into the back seat of the car herself. Toni had long ago found it was a waste to buy expensive luggage – they got wrecked no matter what they cost.

'You may not be able to park,' said Adonis, openly admiring all Toni's expensiveness. 'There is the car park but parking on the road this moment is . . .' he shrugged, every movement fluid, 'impossible.'

The word was dragged out luxuriously. Imposseeble.

'Right,' said Toni crisply, ignoring the admiring gazes Adonis was getting from the other women in the car. They had both woken up from their dreamy looking-out-of-the-window phase.

Toni didn't care if Adonis had abs like a washboard and could make love all night long with the rhythm of a metronome: she was over the male of the species in all its forms, even when it came in the Italian Male version, which was evidently a primo version. Men were the enemy. All the most aggressive drivers on the way from Catania airport to Syracuse had been men. Oliver was a man. Gerry Lanigan was a man. Enough said.

Toni gave Adonis a glare that she hoped would freeze his veins even through her sunglasses. 'I drive straight and then turn right?'

'Yes,' purred Adonis. 'See you around.'

Toni gave him a tight nod and pushed down on the accelerator.

As they raced towards the bridge, Lou was aware that normally, she'd have looked at her sister in alarm, or at least said something along the lines of 'Slow down, perhaps . . .' in a persuasive way. Heaven forbid she'd say anything like 'Are you trying to kill us?' which might have been reasonable because Toni had already reached sixty kilometres in a forty-kilometre zone on two separate occasions on the drive from the airport. But today, in the blissful heat of Sicily, with the car windows open and the scent of the fresh saltiness of the sea wafting in along with smells of ripening lemons, ground coffee and something that could definitely be frying onions and garlic, Lou felt nothing but a languorous heat in her bones.

Toni would drive the way Toni drove. Lou had no power over what happened. No power at all, she thought dreamily, her face catching the sun through the open window.

Since they'd got up that morning, she'd felt most unlike herself, as if the old anxious Lou Fielding had been left behind with all her proper summer clothes. This new version did not have the right bras, or long flowing kaftans to cover up her body, which was her normal holiday behaviour. She had only clothes belonging to her sister and a few things they'd bought at the airport, including black Perspex sunglasses that made her look like a 1950s movie star.

This Lou had done none of the things she normally did before she so much as went away for one night: she had not cooked meals for Ned or her mother. She had not written complex emails for work detailing what needed to be done by whom and when. Instead, she'd sent a long chatty text message to Emily, who'd be in classes, then had a lazy shower at Toni's and smothered her body in Huile Prodigieuse golden body oil. Then, she had rambled through the airport with her sister's vintage canvas carry-on over one arm, wearing Toni's stretchy coral pink maxi dress and her own orange and aqua Havaianas with her toenails painted Ibiza Party Pink by Trinity, who said she'd once done a weekend course in nails.

'I was working in a shop when I was in college, but I thought it would be a handy way of making extra money,' Trinity said idly.

'Clever idea,' Lou had replied, feeling that if Trinity kept dropping titbits about her life into the conversation, she'd soon find out what the younger woman was running from.

'You have lovely feet,' Trinity had said in Toni's house as she folded up bits of tissue paper and wrapped them between Lou's toes in a very professional way.

'They're long and thin,' Lou had said, admiring them. 'Totally different from Toni's. She has enormous big toes.'

'I heard that,' teased Toni, who was packing. 'Are you slagging off my ginormous toes?'

'No. But I do like my feet,' Lou went on. 'Lillian has narrow ankles but my feet are—'

'Very Italian looking,' Toni agreed, peering over Trinity's shoulder as the first coat of polish went on.

'How can feet be Italian?' asked Lou, snorting with laughter.

'Narrow, elegant, perfect for fine leather shoes,' Toni said. 'Mine are Irish. Pale and prone to retaining water after long flights.'

They all laughed, but the idea that she had different feet from the rest of the family stayed with Lou. There were so many things about her that had been different from Toni: Toni was decisive, never appeared to worry about anything, and was a sleek tall woman with fair hair, albeit helped along with hefty doses of hair salon bleach. By contrast, Lou put on weight if she so much as looked at a carbohydrate, had felt anxiety and depression her whole life, and her eyes were a deep brown unlike anyone else in the Cooper family tree.

Nobody else had depression. Her mother was brusque whenever Lou was outwardly down, having not ever actually said 'buck yourself up', but she'd certainly come close. Lou had never felt up to explaining to any of her family that depression was not something one could choose to recover from. She'd thought of saying it to her mother once: 'It would be like asking someone with two broken legs to suddenly start walking. You wouldn't because they can't walk. Depression is having two emotionally broken legs and you can't walk, no matter how much you want to.'

Obviously, she'd never said it. Instead, she'd simply felt different, wrong. Suddenly all these differences were making sense. The things she thought separated her were there because she had more family. There was more to her that she didn't even fully understand yet. She was not missing something; instead, it was like she had something extra. Not less but maybe . . . different? How utterly bizarre. The realisation felt so huge, so new, that she almost couldn't think about it for too long at once. As if it needed to seep slowly into her consciousness and could not be rushed.

Toni was keen to start searching for Angelo as soon as they landed in Sicily and had been bitterly disappointed to find he had no presence on social media. 'We'll track him down,' she said.

Lou hoped it would take time.

At the airport, Lou had bought three Brazilian bikinis, two in mad florals and one in pale leopard print in one shop – it was years since she'd donned anything but a sensible suck-it-all-in one-piece – and five novels in the bookshop, picking them as if she'd been picking sweets, for their deliciousness and promise of joy. She'd bought a bar of white chocolate and ate it all as she meandered through the shops, not allowing herself to feel a hint of guilt because she wasn't having just the two squares of dark chocolate as all the diet guides instructed. What was the point of dieting? This was her shape. Perhaps even her genetic shape?

She'd bought a glossy expensive lipstick in duty-free: a cherry red, not her usual colour at all. When applied, it made her mouth look luscious and full. Normally, Lou didn't go for anything sexy in the lipstick arena. Her mouth was full, like her rounded cheekbones. But she never emphasised it to such an extent. Until today. Today was different. Warmed by the sun, peaceful in this blissful island city, she gazed around her with a peace she rarely felt. The island was truly a place of magic, a wild Mediterranean magical site dusted with sand, ancient history and stone buildings that had been there through all the great epochs of history.

In the same way that Lou had felt something fey and otherworldly in the old Mulraney place in Easkey, some sense that the people there had truly seen the world, she felt that Sicily herself was a wise goddess sitting in the sea, watching the world around her and remembering all she had seen in the past. The Sicily goddess was enlightened, knew that men had fought for centuries over this jewel in the Mediterranean, and knew that, despite their menfolk's battles, the women were keeping everything going: caring for their bambinos, cooking pasta in salted water, and pouring wine from goatskins when the days' work was done.

Lou let the honeyed warmth of Sicily sink into her very being and idly wondered if she was having a strange out-of-body experience brought on by all the shocks.

Ned had let her down. Oszkar and Bettina had let her down. Her mother had let her down. They had all made her question her identity: who was she if she wasn't Lillian Cooper's dutiful daughter or Ned Fielding's easily placated wife? Who had she become as she'd filled all these roles? And stretching back furthest was the trickiest thing to navigate of all: who was she now that she was no longer the mother of a daughter who needed her all the time?

Emily was a grown-up at university and had her own life. Lou, who had put every part of herself into nurturing Emily and all the loved ones in her life, was left with a gaping hole that might have been filled by her husband, her work, her relationship with her mother.

The loss of all of these made her realise that she was on her own. She was still a mother but her child no longer needed mothering in the same way. The family she'd thought was hers, wasn't hers anymore. Not in the same way.

It felt as if darling Mim was talking to her from her unicorn: *You need to take charge of yourself, Lou. Rely on yourself. You can do it!*

Lou wasn't sure if Mim was truly speaking to her or if she was merely channelling the sort of wise and strong thing Mim would say, but the upshot was the same. Lou had the strangest sense that now, here, she had the chance to reinvent herself. In Sicily's balmy heat, she could become someone else, the person she'd always wanted to be.

Perhaps the Lou who jumped out of her skin at the noise of a passing truck was not who she was, really. Perhaps she could be someone else. Someone stronger, someone who could feel the joy of her life and not just the fear.

Chapter Fifteen

'We're here, Lou.'

They were parked in a tiny space overlooking the sea and a seabird sat on the car park's low wall, staring in at them quizzically. Ortigia was made up of even tinier streets than the rest of Syracuse. It was lined with more ancient amber-hued buildings and tourists lazily meandering along from narrow pavement onto narrow roads as if they hadn't a care in the world.

'Are you getting out of the car, Lou?'

The Sicilian version of Lou smiled lazily at her sister. Toni's every nerve seemed stretched tauter than an elastic band. Toni was the one who was falling apart now.

'Yes, I'm getting out,' she said, arching her body luxuriously in the little car seat and stretching like a cat.

'Are you too hot?' asked Toni, half concerned. 'It's not supposed to be this hot in April, but today feels boiling. At least twenty-one degrees.'

'This is perfect,' said Lou, opening the car door, putting out a long limb and admiring her Ibiza Party Pink toes. Italian feet. She had Italian feet. And possibly Italian legs too, she thought delightedly.

They grabbed their luggage and set Google to tell them where to go for their Airbnb. They walked for five minutes along a narrow road, then turned right and right again until they were on a sinuous lane outside a three-storey building with an arched door and a coded lockbox that contained their keys.

Toni opened the arched door and they were in a cool courtyard with two doors off it. Theirs was to the left, Toni unlocked it and they climbed up a few stone steps into a beautiful apartment. It was both compact and airy, with a large single marble-floored room decorated with vast plants, conte crayon drawings of the local ruins on the walls, as well as old framed maps of Syracuse, Catania and Ortigia itself. There was a black upright piano against a wall, leather-bound books in a big bookcase and an old record player along with a small collection of actual vinyl records.

Between two towering pots of feathery ferns were two ochre-coloured couches along with a 1960s hanging bubble chair, fatly acrylic and with a white leather cushion.

'Ooh look,' said Trinity in delight, racing over to the chair and settling herself into it carefully, then swinging so that she twirled in it on the heavy metal chain that kept the chair tethered to the high ceiling. Side tables of old dark wood contained lamps, mosaic coasters and bowls of shells. A paperweight of opalescent Murano glass sat with an old black typewriter on a small writing desk, and to one side French windows opened onto a small balcony with filmy muslin curtains.

Lou went out to the balcony and when Toni joined her she found that they were at the edge of the island city, staring straight out to sea. If she looked to the left, she could just see a rocky quay where people sat and looked down into the sea. Further out was a swimming platform swamped with bathers laughing and dangling their feet in the dark azure waters.

'This holiday was a brilliant idea,' Lou said and hugged her sister.

For a moment, Toni thought of remarking irritably that this wasn't a holiday, it was more of a Sherlock Holmesian quest to find Lou's biological father – but if Lou wanted to think of it that way, who was she to question that.

Leaving Lou to gaze out to sea, Toni kept exploring. The kitchen was tiny, more of a room for making coffee than dinner. Lemons sat in a little fruit bowl along with three limes so gloriously fat and ripe that Toni began to think of making lemonade with limes just to taste how beautiful they were. As Lou exclaimed about how much they could see from their balcony and Trinity was still twirling in her chair, ever-present headphones in as she listened to music, Toni began to climb the marble staircase to the upstairs. She somehow felt like the grown-up who'd brought two teenagers on holiday, and she was examining their lodgings while said teenagers were squealing with delight over random things.

There were two bedrooms and opposite them was another French window. This led out to a large terrace with dark wooden boards underfoot, a mosaic table in indigo colours, sun loungers and painted terracotta pots containing lavender, basil plants, and cacti such as Toni had never seen. A striped canvas awning in blue and white kept the table in the shade and along the prettily shaped railings nearest the sea was a bench carved in stone with a long blue-and-white cushion on it.

Toni sat down, breathing a deep sigh of relief. They had made it. They were here.

The sound of loud music suddenly interrupted the peace of the evening, and Toni sat upright with a jolt.

'Disco Inferno!' Lou's voice squealed as the beat began to penetrate Toni's skull. 'I love this! Let's dance!'

Definitely two teenagers.

Lou woke early the first morning. The room was dark, but she could see hints of light from under the blackout blinds. Toni was fast asleep in the bed beside her, starfished in the bed, face down. Utterly out for the count.

Lou felt energised. She wanted to get out and see Ortigia.

She knew why she was here: to find her father, but now that she was in Sicily, she wasn't going to waste a moment of this. A spark of a new Lou was growing inside her. A Lou who didn't do what people expected her to do. A Lou who rubbed golden oil on her long legs and sashayed in Brazilian bikinis. A Lou who didn't phone home to talk to all the people who expected her to run around after them.

Grinning to herself, she wriggled out of the bed, snagged a sarong and pulled it on around her waist and went out of the room. Trinity was sitting on the little balcony downstairs with a cup of herbal tea. She was wearing a baseball hat, sunglasses, and her skin gleamed with the zincy whiteness of a red-haired person who'd just covered themselves in sunscreen.

'Good morning,' said Lou delightedly. She did love this, starting the day with a gorgeous young person who was pleased to see her.

She'd tried so hard to ignore the empty nest that she'd practically blocked it out. But spending time with Trinity made her realise how much she missed Emily and missed being a mother. A mother with a daughter who needed mothering.

'Lou,' said Trinity, and reached out her slender, white arms for a hug.

'I'm a bit sticky with sun cream,' she added, pulling out her earbuds. 'I really burn. You look like you get very brown.'

'Yeah,' said Lou, and paused. 'I always wondered why I had such olive skin and now it maybe makes sense. If I really do have a Sicilian birth-father.' Her mothering instinct kicked in: 'Did you get breakfast?'

'Can't quite face breakfast at the moment,' said Trinity, 'but I will in a minute.'

'Coffee?'

'No,' said Trinity quickly. 'I'm very happy with my herbal tea. I'm not into caffeine.'

'Probably healthier,' said Lou cheerfully.

She loved how young people took care of their bodies. When she'd been in her twenties, she'd drunk lots of coffee to get her going in the morning and Toni had consumed caffeine tablets like sweeties in college. But Emily's generation truly took care of their bodies in a sensible way.

She came back to the balcony with coffee and toasted bread with butter and honey, a piece of which she gave to Trinity.

'You don't have to eat it,' she said, 'but I have the mother gene in me. It's a terrible habit of wanting to fill people up.'

For a brief second Trinity's beautiful Celtic eyes welled up and Lou was afraid she'd struck a painful nerve.

'I'm sorry, lovie,' she said. 'Did I say the wrong thing?'

'No. No,' said Trinity. 'No. Thank you. It's nice being mothered. I miss it.'

Lou felt the ache of wanting to look after her. She had been very careful not to probe too much but she wondered was this the right time to find out why Trinity was running away and what she was running away from?

'Is everything all right with your mum and dad? Do they know you're here?'

Trinity hesitated. 'I've told people that I've come away for a few days, but they think I'm still with my ex,' said Trinity. 'Pete.'

'Do they like Pete?' said Lou carefully.

This Pete could be a total nightmare. Not that they'd heard anything about him, but what else could make a girl suddenly run like that, and want to leave the country?

'Is he . . .' Lou paused. She wasn't quite sure how to put this. 'Is he looking for you?'

The Catastrophe Creator in her head was already setting the scene with an enraged hulking boyfriend looking for Trinity. This happened often enough, she knew. Outraged exes were getting more and more dangerous.

'Doubt it,' said Trinity, nibbling the toast. 'I left him a note. That'll be enough. He'll be fine.'

'He won't come looking for you though?' Lou probed carefully.

'Oh no,' said Trinity. 'He won't. It's over. He'll understand.'

'OK,' said Lou doubtfully.

She was pleased the girl was eating breakfast, at least. Trinity was too skinny.

Stop, Lou told herself firmly. Trinity was not her personal project to fix. It was enough that they were there together.

'Would you like to take a little walk around the island? It apparently only takes fifteen minutes, but there are so many historical sites and cafes that nobody ever manages to do it that quickly.'

'I'd love to,' said Trinity.

Outside, it was still cool, but the sun was creeping up the sky and the internet weather app was forecasting a day far hotter than usual for the time of year. Even at nine, the streets of the old city, as the island was called, were busy with people walking quickly, tourists heading off for a spot of sightseeing, local people in work clothes, children too small to be in school scampering along. There was a sense of busyness about the place; women hurried along with bags full of groceries and fruit, while old men stood in arched doorways enjoying a coffee and a cigarette with their neighbours, setting the world to rights. Lou found herself looking at the faces of the people she passed who seemed like locals – looking for someone she resembled.

Now that she was here, she felt an awareness that her real father was here on the island. Could he be walking around nearby?

Would she see him and instinctively know him?

She both wanted to see him and yet was anxious about it, something she couldn't explain to Toni.

'We should bottle this air and sell it back home,' said Trinity breathing deeply.

'Yes,' agreed Lou automatically.

She consulted the map she'd found in the apartment with details of both Syracuse and Ortigia's sites. 'I'm not great with maps, but I think if we go round this corner and take that street, there are some ruins.'

They trailed around in the growing heat, until Trinity said she needed a gelato. Under her sunhat, she was pale despite the sun.

'You sit and I'll get you one,' said Lou, and Trinity perched on the edge of a tiny fountain with a pretty fish flashing its stone tail at her, scales beautifully delineated by the sculptor, while Lou joined the queue.

If Trinity had been one of Emily's friends, Lou would have been careful about getting too involved because young people did not necessarily want older people, or their parents' friends, trying to 'fix' them. It was insulting, the implication being that the young people did not know how to handle their own lives.

Lou looked back at herself at twenty-three. She'd long since given up on college and for a moment, she felt a frisson of loss at not having gone. Lillian had needed her but was that the right thing to have done? To have given up her dreams of a third-level education because her mother had needed her. Wasn't it also a little selfish of her mother to have asked Lou to do so . . . ?

No, she wouldn't go there, she decided. That was all ancient history and on this beautiful piece of Italian history, she would not regret what she hadn't done. But at twenty-three, the same age as Trinity, she'd been so innocent, so eager to please. And if she'd been with a boyfriend who had been in any way abusive, would she have had the courage to have left so confidently, so determinedly? Lou wasn't sure she would have.

They sat in a patch of shade and ate their ice creams, Trinity looking around happily admiring the beautiful architecture, and the fascinating people walking up and down.

It was truly lovely to be there with her. It was almost like having, briefly, another daughter. Lou had missed it. She wished her mother had told her what it was like to have a child leave because Toni had left very determinedly and that must have been hard for Lillian. Being a parent to a young adult was painful. One moment, Emily had been the focus of everything and then suddenly, Emily was gone. Grown up. And what was left?

Someone who could no longer define herself as a mother but was instead a woman whose husband forgot her birthday, a woman whose mother destroyed her birthday, a woman whose career suddenly became a job with added demotion.

That's what was left when motherhood ended. But Lou was no longer prepared to let herself be defined that way.

Toni's plan to come here had been a good one, as crazy as it had seemed. It meant Lou was sitting here now in Ortigia peacefully, the sun reaching its zenith, smelling the smells of the Mediterranean and the heat rising from the beautiful stone buildings built thousands of years ago. She could reassess her life. She could meet her birth father and decide what she wanted to do then. For now, she would enjoy what she had. Wasn't that the secret to happiness, according to all the self-help books she'd read? Enjoy the now and don't worry about the future because you can't control it.

Easier said than done.

Emily felt the ping of the message as her phone vibrated.

She was in the college library and phone noises were strictly forbidden but her phone was in the front pocket of her sweatshirt. She pulled her phone out and saw with delight that there were photos from her mum in Sicily.

Wish you were here, Mum had written underneath several photos of a ruined temple. The Temple of Apollo.

Typically, Mum had included a white cat in the foreground, posing against the backdrop of crumbling stone. Her mother loved animals and was forever petting random dogs when they were out and worrying when she saw a skinny animal in case it wasn't getting fed enough.

Wish I was there too, Emily texted back, *but I have too much to do and you need this time with Toni*.

Mum had been wildly apologetic when she'd phoned to say that she and Toni were going to Sicily.

'We've connected with this girl, she's a bit older than you. Her name's Trinity and she's possibly running away from someone – could be an abusive ex. I hope you don't feel left out—'

Emily had stopped her mother there.

'Mum, it's OK. I'm not jealous. I'm a big girl now. If Trinity needs help, then she couldn't be with better people than you and Toni. You'll take care of her, and I'd back Toni against a jealous ex any day! I just hope he has health insurance.'

They'd both laughed at the thought.

It looks gorgeous, Mum, Emily texted back to her mother now. *You and I can go back another time. I love you and I miss you, but I'm happy you're taking time out for you*.

She pressed send and looked back at her laptop to the essay on Constitutional Law. Her brain was still fried after a week of intense work on macroeconomics. Second year was still enjoyable, but it was definitely more pressure than her first year, where people were still finding their feet.

Her stomach rumbled. She had a lot more work to do on this essay but a break and possibly a chocolate bar would help.

She had a plan formulating in her mind. A plan that would fulfil a long-held dream for her mother.

Chapter Sixteen

Toni woke up alone in the bed with no sign of Lou. The sheets were rumpled and the room was dim from the blackout blinds the owners used to stop the early Mediterranean sun from waking holidaymakers. It felt different from her bed at home where Oliver would be slumbering, a mound on the other side of the bed.

At home, she had high-thread-count sheets. Frette. Oliver adored them. So did she – but they'd been mad to spend the money on them.

She fumbled for her phone on the small nightstand beside her and Lou's bed and saw that it was after ten. She couldn't remember the last time she had slept that long. Shame clearly made a person tired.

Never had she felt such shame. How could she not have *seen*? It was her job to ask people the tough questions and she'd thought she was brilliant at it. She'd had confidence in her abilities as an interviewer. She was a mentor, a consummate professional, capable and successful. She'd always thought she had a very good sense of other people: who was hiding things, who was not, who was comfortable being interviewed, who was deeply uncomfortable and desperately trying to fake both confidence and competence. Yet she'd missed all the signals that her husband was a gambling addict.

Which was worse – him losing all their money, or her having no idea it was happening?

Toni didn't know. She threw back the bedclothes, pulled on some shorts and stomped downstairs to get some water. She poured some cool water from the fridge, then emptied out the coffee grounds from the elderly red Moka coffee maker, filled it with fresh coffee and water and set it on the stove – tapping her fingers on the countertop as she waited for it to boil, and trying to calm her spiralling thoughts.

Toni still didn't know how much money was gone because she was terrified of calling Liam, the investment expert, back. What could he say?

You're broke and you'll never recover financially, not unless Bill Gates hires you and puts an extra zero on your salary by mistake and nobody notices.

Toni gazed glumly at her phone. There were many missed calls. One from Ned.

Having heard Lou on the phone to him the night before, Toni wasn't surprised he was ringing her.

'No, I don't want to talk about it, Ned,' Lou had said. 'There's nothing to talk about.'

There had been a pause while Ned tried to put his side of the story.

Clearly, Lou wasn't buying the whole the-dog-ate-my-homework vibe coming from Whitehaven.

'Ned, I always buy all the gifts we give to people, yes I do know that. But for my fiftieth birthday, all you had to do was walk into a shop and purchase something. That was all you had to do. The problem is that you didn't think you needed to. You're right, Ned,' she went on, as if interrupting him, 'I've never said anything like this before. I'm saying it now, OK? It's not about the price of a gift, it's about you making the effort to get one. I have to go—' and she'd hung up abruptly.

'You are changing,' Toni had said in admiration.

Lou had nodded.

'Ned seems to think I'm having a mad hormonal surge and that if he says sorry enough, it'll all be fine, but it won't. If he can't grasp that he hurt me deeply, then I'm going to avoid talking to him.'

'I don't know if avoiding people helps,' Toni had replied, and then realised that this was a case of the pot calling the kettle black.

Her phone showed several missed calls. Two from Cormac, one from Liam and a startling twelve missed calls from Oliver. She hadn't spoken to him since that Thursday night. What more was there to say? She hadn't been able to look at him by the end.

'I can get help, Toni,' he'd said, after his confession, coming to kneel on the floor in front of her. 'There's rehab for gambling. I can book myself in and I'll get better. I know I can. It's just the money is the problem and all I owe, but you love me, don't you?'

Toni had sat in her chair, cold green tea in front of her, and stared at her kneeling husband. At that moment, he disgusted her. He had ruined them. He'd betrayed her, he'd lost everything, and she had never even seen what was happening.

'Get off the floor,' she'd said furiously. 'It's too late to crawl now, Oliver. Why did you wait so long before telling me? I could have helped a long time ago, if only you'd trusted me. You've destroyed us.'

'No, please,' he begged. It was the first time she had seen Oliver beg in real life. It was different from his onstage begging in theatre or his film begging in movies. They were begging-with-dignity. This was begging without dignity, true pleading.

'Oliver, I don't know where you're going to stay tonight but get out of here right now because I can't bear to look at you. Don't touch another penny of our money while I figure this out.'

'I promise,' he'd said. And yet within forty-eight hours he'd removed nine thousand euros from her credit card.

Toni poured espresso from the Moka into a small cup and, coffee in hand, went into the airy living room and sat in the bubble chair that had so enchanted Trinity. She could understand how Lou felt hijacked by the news that their father wasn't Lou's biological father. It had shifted Lou's view of the past. Toni felt precisely the same about her marriage to Oliver. She'd thought she'd known and understood him. The Oliver she'd thought she was married to was a very determined man: determined in his pursuit of her and his pursuit of roles. Oh yes, and in the pursuit of the right things. She thought of their beautiful home and its Japanese art, the handmade rug, the correct couch, the many original paintings.

There were paintings he'd bought because he thought they were impressive by their very strangeness. If it looked like someone out of their head on ayahuasca with access to a full set of acrylic paints might have done it, Oliver would buy it. He liked to pretend that he liked art and bought as a connoisseur. It was not a side of him that Toni had liked, but then people's insecurities often made them do strange things. There had been no money for art in his home as a child. As an adult, he'd made much of his love for paintings.

'I buy what moves me,' he would say when they held parties, and they held a lot of parties in the house. It was the perfect house for entertaining. All that open space for people to walk around clutching beautiful Riedel glasses of wine or a selection of the exquisite cocktails made by the Cocktail Cocteaus, a couple of mixologists Toni had found who brought their cocktail bar from house to expensive house. She closed her eyes at the thought of just how costly these parties had been.

People had wandered around happily, dressed in their finery and admiring the ayahuasca pictures and the obligatory sculpture by her mother. She'd paid her mother for one of her pieces. Trust Lillian to insist that there were no discounts for family.

Toni finished her coffee, then went back into the kitchen to make another, this time with sugar, even though she'd given it up years ago – sugar was good for shock, she'd heard – and took the cup upstairs to the wooden-floored balcony with the jungle of plants leaning over the array of sunbeds and the turquoise and indigo mosaic table.

She lay down on a lounger, not wearing sun cream, sunglasses or a sun hat. She didn't care if she got lines. All these years she'd been taking care of her face, using Factor 50 SPF, getting Botox, having IPL to remove sun blemishes – and what had been the point? Her career was now over as well as her marriage. All the beautifying in the world could not save you when you were both cancelled and broke. She'd end up like one of Oliver's paintings, one she hated: a particularly ugly nude that hung in the cloakroom in their hall. The room itself was where Oliver kept the most precious of his awards. They were high up on shelves in the most clichéd room in the house, displayed carelessly between books and copies of the *New Yorker*. As if to say, 'I am so cool that I can keep these in a tiny loo because I don't need them to prove I'm brilliantly talented.'

But of course he needed to see his awards. He needed them like he needed the house, the money and the adulation. And he needed other people to see them and think he was clever, worldly, artistic, all the things he'd actually felt he wasn't.

She hated the ugly nude he'd hung in the loo. It was definitely painted by somebody who didn't like women. The curves of the nude's shape were dimpled and shaded with bruised, lumpen purples as if the artist had secretly loathed his model and wanted to highlight all the frailties of ageing womanhood. The artist had highlighted every curve of the full breasts that had drooped with age, every dimpled bit of skin in the belly that had grown slack. In someone else's hands, the model would have been a beautiful older woman, but for this artist, she was ugly.

Toni had never understood why Oliver thought she'd approve of the picture. In his business, he could grow older and get roles, but women actors could not. Nor could women in her business, yet he seemed to think that this painting was perfectly fine in its cruel portrayal of the effect of age on the sex who were most expected not to age.

He hadn't understood, but then, she hadn't understood either. Not when it came to the gambling.

Her husband was an addict.

Sitting in the sun with her coffee, Toni found her phone, angled the sun lounger so she could see the screen without glare from the sun and looked up gambling addiction websites. It all made horrific reading. The signs included increased gambling when money was lost; obsession with going back to the gambling location or site; depression; irritability and secretiveness over losing money. He'd certainly nailed the secretiveness so well that she hadn't even known he was a gambler. The things to watch out for were of no use to a woman who hadn't noticed any of this stuff. None of it. If only she had . . . If only she hadn't been so concerned with her own career, then she might have noticed and they wouldn't be in this mess.

The phone rang and Toni almost dropped it in surprise. Before she knew what she was doing, she answered it.

'Toni, is that you?' said a voice.

It was Michelle, one of the suits from her show, a senior executive producer from the money side of the business.

'Hi Michelle,' she said brightly, wishing she could come up with an instant lie to get her out of this but for some reason, her much-vaunted ability to lie on any occasion had deserted her. Now, of all times.

She felt quite emptied of all the abilities that had made her successful in her career.

'I've been trying to get in touch with you for the past couple of days,' said Michelle, who was a serious and bespectacled woman of around Lou's age and who was best known to Toni as a woman who wore nothing but Comme des Garçons clothing purchased on vintage shopping sites. Fashionable, clever and earnest were her three words.

'I assume you know what it's about.'

'Yes.'

'Mr Lanigan's people have been on to us. Apparently he is considering making a formal complaint about your treatment of him. It has been intimated that there is a recording of you and him in the office car park here and that this might be made public.'

'You know he can't make the recording public in any legal sense,' said Toni bluntly. 'He didn't tell me he was taping me, he hid his phone from me, therefore it's illegal. Any release of it would have to be subtly done by a "friend".'

Toni guessed there were loads of 'friends' who'd do it.

'I know,' said Michelle evenly. 'We would hope to . . .' she paused, 'and I say this cautiously, Toni, we would hope to back you once we understand what actually went on. We need to know your side of the story and, so far, we haven't heard anything from you. Cormac Wolfe has talked to me, and he has explained that Gerry Lanigan leapt upon you in the car park and frightened you.'

Good old Cormac, thought Toni.

'Yes, he did frighten me,' she said, thinking of his finger jamming into her breastbone.

But nobody had seen that: it would be her word against his and he had the tape, after all.

'He loomed out of nowhere – and he's a big guy, Michelle. The encounter was certainly scary,' Toni said. 'But that would be me using the "I'm a woman and I was scared" defence, and the right wingers would make mincemeat out of me for that.'

She sighed from somewhere deep inside her. Her fear could mean nothing in this story because the law was still many years behind reality when it came to male strength and aggression used against women. If she said anything, she'd be demonising Gerry Lanigan when, in reality, he'd threatened her physically and they both knew it.

'I reacted badly, for sure. But I did say those things. I shouted at him and said I would finish his career. It might have been fear talking, but that's irrelevant when it comes to a recording that could finish *my* career.'

'You should get legal advice, Toni.' Michelle sounded more cautious now.

'Are you taping this?' Toni asked, feeling suddenly paranoid.

'No, I am not. I am phoning to say we are essentially behind you, but we need to know what happened. We want to get a vision of what we are defending if we are to defend it. You're a brilliant presenter and the interview in question was broadcast on Epsilon Radio, so we are not liable for that. Our issue is to do with your continuing employment with the TV show.'

'I get that,' agreed Toni. 'Things are a little unclear at the moment.'

Understatement of the year, she thought. 'There have been some personal issues which may have affected my lashing out at Mr Lanigan in the car park. But I was scared by his appearing beside my car unexpectedly when I was alone and that was a factor too.'

'Cormac didn't mention any personal issues,' said Michelle in surprise. 'Are you all right? Are you ill?'

The part of Toni that could expertly gauge the news cycle knew that if she had been seriously ill, she'd have a get-out-of-jail card for anything said to a bullying man in the TV car park. *I was ill – big man scared me.* Problem over. The simplistic view would give her an out, but Toni wanted to play this authentically, even if that was a truly stupid decision.

Despite herself, she smiled.

'No, I'm not ill. It's something between myself and Oliver and . . .' She paused. How did she explain any of this? The answer was that she couldn't, not yet and certainly not to Michelle. 'I need to talk to a lawyer.'

'Good plan. Lanigan is certainly out for blood. We will not tolerate being bullied, but we have to have a plan in place.'

'OK,' said Toni. 'Can I come back to you?'

'Of course. Are you in Cork? You were at your sister's party or something?'

'No.' Toni gazed over the balcony railings at the stunning view of the Mediterranean. In the distance, a yacht was passing elegantly by. Toni couldn't see the passengers but imagined people in shorts, T-shirts and deck shoes discussing a dive later and wondering which part of the island they'd head to for a leisurely dinner. She wished she were living their lives.

'I'm not in Cork. We'll talk soon,' she said, thinking that this promise might be fake because she really had no idea what she wanted to do next.

She hung up and decided that there was nothing for it but to make all her phone calls. She rang Cormac.

'Where are you, Coop?' he said, answering on the second ring.

'Sicily.'

'Sicily? Seriously? You on holiday or on the scoop of a lifetime? Is it nice at this time of the year?'

'Fabulous. We're in the middle of a heatwave. I can see a swimming platform from here and everyone is flinging themselves into the sea with wild abandon. But I'm not swimming, Cormac. I came here with my sister, actually. It's a personal thing.'

'Lots of personal stuff coming up in your life, Coop,' he remarked.

Toni laughed. 'You have no idea,' she said, managing to keep the bitterness out of her voice. 'Can you talk?'

'Gimme a minute. I'll go out into the corridor. The walls have ears around here.'

She waited, hearing the familiar sounds of the office with people on the phone interspersed with 'Hello, how're you doing?' remarks as Cormac made his way somewhere private. The whole open-plan office space was detrimental to secrets, no doubt about it. Toni herself sat in the car if she needed a private conversation. Open-plan offices gave one no place to vent, talk to a loved one or get the result of a worrying blood test. Unless one wanted it all round the office.

'Right. I'm alone. Spill.'

Toni finished her coffee and, despite the caffeine buzzing through her veins, felt a hint of a deeper unwinding begin somewhere in her solar plexus. She could trust Cormac Wolfe with her life. Her gut knew it and the gut was always right. If only her gut had tuned into Oliver's gambling.

'Where do I start? When Lanigan got me in the car park, I'd had bad news the night before.'

'I thought you were off that afternoon,' Cormac said sagely. 'You were still good, obvs, but quiet.'

Toni felt a vague hint of pride. At least she'd been able to hold things together at work.

If she wrote her memoirs, she could add that: 'My world collapsed but hey, I kept smiling and waving!'

'Oliver told me that he's addicted to gambling,' she said in a rush. 'He told me he's lost all his money – and all my money too.'

'Shit! No wonder you went off the rails. I wonder you didn't throw a punch at him.'

'Oliver or Lanigan?' joked Toni.

'Both of them.'

'Both of them deserve someone hitting them over the head with something solid,' agreed Toni, 'but it better not be me. I don't want to add attempted murder to my current problems.'

'That wouldn't be a good plan,' agreed Cormac easily. 'Lanigan's a nasty bastard, but Oliver . . .' He paused. 'I didn't see that coming.'

'Neither did I,' admitted Toni, and allowed herself to talk freely. 'I had no idea, Cormac. None whatsoever. He's been lying for years.'

Who knew how many years. Addictions could take time to grow. How many years had he lied to her, and how would she ever forgive him? Could she?

Toni closed her eyes at the thought of all the money she'd had in investments and how long it had taken to grow it. She'd worked so hard, had done endless shifts and back-to-back weekend corporate gigs to build up that money, working without a day off for weeks at a time because she knew her earning power years were limited. She would never be able to make that much money again. Her security was gone and her marriage too, she felt.

'I've lost everything,' she said, eyes still closed.

'Shit,' said Cormac again. 'I am so sorry, Toni. How much is gone?'

'I don't know how much, but we have joint bank accounts, joint investments . . .' She couldn't mention the money lenders, not yet.

Cormac was uncharacteristically silent for a beat.

'There's a lot to be said for not being attached,' he said finally.

'Ha!' she replied. 'You're attached, Cormac Wolfe: only you're attached to a different woman on a six-month rota system.'

It was an office joke the way Cormac had a different girlfriend twice a year: once for Christmas and then, by summer, he'd have a different one. He never seemed to settle down and it never made any sense to Toni because he was decent, charming, funny, good looking and, as she'd said many years ago, hot. He'd been married once in his early twenties and had a grown-up daughter he was close to. He was never, as he always said when people teased him, getting caught again.

'I just had a call from Michelle in the office and she suggested my getting a lawyer.'

'I don't know about that,' Cormac replied thoughtfully. 'Getting a lawyer sometimes implies that you have a reason to get one and I don't think that Lanigan is going to take any legal action against you. He's simply blustering because he's embarrassed and he has to hit out. You need damage limitation, which is totally different. I know a firm you could use for that. Regarding Lanigan, I'm sure he's not as squeaky clean as he makes out. There's more than a whiff of the bully boy about him.'

'There sure is,' said Toni thoughtfully.

A sliver of an idea came into her head: anyone who could hijack her the way Lanigan had must have a few skeletons in his closet. Perhaps it was time the old Toni Cooper started investigating him? The one who worked night and day on a story: that Toni. There still might be a way out of this mess, because he would not go down without a fight.

Cormac was still talking.

'I want to help,' he was saying.

This statement, delivered with a kindness absent from everyone but Lou, made the words flood out of Toni.

'Lanigan jabbed a finger in my chest the other night. Hard, Cormac. He hurt me.'

'What?' exploded Cormac.

For a moment, Toni couldn't speak. She had shared this with nobody because who could she tell? Not Oliver and not Lou, who was going through so much. So to say it to Cormac and have him be angry on her behalf was comforting.

'He just poked me,' she said, but try as she might, her voice still shook just a little.

'That's assault,' growled Cormac. 'He's twice your weight. The coward.'

'Don't say anything to anyone,' Toni begged. 'It'll be my word against his, you know that. I'll be too hot for any broadcaster to touch if he releases that tape. Nobody will want to hire me, and right now, I need money.'

'I understand that, but I think damage limitation is what you need. Hey, Toni.' His tone was softer now. 'Take care of yourself. Phone me anytime to talk. This isn't easy, any of this. The stuff with Oliver – I'm really, really sorry that you're going through that.'

For some reason, the last few words were the ones that were her undoing.

'Thanks, Cormac,' she said. She pressed *end* and Toni Cooper, tough bitch extraordinaire, began to cry.

Chapter Seventeen

Gloria Cooper had been raised to be both kind to others and ladylike but neither thing made her a pushover.

She had angry things to say tonight and didn't think her little dog Sugar should witness any of it. So she left her beloved little dog with her neighbours and drove to Lou's house.

Without the presence of her beloved niece, Lou's house looked somehow less than. The bird feeders in the garden were nearly empty and the curtains in one upstairs room were still pulled shut. Funny how a place could look neglected after only a few days.

Ned answered the door. He was clearly just home from work and was still in his lecturer clothes of shirt, tie and jacket.

'Gloria!' His eyes lit up at the sight of her. 'Come in, come in . . .' He paused in his welcoming. 'You know that Lou hasn't come home yet?' he said cautiously.

'Yes, I know,' said Gloria, walking in.

Louise's home was an extension of her personality: warm, friendly and usually scented with either flowers or Lou's treasured scented candles. Tonight, there was no lovely smell apart from one which hinted at windows not having been opened for a few days.

Emily had her mother's knack of making a house a home too, but it was obvious she was back in college.

As if he realised that the house was somehow less than welcoming, Ned rushed to switch on the table lamps in the living room and swept a pile of newspapers from the coffee table onto the floor where he clearly hoped Gloria wouldn't see them. She said nothing but smiled, and walked in.

'How are things?' Gloria said, settling herself down in the most comfortable chair.

'Er . . . things are OK,' said Ned.

He liked Gloria, but he never entertained her on his own. She was Lou's aunt, Lou's relative. He was hopeless with old ladies. Completely hopeless with his own mother, who was, it had to be admitted, a nightmare even in the elderly lady stakes. Gloria was not a nightmare normally, but Ned felt this wasn't one of her convivial visits.

'Have you been speaking to Lou?' Gloria interrupted his thoughts.

'Yes, and no. I mean, she hung up on me and since then, I've left her messages, but she hasn't got back to me,' said Ned helplessly. And even as he said it, he knew it sounded like a dreadful excuse.

'She was very angry when she left.'

He *thought* she was angry when she left because, frankly, a lot of the night was a haze. It was the Heart

237

Starters. If only Tommy hadn't been so insistent on them. Ned didn't think he'd ever had a hangover like it.

When he woke up on Saturday morning to discover that he was fully dressed on the couch, with a murderous headache, a sick stomach and a wife who had gone AWOL, he resolved never to touch another Heart Starter.

'Just messages?' said Gloria.

'Yes,' said Ned, realising too late that Gloria, for all her easy-going appearance, was another of those women who could pin you to the wall with a sentence. 'I can't reach her. She's not taking my phone calls.'

'Oh Ned,' said Gloria, with a hint of weariness. 'You're going to have to do better than that, you know.'

'I know,' he said. 'It's just I'm hopeless at presents and—'

'Don't be ridiculous,' Gloria said, enunciating every word crisply. 'This is not about presents. This is about paying attention. This is about someone you love very much. Someone you've neglected.'

'I do know,' Ned said, irritated.

'There's no point telling me you know if you're not doing anything about it,' Gloria pointed out. 'You need to have a proper conversation with Lou. I know you love her, and I know she adores you, but marriages drift apart when one person lets the other one get on with doing all the work. And she does all the work, doesn't she? She does the taking care of, the fixing things, the buying gifts for your mother—'

'You know she buys things for my mother?'

'Of course she does.' Gloria was brusque.

'You mean she told you?'

'She didn't have to tell me, it's perfectly obvious. If you are not able to buy a single gift for your own wife on her fiftieth birthday, it's pretty obvious you can't buy your mother things, so of course, Lou buys everything.'

'Am I that transparent?' asked Ned, slightly horrified.

It was one thing to rely on one's wife to do everything. Another entirely for everyone to see this clearly. He felt like a big child playing at being a grown-up.

'Not transparent dear, just a little predictable. And perhaps a little lazy? The thing is, Lou doesn't complain. It doesn't matter if you're predictable if everything else in her life is working and people are looking out for her. However, everything else in Lou's life hasn't been working. And that's the problem. It would be fine if Oszkar and Bettina weren't treating her abominably. And it would be fine if she didn't have Lillian as a mother. But they're two big obstacles to overcome. Add all of that to your not being precisely present, and perhaps taking her for granted, and of course there's a problem. I don't like to interfere—'

Ned snorted. That was the sort of thing his mother said all the time right before she interfered.

'Honestly, I don't,' said Gloria, 'but I feel you need to do something or you will lose Lou. And think of what an example you're setting for Emily. You're showing her that this is how husbands treat wives.'

'Now listen,' said Ned angrily, 'I love Emily—'

'I know you do. But you're showing her that husbands don't have to bother, that only wives bother.'

Ned's lips tightened as he listened.

'You need to be a part of this marriage, Ned, to contribute to it. I don't mean money. I mean time, energy, commitment. Stop sitting back and thinking that, because you're married, you can stop trying. I know,' she added, 'I'm old and never married and you think, what does she know about all of this? When you're as old as I am, you've seen scores of marriages come and go. I'd hate to see you and Lou split up because you treat her like an old armchair you can fall into. She's such a precious person.'

'What am I supposed to do?' demanded Ned. 'She's not answering her phone to me.'

'Take some action. Talk to Toni. Toni will have an idea what to do. They're in Sicily – no reason you can't fly out there.'

'But I've stuff on,' protested Ned.

Gloria got rather stiffly to her feet. 'Of course you do, dear,' she said, with only the faintest hint of condescension. '*Stuff on*. Good luck with that, Ned.'

After she left, Ned felt both churlish and dissatisfied.

What right did Gloria have to come in and tell him how to live his life? Just because Lou was upset because her mother had been narky. There was no reason to take it out on him. He'd buy her flowers and earrings or whatever. It'd be fine. Lou would be fine. Sure, she sounded annoyed on the phone from Sicily, but she'd come round, wouldn't she?

Gloria never arrived at Lillian and Bob's house without feeling a pang of loss for her brother.

Bob had made this house a home. He'd tended the garden, painted the woodwork, wallpapered the girls' bedrooms when they'd both chosen wallpaper in an old house where the walls were anything but straight.

Lillian had said it was madness.

'Tell them no,' she'd said, surveying the first roll of wallpaper up in Lou's bedroom, a prettily floral, old-fashioned paper that was obviously hanging at an angle because there wasn't a straight wall in the entire house.

'I said they could have wallpaper and they will,' Bob had said calmly.

'Suit yourself.' Lillian had stomped off and Gloria had taken over helping, even though she had never been all that good at DIY.

This evening, Valclusa looked even messier than usual from the outside. There were weeds growing between the paving stones, and sand all over the driveway. It was obvious that Lillian had been driving in and out without having made any allowance for said sand, most of which was still in a sugarloaf pile outside the house, so that it had spread.

Lillian's dented car was parked half in and half out of the gate. Gloria parked her own small car neatly outside and carefully made her way past the boulders and the rivulets of sand.

She had a key, of course, but she hadn't used it in years. Not since Bob had died.

In those last months, Gloria had cared for him and she and Lillian had managed a rota system with Toni and Lou so that he would always have someone nearby.

It was the only time Gloria could remember her sister-in-law putting something before herself or her art.

At Bob's funeral, Lillian had made Gloria walk with her, Lou, Toni and Emily into the church.

'We'll go in together,' she'd said, strangely dignified in widow's black and without her trademark bright red lipstick.

Bob had hated that lipstick, Gloria knew. At his funeral Mass, Lillian had honoured him by not wearing it.

She took Lillian's hand and held it as they walked slowly up the central aisle of the church to sit behind Bob's coffin.

'Lillian,' she called now, pushing the doorbell and wondering if it worked.

A moment later, Lillian appeared, clad in her working clothes: an over-sized painting shirt and skinny ankle-length trousers. She was barefoot, her hair was tangled up at the top of her head in a knot and she looked every inch her age. Yet she still had the appeal she'd had over fifty years ago when Bob Cooper had brought this sexy, mini-skirted girl home to meet his family.

'Can I come in?'

In reply, Lillian opened the door wide.

'I've just finished and was about to make dinner,' Lillian said.

'I've eaten,' said Gloria.

'Course you have.'

Lillian led the way into the big living room, which was in full chaos mode. Lillian had never had anyone in to clean the place: Lou did it for her. Gloria felt the surge of anger towards her sister-in-law at how she took advantage of her daughter.

Lillian's eyes narrowed as she saw Gloria taking in the dishevelled space.

'I don't have time for mundane things like tidying—' she began.

'Not when you have a willing daughter to do it,' said Gloria sharply.

Lillian's mouth tightened and she moved to the drinks trolley, which groaned under the weight of bottles.

'I wasn't going to have anything to drink tonight but ping! There goes that plan,' she said in sarcastic tones and poured herself an almost full tumbler of gin from the blue bottle. She added a dash of tonic and raised it to her lips.

'I'm not an alcoholic,' she snapped.

Gloria shrugged. 'It's not my place to judge.'

'Oh you judge, all right,' hissed Lillian. 'Don't give me that crap. You've always judged me.'

'What you mean is that you *felt* judged,' Gloria replied with steel in her voice, 'and you are not the sort of person to feel that unless you know you've done something wrong. There are people who hold themselves to very high standards, like darling Lou. Then there are people like you who never feel responsible for anything. So if you feel judged, Lillian, then you are fully aware of your . . .' she paused, searching for the word, 'misdemeanours.'

'Misdemeanours!' Lillian took a giant gulp of her drink. '*Living* is a misdemeanour in your prissy little copybook. Having sex, having a life, having friends: they're all misdemeanours!'

Gloria felt the beginnings of a headache.

She had handled this all wrong. Lillian did that to her – made her lash out in a way she never did with other people.

'I came to ask you to talk to Lou and to try to fix things. Your outburst at her party was very painful for her. She needs you. You're her mother.'

'You wish you were her mother!' shouted Lillian.

Gloria was in full control of herself now.

'I don't,' she said truthfully. 'I'm her aunt and I love her. This is a pivotal moment in her life. She needs you, Lillian.'

'If she needs me, why did she leave?'

'Because you broke her heart.'

Lillian glared at her sister-in-law but took a large glug of her drink just the same. 'Lou's too soft,' she snapped. 'Not like Toni.'

'That's because Toni can see through you and doesn't take any of your shit,' Gloria said and was amused to see Lillian's eyes widen momentarily.

'Yes, I can swear,' Gloria said. 'I'm flesh and blood, Lillian, even though you like to think I'm an old crone with no feelings. Thinking that makes it easier for you, doesn't it? It made it easier for you fifty years ago. I let you get away with it then but not now. If you don't fix this with Lou, you will lose her. I can't say I care for your feelings, Lillian, but I care about my niece. She needs you. If you can drag yourself out of gazing into the mirror of self-obsession for long enough.'

Lillian glared at her and was about to launch into something, but Gloria had had enough.

'I'll go,' she said now, and swept out of the room, letting herself out of a house for the second time that evening. Peacekeeping was a tough mission, no doubt about it.

Chapter Eighteen

The next morning brought another blisteringly hot Sicilian day and, armed with an ice-filled glass of water, Trinity lay on her back in the small single bedroom and checked her messages. Nothing from Pete. Her aunt Dara and new husband Marc had sent a chatty email of the round robin variety to all their friends detailing their honeymoon trip.

They were staying three nights in a resort in the Son Tra peninsula and then, would head to Ho Chi Minh city and stay near what Dara called the 'historic Saigon post office'. Trinity wasn't sure why it was historic but didn't want to ask.

Dara had also included some early photos from the wedding photographer.

'We all look fabulous! You should see us now – I live in my old khaki shorts and T-shirt. Travelling light is hard!'

Trinity stared at the shots of Dara and Marc's wedding three weeks previously.

Dara, red-haired like Trinity, also petite and slim in a silk column dress with Trinity on one side in fern-coloured satin, and Marc on the other side, tall and beaming with pride. Pete had been roaming around too, delighted to be at the party, having brought his acoustic guitar along in case there was a session.

Trinity had known then and she'd desperately wanted to tell Dara because her aunt had taken care of her all her life.

Mum and Dad had always been hopeless. Sweet but immature. Trinity no longer got angry over the way they'd behaved – the careless way they'd brought her into the world and dragged her around in their untethered, immature life without thinking for one minute if this was right for a small child. Things had changed when she'd gone to live with her aunt Dara in Limerick. Dara was her mother's sister and was everything Trinity's mother was not. Focused, organised, prepared to do anything for her small niece.

Trinity got off the bed and peered out her window at the city spread behind her. This was lovely, an unexpected holiday, but there was no escaping the reality. Her desire to run away made her think she was more her mother's daughter than she'd ever believed before. But she had to decide what to do at some point. Soon.

Downstairs, Toni seemed eager to make progress with finding Angelo Mulraney.

'It's why we came here after all,' she said.

'Yes,' agreed Lou slowly. 'How are we going to get in touch with him?' she asked. Being in Sicily, being away from all her troubles, felt so freeing. Finding Angelo – a task she was actively ignoring – would take away that freeing feeling.

But Toni, once on a mission, was not to be thwarted.

'I've been online again this morning and I've found a gallery that exhibits work by an artist, Angelo M. It's got to be him. It links to a website – which has ludicrously little detail – and an email. I have looked at so many artists and this is the only person who fits. Do you want to see the paintings?'

Lou shook her head and wished she wasn't so conflicted about this. It was why they'd come to Sicily, after all.

'I'm sending an email,' Toni announced. 'Look at what I've written and tell me what you think.'

Lou shivered. 'I'm not sure I want to see it,' she said. 'An actual message makes it feel so real.'

'It's real,' said Toni briskly.

Lou knew that her sister's mind was full of bankruptcy and career suicide. She had absolutely no time for life's niceties. They were in Sicily to find Angelo, therefore that was what they would do.

'Look.' Toni held out her phone.

Hello, I'm trying to get in touch with a painter by the name of Angelo Mulraney and apologies if this is not you. My name is Toni Cooper and I'm on holiday in Ortigia with my sister, Louise. We heard you once knew our mum, Lillian Cooper, when she was living in Whitehaven in Cork, and it would be lovely to catch up with you if possible?

'It makes it look as if we just happened to be here and thought of looking him up,' Toni explained. 'If it's not him or if he's got a wife and ten kids, then they might go mental if we turn up out of the blue and say "Hey, you're my dad!"'

Lou winced. Earlier, meeting with her father had seemed somewhat natural, as if they'd drift across each other's paths on this glorious island, share a walk on a beach and then part: two threads of life simply passing by each other.

But now – this felt very immediate.

What if he *did* have a wife and ten kids and nobody had ever known of her existence? He wouldn't want an unknown adult daughter materialising out of nowhere. Who would? Plus, had he known about her? If so, why had he never looked for her? It would feel like such a rejection – that this man, her birth father, had known of her existence and had not reached out to find her. She was nothing to him.

But if he hadn't known?

'I'm hitting send,' Toni announced, and one finger pressed a button on her phone.

No, thought Lou wildly. *NO! Take it back, delete it . . . if he doesn't want to see me for whatever reason, how will I cope?*

But she said none of this because Toni had already moved on.

'Let's go out and get food,' she said brightly.

They put on sun cream and hats, and headed off into the sun, looking for somewhere to buy groceries.

'You OK?' Lou asked Trinity, who'd been very quiet all morning.

'Fine,' said Trinity in a voice that led Lou to believe she was nowhere near fine. But then, it wasn't her place to intrude. Perhaps the younger woman was simply tired.

'I love this place,' added Trinity, seeming determined to talk to prove that she was OK.

The three of them walked along a narrow street where creamy stone buildings were built close to each other and giant leafy green plants spilled from containers from arched doorways and iron balconies. 'It's easy to forget about another life when you're here,' she added wistfully.

'Normally, I do forget about other stuff on holidays,' Toni replied, 'but not so much now.'

Lou forgot her own fears and put an arm around her sister's waist. Sicily was performing its subtle magic on her again. Her breathing was even, the Barking Dog and Constant Catastrophist were quiet. She allowed herself to briefly wonder, again, what other life Trinity was trying to forget and then told herself that she was not in charge of this young woman.

She could not fix Trinity any more than she could fix Toni, her mother, or anyone on the planet. She could only fix herself. Worrying about the future never solved anything either. What would happen with Angelo would happen whether she worried about it or not. They might never find him. If that happened, so be it.

They walked past a tiny boutique that glittered with gold and pretty necklaces. There were exquisite little evil eye charms in sequins, in enamel and in delicate beads on vermeil chains. It was exactly the sort of shop that Lou and Mim had loved.

'Let's go in,' Lou said delightedly.

Inside, she felt as if Mim was with her in spirit. There were ankh necklaces, the symbol of life from ancient Egypt that Mim adored. There were also starfish charms in all sizes dangling with coral-style stones and crystals on beaded necklaces.

She might not have a job anymore, Lou decided, but these things made her happy and she would buy them for her beloved sister, for Emily, for Trinity and for Simone, Mim's daughter.

When she got home, she'd find another job where they appreciated her. She might even investigate doing a part-time degree. Then she'd be able to take on any managerial job. Then Oszkar and Bettina would see how useful she'd been and how she'd have been able to make strategic plans to beat the band. Beaming, she began picking up necklaces, deciding who would get what.

They left the shop twenty minutes later, each wearing a few necklaces, all laughing and admiring each other's jewellery.

'These are so pretty,' said Trinity, holding up the ankh she'd chosen, along with a cowrie shell bracelet decorated with tiny golden cowries. 'Pete's mother would not approve.'

'Pete's mother? Why not?' said Toni.

'She's religious and she says these things are heathen.'

Toni gave a cynical laugh. 'Cowrie shells were used by ancient Chinese cultures as money, by North American native tribes as protection, and by ancient Africans as symbols of the goddess of fertility. These and the ankh all pre-date Christianity. It's absolute bigotry to despise these pre-Christian symbols and expect reverence for her own religious beliefs. Don't get me started on the Christian symbols and religious holidays which were taken from the so-called pagan religions.'

Trinity laughed. 'I'd love you to meet her and tell her that.'

Toni's eyes gleamed with a look Lou recognised: the 'watch out fundamentalists' look.

'I'd love it too,' said Toni.

They found a market and bought a few things for lunch, including fresh prawns that Toni said looked too glorious to leave behind.

'We don't have a cold bag,' said Lou, with a wild return of Lou the worrier.

'It'll be fine,' said Toni, waving a hand.

On the way back to the apartment, they stopped by a huge fountain dedicated to the goddess Diana, with a mermaid riding a giant open-mouthed sea monster that would have been terrifying if it had come to life.

'Diana would kill it,' Trinity said, giving the giant monster a wide berth and gazing up at a very serene Diana who was overseeing all the chaos of monsters and naked ocean riders with an unmoved look on her stone face.

'Let's get a coffee over there,' suggested Toni. 'I feel the need for a pastry before lunch.'

'The prawns—' warned Lou.

'They'll be fine.'

Lou was about to say she'd rush home with the prawns and put them in the fridge and then thought again. She was not the whole world's mother/fixer. Toni could make her own decisions.

For lunch, Toni cooked the prawns with garlic and olive oil, but Trinity and Lou ate avocados and salad instead.

'Cowards,' said Toni afterwards and the three of them sat on the second-floor balcony. The sisters sunbathed while Trinity sat under the canopy and read her book. Lou had moved the record player so that they could hear it as they sat outside with the lemonade Toni had concocted, and the afternoon passed while they listened to disco music and Trinity laughed at all the silly song names.

'"Ring My Bell"?' she said, laughing. 'That's soo funny.'

'It made sense once,' Lou said, grinning. 'I used to tease Dad about a song called "Be-Bop-A-Lula".'

She and Toni looked at each other, remembering their beloved father. No matter what, Lou thought with a stab of pain, he would always be her father. No matter how things worked out with Angelo, Bob Cooper had been her father and that was that.

That night, languorous from a day of sunbathing, they ate dinner at a street restaurant beside a huge mediaeval wall. Trinity and Toni had pizza while Lou ate seafood pasta and the two sisters drank smoky red Etna Rosso. Giant heaters warmed them against the chill of the evening air and street entertainers, including violinists and a woman with tiny brightly coloured canaries who sat on people's shoulders, wandered among the diners.

Trinity beamed as a tiny pink one, called a cinnamon canary, sat on her shoulder and tweeted happily. Lou had a bright blue bird on her arm.

'They are adorable,' she said.

On the way home, Trinity leaned against Lou and said she was so tired, she might sleep on her feet.

'Nearly there,' said Lou, wrapping her cashmere throw around them both to keep them warm. The heat of the day had been replaced by a soft breeze and Lou was thinking that the weather was perfect when her phone began to ring shrilly.

'It's Lillian,' she said in amazement when she retrieved her phone from her bag.

'Lillian, hello—' she began but a diatribe interrupted her greeting.

'I have sand all over my front garden and where the bloody hell are you?' shrieked her mother.

Shocked, Lou stammered: 'Lillian, I'm away and I didn't know they were coming—'

'You always come to me that day,' interrupted her mother dramatically. 'I was exhausted, utterly exhausted and I had told you I was getting sand. It's not too much to expect you to do one little thing. I don't know why you ran off. You're being overdramatic, as usual, and Gloria said—'

Toni, who was suddenly looking slightly green, grabbed the phone. 'Lillian,' she snapped. 'We're away. This can wait. None of us can help you right now.'

'Toni, where are you?'

The tone of their mother's voice had changed and Lou heard it as clear as a bell. She wondered how she had never noticed this difference before. Lillian spoke to her in two ways: either as sweetie, milk of human kindness, or as if she were a Victorian scullery maid who could be screamed at.

Toni had somehow managed to get their mother off the phone at high speed.

'Why—' began Lou, but Toni interrupted her.

'Can't talk,' she said, looking even more green. 'I think I'm going to be sick.'

'The prawns!' said Trinity, horrified.

Toni clamped a hand over her mouth and began to run to their door.

After an hour of going in and out to Toni in the bathroom, holding back her hair as she was sick and supplying her with face cloths and water, Lou came in with more towels and water and sat on the edge of their bath.

'Why is Lillian different with you than with me?' she asked, holding onto the rehydration salts that Toni said she couldn't possibly look at now.

Toni leaned over the bowl again, wondering whether the desire to eat would ever return. She cursed all shellfish and the horses they rode in on. Was she going to vomit again . . . ?

'Why does she treat us differently?' asked Lou again.

'You have no sense of timing,' Toni said weakly as the nausea passed. She didn't have the bandwidth to think about their mother's behaviour now.

Sinking back onto the floor, she lay on the bath towel and thought she had never lain anywhere as wonderful. If she was offered the presidency, *any* presidency, she would have to say no because this, this towel and this bathroom floor, was the most wonderful place in the world to lie very, very still, so she would not want to vomit again.

If she promised to some higher deity that she would never eat a mollusc or oyster or anything that crawled along the seabed again, would she be spared? A vision of herself offering a sacrifice to the deity came into her head. What would she have to bring? Something valuable? The vintage Pucci scarf she'd bought in that designer second-hand shop in the Portobello market in London? Her ancient black platform Gucci mules that she'd actually bought new but were now so old that they qualified as vintage. They were older than Trinity. She envisioned Trinity, clad in a toga and flowers, presenting the Pucci scarf and the mules on an altar while a phalanx of Roman goddesses looked down their aristocratic noses at the offerings and argued about who'd get what.

Pete's mother would have a fit, she thought with the limited amount of wild amusement her weakened body could manage.

'I think I'm having a hallucinatory moment,' she said to Lou, who snorted with derision.

'What is wrong with you, Lou?' Toni asked crossly. 'You always take care of sick people. Why not me now?'

'I told you not to eat those prawns,' said Lou with equal irritation. 'I don't care how freshly they were caught or how quickly you meant to come home from the market, you insisted on stopping for coffee, it was twenty-one degrees outside and prawns do not like heat.'

Toni scowled. 'If I didn't love you, I would hate you at this precise moment,' she said.

'If you'd listened to me, you wouldn't be sick right now!' Lou continued. 'Nobody listens to me!'

'I do listen to you,' said Toni wearily. She might as well tell Lou where she'd been going wrong all these years. There was no point in circling around the fact: Lou needed to know.

Not knowing stuff was too painful, as Toni now knew. If someone had told her that her husband was a gambling addict, things would have been very different. She'd have money in the bank and she might still have a viable career. Knowledge truly was power.

'I'm going to be really honest with you, Lou, probably because I'm ill and my electrolytes are all over the place. So don't kill me afterwards, OK? Lillian treats you differently because you allow her to: it's that simple,' she said tiredly. 'You have a co-dependent relationship with her. She'd love to behave that way with me, but I said no a long time ago. I did not want to run around after her and tell her how fabulous she is.'

'Co-dependent relationship?' Lou said, confused. 'With my mother?'

'One person is a caretaker and the other takes advantage of that fact. You take care of other people . . .' She stopped because she could hear Lou's sharp intake of breath.

'You do,' Toni repeated. 'She makes you think you can only be loved if you do everything for her, so you do everything for her. You want to be loved.'

That sounded very blunt, she thought, but it had to be said. 'I mean, we all want to be loved but in co-dependent relationships, one person is so desperate to be loved and approved of. It's not good for you. Not healthy.'

The nausea was passing. She chanced sitting up on her towel and leaned against the bathtub. It was miraculous. The goddesses had obviously decided they would take the Pucci scarf and the mules. Toni didn't care. Anything was worth sacrificing to feel better.

Plus, she had always had amazing powers of recovery.

'I do,' agreed Lou slowly.

'Yes, you do,' agreed Toni. 'When she says "jump" you say "how high?" Or, even better, when she says someone was horrible to her or upset her, she sends you off to fix it. You're like her guard dog. No wonder she never wanted a dog – she had you instead. You enable that behaviour because you like being needed.'

'So it's my fault?' Lou said.

'No. Lillian created the scenario. But it's a self-perpetuating cycle. If you don't do what she wants, she turns her love off, so you're desperate for her approval again and you do whatever she wants—'

'Stop!' Lou sat on the edge of the bath. 'Just stop.'

Toni fell silent and Lou allowed herself to breathe slowly, the way she did when the Barking Dog was at her. Slowly in and slowly out.

'I'm sorry. I didn't mean to sound cruel,' Toni said. 'like that. I hate to see Lillian take advantage of you, but I've grown used to it. I thought you didn't mind it . . .'

Toni paused. That wasn't entirely true. She knew exactly what her mother was capable of. If she was honest, she'd simply accepted the family narrative and let it continue. Was she to blame for never intervening in their mother's treatment of Lou?

'I never realised she was treating me that way. Or that I was allowing her to do it,' Lou said eventually. She was still trying to breathe slowly. It was working. She was able to think. Her mind hadn't gone into meltdown.

'The co-dependency thing – what else does it mean?' she asked tentatively.

Toni closed her eyes as if seeing a research printout for a TV show.

'It means you take care of other people but not yourself. You feel responsible for everything and everyone. You . . .' Toni paused. 'You sure you want to hear this?'

'Yes.'

''Kay. You are very self-critical and you absorb other people's feelings.' Toni stopped. She was glad she'd opened her sister's eyes, but she didn't want to keep going. Hearing self-truths was generally painful. Toni had had too many articles written about her television persona to think that other people's analyses of one were fun to hear.

'There's more,' said Lou, feeling the pain of self-recognition. 'Isn't there?'

'I'm not Wikipedia,' Toni insisted.

'You remember everything. You know you do.'

'Fine! After this you can look it up: you're a people pleaser, OK? Happy now?' Lou slid off the bath and sat on the bathroom's marble floor with her sister.

People pleaser.

That described her perfectly. What sort of an idiot was she?

'I'm really sorry,' said Toni, clumsily patting her. 'It's like clubbing a baby seal.'

'I'm a baby seal?'

'You have very big eyes,' Toni offered.

A people-pleasing baby seal. Was this what she was? Fifty years on the planet and this is what she amounted to? All her current problems filtered down to this. She was a woman who was such an easy-going wife that she let her husband basically ignore her. She was a daughter at the beck and call of a manipulative mother who used her. She was an employee who was so eager to be liked, so eager to be helpful, that she allowed her true value to be disregarded.

At least she still had Emily. Didn't she? Or had she got that wrong too? On impulse, she turned away from Toni to send a quick WhatsApp to her daughter.

Can you talk?

Emily was always so busy with college and who knew when she'd be able to talk to her mother, but at that precise moment, Lou wanted nothing more than to speak to her beloved daughter. Emily, the child she adored who'd grown up into a woman she adored.

The little message ticks went blue.

Yes. Want to phone in five? Am still in library. Big assignment due. Constitutional Law – still! Will go outside to talk.

Bliss!

Lou stood up stiffly in the tiny bathroom, patted her sister's damp head, and went up to the balcony where it still felt warm from the day's sun. She somehow managed to give it six minutes before she dialled her daughter.

'Hello—'

'Hi Mum, are you having fun?' began Emily's warm tones.

'Nooooo . . . well, sort of,' said Lou. 'I just feel . . .'

She couldn't continue. Simply feeling Emily's presence even on the other end of a phone was a balm. How many other people were a balm to her? Very few. *She* was the balm to a lot of people but those who returned the favour – there were less of them.

'Mum, are you OK?' said Emily. 'There's a lot going on—'

Lou interrupted. 'I love you, Emily. I know I did something right when I see you and hear you.'

'If I'm amazing, then I got to be that way because of you!' Emily said cheerfully.

This time, Lou couldn't stop the tears welling up.

'But it's true, Mum. One of my uni friends is gay and she has to pretend to be straight when her mother comes to visit because she feels her mother couldn't take it. It's horrible. Imagine having to hide who you are. Another one has to wear clothes with long sleeves to cover up the tattoo on her arm because her father will go ballistic if he sees it.'

Lou was silent. She felt a surge of love for her daughter. She had been a good mother. Still was. It was wonderful to talk to Emily and feel that, feel the love they shared. 'Some people are so blinkered. You love me for me – not for who you think I should be. That makes you an amazing mum, and I love you.'

'Thank you,' said Lou fervently. 'Love you too.'

Aware that her sister was still in the bathroom and that she should go back to her, Lou said quickly: 'Toni said I was a people pleaser.'

It was like saying she was an axe murderer.

'If being a people pleaser means you're a lovely person and think about others all the time, then yes, you're that. It only matters when you please the wrong people, Mum, like—' Emily stopped.

'Like who?' prompted Lou.

'Like Granny,' said her daughter in a rush. 'I am not calling her Lillian anymore. She's going to be called Granny even if it makes her feel one hundred. She was so hideous to you.'

'Your grandmother is tricky,' said Lou. 'Toni says that my relationship with Granny is one where I try to please her all the time, which is not good.'

'Yeah,' said Emily, 'she does demand a lot from you. It's all "Do this, Lou, clean the house, go to the shops for me, tidy the garden, you're the milk of human kindness and I need two bottles of whiskey while you're at it."' Emily paused in her imitation of her grandmother.

'Am I the only person who didn't see it?' Lou asked, horrified.

'Granny's very self-centred,' said Emily with the acuity of youth. 'And you're kind and caring. Toni's kind too, but she knows when people are taking advantage of her. That's what you need to learn. Toni doesn't take any of Granny's bull—'

Lou laughed loudly. 'Thank you, darling Emily. Currently, your aunt Toni is lying on our bathroom floor after getting food poisoning from prawns that spent too long in the sun.'

'Ouch.'

'Exactly. But she's going to help me be different.'

'I love Toni, but don't become like her,' begged Emily.

'I won't. I'll become a better version of me. One that stands up for me first.'

'Can't wait to see that,' Emily said.

Lou ran back downstairs to the bathroom to see how Toni was doing.

As she hurried, she thought that perhaps this was what her flight to Sicily was all about – it wasn't about finding Angelo: it was about seeing her life from a distance.

With distance, she could see what was wrong and what part she'd played in that. Blaming other people – her mother, Ned, Oszkar and Bettina – was too easy. People treated you how you allowed them to treat you.

In the bathroom, Lou found that Toni had graduated to sitting on the lid of the toilet and was clearly now contemplating the rehydration salts. Toni held up her phone.

'Bingo. The Angelo M painter is none other than Mr Mulraney. He emailed right back. He sent an address. He can see us tomorrow at noon, if we can make it.'

Lou gazed at her sister, who got to her feet shakily.

'That is, he can see us if *I* can make it.'

Lou wondered if *she* would be able to make it. This was it: why they'd come to Sicily. Now that the meeting was set, she felt as shaky as her sister looked. But she said none of this. The new, no-nonsense Lou had to be courageous.

'You'll be fine, Toni,' she said, fixing the pillows so that Toni was a little bit propped up. 'I'll take care of you. But don't be stroppy or it's all off.'

'Get you,' said Toni weakly.

'Yeah, this is the new me,' Lou joked. 'Tough cookie extraordinaire.'

'You're too lovely to be tough,' said Toni sinking into the embrace of the bed as if it was a lover.

'Watch me,' said her sister. 'Just watch me.'

Chapter Nineteen

Lou woke, heart pounding, from a nightmare. Beside her, Toni slept the sound sleep of the exhausted food poisoning victim. Sweating and breathing fast, Lou pushed off their light duvet.

In her dream she'd been in her parents' house, Valclusa, in Whitehaven: the house the way it had been before her mother had built the studio. Then Lillian used to sculpt in a big shed around the back. Dad had been there too. He was old in the nightmare: old, frail, with a drip stand alongside him as if he was still getting chemotherapy for the cancer that had killed him.

In dreamworld, Lillian was bright, vibrant and much younger than she was now, her lips glistening with that Moscow Red lipstick she liked.

'Angelo won't like you, you know,' she'd been saying, her voice the taunting of the brattiest child in the school playground. 'He won't like you. Nobody likes you.'

You didn't need a degree in psychotherapy to work out what it meant.

Lou went quietly downstairs in the moonlight and began to boil the kettle in the tiny kitchen. Camomile tea might help. Lou took her tea into the big main room. It was nearly dawn. She didn't think she'd sleep again. The Barking Dog had been missing for the last few days on the island, but now she could feel it in the back of her head rising up again.

She could hear her mother's voice from the nightmare: *He won't like you. Nobody likes you.*

What if he didn't . . . ?

She had no idea if Angelo knew he'd fathered a child with Lillian, if he'd known that Lillian had been pregnant.

But, Lou thought with new clarity, if he had known, why had he not come looking for her?

Outside, the sky was lightening even though dawn must be some time off. She went into the little kitchen and made coffee.

Toni had said she was in love with the octagonal Moka coffee pot.

'Much better than our huge machine,' she said wryly.

Oliver had bought a giant steel coffee shop beast of a thing that needed regular servicing and possibly several baristas to run it.

Toni said she liked the coffee from the stove-top pot much better.

Poor Toni, thought Lou, possibly for the first time ever.

Toni always knew how to deal with everything and yet here she was in Sicily with Lou, her life in chaos too.

266

Toni was wise though. She'd get out of it somehow.

Her sister understood the world in a way that she, Lou, never seemed to.

What had Toni said? That Lillian was a diva who used people and had totally used Lou.

The only reason Lillian didn't use Toni was because Toni didn't allow it. Emily could see this, so why hadn't Lou?

She took her cup of strong coffee out onto the balcony and let the scent of the sea overwhelm her. It was easier to deal with all of that here on this ancient island. Thousands of people had lived here over centuries and the vast sense of history in the great sights on the rock of the island itself made her own problems seem small by comparison.

The coffee was working, she decided: thank goodness for coffee.

'You couldn't sleep either?'

Trinity appeared behind her, clad in a long T-shirt with bare legs underneath. Trinity's beautiful red hair was tangled and her face was sleepy.

'No,' said Lou gently, feeling the motherly affection that overcame her whenever she was with the younger woman.

Trinity yawned delicately, like a cat.

Lou had a sudden thought. When she and Emily were up early, they sometimes watched sweet shows on Netflix.

All the time Mim had been dying, and Simone had been broken-hearted, she, Lou and Emily had comforted each other by sitting on the couch side by side watching old episodes of *Gilmore Girls*.

'Want to watch *Gilmore Girls* with me?' she asked suddenly.

Trinity beamed. 'I'd love that.'

When they were halfway through the first episode, Lou had a thought. 'You know I'm going to see Angelo today? The guy who might be my father?'

'Yes,' said Trinity cautiously.

'Will you come?'

'You sure?'

Lou grinned. 'Of course we need you with us,' she said, putting an arm around Trinity. 'We're the Three Musketeers. Or else the two dogs and a cat in *The Incredible Journey*.' They both laughed at this.

Inside, she hoped doing everything together might eventually crack open the defensive wall around their hitchhiker, and help Trinity to tell them what really was going on.

But, she reminded herself, that was not her business. She didn't exist to fix everyone.

Not anymore.

They set out for Angelo's house at eleven. Lou didn't want to be late.

Trinity was looking better than she had earlier, Lou thought. There was a light dusting of freckles on her cheeks and she was beginning to glow. The sun was agreeing with her. Maybe that was all Trinity needed: a little bit of time away. But she seemed sleepy.

'We take a left here for several kilometres,' said Toni, eyes narrowed behind her sunglasses as she listened to the satnav lady giving directions.

They'd driven through rich, fertile land on a beautiful road near the sea, taking the less obvious road to Avola, the coastal town south of Syracuse where Angelo Mulraney lived.

'Angelo lives here, which is just before we get into Avola,' she'd said, pointing to the map reference point on her phone. 'This big motorway won't be as much fun. Let's take the scenic route.'

The road they'd taken was close to the coast and for one moment Lou was reminded of the road down to the Mulraneys' house in Easkey. It was very different here. Easkey had been windswept and wild. Beautiful in its craggy desolation. Sicily was warm with fertile volcanic soil and yet sat proudly alone in the Mediterranean. No longer attached to its mother country, it was an island that had had to be strong to survive all the invaders who'd left their ancient buildings and traces of their rich cultures behind. There was a certain craggy similarity to Ireland. The places were so vastly different and yet both were islands.

Toni had always had a theory that the reason Irish people were so friendly was because they *were* islanders and as such, had to get on with neighbours from the great continent they were close to. Was Sicily the same? Populated by people with a rich culture and yet able to assimilate into the rest of the world with ease?

She stared out of the car window at the beautiful landscape and the idea drifted into her head that she could easily live here. Lou, who'd never thought of living anywhere but Whitehaven, a few miles from where she'd grown up, wondered what it would be like to make her home here. Away from her mother, away from the life she'd crafted where she did everything for everyone. It was a crazy idea, she knew. Ned couldn't work that way – his job was in Cork. And Emily would not be able to drop over for weekends as easily as if Lou lived in Whitehaven, but what if Emily moved abroad?

What then? Lou had given her roots and wings and her beloved Emily deserved to use them.

'Are you OK?' asked Toni quietly.

Lou glanced over her shoulder before answering. Trinity had drifted off to sleep in the back – as she seemed to do most days.

'Yes. After last night, I keep thinking over everything – me, Lillian, my job, even Ned, how I let people walk all over me—'

'You don't,' interrupted Toni.

'I do a bit,' said Lou. 'I allow it. That whole "what you allow is what will continue" thing never hit me until early this morning. You teach people how to treat you and I taught them they could treat me any old way.'

Beside her, Toni was silent.

'I love it here, don't you?' Lou said, changing the subject and staring out the car window. 'I was thinking how lovely it would be to' – she checked herself – 'come here more often. Mind you, I might not want to after meeting Angelo.'

'Are you nervous?' asked her sister.

'It feels as if I'm going on the most awkward first date in the world,' Lou said. 'He might look at me and tell me to go away instantly. Which would be devastating.

Although, I had a bit of devastation yesterday and look at me: still breathing, still smiling.'

What would that sort of rejection be like? How could she take it, she wondered.

Then, there was another issue: what if she hated him? She tried to explain this to her sister.

'I also feel as if I have to like him, have to be thrilled with him because he's my father, but what if *he's* awful? What if he's everything I hate in a person and I have to pretend?'

'You don't have to pretend,' Toni said.

'Of course I do!' Lou rolled her eyes. 'What should I do – say: "You're really obnoxious and I think we should pretend we never met".' She shuddered. 'A huge part of me wants to turn the car around and go back to the apartment. I already have a father. Why am I even doing this?'

'We could,' said Toni carefully. 'But you'd have so many unanswered questions and then one day, he wouldn't be around anymore to answer them.'

'Yeah,' sighed Lou. 'You're right. I need to do this. But it's hard. Why is everything hard?' she demanded. 'Why aren't things easy?'

Beside her, Toni grinned. 'What doesn't destroy us . . .'

'Yeah, makes us stronger and impervious to all future pain,' deadpanned Lou. She rubbed her eyes. 'Do you think I never argue with anyone and run around after people because it's easier?'

Toni was silent. Lou realised that this was not the sort of question her sister wanted to answer because any answer would hurt Lou.

'Forget I said that,' she said quickly. 'What I should have said is that people-pleasing means you can avoid facing stuff. That is a statement and not a question.'

'Did you have overnight therapy?'

'Yes. I did a whole psychoanalytical course while you and Trinity were asleep. I know everything now – ask me anything.'

'Will you be able to utilise this new, improved you in all dealings with our mother and your stupid bosses?' Toni asked.

Lou laughed. 'Now *that's* the real question,' she replied. 'It's easy doing it with you, but in the real world . . .'

Toni shrugged. 'It's like being in broadcasting – you might find it hard to stand up in front of hundreds of thousands of viewers and talk at first, but you learn. It's about practice.'

'Are we there yet?' asked Trinity from the back.

'A bit further,' said Toni.

''Kay.' Trinity settled back to doze.

They drove on in silence.

Lou could easily see how a person raised in Sligo with the fierce winds of the Atlantic whipping at their home could decide to relocate to Sicily and spend time with the other side of their family, in a place with the same craggy wild feel but a warmer climate. She wondered where in the family tree the Mulraneys of Easkey had connected with a family in Sicily. Then, her mind went back to thinking about Bob, her real father.

She felt the same pang again. She wished Dad were here, for her to talk to, now more than ever. Would he feel she was betraying him, by meeting Angelo? If Dad had wanted her to know he wasn't her biological father, wouldn't he have told her? It felt so strange to think he had withheld something so important from her – he had always been someone she knew she could count on, no matter what. She remembered Emily's tenth birthday party, when she had organised a picnic party for fifteen children on the beach.

The party had been planned so that there were beachy games that ten-year-olds liked and it was a princess party into the bargain. The only boy coming along was a sweet blond cherub called Jacob, who loved princess costumes just as much as Emily and Simone. The three of them were in the same class in school and adored playdates with each other. Jacob's mother Fifi was coming to the picnic as well as Toni and was the fifth adult.

'I'm thinking of making muffins with butterfly tops and sparkly things on them,' Fifi had said to Lou on the phone.

'Perfect,' Lou had said, thinking that was another thing she could tick off her list.

'I could whip up a batch of Rice Krispies buns as well,' Fifi added. 'I've got purple sprinkle dust as well as the gold and silver I'm using for the muffins. Jacob is really into glittery purple at the moment.'

'Really? You are amazing,' Lou had said.

Lillian was not able to come – she was in Dublin at a grand event where one of her pieces of sculpture was being unveiled – and nor was Ned until the very end.

'We must be mad,' Mim had said. 'Fifteen children, an ocean, it might rain and we've only got five adults.'

'Five is perfect – we've got my dad,' reminded Lou.

Bob Cooper, tall, white-haired and with the kindest blue eyes on the planet and a gentle face that had soothed so many distressed people in his pharmacy, was the perfect person to help.

Lou knew he'd do exactly what he'd always done at her parties: gently shepherd the children in the correct direction at all times and watch with great vigilance in case any of them wandered out too near the water. He had dressed, that day, in his normal summer outfit of soft cornflower blue linen shirt and khaki shorts with his long legs and knobbly knees peering out underneath and what he called tennis shoes on his feet.

Children loved him because he listened to them carefully and treated them with respect. He was the perfect grandfather, and always a hit with Emily's friends. Jacob, in particular, adored Bob and felt he was his grandfather, which made Emily very proud.

'Jacob has to share Granddad because my granddad is the best,' she said.

Jacob's actual grandfather, his father's father, had not seen his grandson ever since Jacob had refused to make his first Holy Communion if he wasn't allowed to wear a white fluffy dress like all his girlfriends.

'They were so angry,' Fifi had told Lou privately. 'So Jacob and I haven't seen them since and I'm not going to see them. Jacob is who he is. If he wants to wear a dress, that's his business, not theirs. They've even had the temerity to say that I made him wear dresses. As if,' Fifi said in anger.

Lillian, who liked to behave exactly as she wanted to, as an artist, was also not a fan of seeing little Jacob in princess dresses, something Lou could not understand. Standing at the beach, she had mentioned this to her father.

'Children will be who they are,' Bob said wisely. 'Your mother has a conservative side if you scratch deep enough. But with children, you just have to accept them on their terms.'

Lou had felt a passionate love for this kind man and a gratitude that he was her father. He'd stick by her no matter what, and she'd always known that.

When the rushing around from the game was over, the children threw themselves onto the rugs and began to dig into butterfly fairy cakes, tiny cheese sandwiches and orange squash.

Tired now, Bob sat down on the beach beside his daughter and accepted a cup of tea from her flask.

'Thank you,' he said. 'You forget how much energy these little people have, don't you?'

'Sadly, they'll have more energy after this because we are basically feeding them sugar.'

Her father laughed, his eyes crinkling up.

'The photos are going to be wonderful,' he said. 'Definitely lots for your photo wall.'

He brought a tiny digital camera for special occasions.

'Here's one of you with Emily,' he said.

'Sneaky. I never noticed you taking that one,' she replied, looking at the little vignette of the party: her and her ten-year-old crouched on the sand looking at a shell, oblivious to the camera.

'You made me look nice.'

'I didn't make you look anything,' her father said gently. 'You're beautiful. No extra effort was required. Silly.'

He put a big hand on her knee.

'I'm so proud of you, darling. You've got good friends and you found lovely friends for Emily as well.'

They watched Toni race after one of the smallest of the group, who had spilled her drink and was speeding to the water's edge to wash her hands. The sea was rougher now and they all knew it was important to keep a close eye on all their charges.

'I wish Toni had been able to experience this: being a parent,' said Bob sadly. 'I can understand that she didn't want it but it's so special.'

'Not all women want the whole child experience, Dad,' replied Lou. 'Look at Gloria. Never married, never had children.'

Her father had stared into the distance. 'Yes, of course,' he'd said, a little absently.

The car went over a Sicilian pothole and jerked Lou out of her reverie.

Darling Dad. She so wished she could tell him she loved him just one more time – but then, she spoke to Mim all the time and why not her father?

Love you, Dad, she said silently. Finding Angelo is like finding a piece in a puzzle, but he will be a piece and you were always much more than that.

'Are we here?' she asked, as Toni slowed down.

Lillian from her nightmare spoke to her again. *He won't like you. Why would he like you?*

If only she could quieten that hideous voice. She could feel her heart rate increase. She had to do this, but it was hard. She reached out to grab Toni's hand.

'It's going to be fine,' said Toni gently. 'If he doesn't like you, he's crazy. Because you are one of the most amazing people I know.'

She stopped the car on the side of the road and turned to look at her sister. Lou knew that if she'd pulled the car over, she was serious – Toni never stopped moving. Her sister's face was earnest, her usual wry cynicism nowhere to be seen.

'Lou – you've been a second mother to me. You've raised Emily to be the most beautiful human being in the world and Ned, for all his daftness and inability to show it, adores you. Plus your real dad, *our* real dad, loved you so much.'

Toni glanced into the back seat of the car, then reached over and smoothed an unruly strand of Lou's wild hair down.

'You're even taking care of Trinity. You are warm, wise and wonderful. But not everyone appreciates that. If they don't, that's their loss. So, if Angelo Mulraney does not appreciate you, we will leave here with our heads held high.'

'Thank you,' said Lou, feeling tearful. This maelstrom of emotions was exhausting but, despite everything, she'd never doubted her sister's love for her.

'Ready?'

Lou nodded.

Her sister re-tied her sleek blonde ponytail, glanced in the mirror and pulled out towards their destination.

Lou breathed deeply. She was going to meet her father. Toni was by her side. Whatever happened, she'd cope with it.

Villa Iascaigh was along a headland of olive trees. As they approached, they could see a stone wall and, behind it, a very simple but large seaside villa with olive trees planted all around and a beautiful path made of old stone in a mosaic pattern.

'This is definitely the right place,' said Toni, smiling. 'Iascaigh is the Irish language version of Easkey – it means "place where there are many fish".'

There was a low gate with an electric intercom, so Toni got out of the car, rang the intercom, spoke and then got back in. 'OK,' she said brightly.

'Who answered? Was it a man or a woman?' Lou leaned out.

She hated the unknown and this was all so unknown.

'Female,' said Toni, 'sounded young, maybe someone who works for him or . . .' she stopped.

A *granddaughter*, thought Lou blindly. Angelo might be there with his wife and his children and his grandchildren. Scads of relatives, all the family he'd had after he'd become her father. People who were in his life after he'd abandoned her mother.

But *had* he abandoned her mother? Had he known? The thought roamed round and round in her head. She wished she knew. He might take one look at them and send them packing. Lou wished she'd had the presence of mind to have asked Gloria more about Angelo. Gloria must have been there when he was around, after all. She'd know.

'Can we phone Gloria?' she asked Toni, who looked at her with horror.

'No!' hissed Toni. 'We're here.'

'Yes, of course,' said Lou, mind racing.

What if he didn't like her? What if he denied everything? What if he said, you're not my child? What if she looked at him and saw absolutely nothing of herself in him? And what if he looked totally different? And then what if he looked the same? What if she finally found someone who looked like her?

She was unconsciously rubbing her fingers together, and now she glanced down and looked at her own hands. Her mother's hands were big. And she had strong fingers, which were amazing when it came to her work with the metals she used in her sculpting.

Toni's hands were like Gloria and their father's: long and slender. But Lou's hands were different to everyone else's in the family. Her forefinger and her ring finger on each hand were the same length, both very long, very slim, with quite large knuckles.

Toni had always loved her sister's hands. 'They're unusual. Different,' the young Toni had said.

Maybe his hands would be like hers.

The three of them drove into the driveway, Toni parked and then they got out.

A woman of perhaps thirty opened the wooden front door and smiled at them. 'Welcome,' she said.

Lou looked her up and down curiously. The woman had very black hair, olive skin and freckles. She didn't look like Lou, but still, Lou began to do insane birthday maths. If this woman was in her thirties and she was fifty, and Angelo was . . .

'Come in,' said the woman.

'Sister?' whispered Lou to Toni out of the corner of her mouth.

Toni poked her with an elbow in return.

'Not now.'

They entered the cool house and the woman brought them to a large low room designed with Moroccan influences, with low archways, the subtle waft of air conditioning and the pale stone walls covered with giant canvases. There was no doubt that this was the home of an artist.

'Hello,' said a deep, gravelly voice and Lou stared up.

This was him. Finally.

Chapter Twenty

Angelo Mulraney was tall and thin, although he'd once clearly been a large muscular man because his shoulders were still broad. He must have been Gloria's age, Lou realised – eighty something – and he wore his age well. Despite the thinness, there was a sense of vitality in him. She looked up into his face and saw a spark of excitement in dark eyes as brown as her own. Without thinking, her hands flew to her face and she could feel her own eyes brimming up with tears.

Her father, she thought. Her biological father.

'You look like me,' she said breathlessly.

His face was masculine but he had the same high cheekbones as she did, the same full lower lip and their eyes were identical: deep set, seeing everything, the rich colour of old wood.

'You look like me,' he agreed gently in a voice that said he spoke English rarely now.

He moved forward with tanned and gnarled hands, very like her own with the large knuckles. He reached out to take Lou's hands, holding them gently, tenderly.

'It is wonderful to meet you,' he said.

Lou knew there were other people in the room, but she could barely feel them. She knew that Trinity and Toni were behind her, was aware that the woman who'd brought them into the room was there and over in a corner sat another woman, an older lady, who was watching it all.

But they were all in her peripheral vision. Angelo was really all she could see, all she could feel.

'I wondered would you ever come,' he said softly.

His words cracked open all Lou's anxieties. He was telling her that he'd known about her and that he'd wanted her to come, that he hadn't wanted to make the first move. She couldn't have said how she knew all that from just one sentence, but she knew: it was obvious from the look in his eyes and the joy on the noble old face.

'I didn't know,' she said simply. 'I only found out last Friday night. It's a lifetime of not knowing.'

'Ah,' he said, nodding. 'I have often wondered if you knew but I didn't want to insert myself into your life. I had done enough already. I didn't want to make it worse. Women do not always want the men who fathered their children to stay around, and I knew that was certainly the case with your mother. Is she dead? Is that how you found out?'

From behind Lou, Toni snorted.

'Hi,' she said, 'I'm Toni, Lou's sister. Lovely to meet you.'

Angelo reached out and shook her hand. 'So your mother is not dead?'

'No,' said Toni brightly. 'Not dead. She'd kept this a secret all our lives and we only found out on Friday at Lou's party.'

'You are fifty years old, then?' said Angelo, looking thoughtful. Lou nodded.

'Yes, it was my fiftieth,' she said.

'You don't look fifty,' said Angelo.

He spoke in the accent of a west of Ireland man and yet the odd inflection was pure Italian.

He went back to her, took her hand and led her out onto a terrace.

Toni and Trinity looked at each other as if unsure whether to follow or not.

'I will make us cold drinks,' said the young woman.

'That would be lovely,' said Toni. There was no book of etiquette on how to behave in these situations. 'Are you Angelo's daughter?'

'No, I take care of the house,' said the woman, as if this should be patently obvious.

'I am Angelo's wife, Renata,' said the lady sitting on the couch, and she rose elegantly to her feet. She had long dark hair tinged with silver and though she was possibly not as old as her husband, she walked slowly with a cane. She looked frail and Toni hurried over to her.

'No, please don't get up on our account.'

'I want to greet you properly, but I am not well.'

'I'm Trinity,' said Trinity, coming over. 'You poor thing. What's wrong with you?'

Toni glared at Trinity. What was it about the young that meant they thought they could say or ask anything?

'I have rheumatoid arthritis,' said Renata, one brown slender hand moving gracefully, many tiny gold bangles tinkling as she talked. 'It's debilitating. This is why Angelo and I have never had children.'

'Oh,' said Toni faintly. There was no answer to this. Asking questions was what she did for a living but this immediate information dump in such a tricky situation was almost too much for her.

'I've always known about your sister. But Angelo did not want to interfere. He said it wasn't his place.' The gold bangles tinkled again. Renata talked with her hands as well as with her voice.

'Was that hard?' asked Toni, sitting down beside Renata.

If Renata wanted to spill, then Toni would listen. In this scenario, she wouldn't have dreamed of asking such questions, but Trinity appeared to have started it all off, so Toni might as well find out as much as she could.

Renata seemed to consider it, turning her fine-boned face away thoughtfully.

She was stunning, Toni thought. All finely sculpted and delicate, yet strong at the same time.

'Difficult? Yes and no. We have a beautiful life here. We make art. We are both painters.' The elegant hand gestured at the walls where many eclectic canvases were hung. 'What will be will be.'

'I'd like to live like that,' said Trinity, sitting down on the couch too. Toni wished she was as laid-back as Trinity. It must be a twenty-something thing, she realised.

Cormac had once said that she was a type-A personality: always working, thinking and planning. If she was type A, then Trinity was the complete opposite. Was there a Type Z?

'You must tell me all about yourself,' announced Renata with a certain imperiousness.

'It's been wild,' said Trinity ruefully. 'My life's been crazy over the past month. A week ago, I was in Boyle in Ireland.'

'You have strange names of places in Ireland,' remarked Renata.

'They're often translated from Irish,' said Toni, determined that no hint of weirdness should attach itself to Ireland, although Lou turning up to find her real father had probably pushed the whole encounter into weird. 'Boyle possibly comes from an old Cistercian monastery and might mean pasture.'

'We have an Emo too,' said Trinity.

'It means somewhere to lie down, I think,' translated Toni.

'We do have weird names.' Trinity shrugged. 'Ireland's fabulous, Renata. We've got a place called Hospital and even a Heavenstown. Irish people are eccentric and can be dotty, my aunt Dara says, but we're a very kind people. Where else would someone like me get picked up by two lovely people like Toni and Lou just minutes after I began to hitch? They saved me because I really wasn't sure what I was going to do next.'

Really, thought Toni, looking at Trinity with interest.

'Have you been to Ireland?' Trinity went on.

'To funerals,' said Renata.

'Ah.' Toni nodded. If Renata had been to any Irish funerals, then she had the gist of the place all right, but possibly a slightly warped view because funerals were such archetypes and made people behave strangely.

'We know how to bury people,' she admitted. 'It can descend into a party, which some visitors find unusual, but at least we accept the whole birth, life, death cycle.'

'In Italy, we do too,' agreed Renata. 'You did not know each other until a week ago?'

Toni nodded. 'There's a lot to tell. It's been quite chaotic over the past week. Lou found out that our father was not her real father. And I found out that my husband had gambled away all our money.'

Trinity swivelled to look at her in astonishment.

Toni bit her lip. The words had just popped out without her even thinking. She had told nobody else apart from Lou and Cormac. The spill-your-guts thing must be catching.

Renata, however, just nodded sagely.

'Interesting times,' she remarked. 'As the Chinese say.'

'Yeah, very interesting,' Toni agreed, feeling an almost overwhelming desire to giggle.

'We're the Three Musketeers,' said Trinity, moving to sit beside Toni and patting her hand comfortingly. 'It's an adventure and we're all dealing with weird stuff.'

Toni knew that if she asked Trinity what her weird stuff was, the younger woman would probably tell her, but now was not the time. She didn't want Angelo's wife to think that his newly found daughter's family were total lunatics.

They were strong women.

Women. *Women in Business.*

A lightning bolt of an idea sparked into Toni's head. How had she forgotten about all the women she'd mentored over the years in her daily life and now in her role in WIB. She could not be the only woman who'd been bullied by Gerry Lanigan. He must have form in this regard. She would ask her women colleagues to help. They would help her. The White Older Rich Men would not win.

'Renata, I am in the middle of a work situation and I need to go outside to make a few phone calls.'

'No need to go outside,' said Renata easily. 'There's a seat and desk in the salon off this room. Help yourself to pens and paper.'

Toni smiled. She loved nothing more than fresh paper on which to make notes.

'Thank you,' she said, and rushed off, her mind buzzing.

There were no princes in life – women needed to rescue themselves and they helped each other. That was one fact Toni knew for sure.

Out on the terrace, Angelo had brought Lou down some stone steps into a beautiful circle set with stone benches and several classical busts set on ivy-covered columns. There were steps in front of them that would no doubt lead down the jagged coast to the sea.

'It's so beautiful here,' she said, 'I was thinking about your home in Easkey when I drove here and how different it was.'

'It's very different,' agreed Angelo. 'But there is the same sense of being on the edge of things. In the West, you're on the edge of Europe facing out into the Atlantic. It's a very powerful place to work. But then so is Whitehaven. Whitehaven was different. I went there to work in the studio of a painter I admired in the 1970s and that's how I met your mother.'

'I know nothing about it,' said Lou simply.

'I'll tell you some of it,' said Angelo. 'My family had links with Sicily. My grandmother came from Syracuse, and, after my time in Whitehaven, Ireland got too small, too painful for me, so I came here to paint and I've never left. Renata and I found this house many years ago and it reminds me of home in a strange way even though the water is warm and the wind is warm.' He gestured out at the sea. 'There is the same sense of staring out at the waves, knowing you're on an island – separate from everywhere else. *Allora*. Tell me about yourself.'

He sat close to her. Again, his hands found hers and he held them loosely.

He seemed to want this connection and Lou didn't find it odd that this man she'd just met was holding her hands. Bizarrely, it reminded her of her other dad. Bob was a tactile person and loved to touch people affectionately.

'My father is dead,' she said. 'I really wish he was alive because I could talk to him about this. I don't want to hurt you, but he is my real father.'

'Of course he is,' said Angelo. 'I am the one who gave you life, but he is the one who took care of that life. That's different. Very, very different. I do not want you to say I am your father, but I would be honoured to be allowed to be in your life.'

'Why didn't you come and look for me then?' Lou blurted out.

Angelo looked pained but Lou had to know. This was the crux of it all. 'I left under a cloud, you could say. Your mother and I were both with other people when we . . .' He paused. 'When we came together that time. It should never have happened. I was stupid. Your mother was angry when she found out she was pregnant. She was . . .' he paused again, 'I don't know what you know. I don't know how to tell you this. It should come from her.'

Lou found a core of strength within herself. 'My mother, and I've only just discovered this, doesn't like to deal with the truth. She could have told me a long time ago. But she chose not to. And when she did tell me, she told me in anger, when drinking.'

'Ah, the old complaint. Telling things in drink is never a good plan,' said Angelo, sighing. 'Never good. She was a complicated person when I knew her.'

'Still is,' said Lou wryly. 'If you could tell me something, I would love to know.'

Angelo looked out to sea. He looked every bit of his eighty-something years. 'It's a difficult story,' he said, 'and I did not expect to be the one telling you. It starts with a woman I was seeing in Whitehaven . . .'

Chapter Twenty-one

'I was in love with her and then, your mother came along—'

He looked out to sea and sighed.

'There was a solstice party. Whitehaven was full of artists then and we liked to shock, you know, so we had a party that was a little wild on the beach. The woman I loved didn't come but your mother did and we came together. I regret it so much because of those we hurt, but never, never, because of you. She told me, eventually, but not for some time. At first, I was sad because we had both betrayed people we loved.

'I am so sorry for my actions,' he said. 'I knew your mother was engaged to your father, I take the blame. I hurt . . .' he paused. 'I hurt the other woman very badly too. I broke her heart. She could not forgive me.'

Lou felt pity for the other unknown woman in the triangle, but had most pity for her father. He'd had to live with Lillian's betrayal.

'Two people were involved,' said Lou. 'It wasn't just you. My mother was engaged at the time.'

'He was a good man, your father.'

Lou nodded, feeling a strange mixture of emotions. 'You're my father, biologically, and yet not my father. That was Bob,' she said. She didn't want to hurt this lovely man who, despite his tanned skin and great mane of thick wiry grey hair, was clearly older than her mother, eighty maybe. But she wanted to be truthful with him.

Truth mattered, she realised. Not always absolute truth. Not 'no, I hate that skirt you're wearing' truth. But the essential truths. This new relationship, whatever it might be, even just an acquaintance, would not be built on the foundation of a lie the way Lou felt her relationship with her mother was.

Lillian had lied – often lied, Lou was now realising. And Lou had let her, sometimes even made it easy for her. But Lou would not take that anymore. When she went home, it would be different.

'When did my mother tell you she was pregnant?'

'Two months later, perhaps? I had gone back to my home, and she wrote. The baby was certainly mine because she . . .' He looked pained. 'Your father thought they should wait till their wedding night.'

Lou shuddered. This was worse than she'd thought. She hoped that Lillian had been drinking wine on the beach and had blindly fallen into Angelo's arms.

'She was distraught,' Angelo said. 'They were different times. Different rules. You cannot imagine it because you live in a world of contraception and choice but then – I said I would come to her, but she wrote to tell me no, that your father would be your father. I was not to come near her.'

Lou could quite easily imagine her mother making such a final decision: once Bob was on her side, Angelo could go.

'I left Ireland because I fell into a long depression,' Angelo went on. 'In those days, treatment was limited. The cure was not easy. It is better now—'

'You have depression?' asked Lou quietly.

He nodded. 'You know it?'

'Yes. Yes.' For the first time ever, Lou laughed at the thought of her depression. 'I thought it was just me, that there was something inherently wrong with me because nobody else in the family has this, but you do too!'

Strangely, it felt a joyful realisation in that moment. Finally, a family where she wasn't the strange or different one.

'I have friends who have nobody in their family with this,' said Angelo. 'It is not like hair colour or the shape of your nose. It is mysterious but, yes, it runs in my family.'

Lou sat on the stone seat so she was leaning beside him, her discovered birth father. The man she seemed to share so much with.

'Where did you go then?' she asked. 'What happened?'

'I came here. You know,' he smiled wryly at her, 'how it doesn't matter how much the sun shines when you are sinking into the depths? Great art often comes from depression. Michelangelo suffered this way: "I live wearied by stupendous labours and beset by a thousand anxieties",' he said.

'A thousand anxieties,' Lou repeated. 'I can relate to that.'

'It's not an easy thing to carry, but I have found that a good listener helps. Not your family. A therapist. To know you are not alone helps, too.'

'I felt that I was different, broken really, by having depression,' Lou said. 'Nobody else in my family has it.'

'They do now,' said Angelo simply. 'I see it as an extra something. Not broken. It's like a scar that pains us sometimes. There's no point in wishing that the scar was gone because we cannot wish away such things, but we take care of the scar. We rub it with oils to heal it. You're not broken when you are depressed. You need to find the oil that will heal you. Be it talking or swimming or . . .' he gestured around him, 'living here. And we come out of the depths, I find. Always.'

Sometimes, Lou had felt her heart physically hurt her chest: Dr Google explained that anxiety could give one chest pains caused by stress-related contracting muscles. As Angelo talked, she felt those self-same muscles soften a little, as if in a hot bath.

'Thank you for this,' she said earnestly. Her hands found his again and they sat quietly holding hands. 'Thank you for all this.'

'Let's walk a little,' he said, letting go and patting her hand. 'My old hips seize up if I do not move and we have a lot to talk about.'

An hour later, they went back inside and Angelo asked would they like to go to a little restaurant he knew nearby.

'I want to bring some of my friends,' he said, happily.

293

Lou, feeling serene after her walk on the beach, calm after the most amazing discussion with Angelo, nodded.

'I want them to meet you,' Angelo was saying. 'My precious new family. Please. Who knows when we will see each other again.'

'Yes,' said Renata, 'Please come. And you know you're always welcome here.'

'I want to give you a painting too,' said Angelo. 'You must pick.'

'I don't know if I could bring one home on the plane,' said Lou.

'No,' Angelo said, smiling, 'I will send it, but you must pick. And you too,' he said to Toni. 'You can be my little step-daughter, as well as you,' he added to Trinity.

He patted her affectionately on the cheek. 'You're glowing, child.'

She blushed. 'I can't take anything,' she said hurriedly. 'It would be wrong. I'm not related—'

'Tish,' said Angelo. 'Think of it as Irish and Sicilian generosity.'

The restaurant was in Avola, ten minutes away. They followed Angelo's car, and when they arrived at the restaurant there were two large round tables packed with people of all ages who embraced Angelo and Renata and then threw their arms around Lou, Toni and Trinity. Toni thought to herself that he must have contacted half of Sicily. She laughed. She could see the similarities with Ireland.

'She is beautiful.'

'They are all beautiful.'

'She looks like you.'

294

'Are you married?'

'Angelo! You dark horse! Trust you to have these beauties as your daughters!'

Soon the three were sitting down, and Toni was doing her best to avoid wine, holding her hand over her glass and saying no endlessly as the waiters seemed determined to provide the party with maximum gaiety.

'I don't think it's a good idea,' she said. 'I have to drive us back.'

'But you can stay the night with us,' said Renata.

'I don't know . . .'

'Yes, you must stay the night.' Renata was imperious. 'I insist. We can get taxis back to the villa.'

'It is done.'

The owner of the restaurant came over and was introduced to Lou, Toni and Trinity. There was so much excitement over their presence that people outside the restaurant kept looking in as if wondering who these people were.

'It's like being famous!' said Trinity laughing, drinking delicious Italian fizzy orange juice. 'I feel as if I'm an influencer or something.'

They spent the afternoon and early evening in the restaurant with Angelo introducing them to everyone, explaining that Lou was his beautiful daughter from Ireland.

'She is my daughter, but she has another father, who brought her up,' he said. 'This is important to know.'

Toni glanced at Lou. Her sister looked at peace and nodded assent.

'I'm OK,' she mouthed to Toni.

'Angelo, thank you,' she said out loud. 'I don't want you to feel that you're not my father.'

'I am the man who gave you life, but the person who brings you up, he is your father. And we revere him.'

Everyone raised their glasses for a toast. There were lots of toasts. Every part of the meal and everyone at both tables was toasted and eventually, Toni was feeling no pain, and was thinking that she was having quite the best time of her life.

A tall, lean man in an indigo shirt with several inches of tanned smooth muscular chest revealed had been monopolising her attention for the past hour. His name was Matteo, he was a relative of Renata's and was a sculptor. At this, Toni had looked at him warily.

'The sculptors I know can be very tricky,' she said. 'My mother is a sculptor.'

Matteo had laughed out loud at this, a deep throaty laugh, 'How many do you know?'

'Enough,' she said. 'Enough not to trust them.'

'But you can trust me,' he said, then resting a finger briefly on the delicate bone on her wrist. 'You have lovely skin,' he said, 'and the fine muscles in your arm would be wonderful to sculpt.'

'Stop petting me,' she said.

'I can't,' he said. 'I am, how would you say, very attracted to you.'

Toni laughed. 'You're at least . . .' she looked at him critically, 'fifteen years younger than me,' she said.

'So?' said Matteo, raising his hands. 'What is wrong with this?'

'I'm in my forties,' Toni went on. 'Women in their forties do not go out with young men.'

Matteo's eyes, almost black, glittered. His gaze was steady.

'Why not?' he demanded. 'Is there a rule for this?'

Slightly high on both his admiration and on the many messages she'd been getting from her businesswomen friends on the behaviour of Gerry Lanigan, Toni grinned. She was getting enough information on Mr Lanigan to bury him. There were many strong women in her life: not just her business colleagues but her sister, Gloria, Renata, lovely Trinity.

'There is a rule,' she deadpanned.

'Ha! You are funny,' Matteo said. 'We do not count years in Italy the way they do in other places. What is wrong with Irish women that they do not like younger men? I am not so much younger. I am thirty-one. What difference does it make? Men see women younger than them in other countries. In Italy, we see no problem with a difference in age for men or women.'

'You're right,' said Toni, 'but I still have to keep my hands off you. I can't explain. Well, I could, but it would take all night. Custom, social mores and the way older women are viewed when they have younger dates – as a talking point and as a way of looking at differing standards between men and women, it's a hot topic. '

She looked thoughtfully at Matteo.

'I sometimes do this thing where I sum up people in three words,' she added.

Matteo's eyes glittered.

He was lethally gorgeous, she thought.

'I haven't been doing it much because my judgement appears to have been so wrong lately that I no longer trust myself or my own three-word descriptions but for you . . .'

Matteo leaned closer. He'd be on her lap soon.

'I can think of three for you,' he murmured. 'Sexy, sensual and beautiful.'

Toni started laughing, then fanned herself with the cocktail menu. Was it hot or was it just her?

'It's generally more broad than that. But,' she grinned. 'That all suits you too. Sexy, sensual and very handsome.'

Matteo beamed. 'I know,' he said happily.

Somehow, when the party broke up, Toni found herself handing over the keys of the car to the restaurant owner, who said he would park it behind the restaurant.

'Taxis back to the villa,' said Angelo, who did not appear to have drunk anything and yet was not driving home. The entire party went en masse back to the Villa Iascaigh.

'Isn't this lovely?' sighed Lou, sitting in the people-carrier taxi beside Toni. 'Today has been so strange. I don't understand how it is that I feel a part of this. Angelo is going to do up a family tree for me to show me who everyone is because I've been introduced to so many people and I haven't a clue.'

Toni searched her sister's face and smiled. She felt as though Lou was being genuine, not just being nice.

'I will do it for you,' said Renata, who was sitting on the other side of Toni. 'Angelo promise to do these things but he is no good. He only does painting. Everything else he does not do.'

Everyone laughed.

'You're OK?' Toni asked Lou as they walked back into the house.

'Wonderful,' said Lou, leaning into her sister. 'He told me the most amazing story about how he was in love with this other woman and then he met Lillian at a solstice party and it just happened.'

'Go Lillian,' said Toni drily. 'I bet Angelo was gorgeous in his day. Was this in Whitehaven? And what about Dad?'

'It was in Whitehaven. Angelo was there painting and the other woman wasn't around and well, he didn't spill the beans but it sounds as if I was conceived at a party on Etain beach. Lillian told Angelo when she was pregnant and then she said Dad was going to marry her and that he was to go away and never come back.'

'Dad was amazing,' reflected Toni. 'He did adore Mum.'

'He was a saint,' said Lou and then giggled with the effect of the wine.

'Total saint,' said Toni, joining in.

'I wonder who the other woman was? Gloria would know.'

Toni shook her head. 'Gloria's far too discreet to ever tell. She kept this secret for fifty years.'

At the villa, it was convivial and relaxed. The guests spilled from the living room on to the terrace, talking and laughing. Toni spotted Lou in the middle of a small group, just calmly sipping her drink, not running around looking after people.

Trinity was sitting talking to a couple of younger women and they were all laughing and staring at their phones, discussing playlists and songs they liked.

'How are you doing?' said Toni, feeling responsible for having brought Trinity into this gathering.

'Brilliant! Fabiola and Daria went on a gap year to New Zealand and they're telling me about it. I can't wait to go!' Trinity's face suddenly clouded. 'Although, I probably won't be able to,' she added.

'Nonsense,' said Toni. 'You're young. This is the time to do it!'

She didn't entirely understand Trinity.

On one hand, the girl was clearly clever and sharp. Yet she sometimes got lost in thought, staring off as if her world was about to end.

There was a mystery there, Toni thought. Lou had been right. But solving other people's mysteries was exhausting and Toni still hadn't solved her own.

Lou might have found her father and her mojo when it came to not fixing other people, but Toni still had a few things to sort.

It was hard to think of financial ruin and career suicide here. The villa was beautiful, the people were so friendly, and it was so lovely that Lou was happy.

Toni walked down towards the beach feeling a little bit tipsy and yet very relaxed and happy. Angelo and his family had taken her darling Lou to their heart. It was wonderful.

She gazed out at the sea, thinking how easy it would be just to stay here, to not go home and face the music. There was a lot of music to face, the music of how much money had been lost, the music of how she'd messed up her job. She couldn't think about it. Today had been a wonderful break from the notifications on her phone, the endless worry.

'Here you are, *cuore mio*,' said a voice.

She turned. Matteo was there with two glasses. 'I don't think I could drink anymore,' she said. 'I'm not much of a drinker, to be honest. I'll get a dreadful hangover and I'm too old for that.'

'No, this is water,' he said. 'Water to make us feel awake again. We must hydrate for energy.'

'Oh, good plan.'

They sat on the beach, took their shoes off and let their toes wriggle into the sand. Matteo's feet were like the rest of him, tanned, elegant, beautiful. Toni looked at him dispassionately and thought that if she wanted to have an affair with a younger man, if she wanted to be a cougar, then he really was a rather fine specimen. But that wasn't the sort of person she was. Definitely no.

'So, *cuore mio*,' said Matteo, 'I believe you are a famous person in Ireland, Trinity tells me, and your husband is an actor.'

Toni looked at him and, in that moment, a decision pinged into her brain.

'My soon to be ex-husband,' she said, trying out the words for the first time.

There really was no other way round it. If Oliver had merely gambled away all their money, she could have possibly borne it. If he'd come to her and told her he was a gambling addict, and could she help him, she could have borne that too. But the fraud, the signing her name on documents, the deliberate deceit. She could never forgive that.

He could have slept with every woman she knew in triplicate and she would have got over it more quickly than this deceit. He'd gone out of his way to lie to her. Was there any coming back from that?

Another decision to make.

'You are getting divorced?' said Matteo.

'Yes,' said Toni, 'I am. I think I am. I haven't decided. I'm on a break from thinking about hard stuff. What is this *cuore mio* . . . ?'

He grinned wolfishly. 'It means, my love.'

Toni howled. 'You fall in love very quickly, Matteo.'

'Yes,' he murmured, leaning closer and beginning to nibble her earlobe, which she suddenly found the most erotic thing in the whole world. 'I do.'

'I'm not that sort of woman, Matteo,' said Toni, stretching her neck so he had access to the whole silky column.

His mouth moved downwards to trail kisses along her neck and onto the curve of her collarbone. 'I understand.'

'I've been with the same man for seventeen years.'

'Lucky man.'

'He has no idea how lucky he is. Or was,' Toni corrected herself. 'I'm rusty.'

Matteo paused. 'Rusty?'

'Out of practice,' Toni corrected.

'Ah.'

The nibbling continued. 'It is like the bicycle,' said Matteo.

'Bike?' Toni sat up straight.

'We don't forget how to make love,' he said, 'in the same way we do not forget how to pedal the bicycle.'

Toni sank back down. Just a few kisses.

Trinity, Fabiola and Daria were watching YouTube on a big TV in the den off the kitchen. Fabiola was obsessed with pandas and watched endless footage of them being raised in special compounds.

'We will go after this,' Fabiola said as they started another twenty-minute video.

'Are you staying?'

Trinity nodded.

'They are your aunts?'

Trinity thought it might be too difficult to explain. She didn't entirely understand it herself. 'Yes,' she said.

When the girls had gone, she found Renata to say goodbye.

'You cannot go,' Renata commanded.

Trinity put her hands into the older woman's. 'I must,' she said. 'I've outstayed my welcome,' she said gravely. 'I know what I've got to do now. I needed time.'

Renata nodded. Trinity was impressed with the way the other woman accepted her decision. 'You go back to Syracuse?'

Trinity nodded.

'I will organise a ride for you. You do not pay. You are young and the young never have money.'

An hour and a half later, Trinity was back in the apartment, which felt empty without Lou and Toni. She'd sent both of them a text message to say she was going back so they wouldn't be worried.

Then she picked up her phone and dialled Ferdie's number.

She'd decided. She couldn't tell anyone else, especially not Dara and Marc, in case it upset their honeymoon, and she didn't want to discuss it with Pete, not yet. Ferdie knew the whole story.

Lou woke in the morning in a beautiful pale green room which looked out onto the sparkling Mediterranean. It had been a wonderful evening, although Toni had disappeared off with Matteo at some point and Trinity had gone unexpectedly back to the apartment.

Late in the evening, Lou had been wandering round the downstairs looking for her sister, while the party raged on all over the large villa.

She'd asked Renata, who'd replied, 'I think she went somewhere with Matteo.'

'Matteo?'

'It is fine,' said Renata. 'He is a good boy. He will take care of her.'

'But Toni is a bit fragile at the moment,' Lou had said worriedly.

'I will find him,' Renata had said.

She snapped her fingers and one of the younger guests came over. After a moment of talking, the guest went off and then returned to report back.

'They are sitting on the back terrace. They are good,' said Renata. 'He will take care of her. I sent the message that Angelo will kill him if he hurts her.'

Lou had laughed. 'Thank you for looking after Trinity,' she added.

'She has come to some decision, I think,' Renata said. 'This makes sense to you?'

'Yes and no,' said Lou. 'I don't know what is worrying her, but I will find out.'

Renata patted Lou on her soft cheek. 'You are very maternal, my dear. What a beautiful way to be. It is a gift. And you have given me a gift – you have made my Angelo very happy.'

Now, Lou reached for her phone, but its tiny percentage of battery had died during the night, so she got up, showered and found that someone had left out toiletries and some clothes, if Lou wanted to change into them.

She left the bedroom and found Renata sitting on the balcony with Angelo having breakfast. Angelo was drinking coffee. He gave her a smile but didn't try to fuss over her.

'Good morning,' said Lou. 'Have either of you seen Toni?'

A smile played at the corner of Angelo's mouth as he shook his head.

'Men,' said Renata, shrugging. 'You did not tell me about your man. Your daughter, yes, but not your husband.'

'Ned,' said Lou.

'He did not want to come on this trip?'

Renata looked so knowing as she said this that Lou wondered if she had a crystal ball and could see into people's souls.

'He might have, but we left without him. He forgot to buy me anything for my birthday,' she added, thinking that as she explained it, the whole thing sounded very childlike.

'That's not all—' she began.

'Of course it is not all,' said Renata with gravity. 'It is a symbol of other things. Those symbols are important because they show respect for you as a person. Otherwise, you are merely furniture. In the house to be ignored until one is needed. Marriage must have respect. No contempt, no lack of respect. He is a good man or no?'

'A good man,' said Lou without hesitation.

'Then it is simple. Explain that you want respect. If he does not understand, he is either too stupid to be married to you or too cruel.'

Lou laughed.

'Renata is very firm on what matters in life,' said Angelo.

'But I am right,' his wife reminded him.

'You are,' agreed Lou.

'You will explain this to him?'

Lou nodded. 'I will.'

Toni moved in the bed. It was really incredibly comfortable and she stretched out luxuriantly. She felt quite wonderful. Sometimes when she woke, her lower back ached, but this morning it felt so limber, as if she'd had a full body massage. She had, she realised, remembering warm, firm hands massaging her, of Matteo telling her he'd thought of studying physiotherapy and of how working with clay gave one very strong hands.

She sat bolt upright in the bed. Matteo was lying beside her fast asleep. Beautiful even asleep. She'd slept with him. She hadn't been drunk. She'd agreed. She'd kissed him. She'd *wanted* him. 'Toni, *amore*,' said a voice.

'Matteo, I don't know what to say,' Toni said. 'I've never done anything like this. I've only had four lovers in my life.'

Why was she explaining this? He was not the keeper of her personal code of conduct. But it felt engrained into her, in some infuriating way: women felt obligated to apologise for having sex with the abandon that men could.

'Only four?' Matteo said, raising an eyebrow. 'That is not enough. Now that you have had me, we must do this again. Come back to bed. It is early.'

Toni looked at her phone which was lying on the floor. It was nine o'clock. Nine o'clock in the morning and she was in a strange person's house with a strange man in bed.

'No,' she said firmly, taking back control. She would not apologise for going to bed with him. She did not need to empty her thoughts out of her head in apology. They'd had sex. It had been great. But it was a one-time gig.

'This will not be happening again, Matteo. Is this your bedroom or my bedroom?'

'It is *our* bedroom, *amore.*'

She laughed. He was fabulous but his mind was on one track – a dirt track.

She blew him a kiss, grabbed her clothes, raced into the bathroom, locked the door in case Matteo came in and slowed her down, and showered. She let water run over her face, washing off make-up and sun cream and any stray feelings of having done the wrong thing.

She came out fully dressed. Matteo was still lying in bed, eyeing her up, his fabulously muscled chest on view. 'You're not coming back to bed?'

'No,' she said, admiring him. 'Thank you, but no. It was lovely knowing you.'

'I will see you again,' he said.

Toni shook her head, smiled and shut the door quietly behind her. As soon as she turned around, of course, she bumped into Lou.

'There you are,' said Lou. 'I was so worried. I couldn't find you. What have you been up to?'

Her sister looked rested but was wearing an unfamiliar T-shirt, her hair wet too.

'Sssh!' Toni said, gripping Lou's arm and walking her back towards the stairs. 'You won't believe what I've done.'

'Slept with that good-looking guy?' said Lou.

Toni nodded. 'Yes!'

'He was nice?'

'Gorgeous,' said Toni. 'Utterly gorgeous. He should set up a company to get women back on their feet after a shock but . . .' She paused in spite of herself. 'I am having an attack of the guilts. I'm still married to Oliver.'

'Oliver who has bankrupted you?'

'Yes, that Oliver. But surely it's better to get rid of one man before clambering into bed with another.' Toni sighed. 'I don't know how to feel. I won't say it was a mistake, but . . .'

'It's complicated,' Lou finished for her.

They met up with Angelo and Renata in the kitchen and Toni grabbed a quick espresso before they left.

At the door, Angelo hugged his daughter tightly.

'I will see you again before you go?' he asked.

'Yes,' she said. 'I'd love that.'

'I have something for you.'

He gave her a tissue paper package and she opened it to reveal a heavy gold necklace, like a lariat with an exquisite profile beautifully carved in gold at the knot of the lariat.

'It is Athena, one of the Sicilian protector goddesses,' he said. 'It is very old and she will protect you, no?'

'I love it,' said Lou and Angelo put it around her neck. The heavy goddess sat on her chest, already feeling warm and settled there.

'I love it,' she said again.

Chapter Twenty-two

Toni's thumb hovered over Oliver's name in her phone contacts. If she called him, it would be the first time they had spoken since that night. The time in Ortigia meant the burning rage had left her. But the memory of their last moments together had been so fraught, so angry.

'How could you do this to me?' she'd raged. 'How?'

'I didn't mean to . . .' he began. 'I never meant to. I love you, Toni.'

'You can't love me,' she'd hissed back at him. 'If you loved me, you wouldn't have done this. You've betrayed me. It would be easier if you'd fucked another woman.'

He flinched at this.

'I would never do that to you, Toni,' he said fervently.

'Spare me your self-righteous bullshit. This is a worse betrayal. You fucked me over. We have nothing, you have ruined our marriage. How could I ever trust you again?'

He had nothing to say to that, and his silence had made her even angrier.

'Get out of my sight!' she'd shouted.

And he'd left.

What was she supposed to say to him now? She couldn't imagine living with him, after everything. She couldn't imagine living without him.

Toni pressed the button. He answered the phone so slowly that she thought he wouldn't.

'Toni?'

'Hello, Oliver,' she said calmly. 'We need to talk.'

'I've been phoning and phoning, leaving messages. Why haven't you got back to me?'

It was odd, she thought: Oliver sounded different. Not the strong, commanding actor she'd fallen in love with but instead a man who'd been weak and who'd let her down. Now that she'd seen him this way, she couldn't unsee it.

'Toni, I'm in bits,' he said. 'I'm afraid to answer the phone in case it's the money lender and I went into the casino the other night—'

'You went *back*?' she asked.

'I thought if I kept the stakes low, I could recoup some of it,' her husband said earnestly.

Toni listened, wondering where the man she'd married and lived with for so long was gone. Nobody hearing Oliver would think that this was the fêted Shakespearean actor, famous around the world. In his place was a man who was lost in a world of addiction, consumed by gambling, sure that it would only take one last win to make it all right.

She wondered was there a version of AL Anon for the families of gamblers. She knew from journalistic stories that families of addicts had to let go, that nobody could make that choice to give up using, drinking, gambling apart from the person themselves.

'Oliver, you need rehab,' she said finally. 'A residential place where you can deal with this. You've said it yourself: you're addicted to gambling—'

'No!' he said brightly. 'I wasn't myself when I said that. I was upset. It was a momentary lapse. I've got it under control, Toni. But I need you with me. If I have you, I can control it. I can get the money back. And nobody's going to attack me for not paying up if I'm living with you, are they? You know every cop in the country, you're protected.'

He sounded so sure of himself that Toni held the phone away from her in shock.

'Oliver! Are you living in cloud cuckoo land? Nobody can say they're protected when thugs come after them. Just because I'm well known and have Gardai friends means nothing.'

She felt disgusted. Not only had he lost everything but he was banking on her contacts to keep him safe. Was this why he wanted to stay with her?

Oliver's world meant he was insulated from the reality of life and how money lenders really worked. If he got beaten up, it might make headlines, but he'd still be in hospital. The truth would come out too.

She couldn't live like that – watching over her shoulder all the time.

Tough love, she thought, from her reading of the gambling websites. Oliver had to face his own truths. She could not do it for him, she could not enable him.

'You need to move out,' she said shakily, 'Oliver, I can't be a part of this. I'm coming home on Monday, please don't be there when I do. I'm going to have to let accountants look at our affairs—'

'Please don't,' he begged.

'Because you defrauded me?' she asked quietly. 'Forged my signature?'

There was a long, long silence after this. In the quiet space, she could hear him let out a shuddering breath. Then Oliver hung up.

Toni closed her eyes. Lou was right: she was fed up with things that weren't destroying her but were supposed to make her stronger. To hell with that. Why couldn't life be easy?

Her phone pinged suddenly with an email.

She opened it and smiled. Another email confirming what she knew: that Gerry Lanigan was a bully. But there was more information about sexual harassment cases in his company. This was coming from several sources. Bullying of one sort or another was all part of his business. Women were tired of it, it seemed.

Toni felt the thrill of finding a good story. Only this one could save her career.

Trinity walked along beside Lou through the ancient streets, the sun hot on their skin.

'I was worried when you left to come back,' said Lou gently. 'Is everything all right?'

'Fine,' said Trinity quickly. *Too quickly*, Lou thought.

'I'd love some ice cream,' Trinity said. 'I'm yearning for something really sweet.'

'No problem,' said Lou.

There were little shops selling ice cream everywhere and they queued up at one with Trinity looking at the pistachio flavour which she adored.

They were next in line when she grabbed Lou and gasped. 'Lou. Look. In English – it says the gelato is unpasteurised. I can't eat it.'

'Why?' said Lou, without thinking.

Trinity's beautiful Celtic eyes were huge as she stared at Lou.

'Because I'm pregnant, Lou! You can't have unpasteurised food when you're pregnant. Has it all been unpasteurised?'

Lou's mouth fell open. Suddenly, it all made sense.

Trinity didn't drink. She didn't touch coffee. She hadn't had any shellfish at dinner even though she said she loved scallops. She'd avoided any of the beautiful soft cheeses that Toni had bought for the fridge in the apartment. Lou had begun to suspect some kind of eating disorder. The truth was much simpler.

'I'm such an idiot! I never thought of that,' Lou said finally, and she put her arms around the young woman. 'Oh, my darling, Trinity, that's . . . you're happy, aren't you?' She paused. Not all twenty-three-year-olds were delighted to be pregnant, but Trinity had been doing all the things women did when they were continuing with a pregnancy, hadn't she?

'It was a shock,' Trinity admitted. 'We hadn't planned it. Pete and I hadn't ever talked about kids, like ever.'

'You're young – people don't tend to talk about that stuff at first,' Lou pointed out.

'Also, I knew I was pregnant at my aunt Dara's wedding and I couldn't tell her. She'd been unhappy when I took a gap year out after college so I could live with Pete in Boyle.'

'Your aunt Dara?'

'She brought me up,' said Trinity. 'I'm sorry. I haven't told you and Toni anything. It's not fair because I know all about you and you know nothing about me but it's all so crazy. I was mulling it over in my head and I didn't want to tell anyone because saying it out loud would make it real.'

'I understand that,' said Lou. 'You don't owe us your life story.'

'But I wanted to tell you. My mum and dad had me when they were very young and they weren't able to cope. They should never have had me – at least, that's what my aunt Dara has always said. Not that she wanted me not to be born, because she's like my mom. But they were young and silly, then they got married and it all fell apart.'

Just, thought Lou, *like the story of Angelo and Lillian.* She wondered if Lillian would have gone ahead and married Bob if she hadn't been pregnant with Angelo's baby.

'So you see when I went off with Pete to live with him, Dara was upset because I said I was taking a gap year after college. It wasn't really a gap year, it was a year where Pete wanted to spend some time with a friend of his who lived in Boyle and he had a recording studio. They were in a band—'

'A band?' said Lou, thinking that she'd heard this story before.

'Yeah, a band. It's like he's stayed seventeen, even though he's the same age as me,' said Trinity. 'When I got pregnant, I thought he'd be so vibed. We've been together for four years and I thought we were together forever. But I said I'd done a pregnancy test, it was positive and he got all wrathy.'

'Wrathy?'

'Upset,' translated Trinity. 'I think he was scared.'

'Understandable,' said Lou, being measured. She didn't want to diss Pete if he turned out to be Trinity's one true love. 'But not very grown up.'

'Exactly. I had to deal with it,' Trinity pointed out. 'I was pregnant. I had to figure out if I wanted a baby or an abortion. One or the other. I had to do the adulting, all by myself.'

She breathed heavily as if she might cry.

'It must have been so scary,' Lou said gently, 'and Pete sounds immature.'

Trinity rolled her eyes. 'That is not the word. He is a KID. I waited a couple of days hoping he'd come round but he was still being the kid. I have a friend in Boyle, Ferdie. He's been so good to me. He knew I was thinking of leaving. So I left my stuff with him and left the apartment and hitched. That's where you met me.'

'Have you told Dara where you are?'

Trinity shook her head.

'Dara got married a month ago, and she's gone off on her honeymoon. She deserves it. She's taken care of me all my life. She's been my mom. My mom and dad are hippies. Basically, they do a lot of dope, hang around festivals and they've checked out of life. I don't know how I'm going to tell Dara. She loves me but it will be like history doing déjà vu. She wanted so much more for me than to be pregnant and alone at my age. She was so thrilled when I got my degree because she thought it meant I was going to have a good life.'

'You're going to have the baby, then,' Lou guessed.

'I think so, yes,' said Trinity. 'I've been thinking of nothing else since I've been here, mostly because of you. The way you talk about Emily . . . You're so close. You're part of her life, but she has her own life, you love her so much, no matter what. You're such a great mum. And I know, from hearing you and Toni and – sorry for overhearing, but your own mum sounds like a bit of a pain and . . . that's made me worry less about repeating history.'

Lou felt her eyes fill with tears.

Trinity, young and apparently naïve, was so wise. She could see what Lou hadn't.

Lost in the fantasy that Lillian was a perfect mother, Lou had assumed that she'd learned how to parent her beloved Emily from seeing her own mother do it.

But she knew now that Lillian manipulated people with guilt, martyrdom and tantrums. Lou had to earn her love and affection, while Lou was the sort of parent who gave love freely, unconditionally. This sudden knowledge felt both shocking and somehow freeing, too. Lou was not a failure. Sure, she liked fixing people, but she could pull back on that. She was a good mother, a good sister and a good wife. Ned might need to pull his socks up, though.

'This trip made me see that I wanted to be a mum,' Trinity finished. 'I mean, I know it's not going to be easy having a baby and trying to do a job. But I can, can't I?' she asked, sounding young again.

'You're very patient, kind and calm,' said Lou cautiously. 'They're some of the main things you need as a mother. Obviously, money helps. We're going home on Monday – what are you going to do?'

'I don't know.'

Lou weighed up her fixing people tendencies and then decided that sometimes, she had to get involved.

'If it was Emily, I'd want to know,' she said. 'You're keeping the baby, so it would be great to have a support system in place. Tell Dara. If she's angry, you can consider what to do next. But she'll find out eventually.'

'You think?'

'I think.'

'I suppose you're right,' Trinity added. 'I thought I'd have more fun time running around the world but . . .' She gently padded her tiny belly. 'This little person comes first. That's the great thing about going away, isn't it? It puts your life back home in perspective.'

Emily had left a voicemail again. Ned was getting to dread the voicemails because, while he loved hearing his daughter's voice, he didn't like the faintly irritated air Emily had. He was her father. He'd bathed her, put her to bed, changed her nappy. She had absolutely no right to be telling him how to live his life like this.

But she wasn't telling him how to live his life, he knew – which was what made it so very annoying. She was being sensible, thoughtful, polite, and he felt entirely in the wrong, which was not an experience he liked. That had been the great thing about being married to Lou: she never made him feel as if he was in the wrong.

His brother Tommy was always in trouble because his wife, Siobhan, felt that a husband's place was in the wrong. Tommy sometimes said Siobhan was one of those women who just needed some PVC clothing, stilettos and a whip to set herself up as a dominatrix specialising in husbands who needed yelling at.

Siobhan's Den of Pain: Ned could imagine it. Siobhan screaming and belting harmless men because of minor infractions. He shivered with horror.

Emily wasn't screaming at him. She was just reminding him to talk to her mother.

Grimly, Ned looked in the fridge. There was now almost nothing in it, some tired-looking cheese and wilted salad. When Lou went away usually, which didn't happen that often because he was the one who went away most to conferences, she cooked things for him. The fridge would be full of carefully labelled meals. She bought him the beers he liked, and nice wine.

Feeling guilty again, Ned closed the fridge, aware that the house was dull and unlived in since his wife had gone. Lou always made it homey. She brought flowers from work and kept all their many plants alive. She lit candles and dusted surfaces, wiped down the kitchen counters in a way he could never mimic. How did she get it so shiny?

Even the garden was listless without her. If Lou had been here, she'd have been out on Saturday or Sunday weeding, tidying and tying up trailing plants, moving the plants on the veranda to make sure they all thrived.

Ned found himself walking around the house a little aimlessly. He ended up in their bathroom, standing at her side of the vanity unit. Some of her creams and ointments were there. Nothing much. She wasn't vain. She had a night cream that had lavender in it, he remembered.

He could have bought her something with lavender in it for her birthday.

He went into the bedroom. Lou's books were in a small bookcase beside the bed. There were framed photographs on the bookcase hiding some of the books. There were pictures of him and Emily, pictures of Toni, Lillian, Bob, Gloria and a lovely shot of Mim and Simone.

He sat down and lifted one of the framed pictures. There were none of Lou herself, just the people she loved. Behind the photos were books that Ned realised he'd never really examined: books on anxiety and depression.

He pulled one out; it was about changing the inner voice. *What inner voice?* he wondered in bewilderment. He read the foreword and it began to make sense. The inner voice was one that criticised endlessly, a voice in a person's head that derailed them.

He thought at that moment about Lou's struggle with depression that time, and how Mim had helped her. He had done very little, he realised guiltily. He'd been there for her but not in a really practical way: he'd said, 'I'm here for you,' but had he done anything? What did saying

'I'm here for you' mean in any real sense? They were just words, he realised.

Lou had called her antidepressant medication her 'anti-mad tablets'. She was funny when she talked about those things. But it wasn't really funny, Ned reflected. She'd been trying to share it with him and he, uncomfortable around sharing emotional stuff, had blandly smiled and not helped at all.

He loved Lou, adored her, but he was hopeless at the touchy, feely stuff. Yet that wasn't an adequate excuse – he spent days lecturing students and teaching them how to extend their learning. That didn't just apply to engineering. It applied to life.

Lou's words on the phone flickered in his head;

The problem is that you didn't think you needed to . . . It's not about the price of a gift, it's about you making the effort to get one.

The memory of her words made him guilty, so guilty he didn't know what to do or how to fix things. He loved Lou but he felt helpless at fixing what he'd messed up. He put the book on the inner voice back carefully and then made their bed. He hadn't been bothering with housework up to now, but he smoothed down the covers and plumped the pillows on Lou's side the way she liked it.

He would nip out to the shops, grab some groceries, put them in the fridge and then go to college. That way there'd be some food when he came home that night.

He parked the car and was walking down Main Street thinking that he might buy steak from the butchers. He wasn't a bad cook although he was out of practice, had become lazy. He only ever did very simple things: steak, grilled fish, omelettes.

He was so busy thinking about his repertoire that he nearly bumped into someone.

'Excuse me,' he muttered and looked up to find Martin, Mim's husband.

Ned floundered instantly. He'd seen a lot of Martin when Mim was alive but much less so since she'd died. Lou handled all that. Lou handled everything, didn't she?

'How are you?' said Ned awkwardly, realising in that instant that he didn't want to know. He couldn't handle talking to Martin because he never had the slightest idea what to say.

'Grand,' said Martin easily.

He'd put on weight. Comfort eating since his wife died? Age?

'Er . . . I didn't see you at Lou's fiftieth,' said Ned desperately.

How would he have seen Martin? Wasn't he paralytic on Heart Starters. And would Martin have come anyway? Going to the fiftieth birthday party of your wife's closest friend would just remind you that your wife was no longer around, would never be fifty.

'No, I couldn't come. Was it a good night?' said Martin.

Ned thought wildly of the night. It had been chaos.

'It was interesting. Lillian kicked off a bit.'

'She was always wild,' said Martin. 'A colourful character, isn't she?'

Ned nodded. 'She sort of lost the run of herself with a few drinks, though,' he said, because Martin, no matter how closeted his life was now, would surely hear about it.

'Drink does take some people like that,' agreed Martin.

Ned was stuck now. He couldn't ask about Simone's presence at the party because she was his daughter's best friend and he should have known if she was there.

'Simone said it was enjoyable,' Martin went on.

If that had been her description, then Simone ought to apply for the secret service, as she was world class at keeping secrets, Ned decided.

'She's talking about going abroad when she's qualified,' Martin was saying. 'It's going to be difficult without her. I've come to rely on her.'

'That's tough,' said Ned.

If Simone left . . . Martin would have nobody.

Mim had been a truly amazing woman. A beautiful person and an amazing friend. What would his life be like if Lou was gone, Ned thought suddenly. If she decided she'd had enough.

Ned stared at Martin. He wanted to ask things, but he didn't know how – this wasn't the sort of thing he liked to talk about. And yet, the words were determined to squeeze themselves out of his mouth.

'How do you cope?' he found himself asking.

Martin did not fall over in shock at the question.

'It's difficult sometimes. My friends say I should start dating again. I can't imagine seeing anyone else. Mim was everything to me – we were supposed to be forever always,' he said. 'At the end, Mim made me promise that I would go and find someone else,' he added, almost brightly.

'She was full of plans in those last days in the hospital. It was the drugs, I used to say to her. She said myself and Simone should go on holiday. Not sell the house or make any big decisions in the first year, because apparently that's a bad time to do it. But me finding another woman was on the list.'

'Really?' said Ned hopelessly.

'Yep. She wanted me to be happy. She was amazing. She loved your Lou. Loved her like a sister.'

'I know,' agreed Ned.

'How is Lou?'

'She's gone away to Sicily with Toni.'

Ned was about to lie and say it was a pre-arranged girls' thing, but he could not lie to a man whose wife had died of cancer. It was as if some lasso of truth was wrapped around him.

'At the party the other night, she had a bit of a shock,' he said. 'Lillian got pissed and told Lou that Bob wasn't her father, that another fella was her father. And I forgot to give her a present.'

Putting it like that, he understood in the coldest, clearest terms why his wife had left the country.

'For her fiftieth?' said Martin.

'Yes,' Ned said, feeling worse and worse. 'She left with Toni the next day to find her real father. Proper father.' He ran his fingers through his hair. 'I don't know what the word is. But anyway, he lives in Sicily. So they've gone there to find him.'

'Why didn't you go?'

324

'She won't talk to me. She was angry with me because I was taking her for granted, just like her mother. I've really screwed everything up. I might have lost Lou by being a moron.'

Martin looked at him for a few moments, then said quietly, 'If I was you, I'd try and sort things out. Because you don't know what you've lost until it's gone. You *think* you know, but you don't really. During those last few months with Mim, I became more and more aware of who she was. Her dying left a crater in our lives that no asteroid could make if it hit the earth. Nothing will ever fill that hole again. So, yeah, talk to Lou. See you around, Ned.'

Ned stood in the street and tried to remember what shop he'd planned to go into. He felt entirely thrown. Martin said you didn't know what you'd lost until it was gone, and he was *right*.

Ned had to fix this. But – how?

The luggage seemed heavier as they dragged it down the steps and put it into the car.

'What did we buy?' asked Toni, panting.

'Bits and bobs for everyone,' said Lou happily.

Her soft skin was tanned, she was wearing a new coral-coloured sundress that clung to her sinuously and the golden necklace from Angelo hung around her neck. She looked different, Toni thought admiringly. Not like the Lou from the night of her fiftieth, but like a totally different woman. It wasn't the clothes or the tan: it was the essence of her, as if Sicily had been there when Lou entered a new chapter in her life and the island had opened up a whole different world to her.

Lou even walked differently now. She had a sexy lilt to her step, as if she'd embraced the Mediterranean side of her heritage with gusto, no longer muttering that she had to lose half a stone but instead, enjoying her body, glorying in it. Italian men called to her as they walked through the town and, whereas once Lou would not have noticed, now she laughed at them, and flicked her gaze away. *I am woman – hear me roar*, Toni thought.

Even Trinity had luggage now. Toni and Lou had brought her to a store that sold pregnancy clothes and got her elegant Italian jeans with a soft baby pouch. The store had a cushion that customers could put under their clothes to simulate the look of pregnancy with various outfits. Trinity had wanted to buy the cushion.

'I want to see my baby bump so much,' she'd confided to them.

Lou had laughed. 'You will soon enough,' she said.

The drive to the airport was speedy and they left the car windows down so they could smell the sea one last time.

'We're coming back here,' said Lou. 'I'm bringing Emily here.'

'But not your mother or Ned?' said Trinity cautiously.

'Ned can come if he plays his cards right,' said Lou. 'The jury's still out on that one. And as for our mother—'

The sisters laughed.

'I'd like to see Renata do battle with Lillian, though,' Toni admitted. 'That would be worth the price of the plane ticket.'

326

'Mum's not that bad,' said Lou automatically.

Toni patted her sister's leg. 'You truly are the milk of human kindness,' she said.

They sat on the plane in the same positions as before: Trinity at the window, Lou in the middle and Toni on the aisle.

A woman walking down the aisle from the toilets recognised her: Toni could see the signs, could hear the woman whisper, 'You'll never guess who's on this flight!' to her friends a few seats back.

Yeah, thought Toni: *Toni Cooper, wife of disgraced actor Oliver Elliott and woman who used to be the most likely to succeed.*

Then she shook herself.

Lou had grown in stature in Sicily while she had merely run away. It was time to stop running and fix things. She reached under the seat in front, hauled up her handbag and found her ever-present notebook. Lou wasn't the only one who made lists.

Career – options: she wrote, and began to think.

Toni Cooper was not going down without a fight. She now had ammunition on Mr Lanigan to make his bullying threats go away. She needed to reconsider her work life. It depended on her being able to see the person behind the facade, and if she hadn't been able to see Oliver properly, then was she in the right job? Did she need to take a break from television? From the sort of life she'd lived before? And from Oliver?

* * *

There was a crowd waiting for them at the airport.

'Mum!' yelled Emily as soon as she spotted the threesome.

She rushed past the other people at Arrivals and grabbed her mother.

'I've missed you!'

Lou sank into the embrace. She was so very lucky. She had Emily.

'Lou, I am so sorry.' There was Ned beside their daughter, and Lou could swear he had tears in his eyes.

Ned – crying? She hadn't seen Ned cry since they'd mistakenly watched *Marley and Me* on the TV.

He had a bouquet of flowers in his arms, a bouquet so big that his credit card must have winced when it went through the machine.

'I am so sorry,' he was saying. 'I didn't know how to support you or anything, and I'm a hopeless husband, but I'll be better.'

Lou stared at him in amazement. She had not expected this.

Her plan had been to have a sit-down with her husband and tell him, calmly and like a grown-up, that she did not want to be in a marriage where she gave everything and received nothing. That there had to be balance, that he had to make an effort.

Ned had scuppered this lovely, well-thought-out plan by arriving at the airport with flowers and apology written all over him.

'It's my fault,' he went on, as if he couldn't get the words out fast enough. 'I take you for granted, I let you do everything in our marriage – and look at Martin! He lost Mim and what would I do if I lost you? I am so sorry, Lou. Please forgive me.'

'Where is Ned and what have you done with him?' she joked, to hide how jolted she was.

'I'm serious,' said Ned. His eyes sought hers. 'Please?'

For a moment, Lou couldn't speak. She just nodded and then Ned was hugging her and someone had taken the giant bouquet from him so he could put both arms around her.

They were both crying then.

'I've missed you,' Ned said.

'I think I've missed you for longer,' said Lou meaningfully.

'You're right.' He was rueful. 'It won't happen again. Promise.'

Finally. He let her go and she was able to hug Emily again. 'You look fabulous, Mum,' said Emily, standing back. 'Totally amazing.'

'Amazing,' agreed Simone, who was now holding the flowers.

'Oh darling.' Lou hugged Mim's beautiful daughter.

'Evan came too, but he had to stay in the car,' said Emily. 'He's taking care of something.'

Before Lou had a chance to ask what, Toni had arrived beside them and they were all hugging again, then they had to meet Ferdie, a tall boy with wildly peroxided hair who was dressed exquisitely fashionably.

'I love your show,' Ferdie said to Toni, touching her hair thoughtfully. 'I can totally see you as a brunette. Do you mind me saying that?'

Toni laughed. 'I'm always up for a total life change,' she said.

Ferdie carted Trinity and her bags off to his car and Toni grabbed her case to head off to hers.

'Do you want us to come home with you?' Lou asked her sister before she left.

Toni shook her head. 'No,' she said. 'I've got an agency coming in tomorrow to pack everything up into storage, before it leaves the premises by other means. I'll be sorting my stuff out tonight. I need to face it myself. Love you, talk later.'

'We've got a surprise for you,' said Emily as they took the lift up to the third floor of the airport car park.

'Not more flowers,' said Ned, who was holding his wife's hand as well as pulling her suitcase.

The surprises were being taken care of by Emily's boyfriend Evan: two small and slightly outraged dogs who obviously felt that the car was not big enough for them.

'They ate all the biscuits,' said Evan as Lou stared in amazement.

'This is Boo,' said Emily proudly, holding up a small grey dog who had a bit of whippet in her parentage along with some terrier. 'And this is Lola.'

Lola, all terrier, white and caramel, threw herself out of the car and onto Lou and began to lick her new mistress soundly.

'She licks a lot,' said Emily.

'My jeans are totally wet,' agreed Evan, displaying one leg where his trousers had a big wet patch from canine licking. 'Does that mean she thinks I'm her puppy?'

Emily ignored him to continue the tale of the two dogs.

'Gloria's neighbour has been trying to re-home them, but they had to go together. We've had them for twenty-four hours and they own the house already.'

'Our house?' asked Lou, just to be sure.

'Our house,' said Ned. 'Welcome home, love.'

Chapter Twenty-three

'I can't believe you even *want* to see Lillian,' Emily said, outraged. 'I mean, Granny.'

'Granny?'

'Yeah.' Emily smiled. 'She's Granny now – and she *hates* it.'

Lou laughed. It was evening and they had just arrived home, and after letting the two dogs tear around the garden and then feeding them, Lou had decided it was time to drop in on her mother.

'This is the longest I've ever gone without speaking to her,' she said. 'It feels weird.'

But it wasn't just that. After everything that had happened, Lou needed to see Lillian – to show herself that she really had changed. Her mother was the litmus test for the rest of her life: if she could stop Lillian from walking all over her, then nobody else would ever be able to.

For the first time in nearly two weeks, Lou made the drive up to Valclusa, letting herself in as she always did

– although she'd had to clamber over a lot of sand to get in, which was new. She found herself taking in all the familiar sights as if she'd been away for years rather than days. Nothing had changed, except it now looked as if every glass in the premises was stacked in the sink.

'Hello, sweetie,' said Lillian.

For a brief second, Lillian looked her older daughter up and down, taking in the tanned body and the very un-Lou-like bare legs and curvy body in the knee-length coral T-shirt dress, which fell beguilingly off one rounded shoulder. Lou was still wearing her 1950s movie star sunglasses, her glossy sexy lipstick and the heavy Athena necklace Angelo had given her.

'You look different,' said Lillian in a voice that might have been saying *I don't like it.*

Lou smiled tightly and said, 'Do I?'

Inwardly, she marvelled at this new version of herself who was able to speak to her mother in a normal way.

Don't be a people pleaser, she told herself. *Don't be co-dependent.*

Lillian began to walk into the living room.

'Drink?' she said.

Normally her mother never offered her a drink.

'I'm driving,' said Lou.

Lillian poured herself something, then settled into the couch. 'Goodness, I need a holiday. I can't think when I was last away. Very clever of you and Toni to think of doing it . . .'

Her words left a pause as big as a sinkhole and Lou fell right into it.

'It didn't start as a holiday,' she began. 'It started as something completely different.'

She paused, finding herself unable to carry on. No matter how much work she had done on herself, this new way of being with her mother was very strange and she wasn't yet ready for speaking her mind. Saying 'it started because you dropped a bombshell into my fiftieth birthday party' was going to take some time.

'I understand,' soothed Lillian. 'Sometimes one needs time out. I felt the same way after I heard about the Kennedy Art Prize. I mean, to have one's life's work ripped away like that, it was almost a death. I thought I could have a heart attack. My heart has been very dicky lately. I did go to Dr Ali and he says I should see a cardiologist.'

'Lillian!' Shocked, Lou sat down beside her mother, all thoughts of behaving differently gone.

'I didn't want you to worry, sweetie,' Lillian went on. 'I'm quite ready to go if it's my time.'

'Lillian, Mum . . . Please don't talk like that,' said Lou, genuinely horrified. 'Heart issues can be so well managed . . .'

Mim's father had had all manner of heart issues and open-heart surgery and he was doing incredibly well now. Imagine Lillian having open-heart surgery – Lou felt her own heart flutter with the anxiety of it. How could she possibly have kept her mother at arm's length when this was going on? She must have been mad; Lillian was her *mother*, the person she had looked after all her life. Lou felt the guilt flood her and all plans to remain coolly indifferent went out the window.

'No, really, I am fine,' said Lillian, beginning to sound anything but fine. 'I'm fine, sweetie. All I need is a little rest. A holiday. It was such a lovely notion to go out to Sicily. Clever old you and Toni.'

Another blast of guilt hit Lou. Sicily. Should she have gone . . . ?

'Tell me exactly what the issue is,' she said.

'Dr Ali suggested some tablets. I wish you'd been with me . . .' said Lillian with a little sigh. 'One does need someone in these very difficult traumatic moments in doctor's surgeries because one forgets things.'

'Of course you do,' said Lou, pressing her hands.

Had Lillian got thin? She anxiously scanned her mother and there didn't appear to be anything different, but she was pale around the eyes . . . was that it? Of course, everyone in Sicily had looked in the rudest of health thanks to the glow of the sun and their tanned skin.

'Have you been eating properly? I know I didn't leave anything for you when I went. I normally leave meals in your freezer.'

Lou's guiltometer was reading very high now.

'It has been a bit tricky,' admitted Lillian.

Lou noticed that she was wearing a very beautiful golden cuff bracelet on one arm. It was new, Lou was sure.

'Lillian, that's so pretty,' she said, pleased to have something to praise.

'A gift,' said Lillian quickly. 'Peadar and the boys thought I needed cheering up after the art prize. It was so difficult. I know you understand, sweetie.'

'Of course I do,' said Lou.

In the back of her head, the Barking Dog reared and began to howl. What else had Lou missed by being away? Emily seemed to be doing terribly well, but if there had been an emergency Lou wouldn't have been there and Ned, well Ned managed things on his own, but she was his wife and work . . . Blossom. Oh gosh, a slush of fear and anxiety washed over her. Blossom . . . how could she have walked out? What disasters might have happened in her absence? That was completely insane. What had she done?

'I don't suppose you could cook something for me, sweetie?' asked her mother. Lou dragged herself out of the morass of anxieties, guilt and roads not taken, to concentrate on her mother.

'Of course,' she replied automatically. It had all felt so different earlier. She knew what she was going to say. She was going to say that if she had known about Angelo earlier, when Dad had been alive, she'd have been able to talk to him and reassure him that he was her real father. That would have helped her so much. She was going to say that how Lillian had broken the news was so hurtful. She was going to tell her that their relationship was going to change.

But with her mother sitting beside her, clearly worried sick about her health, things were different.

'Let's not talk about any of that, Lillian,' she said. 'The important thing is that you're here and you can have a little break and we can talk about your health.'

Now was not the time to say anything about Angelo, Sicily or changing their relationship. There was time enough for that when Lillian was better.

Toni had been interviewed by people who could talk for five minutes without ever asking a question. She was extremely good at waiting for the actual question to be asked instead of many random comments, where the reporter was just hoping she might jump in with a sound bite.

Elaine played no such games.

'This morning, we have Toni Cooper with us and Toni, host of *Tonight with Toni,* is on to discuss the fallout of a panel interview on a radio show where she clashed with one of the country's top executives and which has left some people questioning her position here. Good morning, Toni. Tell us exactly what happened.'

No waffle there, Toni thought, grinning at Elaine.

'Good morning, Elaine,' she began. 'It's great to be here to be able to put the record straight.' Without waiting for any prompts, she dived in: 'One of my roles, one for which I receive no salary, is as chair of Women in Business, which is an organisation set up to help women achieve similar success in the workplace to their male counterparts. As listeners know, women still don't have equal pay for equal jobs in a lot of the world and WIB is trying to redress that in Ireland. We're not a lobby group; instead, we mentor women and use the WIB as a networking tool to help women who are trying to gain foothold in positions of power in businesses. As part of that work, we share information on pay rates in companies that are proactively hiring women and those that are not proactively hiring women.'

'That does call into question the issue of workplace privacy. Some companies don't want salaries revealed,' said Elaine.

'You are entitled to reveal your own salary,' explained Toni. 'Not anybody else's. However, if we take it that there are more males in executive positions in companies, then we're in a system where a company can say women are paid equally to their male counterparts, but the reality is that we're not playing rounds of golf with the boys, we're not going to international rugby matches, we're not going on' – and she couldn't help herself here – 'team-building weeks in Donegal, where we stay out for a night to prove how hard we are.'

Across from her, Elaine smiled.

'We're women, running businesses, juggling lots of things, fighting against the glass ceiling every day,' said Toni. 'So, Women in Business is our men's club. It wasn't set up as an organisation to libel anyone or to slander anyone. It's about mentoring, advancing women in industry. It's about sharing information. It's about networking. It's a resource for women in the world of business.'

'So what went wrong on the day you were interviewed on Epsilon Radio?'

'What went wrong,' said Toni, 'was that I was on a panel with a CEO who felt that WIB was not needed. This person's opinion was that women were getting just as many managerial jobs and were paid the same amount as men. That's not true, not generally, and not in this particular business.'

'But how did you know that?' said Elaine.

'I had researched the company,' said Toni.

It was the only safe way to put it. She'd spent so long going over this with Cormac and his damage limitation people on the phone the night before that she had a headache trying to remember the right words to use.

'So I disagreed with the CEO.'

'And then what happened?'

'He insisted that his company was very female friendly. I disagreed with this analysis. We had a row. The next day, he confronted me in the car park of the TV station as I was leaving work after recording my show. I have to admit to being a little anxious when he confronted me because I was alone and felt vulnerable. He was very angry. And I said things I shouldn't have said.'

'Do you regret this?'

'Yes, of course I regret it. I regret that I allowed my professionalism to desert me,' said Toni, 'I regret that I lashed out – I should know better. But I was dealing with a personal matter at the time, and I lost my head.'

'This CEO, who refused to come on the radio this morning and take part in the show, is very unhappy about the treatment, and says that you targeted his business particularly.'

'I didn't,' Toni said simply. 'I was put on the show with him, and I did my research in advance. It could have been anyone. He has not, however, taken any legal action,' Toni pointed out.

'True,' said Elaine, picking up a piece of paper. 'His comment is that he wants to move on from this.'

Toni smiled inwardly. Gerry Lanigan absolutely wanted to move on from this. He had so many fires he was trying to put out right now that he had neither the time nor the heart to go after Toni Cooper. The three sexual harassment claims his company was facing were keeping him busy. Toni's female friends had told her about the phone recording of the Lanigan's Christmas party where another executive tried to assault two separate female employees in the women's loo. The company had tried to hush it up, but it hadn't worked. Said executive was currently assisting the police with their enquiries and Women in Business were going to commission a report on sexual harassment in the workplace and look at how often such cases were actually reported because women were afraid of the repercussions for their careers.

'I regret my comments in the car park, but his way of approaching me was not right – and it is part of the problem. Luckily, I work in an industry where women can rise to the top and have big careers, but there are many other women for whom this is not the case. When company bosses say Women in Business is too "woke" and isn't required, when they pretend there are already enough women executives, that women are already being paid equally, they are shutting down the conversation and they are part of the problem.'

Toni knew she was on thin ice here.

'We need organisations like Women in Business to help women thrive. WIB can take the place of the golf club, the rugby outing, whatever place or outing where guys go and network. WIB can also allow women to share real experiences of working in male-dominated office spaces – that includes sexual harassment.'

Elaine said nothing about this statement. Before they'd gone on-air, they'd discussed the libel implications of saying anything more and had erred on the side of discretion. Nobody wanted to be sued.

Instead she remarked: 'You obviously have a lot of plans for the organisation, Toni?'

Toni took a deep breath. 'The thing is, I'm not the correct person to be mentoring for Women in Business anymore,' she said. 'I believe in personal responsibility, and in losing my cool in this encounter, I feel I have failed the women I work for. The staff need to be beyond reproach, so I am standing down from my position.'

'You're standing down? When did you make this decision?' asked Elaine.

'I took some time out, I went to Sicily with my sister,' said Toni, thinking that 'I went to Sicily with my sister,' was a very limp phrase for what had been an enormous life-changing event on so many levels for both of them.

'There have been changes in my personal life and I decided that it would be wrong of me to continue in the job when I had made such a professional error by allowing myself to shout at someone. That is not the way to change how women in business are viewed. Plus, if the discussion is about me, then it takes the focus off what we do. So I am resigning.'

It was the right thing to do, she knew. The revelations she'd uncovered about Lanigan and his bullying behaviour would soon emerge and would result in more controversy. Toni would inevitably be asked about him, and she firmly believed that if the focus was on her personally instead of her organisation, then she would be failing the charity.

'Well, you heard it here first, folks,' Elaine said. 'And your TV show?'

'Oh, I'll still be doing that,' said Toni, without a moment's hesitation.

Gloria walked down the street with Sugar trotting neatly along beside her. Behind her house was a square where stately oaks grew, small children played on seesaws and swings, and people with dogs let them race among the shrubs sniffing and running after each other.

Gloria hadn't wanted to adopt little Sugar five years ago. The small dog was rescued from the side of the road, covered with mud. 'I'm too old for a dog,' she'd said. 'I always said I'd never have another dog after Benjy died. It's not fair to them if you can't walk them, and look at me – I'm a crock!'

But after one night with the delicate creature snuggled against her, Gloria had known that Sugar was never going anywhere else.

'Are you tired?' she asked once she and Sugar completed their second stately walk around the square.

Sugar looked loyally up at her mistress as if to say yes. They were both a bit physically fragile, Gloria thought, which meant they suited each other perfectly.

'Aunt Gloria,' said a voice, and Gloria turned to see her niece walking towards her. 'I hoped I'd catch you. Hello, Sugar.' Lou bent and petted the little dog and then hugged her aunt.

'Welcome back,' said Gloria. 'How was it?'

Her tone was cautious. She wasn't really sure she wanted to know. Lou had messaged her from Sicily to say she'd met Angelo.

He's a wonderful person but he's not Dad, Lou had written, which had made Gloria so relieved.

She missed her brother, Bob, and she'd felt so protective of his memory, knowing Lou was meeting Angelo. Thank goodness Lou seemed to understand the difference between a biological father and a present one.

'Wonderful. I've a lot to tell you,' Lou said.

'It's a beautiful day. We could sit in the garden and have tea?' said Gloria. 'Or are you rushing? I know a person always has lots to do when they get back.'

'No, I came to see you and tell you everything,' said Lou happily.

Her aunt looked tired, Lou thought, and once they were back in the big house, she insisted that Gloria sit in the garden while she prepared the tea tray, with the pale blue enamel teapot her aunt had used since the year dot.

Gloria's back garden was mainly paved now, great stone slabs with raised beds here and there so that her aunt, who could no longer bend easily, could tend her flowers and herbs. Looking out the window, she saw Gloria shiver as a breeze rippled around the garden and called out: 'I'll get you a cardigan.'

Lou ran upstairs, mentally listing all the things she had to do that day: she planned to redo her CV and start looking for a new job. Not that she'd resigned from the old one, but she was working her way up to that. She was popping into her mother's later too, to do some tidying.

Lillian, true to form, hadn't so much as lifted a duster while Lou had been away and the surfaces were all sticky with drink rings. Lou itched to get it all clean again.

She hurried upstairs, up to Gloria's bedroom, which was, as ever, perfectly tidy. There was a tiny white orchid in a crimson pot beside the bed where Gloria's stack of books and her reading glasses lay.

Cardigans, thought Lou, looking around for one. Gloria normally had a couple of soft shawls and one of her cardigans on a chair by her dressing table. There. Lou picked up a soft grey one and was about to hurry out of the room when she stopped.

The painting . . .

She turned to look over the bed again. She'd glanced at the painting that had hung for years over Gloria's bed when she'd entered the room but, in the way of things a person had seen forever, she'd barely noticed it.

Gloria had lots of old pictures in the house: mainly ones from her parents' day but lots of pretty watercolours and amateur oils, things she'd bought at various Whitehaven events over the years. The painting over the bed was different, though: a large canvas in an old-fashioned white frame, it was clearly a scene of the Atlantic with a beach and a peak in the foreground, crashing wild waves in the distance.

It had been there ever since Lou could remember. It was easily recognisable as Whitehaven Beach and Mermaid's Peak. But now, with new eyes, Lou could recognise the style. The confident brushstrokes, the way he painted clouds and the wild drift of the ocean. The painting over Gloria's bed had been painted by Angelo Mulraney.

Late May 1973

Gloria Cooper freewheeled down the road on her bike, enjoying the sense of the sun on her skin and the wind blowing back her fair hair. She had a few days' holiday and she was going to head down to the beach and find somewhere nice to sit and sketch, maybe even play with her watercolours. On the beach in the right place, nobody would notice her or come up to see her work. Having a degree in fine art meant a person was very aware of their inadequacies as an artist and Gloria was in no doubt as to her abilities.

'I know I'm not very good,' she always said to her brother, Bob. 'But I love it.'

Bob had looked at her thoughtfully. 'It's not important that we're good at everything,' he said. 'It's important that you enjoy doing it. I'm not very good at dancing and Lillian tells me that often enough,' he said ruefully. 'But I enjoy doing it. I love music.'

Gloria smiled. She adored her older brother. He was so kind and gentle. She worried about him. In particular, she worried about him and Lillian Foyle because Lillian was cut from far harsher cloth than Bob Cooper.

Lillian had come to Whitehaven the year before and had caught gentle Bob Cooper's eye immediately. She'd been to teacher training college but was taking time out and working in the local hotel as a chambermaid, so she could build up her portfolio. She still had hopes of a career in art.

Gloria had been astonished at Bob's new girlfriend. This girl, with her mini skirt, vertiginous white platform boots, and a bolshie attitude that nobody could ignore, was very different from Bob's normal type. Until now, Bob had dated girls he'd known for years, but he'd never found the perfect person, he said.

'It's very difficult,' Lillian told both Bob and Gloria, the first time he introduced her to his sister. 'The art world's all male-oriented. Nobody's interested in women artists. Feminism hasn't hit Ireland yet,' she said angrily.

Feminism *had* hit Ireland, but in the seventies the country still had a way to go. Still Lillian didn't seem that pushed about feminism for other women. Only for herself. When Gloria tried to interest her in raising funds locally for the unmarried mothers' group that Gloria volunteered for in Dublin, Lillian had said she was too busy.

'I don't have time to help girls who get knocked up,' she said with a sniff. 'I'm either being worked to the bone by that old cow in the hotel or I'm trying to paint. You can't do other things when you want to be a painter. You have to give everything to it.'

Gloria had marvelled that her brother could like this selfish girl. Feminism meant helping women who were marginalised, and none were so marginalised as those unmarried pregnant women who were treated with callous disrespect by so many in society.

But there was no point discussing this with Bob. He was besotted and Gloria could see why. Lillian was very beautiful. Sex appeal rippled out of her like it was a scent that could be touched. She had that certain something that meant people didn't notice her selfishness. Instead, people looked at her and bathed in her charisma. Gloria, who'd never been blessed with such a thing, felt a hint of envy towards the younger woman. What would it be like to make men follow her with their eyes?

Sighing, because there was no point dwelling on what was never going to be, Gloria brought her bike right down to the beach to keep it safe. It was a battered old black thing and nobody would ever want to steal it. Still, you could never tell. Whitehaven was a tourist town and people took the maddest things. Only the other day someone had stolen the teapot sign that hung above Mrs Rafferty's tea shop. Gloria had come upon her standing outside in the street staring up at where the overhanging blue painted metal sign used to hang.

'Why would they do it?' said a bewildered Mrs Rafferty. 'I don't understand it. Why, in the name of all that is holy, would anyone want a giant teapot? It's riddled with rust. It's no use to anyone.'

Gloria suspected it might have something to do with too much drink the night before and people having a wager on what insane things they could steal but said nothing.

'Do you want me to call into the police station and get the sergeant over?'

'I suppose,' said Mrs Rafferty thoughtfully. 'I might get a guard dog. What do you think?'

Gloria wheeled her bike along the sand. She waved to people, petted the odd dog and looked a bit nervously at a few people who were swimming quite far out. The currents were strong in Whitehaven Bay. Just because it looked calm and beautiful didn't mean that it was safe.

She'd keep an eye on them. Father always said she had an overdeveloped social conscience.

'Pot kettle black!' Gloria liked to say.

The town doctor had no right to be talking about overdeveloped social consciences because Dr Risteard Cooper had dedicated his life to public service.

Finally, she found the right spot. There was a little curve in the beach where there was a handy flat rock which meant she could sit down, fix a portable easel and if she worked quickly enough, could get both the boats and the beautiful midday sun. It was hidden so that nobody could creep in behind her and look at her work unless she wanted them to. She set up quickly and was soon speedily sketching her seascape. An hour later, it was almost done. You had to work fast with watercolours because everything changed so quickly, and long experience of Whitehaven meant that Gloria knew the rain could come down at any minute. Summer showers could come at speed and go again as quickly but they played havoc with watercolour paper.

She was just kneeling down and packing away her paints when a low, deep voice said: 'I like it.'

Gloria whirled around.

'Hello,' she said, taken aback. 'You crept up on me, Angelo. It is Angelo, isn't it?' she said.

'Yes,' he said, 'and you're Gloria, Bob's sister.'

Gloria coloured. She had no problem talking to people anywhere. But talking to men, or men she found attractive, was very difficult. She knew that she and Bob were reserved. They'd been brought up that way. But Bob had somehow got past this when he'd fallen for Lillian. Or perhaps it had just been that Lillian knew what she wanted and had pushed past that reserve.

Lillian spent a lot of time at the artists' centre where Angelo was working. The young artists spent a lot of time together, drinking pints in Maguire's Lounge and Bar, with the female artists scandalising old Mr Maguire by ordering pints of stout instead of just glasses. Gloria had seen Angelo with them.

'I like your seascape,' he said now.

'It's not great,' said Gloria self-critically.

'Perhaps not amazing from the point of view of precision,' Angelo said, being truthful. 'But you have captured the sense of the place, the wildness, the beauty and the light. That's what I love about here. The light. There's a clarity of the light that comes in from the Atlantic and then, when the clouds move in, I love that lowering darkness it casts over the beach.'

Gloria never knew why but at that moment, she felt as if she was falling in love.

It was ridiculous. She was Gloria Cooper, spinster of this parish, a woman who had lived on earth for thirty-four years without falling for any man and without any man falling for her. She didn't do this type of thing. But in that moment, she wanted nothing more than for Angelo to sit down beside her on her flat rock, talk to her and touch her face. Perhaps the way Bob touched Lillian's face.

He might ask her out and . . .

'I was coming to paint, but do you think you might come for a little lunch with me?' said Angelo, gazing at her. She couldn't quite place his accent. It was west of Ireland with a hint of something else.

'Where are you from?' she asked suddenly, and then was a little shocked at her brazenness. She was behaving differently with this man.

'I am one quarter Sicilian, which is different from Italy, better,' said Angelo. 'My mother's mother was from Sicily, and she lived with us.'

'That explains it,' said Gloria delightedly.

Gloria had never known a summer like it. During the week she went to work in Dublin, working in the college library and sometimes giving extra lessons on art history to college students. At weekends, Angelo came to fetch her in his battered old Volkswagen and they drove down to Whitehaven together. Those trips were magical. They'd have a picnic in a field. Sometimes they'd find a pub along the road when they were nearly home, where Gloria would drink a gin and tonic while Angelo made do with shandy. 'I can drive,' she said to him.

'No, I shall look after you, *carissima*.'

She loved when he spoke to her in Italian. He was fluent because his grandmother had taught him.

'The others didn't want to learn but I'm a painter and every painter wants to go to Italy, right?'

At weekends, they'd sometimes spend a whole day in bed in the tiny cottage he was renting from one of the farmers outside the town. Gloria loved those times in bed, feeling Angelo's hands on her skin. She felt beautiful in his arms, in a way she'd never felt before.

'You make me feel loved, beautiful,' she said one day, sitting on the bed with Angelo behind her, both of them naked, staring into the mirror, his arms around her caressing her naked shoulder and her naked breasts.

'I would like to paint you like this,' he said.

'Angelo, I think my parents would have a heart attack.'

'They must know what we are doing here, *carissima*,' he said.

'I think we're operating on a don't-know-don't-tell basis,' Gloria said wisely. 'Both of my parents are pragmatists. They have to be after years of serving the town. But still, they would prefer to see me . . .' She stopped. She'd been about to say *married*. The revolution of the sixties and seventies had been slow to reach Whitehaven. Her parents would not acknowledge that their daughter was sleeping with a man she wasn't married to.

But Angelo had never mentioned marriage or indeed anything long term. Gloria accepted this. She knew he wanted to travel the world and paint, and she thought that perhaps she might go with him. It was 1973. It was a different world. People did not have to get married to live together. People had children outside wedlock. All these things were possible.

Angelo, being an artist, was not bound by the constraints of the time that she thought about. He made sketches of her and Gloria loved the way he portrayed her body. She had never thought herself in any way beautiful. And yet, in Angelo's eyes, with his fingers flying over the page, sketching her, she was.

Of course it could not last. She'd known.

Lillian had noticed. Lillian who had her own man and yet wanted everyone's eyes on her, as if she could only exist when she was the brightest star in the firmament, the one everyone gazed at.

'I see you spending a lot of time with Angelo,' she said silkily one evening at the Coopers' as they sat around the table for dinner. She and Mrs Cooper had been discussing bridesmaids' dresses for Bob and Lillian's forthcoming wedding. It was to be the end of August, a Saturday, and then they were going to travel to Paris for their honeymoon.

Lillian's plans were for a wedding the like of which Whitehaven had never seen. Her own family, the Foyles, had been pushed into having the wedding in Whitehaven. Lillian had no desire to marry in the small country town in Kerry that she came from. She had no respect for her decent farming parents and preferred to get married from the doctor's house in Whitehaven.

Lillian's grand plans included an expensive and sleekly beautiful wedding gown for herself.

Gloria knew that the bridesmaids, of which she was one, were to be clad in pouffy dresses in giant florals so as not to take from the beauty of the bride.

'Angelo's a very interesting person,' went on Lillian.

'Yes, he is,' said Gloria politely.

She had tried her best, but she found it hard to get on well with Lillian. No matter how many overtures of friendship she made, Lillian wasn't interested in being nice to her future sister-in-law. It was as if Lillian was jealous of her, Gloria thought, and as to why that was, Gloria had no idea.

'He's very talented,' said Lillian idly. 'Lots of sex appeal.'

Dr Cooper looked over his spectacles at his future daughter-in-law as if to say, 'We do not discuss such things at this dinner table,' but Lillian, characteristically, didn't appear to notice the froideur.

'He has such a way with the ladies,' she went on as if wildly amused at such a thought. 'We had some tourists in the studio the other day. He was all over them. It's the Italian thing. He's half-Italian or something. They can't help themselves. They'll flirt with anyone.'

'A quarter Italian,' said Gloria and regretted it instantly.

'Really? So you do know him well,' Lillian said.

Gloria flushed, and under the table she clenched one fist so that her fingernails stuck into her palms. She would not respond. Lillian was taunting her.

The summer solstice was when it all went wrong. A group of people decided to hold a celebration out at Etain beach, a tiny curve of white sands named for the Celtic goddess of the summer solstice.

Quite a lot of people in Whitehaven were outraged at the idea.

'All that pagan carrying on,' raged the Coopers' neighbour, Mrs O'Brien. 'It's not right. I don't know why the bishops don't put their foot down and ban it! Far from Celtic festivals that lot of young pups were reared.'

Since Mrs O'Brien disapproved of singing, disco dancing and the heathen carry on of horoscopes, her views meant nothing to the younger people.

There was going to be a big party with the bonfire to celebrate the solstice, with drinks and some traditional music and nobody managed to put a stop to it in time.

'I hope you're not going to that,' Mrs Cooper said to Gloria, on the night in question. 'I know you're thirty-four, Gloria, but it's going to be a bit wild. There're going to be drugs, you know there are. Your father sees enough of it in his work. People think drugs can't get out to Whitehaven from the cities, but they should see what your father sees. The real world is here too.'

Gloria was desperately torn. She was an adult and if the solstice was happening on a Dublin beach and Angelo had asked her, she'd have been able to go along.

But here in Whitehaven, when her father and mother were so against the idea, when half the town was so against the idea, she felt as if she'd be letting them down if she went.

'Why not?' said Angelo, confused. 'We were pagans long before we were Christians,' he said. 'You don't have to drink and take drugs. I'm not bringing the car so I'll have a whiskey or two, but that's all. Reefers give me a headache and stop me working. I don't like them.'

'I don't know, Angelo,' Gloria had said. 'It's tricky. I'm from around here. You're not.'

He shrugged. 'I will not tell you what you can do, *carissima*.'

They separated with her feeling miserable and him quiet.

'Is Lillian going?' Gloria asked Bob.

He looked at her uncomfortably. 'She wants to and I can't stop her.'

The notion of Lillian going to the party infuriated Gloria for reasons she couldn't quite express. Lillian was younger and yet she had all this freedom, freedom she liked to wave around like a flag.

She'd taunt Gloria about the solstice party too, Gloria knew. To Lillian, Gloria was a prude. If she knew about Gloria and Angelo's relationship, she wouldn't think that, but then Gloria couldn't tell her. What did Bob see in the bloody girl apart from the obvious?

The evening of the solstice, she and Bob went for a long walk through the town and out the city side, then back. The older people nodded approvingly at them, pleased to see the polite and well-behaved doctor's offspring at home on such a night.

'I feel as if life is going to pass me by,' Gloria said restlessly. 'You're getting married, Bob, and what am I doing? I'm running up and down here every weekend from Dublin, like a kid who still lives with her parents and still ruled by their wishes . . .'

'If Angelo cared, he'd understand that you can't go,' said Bob, and Gloria had glared at her brother.

'So it's different for Lillian?'

Bob had sighed. 'Lillian does her own thing. We're going to get married. And I feel as if this is her last big blowout. We've talked about it. She's going to work, get a job, an ordinary teaching job, because if we have children, she can't live that crazy life then.'

'Oh Bob,' Gloria had said, feeling protective on his behalf. She had to say something. 'Lillian is never going to settle down.'

'She is,' he insisted. 'She is because she loves me.'

The weekend passed slowly with no sign of Angelo. Lillian had turned up at the Coopers' family home on Sunday afternoon just before Gloria headed to Dublin. Lillian had been bright-eyed, skin glowing. Her dark hair rippled around her shoulders and her eyes had careful kohl at the edges, emphasising their catlike shape. She wore a seersucker dress in simple white with no bra, her tanned shoulders gleaming from sitting on a sun-soaked beach.

'How was your trip to see your mother?' Mrs Cooper asked.

Gloria looked around in shock.

Lillian had lied about going to the solstice party and Bob had been complicit in this.

'It was lovely, Mrs Cooper,' lied Lillian, 'Just lovely. We went into Tralee to see my friends but it was a quiet weekend.'

Gloria just stared at her. To lie so blatantly . . .

There was no phone call from Angelo during the week in the hall of the Rathmines house where Gloria lived. All the flats used the same coin-operated phone in the hall and when it rang, they took turns in answering and yelling up to the flat in question to say there was someone on the line for them.

Nobody phoned Gloria from Whitehaven. Was it over?

But Angelo appeared at their usual spot on Friday evening to drive her home. He looked different. Paler, tired and when he looked at her his eyes were sad. Instinctively, Gloria didn't ask what was wrong. She didn't want to know. But she knew all the same. Something was broken but if she didn't talk about it for the journey, then she could still exist a little bit longer in the mirage of their love.

They stopped briefly for tea and sandwiches along the way. But it wasn't the fun picnic they normally had. When they got to Whitehaven. Angelo drove to Mermaid Point instead of to the Cooper family home.

'I need to talk to you,' he said.

'About what happened at solstice?' asked Gloria.

Angelo said nothing for a while. 'I slept with Lillian.'

And Gloria felt the dread that had lived inside her all week finally settle in all its darkness.

'I knew it,' she whispered.

Lillian had wanted him, not just because he was beautiful, sensual and gifted, but because he was Gloria's.

'We're finished then.'

It was broken. Over.

'No, please,' Angelo said. 'Please no—'

'I can't forgive you that,' Gloria said, eyes blinded with tears. 'I wish I could, but I can't. Goodbye, Angelo.'

Somehow, she got out of the car, pulling her small weekend bag with her. He didn't try to come after her because he knew there was no point. It was over. The weekend bag was heavy and she held it to her chest as she walked, letting the tears drop onto the canvas.

What could she do now? Confront Lillian, who would no doubt deny it? Tell Bob?

She couldn't do that. Gloria walked slowly, climbing over the stile so she could walk along the fields in case Angelo drove back that way. If she saw him again, she wasn't sure she'd be able to resist him. And she had to.

Lillian might have wanted Angelo, might have done her best to entrap him, but he was a grown man. He had the ability to say no. They were both to blame. She couldn't stay with a man who would betray her.

But Bob . . . she wasn't sure if she owed it to him to tell him. Or owed it to him to say nothing. If she did that, he would marry Lillian and she would have to watch. But she'd never forgive Lillian. Never.

Lou stared at the painting and felt a whole well of sadness open up inside her.

There could be only one reason why Gloria would have such a painting by this man hanging over her while she slept.

She was the other woman in the story of Lillian, Angelo and Bob.

Angelo had betrayed this other woman but hadn't named her. He'd hurt darling Gloria.

But Lillian, capricious, charming and selfish Lillian, had stolen her nearly-sister-in-law's man and hadn't cared less. Lillian had been playing with other people's lives for years and had no regrets. An icy calm descended upon Lou. The last bit of filmy curtain in front of her eyes fell to the ground. She could not change her mother's behaviour, no. But she could change her own reaction to it.

Lou went into the garden and handed the cardigan silently to her aunt. She brought out the tea tray, set it down, then poured.

'You weren't ever going to tell me, were you?' she asked, still feeling remarkably calm.

Gloria looked up, startled, then awareness came over her face. 'Angelo told you?'

Lou shook her head. 'I've only just realised: I saw the painting over your bed.'

'Ah.' Gloria smiled. 'You've seen that painting so many times. I should have sold it, but I couldn't. I'd loved him . . .'

'Oh Gloria, I'm so sorry. I never asked you about the lost love. I never asked!' said Lou, deeply upset. 'Angelo's such a lovely man and you would have been so happy together . . .'

'I am happy,' Gloria said simply. 'I learned to love the life I had. I had you and Toni and Bob. Then I had Emily. I had my charity work in Whitehaven, my little dogs.' She looked down at Sugar with love. 'I could have wasted my life in reproach and bitterness but why? No, Lou, I've been happy. And . . .'

She hesitated.

'Angelo. He's happy too? Married, Toni tells me, with a beautiful wife.'

Lou nodded.

'Why didn't he tell me it was you?' she asked.

Suddenly Gloria's eyes glittered with unshed tears.

'He knew me, knew I'd never hurt Bob by saying anything. If you didn't know that I was the woman he'd cheated on, then I knew he'd realise that I hadn't wanted you to know because of all the hurt it would cause. He would have known Lillian would have said nothing about it all. He understood your mother quite well, I think.'

'I was the one who didn't understand her. I do now,' said Lou grimly.

'It's the past,' said Gloria. 'I have been happy, Lou. Please don't think otherwise for a moment. My life has been full and rich. There are many paths for us. Mine wasn't with Angelo but oh my goodness, it's been a happy one.'

'You are a truly wise and forgiving woman, Gloria,' said Lou, her voice quivering. 'Like Dad.'

Gloria's tears began to fall now.

'Bob was such a darling man. I miss him.'

Lou sighed. 'He was my father, my true father, and it will be lovely to have a relationship with Angelo because he's part of my DNA. Toni says I should have counselling about it and I'm going to. But . . .' Lou poured the tea and her hand shook with suppressed anger. 'I do not forgive my mother.'

She thought of Trinity, her fear of telling her family, her worry that she wouldn't be able to do it alone. It was Lillian's story fifty years later. There was still so much shame attached to unplanned pregnancies, and women had to carry it all.

'I don't blame her for getting pregnant, not at all. But I do blame her for keeping this toxic secret, for cheating on you and my father, for ruining my birthday. For making me run around after her all my life.' Lou inhaled deeply. 'Yes, I definitely blame her for that.'

She stood up. She needed to visit Lillian now. She had let her mother manipulate her one too many times, now. It was time for the cycle to end.

The sand outside Valclusa was worse than it had been the evening before, like a bunch of wild animals had been playing games on it: deranged squirrels or pigeons having races. It made getting to the house even more difficult, and Lou's frustration grew.

'Mum!' she yelled as she let herself in.

Lillian appeared, still in her nightclothes, a filmy heliotrope negligee thing, a lilac camisole and beige silky pyjama pants. Her hair was unbrushed but she was wearing her trademark lipstick, which she only wore when there were guests or when she was going out.

She looked displeased at the sight of Lou.

'You're here early,' she said.

'Is someone here?' asked Lou as she heard a noise from upstairs.

Lillian appeared to be thinking about lying but then they both heard the upstairs loo flush.

'Mum—' Lou started.

'Why are you calling me Mum now?' snapped Lillian.

'Good question,' snapped Lou. 'You're right. Lillian works better.'

She went into the hall and yelled up the stairs. 'Hello! Do you want coffee?'

'Yes,' roared a masculine voice.

'What are you doing?' snapped Lillian crossly.

361

Lou felt years of anger cascade inside her. Her father, Angelo, poor Gloria. She thought of her beloved new dogs and felt afresh the anger at not being allowed to have a dog as a child.

'How dare you steal Gloria's man?' she snapped. 'How dare you betray my father, how dare you ruin my party by telling me then. How dare you not tell me years ago when I could have made peace with Dad. How bloody dare you for all of it, but worse—'

'Where's the coffee?'

Peadar, who seemed very skinny in an old dressing gown with a pipe in his mouth, appeared.

'Peadar, not now,' said Lillian.

'No, now is fine!' said Lou. 'An audience is always nicer for this type of thing, don't you think, Lillian. How do you think my mother's heart is, Peadar? Is she taking a lot of tablets? Resting a lot?'

Peadar laughed good-humouredly. 'Resting? You know the old girl – she never rests!'

'All the Dr Ali stuff was a lie, wasn't it?' said Lou.

Lillian's lips tautened as much as they could with all the filler. 'You just hate that I have an active sex life,' she hissed at her daughter.

Peadar paled and fled to the kitchen to get away from all this family drama.

'I don't care about your sex life,' Lou shouted fiercely. At this, Lillian finally backed away. 'You can have men coming out your ears for all I care. Women have just as much right to enjoy sex as men. But what I do hate is your lying, your manipulation, how you twist everything so that I've been running around after you for years! And what do I get for that?'

Lillian said nothing.

'I get you ruining my birthday party because you're a spoiled cow. You have to be the centre of attention, always. Well, it's over now.'

'I suppose Gloria told you about it,' said Lillian savagely.

'Neither she nor Angelo told me,' said Lou. 'They protected you. But I found out another way.'

She didn't want to talk about Gloria's precious painting. That was too private to share with Lillian.

'Oh by the way, I've got two dogs now. So I won't be cleaning your house anymore because I'd have to bring them with me and you're frightened of dogs, aren't you?'

'Not really,' said Lillian warily.

'Don't you mean "No".'

'Fine. No!'

'Why did you lie so much?'

'I don't lie,' began Lillian. 'I just embellish. I mean, dogs are messy. Oh sweetie, you like looking after me. All great artists have people who do things for them—'

'Great artists, maybe,' snapped Lou, 'but your greatest act of creation is the invention of yourself: the fabulous Lillian Cooper, glamorous and sexy. Be as glam and sexy as you want, Mother, but you can buy your own lipliner on the internet from now on. Or get Peadar to do it for you.

'You can move in, Peadar,' she yelled in the direction of the kitchen. 'As long as you're good at cleaning.

Mother doesn't like scrubbing the bath, changing sheets or washing clothes, so if you can do that, you've a place to stay. Otherwise, welcome to squalor.'

'I don't want Peadar staying!' hissed Lillian.

'I heard that,' he said, appearing at the door and looking aggrieved. 'I'm off.'

They heard him stomping upstairs.

'Now look what you've done!' said Lillian petulantly.

'You've lots of male friends,' said Lou. 'Phone someone else.'

All of a sudden, the fight went out of her.

She was tired of it. She wanted to be Lou, the real gentle Lou. Fighting with her mother was not the way to honour who she really was.

'I'll talk to you during the week,' she said, and turned to leave.

'That's it?' said Lillian, standing forlorn in her negligee. 'You've insulted me and now Peadar's going, and the place is a tip!'

'There are dusters in the drawer under the sink and cleaning products in that cupboard beside the freezer. You're a survivor, Mother. You'll be fine. I'm going home to my family.'

Chapter Twenty-four

Lou had got into the habit of walking along Whitehaven Beach in the mornings.

She had a new watch which tracked her steps and she was enjoying hitting ten thousand every day. Boo and Lola adored their morning walks and Lou wondered how she'd ever lived without dogs as she watched her beloved pooches racing around in the sand. A few times a week, she took Sugar for Gloria and brought the little dog back to her aunt in a state of exhaustion.

Sometimes Ned managed to walk with her. In the beginning, she used to say: 'You don't have to walk with me, darling. I can walk the girls on my own.'

'I want to walk with you,' Ned would say. 'I like being with you.'

He said this a lot now. In the beginning, Lou used to wonder if Emily had put him up to it, and then she realised her daughter had nothing to do with it. Ned had changed in a way that was very subtle. He wanted to be with her and he wanted her to know this.

He was making a Herculean effort at their marriage.

Lou was not sure if her leaving for Sicily had given him a shock or what had affected him, but Ned was a different man. She loved walking with him. They'd park on Mermaid Point, get the girls out of the car, and walk down onto the sands together, holding hands, but then they'd let go and stride along, laughing about how many steps they could manage.

Occasionally they'd meet other walkers with dogs that ran out into the waves. Lou found as a new dog owner she now knew the names of all the dogs because people called out the dog names.

'Prince, stop drinking the water,' someone would shout to a particularly energetic border collie.

Lola and Boo adored running into the water too, but Lola only danced around the edges.

'She's not waterproof,' Lou told Ned, who laughed.

When she was there for the weekend, Emily always joined the walks and mother and daughter loved their time alone on the beach, walking miles over the headlands and talking about everything and anything. Emily sometimes talked about travelling after she got her degree and, nowadays, Lou found she could cope with the idea.

'You need to travel,' she said firmly. 'There's no point in me teaching you to be this independent woman if I cling to you.'

'Mum, you don't cling,' said Emily. 'We love each other. Do you know how wonderful that is?'

'Yes,' Lou said and squeezed her daughter's waist.

Trinity and her aunt Dara had even come for a weekend. Trinity was blooming in pregnancy and had decided that she'd do a masters over the next couple of years.

'Makes sense from a career point of view,' she'd said proudly to Lou.

Her aunt was dying for the baby to be born: 'Trinity was like my baby, but I didn't have her in the actual baby stages,' Dara confided. 'I can't wait to be a proper granny.'

Whenever she could, Toni would join Lou and the dogs on the beach too. Toni and Oliver's Dublin house was for sale. At least, Toni said, Oliver hadn't managed to put a double mortgage on it so that, once it was sold, she'd have some money. Toni herself had moved out and was renting an apartment in Greystones. It was near the sea on the top floor of a three-storey block.

'I love being near the water,' she said. 'The old house was too far from the sea. That'll never happen again. I need the water.'

She now worked two days a week in Academy, the PR company run by Cormac's friend, who'd given her such good advice on damage limitation.

The work was interesting. And well paid. She still had her TV show, but she was considering stepping down from it to work on documentaries.

'My heart's not in that sort of confrontational broadcasting anymore,' she told Lou. 'I like the idea of doing big, long stories where I can really take people into the details of something.'

She told Lou that she'd be working for a long, long time before she could make back even half of the money Oliver had lost.

'He says he's sorry,' Toni said one day as she and Lou walked at speed along the curved golden sands of Whitehaven, Boo and Lola prancing around in front of them. 'He knows it was an appalling thing to do.'

Oliver had gone to Los Angeles and was working in the film industry. He was not getting huge roles but there were small jobs out there and he was, he'd told Toni, determined to make their money back. He was still gambling and that made her heart ache for him.

'You won't make the money back, you know,' she'd said to him on the phone when he rang her the night before flying to LA. 'You won't make the money back. You can't.'

'I can try,' he said, sounding a little like the commanding King Lear he'd played in his last big play.

'Oliver, you're a gambler, you need help,' Toni replied. 'I'd love to have the money back. But be real about it. Don't live in a fantasy world thinking you'll get it all back the way you did every time you lost money. That's what got you into this scrape in the first place. Please get help.'

'I want to get the money back for you,' said Oliver. 'I'm home in a few weeks, Toni,' he said, 'and—'

'No,' said Toni, holding up a hand even though he couldn't see it. 'I can't see you, Oliver. As far as I'm concerned, we're over and I want my money back if we can manage that, but I don't want to hear about your life. I don't want to be a part of it.'

'You've been very good to me,' Oliver said in a low tone.

'Because I haven't outed you for being a gambler and losing every penny I had?' she said.

'Yes, that too,' said Oliver.

'It's not the sort of person I am,' Toni said.

'It sounds like you've forgiven him,' said Lou, now.

Toni considered it. 'It's not that I forgive him, as such,' she said. 'Sometimes in the middle of the night I wake up and I beat myself up over the fact that I didn't know what was going on. I go into that "if only" stage when I think of how life would be different if only I'd noticed he was gambling and if only I'd talked to the investment guy, or if only . . .'

She sighed in a way that said she had gone over this many, many times before.

'He deceived you very well,' Lou pointed out. 'You're supposed to be able to trust your partner.'

'Yes,' Toni agreed. 'And there's no point holding on to the resentment or the anger. It was eating me up. I worked so hard for that money, for that security. That everything can be taken away so quickly was shocking, but,' she shrugged, 'that's life. It can be taken away quickly. Anything can be taken away quickly from us. Your job, your home – I'm not the first person to lose them. And look at Mim, losing her health, her life. If I'm going to move on, I've got to make peace with it.'

'Zen Buddhism?' asked Lou, unable to stop herself making the joke.

'No,' said Toni. 'Practical, down-to-earth womanhood. It's the betrayal that kills me most. That he could do that to me – that I didn't spot it – it will take me time to get over feeling the shame of *that*. If I do start making documentaries, I'd want to do one on betrayal first.'

'No research will be needed,' joked Lou.

Betrayal had been huge in Lou's life too. It was something she talked to her therapist about. She was seeing her for a range of things, including discovering that her father hadn't really been her biological father. Even better, she was talking about her depression for the first time ever. Not just to her therapist, but to Ned, too. Ned had read a book on depression that her therapist had recommended, and he emerged after reading it with a hugely sad expression on his face.

'I am so sorry, Lou,' he'd said, and she'd been astonished to see that he was close to tears. 'I was ignorant, I didn't know what you went through. Emily did, but I never bothered. You must have felt so lonely.'

'Depression is inherently lonely,' she said, with the confidence she'd found these past months, 'but you understand now. That's huge.'

She'd left Blossom.

Two days after her return from Sicily, she'd gone into the shop in the city and found Oszkar shouting at a young woman.

'Mindy, this is not how we do it!' Oszkar was shrieking.

'I don't care!' Mindy was shrieking back. 'I'm leaving. I'm going back to my uncle's business. You're all mad here. You expect me to know what's in your head without telling me!'

'Lou!' said Oszkar in relief, spotting her. 'You're back!'

'No,' said Lou calmly. 'I'm here to clear out my desk.'

'You're Lou!' said Mindy in surprise. 'How did you stand it? By the way, we lost that big wedding because I said I'd been hired over you and the woman, the one on Insta, said she couldn't believe you weren't in charge and—'

She paused for breath. 'I'm sorry I took your job.'

'You didn't take it,' Lou said kindly. 'They gave it to you because I let them. I let them walk all over me.'

'I am sorry, it won't happen again,' promised Oszkar.

'It won't,' agreed Lou. 'Because I'm not coming back. Bye, Oszkar.'

Through Toni, she'd found a job with a charity in Cork which was helping women who wanted to get back into the workforce after taking time out to care for their children. She loved it. There were women from all walks of life trying to get back into any area of work, and helping people achieve their dreams gave her such a thrill.

'It's fulfilling and I can help them not get ground down the way I was,' she told Toni eagerly.

'I'm so glad,' Toni said. She had never seen her sister so happy – she had never felt so happy herself. She had more time off, time to spend in Whitehaven, walking the beach, time in her own cottage garden.

She'd surprised herself by going out on a few dates with Cormac Wolfe.

'He is devastatingly hot,' Lou said when Toni showed her a photo of him.

'Yeah, let's keep him away from Mum!'

They laughed. Lou could do that now. It had taken a while, but her relationship with Lillian was improving.

'She still tries it on with me,' Lou told Toni. 'If I drop in, she says things like "Can you run the wine glasses under the tap . . ." and then she remembers that those days are over.'

'I bet you wash them anyway,' said Toni, who knew how soft her sister was.

Lou laughed. 'Yeah, I do. But only because I want to. Not because she's guilting me into doing it. Did I tell you she made me a sculpture for the garden for my birthday?'

'Is it a variation on the controversial one for the local library, "Woman: self-pleasure"?'

They both howled so much that the dogs ran back to see what was wrong.

'No, it's almost normal. It's a tree of life and she said one part is in a bronzed metal to signify my Italian heritage and the rest is hammered steel for Ireland. She made one for Gloria too, a smaller one. I think it's an apology.'

'Lillian can't ever simply say sorry,' said Toni. 'Always the grand gesture.'

'You can't change people,' said Lou, shrugging.

'Yeah, you can only change how you react to them,' finished her sister. 'How do you think she'll react to Angelo when he comes here to visit?'

Lou laughed. 'I'd back Renata over Lillian any day.'

'And Gloria, is she OK with the whole idea of Angelo and Renata coming to Whitehaven?'

Lou thought about it. 'I asked her before I issued the invitation. She said she'd be perfectly happy to see him again and to meet Renata. She's remarkable, really. She's found peace in her life in a way Lillian never did.'

'It's an inside job,' said Toni. Toni began to run along the beach with the dogs racing after her. 'Last one to the big rock is a rotten egg.'

Lou began to race and she felt herself run faster and faster, uncaring that her hat had fallen off or that several dogs were now joining in, belting along beside her. It was like running as a child: freewheeling down a hill with arms and legs racing, letting the wind and sheer childish exuberance flood through her.

She felt alive, happy and so very full of joy.

Toni got to the rocks first, blonde hair flying out behind her before she juddered to a halt.

She whirled around as Lou arrived to see her sister's face blazing with happiness.

'Let's call it a tie,' said Toni, beaming.

The gaggle of dogs began to dance around delightedly, waiting for the next game.

In the distance, the gulls soared and cried to each other. The gentle lapping of the waves proclaimed that today, the Atlantic was playing at being a nice calm ocean. Lou felt the tang of seaweed and salt spray in the air.

'No,' she said, always the older sister. 'You won.'

She sank onto the sand and stared out to sea, letting the mild sun warm her skin. If life was to be measured in winning, then they were both so very lucky. They had everything they needed: everything anyone could ever want.

She looked up at the sky, hoping that Mim was there looking down: seated on her unicorn and eating an ice cream or casting a rainbow out of thin air.

'Thank you for everything, Mim,' she murmured quietly. 'Love you, darling girl.'

Acknowledgements

If it takes a village to raise a child, I am not sure how many villages or villagers are needed to write a book, nurture the book to publication like a duckling leaving the nest and then nurture the writer when said writer gets cancer just when the book stuff is getting fun.

Sisterhood is an incredibly special book for me – the first book back with my dear colleagues in HarperCollins and it has been a joyous homecoming.

Then cancer threw a grenade in there and everything changed in an instant.

But really, if stuff didn't happen to us, then what would we write about? To borrow shamelessly from Nora Ephron, 'everything is copy'.

Thanks and so much love to my holding-my-hand family, PJ and my darling sons, Dylan and Murray. I would not have got through these months without you. Cancer is a family disease and when you are lying in bed unable to move, someone has to walk dogs, make dinner, and my darlings, you did it with such love. Love to Dinky – who went through chemotherapy with far more grace than I did, little warrior princess, love to Scamp, who loses battery when dinner is late, to Licky, who wants to write her own book, and to Juno, who surveys the people and the three Jack Russells from the glorious heights of her Winter Cat Palace. Speaking of which, how did we get mice who ate the central heating pipes . . .? Three terriers and a cat? Just asking.

Love always to my darling sister, Lucy, who is the funniest person I know and the dearest. Love and thanks as always to dear Mum who really should have written her own books. Here's hoping! To Dave, my brother-in-law who remembers every appointment I have and sends me encouragement every day, and special hugs to Princess Lola who is the squishiest girl ever. To Francis, big brother who always knows the answer to all questions and will drop everything if I need him. Always there: much love, Fran. To dearest Laura, Naomi, Emer and Anne for encouragement and love. Did I ever tell you how proud I am of you three girls? Besotted aunt.

Love to Robert, Rory, Katie and Spike. Armfuls of love to my dear Emma, Richard, Kit, Ahir and Angie. Thank you, Ahir, for all the footage which meant I could see the wedding when I was stuck at home being all cancery. Thanks and so much love to darling Lisa Lynch and Wanaka who make the world a better place and would move mountains for me. Hugs to my darling goddaughter, Annmarie. If I ever have another business, you and your mother are running it! I do not know how I would function in the real world without this sisterhood and love of Gai Griffin: you are an angel. Aisling Carroll, you came into my life like a whirlwind over twenty years ago and you're still whirling with vitality. Love you. To Lynn, who is as beautiful and wise a friend as one could ever have and is a joy on my life.

Love and hugs in vast quantities to Tiggy, Nell, Alan, Richard, Cindy, Dorothy and Matt who are truly among my most favourite people on the planet. To darling Bea, Katie, Kiki, Pickle, Pebbles, Lucy, Jim, John, (going after the dogs in an acknowledgement list is FINE, guys . . . I dedicated a book to my beloved Tamsin, a little Labrador). To the combined forces that make up the wonderful Extendables, who are all angels, with special mentions to Satara, Carol, Lizzie and Bridget and a huge swooping hug for Vickey, Portia and Harry and the dogs.

Thanks for evermore to darling Cindy, Georgina and Caroline, to dear generous Lottie and darling James who still lets me hug him. Thanks to Karen and Eleanor for checking in on me so kindly. It so helps. Thank to my darling Clodagh Finn, a brilliant writer, a brilliant person. Thanks to Michael McNiffe and dear Molly! To beautiful Joanne McElgunn and let's not work out how long we've known each other. Thanks to Alyson Stanley and Stella O'Connell, two angels, Jane O'Neill, Gerry McGuinness, Felicity Carney and Wendy Hutson for being there. Thank you to the gifted Aidan Storey and his equally gifted – but much better at golf! – husband, Murtagh, for being such good friends to me always.

Thank you for being there as ever to LisaMarie and Laoise, Susan Zaidan, Niall, Martina, Kelly, gorgeous Lou and the exquisite Sienna who is just the best reader ever! My life would be the poorer without the steadfast and true Stephanie, Debbie, Charlotte, Anne, Judy, Mary-Pat, Trish, Carey, Louise, Bridin, Tara, Barbara, Janet, Mandy, Sheila, Chris, James, Aidan, and dear Jean.

There are people who've been on every acknowledgement list I've ever written, people like the Fabulous Ms Patricia Scanlan, who is Irish royalty, darling Dr Marian Keyes, ditto. Why don't we have medals . . . ? Just asking. Thanks to Sinead Moriarty, who is just the kindest friend, Sheila O'Flanagan for being one of the four office lunchers,

Erica James, Belinda McKeon, Hazel Gaynor, Kate Kerrigan, Carmel Harrington, Susan Lanigan, who has come through her own cancer battle, the fabulous Monica McInerney and everyone in the writing community who has said hello and sent me virtual hugs.

Cancer brings different people into your life, wonderful people who help you navigate this landscape: You need to meet people who will help you though chemo and tell you that no you are not going mad. I am lucky to have so many wonderful new friends. Thank you so much to JoAnn Connolly, Vicki O'Mahony, Frances O'Gorman, Pauline Mulroney (old pal, new world), Gert O'Rourke and dear Anne Marie O'Sullivan.

Thanks in enormous measure must go to the incredible staff at Ireland's BreastCheck, St Vincent's University Hospital and St Vincent's Private Hospital. In the many months since I've been diagnosed with cancer, I have spent a lot of time in these places and the kindness and dedication is second to none. Without them, I wouldn't be here. From the lady who cleaned the floor when I had pneumonia and was lying on the bed like a slug, just about breathing and not even capable of speech, to my oncologist, dear Professor John Crown, I just want to say thank you. ARC Breast Cancer services were incredible too. Thank you, Sinead! The acupuncture was glorious!

Thank you to the combined forces of Ark Vetcare and My Vet Lucan who looked after Dinky like the tiny dynamic princess she is. You were incredible, thank you all. She is so precious to me.

While I was being sick, the wonderful team at Curtis Brown were making the world ready for *Sisterhood* and a huge thank you to the whole team, led by the dashing Jonathan Lloyd, ably assisted by Lucy Morris, genius, and Olivia Edwards, fabulously chic in vintage. The CB team has been in my life for so long, and they work so hard – thank you.

Finally, coming back to HarperCollins really has been the loveliest homecoming. I love turning a corner in the new cool building and seeing someone I remember from fifteen years ago and we shriek, and say hello, like mad magpies! I love it! It is always a joy to work with my HC family and, cancer story permitting, I will be winging my way to parts of Australia and New Zealand to see my beloved friends in HarperCollins Aus and NZ very soon. Karen-Maree, can't wait!

So with this in mind, thank you for all your help, dear Lynne Drew, publisher, and it's such a joy to have this wonderful friendship back again. We can change the world. Will we shop first, though...?

Thank you to Lucy Stewart, editor extraordinaire, to Kate Elton, who is always calm and exudes the sense that all will be well. I want some of that, Kate! Thank you to darling Kimberley Young – we will miss you, but mountains must be climbed. Dear Roger Cazalet, thank you for everything and for always being such glorious company. To Charlie Redmayne, I am so thrilled we are doing this! Thank you to the combined brilliance of Sarah Shea, Jo Kite and Maddy Marshall in marketing, to dear Felicity Denham in publicity, to Holly MacDonald in design for the exquisite new cover, to Fionnuala Barrett for the audio (can't wait to hear Angeline Ball), to Bethan Moore in international sales, to the Irish team of Tony Purdue, Patricia McVeigh and thank you a million times to my dear friend, PR genius Aileen Gaskin who can genuinely turn a PR plan around in about an hour. You are breathtaking, Aileen, and it's a pleasure to work with you.

Thanks to Karen-Maree Griffiths, Jim Demetriou and Michael White in Australia, Peter Borcsok in Canada, and everyone who works in the HC family round the world. I'm coming soon but keep me out of the craft shops because my new hobby is just buying wool/embroidery threads!

Now, I have chemo brain, which is a thing. It means you forget stuff. For example, I currently take an anti-nausea drug and I cannot for the life of me remember its name. Nor what letter it begins with. I take this thing three times a day and I call it . . . 'Reb . . . ?' No. So on that basis, if I have left you out and I will have because . . . chemo brain . . . I apologise. I am so lucky to have such glorious friends and family and to work with such wonderful people.

I am also lucky in that I have amazing readers who keep coming back to my books. You have no idea what an honour that is and I still can't believe it. Can I send you a heartfelt thanks.

I hope that my books help the way other peoples' books have helped me.

And thank you to all the wonderful booksellers and librarians who get books into the hands of eager readers.

Finally, I thought I understood how hard cancer was because my best friend, Emma Hannigan, had battled it so bravely for so many years but, living with cancer, I realise again what an amazing human being Emma was for making the impossible look so effortless. Love, as always, to Kim, Sacha, Philip and Denise.

Love, Cathy